FLESH AND BLOOD

Also by David Mark

Novels

THE ZEALOT'S BONES *(as D.M. Mark)*
THE MAUSOLEUM (aka THE BURYING GROUND) *
A RUSH OF BLOOD *
BORROWED TIME *
BLOOD MONEY
INTO THE WOODS
SUSPICIOUS MINDS *
CAGES *
ANATOMY OF A HERETIC
THE WHISPERING DEAD *
PIECE OF MIND

The DS Aector McAvoy series

DARK WINTER
ORIGINAL SKIN
SORROW BOUND
TAKING PITY
DEAD PRETTY
CRUEL MERCY
SCORCHED EARTH
COLD BONES
PAST LIFE *
BLIND JUSTICE *

* *available from Severn House*

FLESH AND BLOOD

David Mark

SEVERN
HOUSE

First world edition published in Great Britain and the USA in 2023
by Severn House, an imprint of Canongate Books Ltd,
14 High Street, Edinburgh EH1 1TE.

severnhouse.com

British Library Cataloguing-in-Publication Data
A CIP catalogue record for this title is available from the British Library.

ISBN-13: 978-1-4483-0937-5 (cased)
ISBN-13: 978-1-4483-0938-2 (e-book)

All Severn House titles are printed on acid-free paper.

MIX
Paper from
responsible sources
FSC® C013056

Typeset by Palimpsest Book Production Ltd.,
Falkirk, Stirlingshire, Scotland.
Printed and bound in Great Britain by
TJ Books, Padstow, Cornwall.

Praise for the DS McAvoy novels

"David Mark has put Hull on the map . . . and placed DS
Aector McAvoy as one of the most interesting and
likeable British detectives"
The Times

"Deliver[s] the kind of grisly torture and murder scenes that
have rightly linked Mark's work with that of Val McDermid"
Booklist on *Blind Justice*

"Polished prose, lovable recurring characters, and
a stunning revelation make this a mystery to savor"
Kirkus Reviews Starred Review of *Past Life*

"A fine police procedural . . . Ian Rankin fans will be pleased"
Publishers Weekly on *Past Life*

"[Mark is] on the level of Scottish and English contemporaries
such as Denise Mina, Val McDermid, and Peter Robinson"
Library Journal Starred Review of *Cruel Mercy*

"To call Mark's novels police procedurals is like calling
the Mona Lisa a pretty painting"
Kirkus Reviews Starred Review of *Cruel Mercy*

"Strong prose, intriguing characters, and high tension
make this a standout"
Publishers Weekly Starred Review of *Dead Pretty*

"Excellent . . . weaves a complicated web of deception,
betrayal, and violence as the action builds
to a stunning conclusion"
Publishers Weekly Starred Review of *Taking Pity*

About the author

David Mark spent seven years as crime reporter for the *Yorkshire Post* and now writes full-time. A former Richard & Judy pick, and a *Sunday Times* bestseller, he is the author of the DS Aector McAvoy series and a number of standalone thrillers. He lives in Northumberland with his family.

www.davidmarkwriter.co.uk

*Mam, with love, thanks and a marked
absence of sarcastic comments.*

PROLOGUE

St Oswald's Church, Buckton, East Yorkshire
February 9th
2.15 p.m.

He walks with both hands behind his back, coupled at the wrist, as if wearing handcuffs. He stoops a little, but it's habit rather than old age. He's lived here longer than he's lived anywhere else and has long since learned to watch where he puts his feet. This is a landscape of hidden edges and sudden dips: where loose-rooted trees and shards of hefted rock hide lethal shafts of glistening blackness. The sea waits at the foot of the crumbling cliff, taking bites out of the land with each new tide. Abandoned bungalows and teetering mobile homes stick out over nothingness; sewage pipes and electric points jut out from the wet earth like the guts of the disembowelled.

Even here, tramping along the pitted trail towards the church, he has to be careful not to turn his ankle. Lately he's become brittle. He feels the cold. *Him!* A copper, once. A good one, too. He caught villains. Killers. He was never a thug the way some of his colleagues were. Never put the boot in. Clever, too, in his way. Insightful. Shrewd. A good judge of character, that was never in doubt. Could spot a wrong 'un a mile off.

Moodily, he wonders what his younger self would make of him now. Considers that wee lad, who used to plunge into the frigid black waters off the headland at Flamborough while whip-crack winds churned the surface. Him; who wore damp shorts on frigid December mornings and played football on the tops at Filey wearing metal-belted clogs, snow stuck in the caulkers so it felt like playing in skis. *Him*, who carried a concussed tup five miles home to their little terraced house in Skipsea in the hope that a night in front of the open fire might bring it round. Him. Tom Spink.

Tom catches a glimpse of himself in a puddle as he trudges through the mist towards the church. Scowls as he takes himself

in. He'd expected to start looking like his father as he approached
the final chapters of his life. Instead he has found himself morphing
into his mother; wrinkles in his top lip and damp, yellowy eyes.
He sometimes feels genetically short-changed, having already
inherited his father's stunted stature and early onset baldness. His
ruddy head is almost ovoid and protrudes from a ring of downy
white hair so that from certain angles his mottled head looks like
an egg not yet fully liberated from a hen. He walks bandy-legged,
sucking at his lower lip like a baby with a nipple. He was handsome until a couple of years back: still straight-backed and twinkly
eyed. Old bugger, now. Old and done in. Ready for it to end, if
he's honest with himself. Ready to drop off one night and not
wake up. He'll be missed, but he'd rather go before he becomes
a burden. The wife's already in and out of respite care, her mind
unravelling so that she doesn't know whether it's last Tuesday or
Christmas '79. She'll have to mourn him afresh every time somebody tells her that he's gone. And there's Trish, of course. Trish,
who he loves with a quiet ferocity; Trish, who's been something
between a daughter and a best friend for the past thirty years. But
she'll be glad, deep down. She won't want to see him infirm.
Won't want to see him wetting himself and eating pre-chewed
food from a plastic spoon. No, better spare them all that. A night
in front of the fire, a good bottle of malt, and enough sleeping
tablets to kill a wildebeest – that's the way to play it. Next week,
maybe. Perhaps the month after. A few things to sort out, first.
There's the book to finish. He writes local history pamphlets to
keep his mind active. He contributes to the occasional poetry
journal. He's written about some of the big cases he was involved
with. And here's the podcast, of course. 'Good Murders, Bad
Deaths'. He'd like to hear his own contribution. There's still plenty
of life in his ego and he can't bring himself to check out before
he makes an appearance on the most downloaded true-crime
podcast of the year.

'Rex,' he yells: the word emerging from the good side of his
mouth. 'Rex. Rex!'

He stops himself. Spits and wipes his chin with his cuff.

Dog's dead, yer daft sod, he reminds himself. *It cost you ninety
quid, remember. You asked the vet if he'd do the same for you for
an extra tenner. He didn't laugh.*

He feels embarrassed. He glares at the ground as he walks. Starts working his jaw in circles, focusing his slack tongue on a point at the back of his mouth, trying to remove the bramble seed that has somehow lodged itself beneath his lower denture. He burps and has to hit himself in the chest with his good hand before the bubble of blocked belch rises up from his oesophagus. He forgot to take his antacid tablets this morning and can still taste the lamb jalfrezi he'd picked up last night from the Indian restaurant in Beverley. His skin carries an onion whiff, despite the bath he'd taken at his habitual 5.45 a.m. He still likes to rise before the sun. Listens to Radio Humberside on the wireless while he eats his breakfast. Always the same start to the day. Porridge and prunes, then a doorstep bacon sandwich. Two teas from the big brown pot on the centre of the long wooden table. Then he has his first roll-up, leaning in the doorway of the small grey cottage, its garden already given over to the sea. There's a crack running from the back door to the front and a chicken-wire fence blocking him off from the road. He's the last resident of the littler clifftop community: mostly retirees from West Yorkshire, spending insurance payouts and the equity from the sale of the family home to see out their days on this cold, wind-blown strip of paradise. They've all gone, now. All moved inland to be with family. But Tom's stubborn. If the house suddenly slips over the cliff and drops the hundred feet to the shingly beach beneath, he fancies he'll rather enjoy the ride.

He burps. Grimaces. He can discern something unpleasant; bitter and garlic and stomach lining. The health visitor will give him hell when she comes next month, he's no doubt. Will prick him and prod him and take his piss and tell him he's living wrong. She'll tell him she can pull some strings. Get him into one of those nice sheltered flats. He'll tell her he'll think about it, then curse her for an interfering sow once she's gone. He's known too many who've quit the land they knew and been dead inside a month. He doubts he could survive on different air. He'd rather stay and feel dreadful than decamp and die on unfamiliar soil.

He spits, foully, onto the surface of one of the petrol-rainbowed puddles that have formed in the potholes of the pitted, broken path. His wellington boots make a noise like a horse chewing a mint. He wears long hand-knitted fell socks beneath his dark green boots and he has tucked the bottoms of his overalls into their tops, the material bunching up just below his knee so he seems to be wearing knickerbockers. He wears a long coat, its khaki material mottled to a camouflage pattern by twenty years of exposure to the elements.

Tom's somewhere in his seventies, though he struggles to be more specific when asked. He has to go through a complicated set of sums to work it out. Has to remember faces long since dead. Fills his mind with dates that only serve to pitch him into a black gloom. Mum's death. Dad's death. '91, when he met Trish. '98: the year his first wife filled her pockets with stones and walked into the lake.

Tom glances up as a sudden sliver of light pierces the low grey-violet clouds. Wishes he had his stick. Wishes he'd brought a flask of tea and his binoculars. Wishes he had somewhere to go.

He comes to a stop outside the little church, half hidden behind the rise of the clifftop and shielded by huge tangles of grass and reeds and half-dead twists of bramble, coiled like barbed wire. In the next field, two stout, muttony tups are glaring at him, buck teeth working monotonously at a clump of grass.

Tom reaches out and leans on the dry-stone wall that circles the church. Looks back the way he's come. He's a couple of miles from home. Yew trees stand on the lip of the rise like great paper dolls. He leans forward, shifting his weight so that he is balancing on the wooden slats beneath the lych-gate. He glances at the nearest headstone: a big shard of polished black stone. At the base, dead stems emerge from an empty jam-jar. He realizes that he should have brought flowers. Should have put a candle in a bottle and let its flickering light find the shadows in a bouquet of berbera and hydrangea.

He forces himself through the lych-gate. Feels as though there is a weight tugging him down as he moves towards the plot where his dad's bones marble the earth. He cannot help but imagine the day, surely not too far away now, when he will be lowered on mud-caked ropes into a cold hole in the earth. He wonders who will be there to see him off. Whether anybody will pour whisky on his grave the way he did for his grandfather. Whether the sandwiches they serve at the pub in Old Ellerby will contain more than single slice of ham.

Stop it, he tells himself, and hocks back phlegm and tears. Tells himself it's just the wind, causing his eyes to run. Sings himself a little song inside his head, trying to make his feet match the rhythm.

He glances at the church, small and squat: a Monopoly house with a slate roof. The tower has axe-wound eyes. There are monsters scowling from the gutters: gurning goblins and multi-fanged beasts, writing in pagan debauchery atop virgins in flowing robes. A gull perches on the head of a howling woman, talons plunged deep into her eyeballs, tongue probing the bare behind of a leering imp. They are hideous and hypnotic and would be a Mecca for tourists if the church leaders weren't so ashamed. The gargoyles were unearthed by a sculptor a few years back: a handsome, blue-eyed devil commissioned to undo the damage caused by centuries of salt and spray. He'd done more than they asked. He found the truth in the ancient stone, disinterred the goblins and imps that once leered down at parishioners and protected the little stone church from vengeful spirits. God and Satan, Pan and Freya, all are bound in one house of worship. There's stained glass at the far end. On bright days it casts a multi-coloured pattern on the flagstones so that it looks as though jewels have been scattered on the floor. There's a wooden lectern inside: hand-carved by the same craftsman who remade the gargoyles. Tom was married here. For a moment he remembers his wedding day – Gillian so nervous and shy that her teeth chattered like wind-up toys. He'd had to put an arm around her, even with her dad looking on. Had to stand at the front of the church and say his vows hugging her to his chest, promising her he'd look after her and do right, for better, for worse. He fancies he kept his word, more or less.

He grows cold as he approaches the far corner of the graveyard. He glances up and the clouds shift, allowing a shaft of barley-yellow sunlight to spear down and into the churchyard. He glances at the tombstones of men he knew. Tom has never been a sentimental man but it saddens him to think of his own grave untended. He always used to tell the family that he didn't care what happened to his mortal remains. Used to grumble to Trish that they could fly-tip him on the front lawn for all that he cared.

The joke's worn thinner the older he's become. He only permits himself visits to the graveyard a couple of times a month now. He doesn't want to get maudlin. Knows too many old men who have gone funny towards the end; wrapped up in an obsession with mortality, asking big questions about whos and whys and whethers. He doesn't want to be remembered like that. He's still pretty good company on the three nights a week he permits himself in one of the two pubs he can get to from home. Can spin a yarn and handle his drink and hasn't embarrassed himself in front of any youngsters as far as he's aware. He's happy enough to be thought of as he is. He doesn't want to become the morbid old bastard with tears in his eyes. He doesn't pray for much these days. Just says a few thank-yous and asks God to make sure he drops dead before his mind goes or he starts soiling himself.

He pulls a roll-up from his baccy tin, cosy in the pocket of his coat. Lights it with a match. Sucks the smoke into lungs that rattle like a saw working through wet wood.

They've been burying the Spinks here since the church was first consecrated.

He gulps, lustily, upon his roll-up. Feels a kind of comfortable melancholy settle upon him as he looks down at the plot where soon his own bones will rest. He's left instructions. Best brown suit and fresh socks. The comfortable shoes with the Velcro from the specialist shop. Hair lacquered flat, the way the wife had liked it. He wants his baccy tin in his coat pocket. He wants his dentures in, so he doesn't get to Heaven and give gummy *greetingsh* to *Shaint* Peter. He wouldn't mind a few butterscotches in his pocket for the journey.

As he stands in front of the graves of his loved ones, he becomes aware of a high, greasy kind of odour, cutting through the cigarette smoke and the mist. It's at once carnal and organic, like the base of a pan used to fry up chunks of yesterday's veg in bacon fat. It's a smell he knows. He knows how death tastes. He's seen bodies eaten alive by maggots. Was there when they brought up the poor lassie from the bottom of the lake, unpeeling her there on the ice-rimed shore; flesh peeling away like bad fruit. He stood here as the two big, quiet lads from Beverley sunk their spades into the sodden soil and wordlessly worked their way down towards his mother's bones, preparing a space for his dad so he could spend his eternity on top of her. It were always his joke – his idea of Heaven, so he said.

Tom turns from the headstones and wrinkles his nose. It's stronger now he's latched on to it. It's powerful. Stinking. He hocks up a mouthful of something nasty but can't bring himself to spit near the family graves. Swallows it down and grimaces.

Tom pushes aside the soft, damp twigs of the yew. Nudges his way into the quiet, murky chill beneath the canopy of branches and leaves.

He sees the axe, stuck in the ground like a flagpole. Sees the trench of freshly turned earth; all mulch and leaves and fat wriggling shapes. The chocolate brown of rotten wood. The pink and grey of rotten meat. The cloudy white of bone.

Tom steps back. Feels something touch the back of his neck. He feels dizzy suddenly, as if he's stood up too fast in a hot bath. He can't hear properly. He feels like he's underwater, bubbles and swirls of colour dancing in his vision.

He reaches out to steady himself. Grabs for the handle of the spade. It shifts beneath his weight and slips free from the sodden ground.

Suddenly he can hear wasps. Bees. Hornets. Horseflies. Millions of tiny, angry, buzzing pests surrounding him, biting him, settling upon his skin.

He stumbles back. Bangs against a hard mass. Tumbles forward, apologizing instinctively.

'Sorry, sorry . . .'

Tom realizes he's not alone. Shadow devours him like the mouth of a whale. He turns around to see who's joined him here, at the little church that has stood sentry here for five hundred years. He wonders where they came from. Who they're visiting. Whether they know who carved the lectern that stands beneath the stained-glass window. His thoughts arrive in a great rush: his mind still quick and agile. He reckons it'll be one of those true-crime enthusiasts, making a pilgrimage to venerate a monster. It could even be a journalist, though there aren't many of those buggers left. It would be nice if it was Trish, here to surprise him. It's been ages since he saw her or the girls. Too busy with her fancy-piece, he supposes. Can't blame her for that. deserves some happiness, that one. Seen too much . . .

The world lurches left. Sky becomes earth, sea becomes sky.
There's pain, somewhere. Pain and cloud and the buzzing of the
wasps.

The figure who stands above him is familiar: like a reflection in
a fun-fair mirror. Tall. Broad-shouldered. And the face, with its
dark beard and pointed cheeks; dark hair slicked back. And those
eyes. Black as coal. Black as the headstone.

Tom feels his dying heart clench. Grabs the tail of his sanity
and forces himself to reel it back in. Somebody's wearing a mask,
that's all. Somebody's trying to give him a fright. It's a rubber
mask, isn't it? But it's so realistic. It looks like dead flesh; looks
like meat buried underground then hewn from the earth with an
axe.

He's looking at Anders Wilkie. He's looking at the dead husband
of the woman he thinks of as a daughter. He's looking at the man
who once threatened to kill him. Looking at a bad man who
deserved all the misery that came his way. He's been dead for the
best part of two years. A decade crippled and voiceless before
that. But he's here. He's standing tall. He's wearing a soft leather
apron over jeans and a collarless shirt. There are tattoos on his
hands, skin glistening pinkly around the scars on his knuckles.

'Scared me . . .' burbles Tom, gulping, gasping, trying to make
a joke of it.

The figure reaches into the pocket at the front of the apron.
Pulls out a parcel. It's an oilskin roll, an old-fashioned pouch
wrapped up with a leather thong. There are initials monogrammed
on its frontage, smudged with dirt.

RH

'It's inside,' says Tom, still trying to keep things light. 'The
lectern, yeah? He did the gargoyles too. The misericords. They'll
be worth a fortune, shouldn't wonder. Church is locked, but I know
the warden. Shooting a video, or something are you? I can get out
of your hair . . .'

From the mouth of the mask, a great slug of purple tongue. It
elongates. Points. Divides perfectly in two.

Tom feels his face twist in revulsion. Peers at the figure. Stares
through the eye-holes. The eyes are shark-like, perfect black. He
remembers reading an article about body modification: people

injecting ink in their eyeballs; slicing their tongues in two; inserting implants in their foreheads to look like demons. He needs this to be a joke. He feels old, suddenly. Old and frightened.

'By heck, that must have hurt. Rather you than me . . .'

They unroll the pouch. It's full of chisels, each neatly placed inside an individual slot. Tom already knows who they belong to. Knows that he won't need to worry about the pills and the whisky and the best way to say goodbye.

'He sent you?'

They slide a fine-bladed chisel from its sheath. Angle their head. Clink, twice, their eyeballs swallowing the light.

'Not Trish,' says Tom. 'Don't hurt her. I swear to you, whatever you think you're doing, you don't want to go after her. She did her job. She did right by you. It was never what you thought . . .'

Tom doesn't even have time to raise his hands. One moment he's talking and the next he can't swallow, or breathe, and his mouth is filling with hot blood and the reek of iron, and he's falling to his knees; red dripping from his open mouth to anoint the handle of the chisel that sticks out of his throat; red flowers blooming amid the long grass and the churned earth at his feet.

He tumbles onto his side. Raises his hands and bats weakly at the object lodged in his trachea. Feels his fingers slip off the bloody handle.

He's rolled onto his back. The man with Anders' face stands with his feet either side of him. Tom smells sweat and the hot cat-piss reek of his own fear.

He looks past him. He doesn't want the face of Anders Wilkie to be the last thing he sees. Looks for the sun. Sees only the darkening sky.

He feels the first of the chisels go in between his ribs. Feels the second disarticulate his shoulder joint. Another separates his breastbone with the aid of a hammer. Tom watches a gull circling overhead. Hears his breath emerging from places other than his mouth. Feels himself diminishing: becoming less; emptying out into the earth that will eventually devour him. Then slide into the sea.

By the time his killer takes the final chisel to his body, Tom Spink has been dead for half an hour. His killer won't stop until he is told to do so. He has instructions. He has a duty to perform.

He is doing the Lord's work. He couldn't stop even if he wanted to. The Lord is watching. Watching even now, staring out from a little rectangle of mobile phone, sat atop a grave. The Lord doesn't speak. Doesn't offer words of approval.

The Lord just watches, and touches themselves, and enjoys the show.

It takes Tom's killer no effort to drag him by the ankles through the maze of gravestones. His corpse is hefted into the rear of a flatbed truck without any discernible effort. And then he is driven home. Driven to the little clifftop cottage where he has made his best memories. He's taken inside. Deposited on the floor: handles sticking out of him like the bristles of a hairbrush.

The killer listens to the eerie sound of creaking masonry and shifting earth. Crosses to the fireplace and cranks it up the full. Looks at themselves in the little mirror. There's blood upon the unfamiliar face. Blood and earth.

Somewhere deep inside, a voice cries out. Tells him to stop this. Tells him that this isn't what he wants. This is just the beginning. So much blood will be spilled: enough blood to drown her; to flood her; to make her see.

St Fucking Trish, he thinks. *Trish Fucking Pharaoh. They'll see you for what you are. They'll know what you did.*

And then he hears the Lord.

'It is mine to avenge; I will repay. In due time their foot will slip; their day of disaster is near, and their doom rushes upon them.'

The Lord looks upon his disciple's work. Looks out from the little rectangle of plastic and glass. Looks upon the tools sticking out of the old man's body like a woodcut of medieval vengeance.

And sees that it is good.

Transcript: 'GOOD MURDERS, BAD DEATHS'

Episode 13: You'll Meet a Tall, Dark Stranger

Original Air Date, January 4th
GMBD theme song plays

CLEM: And hello to all my murder groupies out there. You're a bunch of sick motherflumpers and I love you. This is the podcast for all you ladies who wet your panties when your phone vibrates unexpectedly but who can only fall properly asleep listening to an autopsy report and a psychological profile on the Green River Killer. I'm Clementine Lippman . . .

FENELLA: And I'm Fenella Warnock, apparently. When I put on a happy face, it's because I've just cut it off a dead clown. My head's as full of gore as Jeffrey Dahmer's fridge. And I'd like to apologize for use of the word 'panties'. What can I say – we have to cater for the Americans.

CLEM: Fenella's the quiet one. It's always the quiet ones.

FENELLA: I'm here for balance. And can I just say, high-five for motherflumpers. That's a word I'm stealing. I'd also like to second the learned lady's contention. I love you all too. You're making us ever so slightly relevant, you're helping us pay back student loans, and you're definitely putting a buffer beneath us and grisly death. That's right, yeah, Clem?

CLEM: Totes. Primarily, we're here to statistically decrease our chances of being murdered. That's right, yeah?

FENELLA: We hate the idea of pain and fear and suffering. But . . .

CLEM: We're addicted to learning about it. Snuffling about in it . . .

FENELLA: We're truffle-pigs for gore, yeah?

CLEM: I'll take that. And we do this because we know there are loads of people out there who are just like us, and because on some level we feel that the more intensely we look at murder, the less chance there is of us falling prey to it. Does that make sense?

FENELLA: Not really, but that doesn't make it any less real a feeling.

CLEM: She's the one with the psychological training, people. I'm just the ex-journalist.

FENELLA: Pin-up girl for the worst people in the world, is that right?

CLEM: I've been known to receive the occasional soiled tissue from Maximum Security, it's true.

FENELLA: And this week we're looking at a killer who's every bit as easy on the eyes as our Clementine, here. Quite the dish. Ladies and gentlemen, let me tell you about Reuben Hollow.

CLEM: This is the Lancelot Complex guy, yeah?

FENELLA: That's what they say. There have been a shitload of academic papers written on this guy. One of the 'syndromes' that's struck a chord with the general public is the whole 'Sir Lancelot' thing. If you've ever dreamed of a knight in shining armour, this is the dude you've been trying to summon up. Be careful what you wish for.

CLEM: So, here's this guy's deal. Imagine you're a young, attractive woman . . .

FENELLA: So easy, right?

CLEM: And you're in a bar, having a drink, and feeling like the whole world is against you. You're in trouble, right? Your boyfriend is beating you up. Or you owe money to your landlord and he's going to take the arrears out of your rear, yeah? Or some drunken prick has run your sister down on a country road and now they're suing her for having the temerity to get in the way of their Subaru. And you're feeling so lost and helpless and small and you're wishing it was like the movies. You're wishing some handsome stranger would come and buy your drink and listen to your sob story and generally tell you that everything's going to be OK now.

FENELLA: Been there, babe. It'd be nice, right?

CLEM: Reuben Hollow's the guy you're trying to conjure up. Reuben doesn't like bullies. He doesn't like bad people. And if you catch him on the right day, in the right mood, and you've got the right story, there's a good chance that the person who's been making you unhappy will end up dead. Brutally killed. Beaten and stomped and taken apart. Removed. Excised. Gone. And you're happy, right, because your problems have gone away, and you never asked him to do anything, did you, so your conscience is clear.

FENELLA: It helps that he's pretty as a picture. Take a look at this guy . . .

CLEM: Oh wow! Do people still say hubba-hubba?

FENELLA: That's a Hollywood face, right? Scruffy wood-cutter guy – rugged and twinkly; the plaid shirt and the leather jewellery and the Celtic tattoos . . .

CLEM: And he lives in a tumbledown little cottage in the woods in East Yorkshire. He looks after his stepdaughter and he carves beautiful lecterns and misericords for local churches. He smokes roll-ups and drinks in his local and listens to people who need a friend. And in his spare time, he's killing nasty bastards with his bare hands.

FENELLA: You're sure they did the right thing catching this guy? You don't think people would behave themselves a little better if they knew this bad-ass was out there waiting to teach them a lesson if they overstepped the line.

CLEM: Too good to be true, as ever, Fenella. He wasn't just bumping off dealers and people-traffickers; sex pests and wife-beaters. Unfortunately for those of you who were about to write to this guy and propose marriage . . . he's got two serious black marks against his name. He's doing life for six murders but two of them are the very same broken and vulnerable young ladies who he set out to help. Adejola Bankole, Bruce Corden, Dennis Ball, Raymond O'Neill. All nasty motherfuckers, right? But Ava Delaney and Hannah Kelly died nasty deaths and had their armpits scalped.

FENELLA: Wait, back up . . .

CLEM: Two of the ladies he helped out – they weren't happy with the whole enigmatic mystery man thing. They wanted more. One of them wanted love; the other wanted money. Both threatened to expose him in order to get it.

FENELLA: So he killed them for it?

CLEM: So he says. Admitted it at trial though he wouldn't answer a single question about those two. Happy to give the police chapter and verse on the others, though there's every chance he's done plenty more than those he confessed to – including some very suspicious deaths among the sex-offender community since he's been in prison.

FENELLA: The armpits thing was a kink, according to his internet search history. His critics say they show his true colours – others that he's got a split personality or an accomplice with a different vibe. Talk about a let-down, right? Why couldn't he just be one of the good guys, yeah? Either way, he's fascinated the psychiatric community.

CLEM: The Lancelot Complex thing, yeah? The Knight in Shining Armour, riding in to rescue damsels in distress. Fuck, this guy's in the wrong century.

FENELLA: He's struck a chord somewhere. The prison authorities say he receives upwards of two dozen proposals of marriage a week. He still gets letters from ladies desperate for him to help them get out from under the chokeholds of whichever bastard is holding them down.

CLEM: My misogyny alarm bells are clanging, babe. Does this guy love women or think we're all too pathetic to stand up for ourselves?

FENELLA: That's the question asked by the detective who caught him. Ladies and gentlemen, you've got to acquaint yourself with Detective Superintendent Trish Pharaoh. Hull Police? Humberside? Fuck it, who knows? But this lady is a proper Queen Bee, you know what I'm saying. Five foot nothing, sunglasses and a leather jacket; black cigarette sticking out the corner of her mouth. She staged the honey trap that got him to confess it all. And she was the honey. Rumour is he fell in love with her during the investigation. Carved these little miniature figurines of her, even while she was trying to lock him up for multiple murders. She still visits him inside.

CLEM: What's her deal?

FENELLA: She made herself vulnerable. Set herself up to be the perfect damsel in distress. He came riding in to the rescue and now he's never getting out of prison.

CLEM: And he's cool with that?

FENELLA: Either that or he's sitting in his cell plotting some dire retribution. There've been one or two true-crime documentaries about this dude but Trish won't be interviewed about it. Probably saving her best stories for a speaking tour when she retires.

CLEM: So, come on. Gory details . . .

FENELLA: Oh, he was a master craftsman. You're going to love this . . .

PART ONE

ONE

He makes a pillow of her chest, pushing his cheek into the warm softness of her tummy. Nuzzles his head beneath her chin: pitching quiet compliments into her belly-button like coins into a wishing-well. His hair is longish, reddish. Her heartbeat punches him in the jaw. She looks down, eyes slightly crossed. Imagines herself to suddenly possess a splendid Viking beard. Giggles, the sound girlish and bright. Chides herself for being such a soft sod; for being such a total fanny. Bites her tongue, and wishes it were his.

'Trish?'

She shushes him. Kisses his forehead and breathes him in, sipping at the soft cocktail of his flavours like a sommelier assessing the tannins of a particularly earthy *primitivo*. She recognizes her own hand cream in his scent. Her own sweat, too. Catches the faint trace of some herby, home-made soap; all mulch and roots and yellow-green leaves. She lifts her nose from his scalp before she can be assailed by shameful mental images; before she can picture the nimble fingers of the perfect little wife who made the lotion.

She lifts his head. Pushes him down a little. 'Again?' he asks, eager to please.

'Fuck, no,' she laughs, the sound harsh in her throat. 'Soz. Knock yourself out if you like but I'll be dozing.'

'I'm sure I can tempt you.'

His breath is warm against her bare skin and although she's too tired and sore to need him again, she feels her body respond. Persuades herself to resist. Her hunger for him is a carnivorous, gluttonous thing. She wants to gorge herself on him; tear at hunks of his big, scarred, muscled flesh. Wants to attack him like a shark devouring a dead whale. But there's a limit to what she can ask of herself.

'You're smiling,' he says, into her armpit.

'How can you tell that?' she asks, running her fingers through his hair. She thinks of fur. Thinks of a big soppy dog having its ears scratched.

He shrugs. Tickles her hip. 'The air around you,' he says, voice muffled, his accent thick. 'The temperature you vibrate at. The frequency of you. I don't know. I see your colours and I know when you're happy.'

She gives a little laugh. 'It's the accent that makes it poetic. If you said that like a bloke from Rotherham you'd sound fucking mental.'

She wriggles herself until she's a little more comfortable. Feels the good ache in her tummy, the bruising of her lips. Loses focus; tiredness creeping in. Looks for the horizon as if trying to fend off motion sickness. Her gaze falls on the laptop, half open on her cluttered dressing table, among the glass bottles, the bangles and beads. She's silenced the notifications but she can't help wondering whether there have been any developments; whether her lies are holding together or starting to fray. She feels like the spider at the centre of a web, sensing the nearness of the storm.

'Trish?'

She doesn't reply. Becomes aware of the cold air drifting from the open window. Sees her own breath rising up; feels her sweat grow cold and experiences a surge of gratitude that she has a warm body to cuddle into for the first time since before.

He shifts his position. Moves down and kisses her stomach; her belly-button; her stretch-marks.

'It's like the sand after the tide has gone out,' he says, softly, stroking his big, rough fingers over the silvery texture upon her skin. He touches her caesarean scar. 'Which one was this?'

'Last one,' she says, glad of momentary distraction. 'Olivia. I was expecting her to pretty much walk out but nope, had to be awkward. Head like a fricking bowling ball so it's probably just as well.'

'She's what? Seventeen now?'

She grunts an affirmation. 'Aye. Pain in the arse but brilliant.'

'You're still arguing?'

'Thinks I'm the devil,' she says, tightness in her throat. 'Made a saint out of her dad since he kicked the bucket. Telling herself fairy tales.'

'Kicked the bucket?' he asks, as if he's never heard the phrase before.

'Don't worry your pretty head.'

She's pleased when he doesn't press for more. She doesn't want to talk about her children. Not here. Not now. Not when she's finally holding her big, red-haired warrior and basking in the warm glow of their coupling. Not now she's finally damning the consequences. It's not as though she's even a proper mum any more. Her eldest has a baby daughter of her own, which makes Trish Pharaoh a fucking grandmother! The two middle girls are away at university making bad debts and good memories. And Olivia, well . . . she hopes she'll find her way back to some kind of equilibrium. She's got a temper, just like her mum. They've always butted heads. She saw too much when she was young. They all did, but Olivia was too young to talk about any of it when it was happening and by the time she'd reached an age where she might understand the accommodations that her mum made in order to do them all the least possible damage, Pharaoh didn't want to dig up old memories. Lies and accusations have flooded the vacuum. Olivia has jumped to all the wrong conclusions and Pharaoh is too damn proud to sit down with her and talk to her about it. So they just argue, and shout at one another: send text messages in capital letters. Occasionally they apologize and manage to have a halfway pleasant breakfast or see a film. But there is a chasm between them – each on a different ledge over an impossible divide. And Pharaoh, if she's honest, has other things to deal with right now. Other problems, far bigger than Olivia's teenage angst. The ghosts of her past are climbing out of the earth. The sins she committed in her youth are demanding that she balance the books. The wrong people are scrutinizing her decisions, her narratives; the carefully woven tapestry of half-lies and omissions that have permitted her to stay one step ahead of her pursuers. This moment, this here, this now, is an indulgence, a longed-for distraction from the unceasing static in her skull. Here, in his arms, she can briefly forget about Malcolm Tozer. About the podcast. About the old videotape. About Reuben Fucking Hollow. Here, with him, she feels able to put herself first. Feels entitled to cushion herself from her anxieties and fears with an increasing number of moments like this. She knows it won't last – that this union is mere intermission, a pleasant pause in which she can draw a breath.

'. . . had it up to here with bloody aubergines, Tristan.'

'This is the business with the avocado all over again, isn't it!'

From somewhere nearby comes the sound of a man and woman arguing. She experiences a memory; the excitement of hearing it all kick off in the street outside her childhood home in Mexborough, South Yorkshire, though anybody getting upset about aubergines in her neighbourhood would more likely have mispronounced a slur against Australia's natives. She used to love summer nights when the neighbours would have too much to drink and launch themselves at one another over the garden fence and she'd be able to sit at the window, shielded by the paper-thin curtains, and watch Mad Mags kick lumps out of her own front door. She had her own share of scraps when she got old enough. Put down bigger and harder when they had the brass neck to tell her she was a stuck-up cow who spent half her life on her back and the other on her knees. She always stuck up for herself. Stuck up for others too. Could never stand a bully, right up until the day she married one.

'I've cut you,' she says, looking down at the scratches on his back. She glances at her fingernails. She had them done for their date, black with white tips: a pint of Guinness at the end of each finger. Two of them are missing. 'That must be sore.'

She feels him shrug. 'I'm not complaining.'

Silence again. Just breathing and the pleasant connection of skin upon skin.

'You still take these?' he asks.

She changes position. Sees that he's picked up a blister pack of her pills from the junk on the bedside table. She's been using them as a bookmark, stuffed into the paperback that serves as a paperweight for bills, print-outs, old photographs and empty biscuit wrappers that form a little mount of modern art.

She nods. '225mg. Tried dropping down a bit but it felt like somebody was jangling keys inside my head. I'll go cold turkey when I have the time.'

He doesn't reply. She's grateful. She doesn't want to answer

questions about the vagaries of her unhappiness or the dosage of her
anti-depressants. Doesn't want a lecture on the dangers of drinking
when she's already cushioning herself with medication. Doesn't
want him thinking that she shouldn't need to take them now they've
truly found one another. She has a packet of diazepam somewhere,
just to take the edge off the anxiety. She doesn't want to be told
that she never seems anxious – that, if anything, she radiates a
confidence and capability that most people would long to possess.
She wants him to see through the act. Too see through it, but not
tell her. She doesn't want to tell him how much of the appearance
she wears for the world is an act. Can't stand the thought of him
questioning whether such a convincing performer can be trusted to
say 'I love you' and really mean it.

'Since he died?' he asks, quietly.

She nods. It's easier. Her husband's been dead nigh on eighteen
months. She's happy to let him think that she grieves.

She hears voices drifting up from the street below. She lives on
one of the wide, arrow-straight Victorian avenues in what passes
for the bohemian, artsy quarter of Hull. They call this place the
Muesli Belt. It's coffee shops and cafe bars; it's wheat beer and
book clubs and mums who bake muffins for teacher on the last
day of term. It's all matching jogging wear and twice-yearly skiing
trips and parents who call their children 'the guys'.

'I'm hungry,' he says, stretching out. 'I could make you
something.'

'I think there's a Chinese underneath that mound of shoes,' says
Pharaoh, nodding in the general direction of the wardrobe. She'd
planned to tidy up for her guest's arrival. Decided that housework
was a patriarchal construct and that she would better serve her
beliefs by leaving the place a pigsty and watching *The Godfather*
while eating cereal from the box instead.

'Is there really?' he asks, a wince in his voice.

'It's probably evolved by now. Primitive life-form. He's called
Alan and works in urban planning. Plays golf on a weekend.'

'I don't always understand you,' he smiles, running his knuckles
over her bare skin.

'Neither do I.'

They lie in silence for a while. She stares up at the ceiling.
It's high. Artexed. There are cobwebs pitching a sail from the

cord of the light fitting. She'll never be able to reach them. She's small. Round-shouldered. Blue-eyed and dark-haired and squishy in the places she wants to be. She reckons she looks OK for fifty-two. She's cut down on the booze recently. Dropped the little black cigarettes and started to vape. Does the occasional workout in front of her laptop, giggling and swearing to herself as she topples over on her yoga mat or falls asleep while downward-facing dogging.

He readjusts himself. Lays his head down on the pillow beside her. She rolls onto her side so she can touch the tip of her nose against his. His big, scarred face blurs; one eye in the middle of his forehead. She giggles. Doesn't mind. She feels happy. Doesn't need to pretend she's somebody else. Doesn't need to be Detective Superintendent Trish Pharaoh. Here, now, she's a woman who might just be in love.

'It's late,' he says, glancing at the clock on the dressing table. It's an antique. Expensive. She likes the tick. Needs it to sleep.

'You're not going,' she says, stiffening. She takes a fistful of the bedsheet. Holds her breath. Please, she says, inside herself. Please don't go . . .

'Going?' he asks. 'Going where?'

She doesn't reply. Rolls away from him. Reaches down into the mess on the floor and retrieves her vape from the pocket of her leather jacket. She inhales deeply. Wishes it was a cigarette.

'What flavour?' he asks, sniffing.

'Chicken Kiev,' she mutters, into her wrist.

'Hey,' he says, gently. She feels a hand on her shoulder. 'Hey, Trish . . .'

She shakes her head. Puts her palms together and places them under her cheek. Pulls her knees up.

'Did I say something wrong?' he asks, pulling himself in behind her. She feels his nakedness. Feels all the desire drain out like blood. 'Trish, why would you think I would go?'

She doesn't reply. A motorbike growls past; a low throaty rumble drifting in from the open window. She wonders if the neighbours heard them having sex. Hopes so.

'Trish?'

'I'm tired,' she says, without emotion. 'You've worn me out. You can stay if you want. I don't mind. Whatever.'

She can sense his confusion. Can't help but enjoy it, even as she hates herself for playing games with his brain. She doesn't know what she wants. Doesn't know how to help him help her.

'I can sleep on the sofa,' he says, his accent stronger as the exasperation takes hold of his voice. 'I don't understand. You asked me to stay. You said you wanted this . . .'

'Don't,' she says, biting the inside of her cheek. 'Don't get weird.'

'Me get weird?' He rolls away from her. She feels the bed move as he sits up and swings his feet out and onto the floor. She wants to roll over and put her palm upon his back. Wants to tell him to stay; that she wants him to stay and never leave – that she's just frightened because she hasn't woken up next to a new man in almost thirty years.

'Me get weird,' he mutters. 'Me? *Andskotans!*'

She hears him moving around, picking up his clothes. Hears the little beep as he checks his phone. Wonders if it's a message from her. From the pretty, perfect little wife who's keeping his pillow warm at home.

Pharaoh rolls onto her back. Pushes herself into a sitting position. Covers her nakedness with the quilt and watches as she pulls on his shirt. He looks upset. Looks confused. He senses her watching him and looks at her with his big sad eyes. 'I did something wrong?'

She sags. 'I don't know where I'm at,' she mumbles, and wishes she could think of a better way to make it make sense. She pushes her hair behind her ears and pulls her knees up. 'I feel wrong. Feel lost, or something. I get moments where it's all good, all brilliant; I'm smiling for nothing, just grinning like a fucking idiot. And then I think about the other stuff – the people who'll get hurt; about where we'll live, what we'll do, who we'll be. They want me to retire. I could, you know. And I have these fantasies about you and me and a little place away from the world. But then I feel like a silly old woman. I mean, you're so much younger than me. And I've done things. I've got secrets. I don't know what's for the best and that's something I always bloody know . . .'

He gives her a gentle smile. Nods his head. Puts his hand out. It's huge, with cracked knuckles and pale, freckled skin. There's a pain in her chest as he pulls her towards him; a sensation of having everything she wants, and nothing at all.

'Trish, I . . .'

There's a loud bang from outside: the thud of metal striking something hard. A moment later comes the screaming-baby wail of a car alarm. Flashing yellow lights throw a soft, gaudy pattern onto the backs of the net curtains.

Pharaoh puts her head back against the headboard. 'Fuck sake,' she mutters, clambering out of bed. 'That's bloody mine . . .'

He pats the air. Shakes his head. He looks out of the window. Turns back with a shrug. 'Throw me the keys,' he says. 'I can try from here.'

'Doesn't work,' she says, her manner one colossal shrug. She doesn't want to think about her car. Doesn't want to go and pick up the pieces of whatever else has gone wrong while she was looking in a different direction. Let some bugger else, for a change. 'It needs recharging. You have to put the key in the lock . . . oh, for fuck's sake. It's OK, chuck me that dress . . .'

He spots the car keys on the dresser. Gives her a smile. 'I'm more dressed than you,' he smiles, gesturing to himself. He has his trousers on. Boots. He's a huge great bear of a man and looks like he's about to go and take part in an underground bare-knuckle boxing match. She grins as she looks at him. Enjoys knowing that here, now, he's hers.

'Thanks,' she says, and settles back. She likes this. He closes the door behind him and tries to shut out the raucous call of the car alarm so she can hear him make his way through the living room and out the door. Listens for the faint thump of his feet down the staircase. Hears the front door open. Takes a suck on her vape and enjoys the sound of popping bubbles. Hears the car alarm fall silent. The soft snick of the door on her old knackered little convertible gently closing. He's so bloody considerate. Such a nice big lump of a man.

She strains to hear. She's comfy in bed. Doesn't want to cross to the window and peek out like some nosy neighbour. But she's a copper. Curiosity doesn't always kill the cat.

Pharaoh is halfway across the bedroom, stepping over a pile of case files, pulling a blanket around her shoulders, when she hears the noise. It's shrill; pained – an inhuman screech of shock and pain. She stops suddenly. Hears three thuds. A fourth; a sound like a cleaver hitting a chopping block.

Pharaoh darts forward. Snatches back the curtain. Looks down to the road.

He's on his front, arms outstretched. In the cone of yellow light that emanates from the streetlamp he looks like Da Vinci's Vitruvian man.

She blinks. Tries to make sense of what she's seeing. Feels her heart clench like a fist squeezing a stone. Feels her throat constrict.

Her instincts kick in. Thirty years of coppering take over. She scans the street. Sees her car, parked up between the little Kia and the estate. Looks across the big houses opposite. There are lights on behind the curtains in one or two of the properties but nobody's looking out. She glances down towards the big fountain that sits in the middle of the little roundabout, a great incongruous assemblage of white mermaids and herons.

Then she sees them. Sees the shape that lurks in the darkness beneath the towering lime tree.

They step out. Step into the next cone of light like an actor stepping onto a stage. She's too far away to make out any details. They're big. Dark clothes. Gloves. She squints through the gloom. Watches, barely breathing, as he raises his head and stares directly up at her. For a moment there is a flash of recognition. For an instant, there is something about him that seems familiar. There's something wrong with his face. There's a blurriness to him, as if he is a smudged Polaroid.

'Stop,' she shouts, swallowing hard. Instinct takes over. 'Stop . . . police!'

He slithers back into the shadows, the darkness closing around him like a mouth.

And then she is running from the room, barrelling down the steps, slipping on the cold stairs. She yanks open the front door and runs down the path, broken glass and tiny stones stabbing at her bare feet. She dashes across the chill, dew-soaked grass to where her man lies. Stops a car length away from him, hands at her mouth.

There are three huge wounds on his back, three axe strokes in his pale, freckled skin. They bleed blackly, oozing blood.

'No,' she whispers, gasping for breath. 'No . . .'

She crouches down. Presses her fingers to his neck. Feels the pulse, weak as a baby bird's, beneath the beard.

'Hold on,' she says. 'Please, don't, please . . .'

She looks again at the wounds. Looks at the horrifying trench cut into the broadness of his shoulder blade. Looks at the ruination of flesh and meat and muscle. Presses her fingers to the worst wound, trying to hold his skin together. It's like trying to pick up a cobweb. Her fingers slide in the gore. Touch something hard. Something that shouldn't be there; protruding from the ruined flesh of the man she thinks she loves.

She can't help it. Can't help but manoeuvre the flesh so that she can see the little object sticking out of the wound like a toy soldier buried in sand.

There are footsteps behind her. The sound of screams. Shouts. The demand to call for an ambulance. There are hands upon her. Hands upon him. A light shining on his back, illuminating the true horror of what has been done.

She sees the little figurine poking out of the wound. She's seen one before. Knows exactly what is staring back at her. It's a tiny wooden sculpture; no bigger than a chess piece. It's female. Sultry. Motherly. It's at once a fertility idol and an immaculate Madonna. It's her own likeness, a perfect miniature Pharaoh rising from the gash like the figurehead of a ship.

'Boss,' she hears. 'Boss . . . they're here, the paramedics, let go, Boss, let go . . .'

She lets herself be steered back. Feels arms around her. Feels a coat around her shoulders. Holds the bloodied figurine in her fist and tucks it, wetly, inside the folds of the blanket.

She only half recognizes the officer. Can't remember his name or rank or whether he's any good. 'Detective Superintendent,' he's saying, over and over. 'Boss, are you OK . . . are you hurt?'

She shakes him off. There's a buzz of static in her head; lights flashing, sirens wailing, tyres crunching over gravel and grass. Two paramedics are kneeling at his side. Another uniformed copper is on his radio, looking down at the dying, half-dressed man. He glances at Pharaoh. Lowers his voice as he talks into the radio. She reads his lips. Sees the wheels in his brain turning. The big, red-haired man; tattoos and scars and muscles like a cage-fighter. Realizes what they're all going to think.

'Jesus,' he's saying, looking down at the broken body. 'I think the victim is Aector Fucking McAvoy . . .'

Pharaoh doesn't hear the rest of the conversation. Her world is all static and grief. She slithers down to the kerb and sits with her feet in the gutter. Watches her world collapse in on itself like a dying star.

TWO

Amberline Haven, Gamblesby, Eden Valley
12.37 a.m.

Aector Fucking McAvoy is feeling unusually good about life when the news reaches him that he's been attacked and left for dead on one of Hull's most well-to-do streets. It comes as a shock and causes a familiar flush of disappointment with himself. Getting killed is just the sort of thing he'd expect from the over-achieving simpleton he knows himself to be. He had believed himself to be enjoying a break with his family, their borrowed bow-top wagon pitched in this green velvet fold of the Eden Valley: this soft pause in the craggy landscape between the Lake District and the Pennines. He had thought himself comfortable by the fire, the echo of poetry upon his tongue and fire-fairies dancing upon the cold dark air. Had thought he was listening to the snap and chomp of the kindling giving itself up to the flame, smiling to himself in response to the occasional ghostly hoot from the owl that stares out with wide, paranoid, *you-weren't-there* eyes in the oak overhead. Had believed himself to be alive and vital: sitting outside the darkened hump of the bow-top *vardo*, his clothes damp with dew and sweat and the soft rain that hangs like mist in this black, black air.

It's not really a holiday, though he's sold it to the children as such. Sold it as skilfully as Trish Pharaoh sold it to him. He has no capacity for lies, but he has a knack for protecting the people he loves from the harshness of unvarnished truth and he found the strength to dissemble. He hasn't beaten himself up for it. Not this time. The kids don't need to know just how poorly Mammy has been. That particular pain is his to hold. Hers too, though she carries the pain of her illness without complaint. Tells him that he's making a fuss, being an eejit, even as her legs give out and her joints ache and she erupts in hacking coughs that engulf her with such ferocity that she can't even find the breath to scream. It's called Familial Mediterranean Fever. Hereditary, though neither Mam nor Dad nor any of her multitude of sisters and brothers have been struck down. It's a condition peculiar to her heritage, found almost exclusively in travellers and those of Mediterranean origin, announcing its previously unheralded arrival in a storm of peritonitis, pleuritis, arthritis and fever. The consultant at Castle Hill Hospital feared it was leukaemia before a senior colleague discreetly pointed out that Roisin had 'a rather gypsy look' and suggested she be quizzed accordingly. The junior doctor had been rather excited to be able to tell that it was FMF. She wasn't dying – just destined to suffer in perpetuity. They'd told her that it would go away, but it would come back, and that this would be the pattern of her life until it wasn't. If it affected more people there might well be a cure but those it strikes have a knack for forbearance and tend to make do with ibuprofen, vodka and stoicism.

These few days in the bow-top wagon are McAvoy's 'Hail Mary', a union of pilgrimage and prayer, of convalescence and cure. They represent his desperate need to do something, anything, that might just help the person he loves most find her way back to herself. It's working, after a fashion. She's smiling again. Can stand to be touched. Can just about raise her hands high enough to brush her own hair.

In this quiet, gentle, fireside moment, before he learns he's a dead man, McAvoy's feeling a mild swell of contentment; a sense of having done something of use. He's not a godly man, but there's something atavistic about the frost and the fireside and the gathering dark and he finds himself giving some unspoken sense of thanks to the elements; to the universe, to the old deities and the new, that he's alive, and here, and that everybody he truly loves is more or less by his side.

The little fold-out chair doesn't look big enough to hold his weight, let alone the added bulk of his seven-year-old daughter,

Lilah, who has draped herself around him like the chains of a lord mayor. She's wrapped in a blanket, her pretty little face poking out to snore hot-chocolate breath against his cheek. She braided his beard earlier: twin plaits dangling down from his chin like the drool-strings of a bulldog. The temperature is only a little above freezing but McAvoy is sweating like a fun-runner in July. He fed the fire before taking his place at its side and the flames dance and flicker like garlands, casting great gusts of hot smoke into the dark, shimmering air. His eyes are stinging, his skin clammy beneath his padded shirt and paint-splashed jeans. But he doesn't want to put Lilah to bed. Doesn't want this moment to end. If he squints he can just about make out the little white shapes above the rise of the hill. He can see Roisin, wrapped in her mother's shawl, pressing her face against the flank of the big grey Clydesdale that's been pulling them around the little network of wildflower-dusted meadows and soft, silent woods. She's been better this past couple of days. The puffiness at her neck and wrists has dissipated a little and there's more colour in her eyes. She's making jokes again. He heard her singing this morning as she cleaned the windows of the little bow-top wagon that's been home these past few nights and where their son, Fin, is currently spreadeagled and snoring, his bones aching from a day of chopping logs and building walls, repairing the chicken coop and shoring up the bank of the river at the bottom of the hill. This place is doing him good. He's been through a lot, has Fin. He's fourteen now; a tricky age for anybody but twice as hard when you're big and ginger and prone to blushing in the face of social interaction. McAvoy breaks out in cold sweats at the thought of being an adolescent in the age of social media.

'. . . and then the rat chewed my toe and said I was a marshmallow.'

McAvoy smiles. Strokes Lilah's hair. His daughter has always talked in her sleep. She has a busy brain and an excellent imagination. She writes stories sometimes, building great worlds of goblins and pixies, werewolves and knights. Some days she'll only answer to the name 'Mariposa' and will only concede to go to school if she's allowed to wear her elven queen costume beneath her school uniform. She scares her teachers. Scares McAvoy too. She and her mammy argue every day – McAvoy and his son watching their

unceasing disagreements with abject bewilderment. To both, it
seems as futile as arguing with a mirror.

McAvoy shifts position. He wonders whether it would disturb
her if he leant forward and picked up his book from the wet grass.
There's just enough light to see by and he'd like to finish the
chapter before he retires for the night. He's enjoying a new trans-
lation of the works of the Syrian poet Nizar Qabbani. It habitually
moves him to quiet tears. McAvoy loves any poetry which feels
like it has been written in the ink which has bled from a broken
heart. It comforts him to know that there are people in the world
who understand how it feels to love truly; to love fiercely – who
know the kind of love that a person will live for, die for; make a
fool of themselves for. He knows love to be an insanity of sorts:
a psychosis as cruel as it is enchanting. Qabbani understands. He
wasn't familiar with the poet until recently. Somebody sent him
a copy, bound in waxy butcher's paper, on his last birthday. There
had been no card. No tag. Just a neat inscription written on the
flyleaf. *To The Only Good Man I Know*. He presumes it was from
Helen, a friend and former colleague who works in London for
the National Crime Agency, and who has become a fan of poetry
since he first loaned her a precious copy of a Larkin. She'd been
right in her assertion that he would love Qabbani. Roisin does too.
He likes reading to her as she curls up against him, shivering and
sweating in turn. She likes his voice when he reads – his low
Scottish brogue somehow a perfect fit for the Middle Eastern
rhythms. He's aching for her now, ready to get everybody settled
down for the night. When Roisin returns from the paddock he'll
kiss her goodnight and take up his sentry position beneath the
wagon, laid out on a plastic tarpaulin and wrapped tight in a too-
small sleeping bag. Roisin had gone into convulsions of laughter
when she'd first seen him trying to squeeze his twenty-stone, six-
foot six-inch frame into the bag. '*Fecking hell*,' she'd laughed,
wiping away tears. '*It's like putting a condom on a horse.*' He
hadn't offered anything but sad eyes in reply, even as he'd felt the
urge to enquire who'd done her research.

'My, that's a sight.'

McAvoy hadn't seen his wife approach. She appears in the
circle of firelight like a ghost. He grins, instinctively, as he takes
her in. Fourteen years of marriage and she still takes his breath

away. She's wearing leopard-print pyjamas beneath the hand-woven shawl. She's barefoot, convinced that feeling the earth beneath her feet will do her as much good as any amount of vitamin supplements and anti-inflammatory drugs. It always comes a surprise to McAvoy that flowers don't spontaneously bloom where she treads.

'Is Bob settled in for the night?' asks McAvoy, quietly. A small, fond smile warms his eyes.

'He's a big eejit,' she says, flicking her dark hair behind her ears. 'Proper soft sod. Size of a bloody battleship but just wants his tummy tickled. I swear, I looked in his eyes and saw my husband.'

McAvoy pouts. 'That's twenty-seven jokes about my similarity to a carthorse. Twenty-seven, Roisin. I've been keeping count.'

'Twenty-eight,' mutters Lilah, opening one eye. 'She actually said something mucky after she made the condom joke. I didn't get it, but there was definitely something in her voice that said it was mean.'

'It was complimentary, actually,' laughs Roisin, pushing Lilah to one side and sliding on to McAvoy's knee. She nuzzles into him, nose-to-nose with her daughter. The wooden chair creaks. McAvoy's bones make a sound like splintering logs. He bears it without complaint.

'Kush brought me a tea,' says Roisin, in the voice she uses when she wants to tease her husband. 'Perfect, it was. Stewed just long enough. Right temperature. Just a stir of sugar.'

McAvoy sighs, put-upon. He'd tried to boil the kettle on the campfire the first night they arrived. It took him four hours and when he delivered the brew to his wife's outstretched hand she'd told him it tasted of the soap he'd used to rinse the mug. He's a sensitive man. It will take a long time for him to forgive himself. He's already slightly jealous of Kush, the long-haired New Age traveller who runs the off-grid paradise between the copse of woodland and the chuckling waterway at the foot of the slope. He lives in a hand-built wooden cabin beyond the paddock: a chaos of wood and aluminium, scavenged sinks and rainbow glass. McAvoy has already accepted that if he dies any time soon, Roisin and Kush will make a lovely couple and this is the environment he wants them to raise their children in. McAvoy and Fin have made themselves useful, helping him with the general upkeep of the place. Lilah, by contrast, has spent most of her time risking life and limb on the horribly unsafe rope swings that dangle over sheer drops like nooses over a trapdoor.

'It's colder tonight,' says McAvoy, pulling his girls closer into his embrace. 'There'll be frost in the morning.'

'You'll be frozen solid,' laughs Lilah, sleepily. 'Mammy, if we have to boil a kettle to thaw him out, can you do it? I mean, you're the expert at all this.'

'I'll just pee on him,' says Roisin, mischief in her voice. 'My daddy used to put his feet in a bowl of his first pee of the day whenever he had chilblains.'

'How delightful,' says Lilah, wrinkling her nose. 'I can help though, if you want. You do the top end, I'll do the bottom . . .'

'Could you not have this conversation please?' asks McAvoy, feeling a little picked on. 'Next you'll be saying "heads or tails". And anyway, you can't leave Fin out.'

'You are so weird, Daddy,' mumbles Lilah, snuggling back in to his chest. 'Seriously, it's no wonder Auntie Trish is always saying you need a good bang on the head.'

Roisin tuts; a standard response whenever Pharaoh is mentioned. 'Aye, she'd bang you right enough. I'm sure I spotted her in the next paddock, as it goes. She looked happy enough. Grazing merrily, so she was.'

'Horse joke?' asks Lilah, sleepily.

'Cow,' explains Roisin.

McAvoy stays silent. He knows it's for the best. His wife and his boss tolerate one another. There's even a grudging kind of respect there. But he fancies that if one heard that the other had parachuted into the whirring blades of a helicopter, the other wouldn't be able to mask their smile.

'Aector! Hello, Aector – I don't want to give you a fright but if I start shaking a tambourine it's likely to freak you right out. Bugger, is that horse-shit? It is. Oh man, right through the flip-flop. Roisin, give him a prod, it's the fuzz.'

McAvoy looks up. Kush is emerging from the darkness: piratical in his boots and neckerchief, his bald head and rhododendron tufts; his earrings and septum-piercing. He's holding a phone, using the light to pick his way between the other wagons. There are six of them, laid out in a semicircle, though the McAvoys are the only guests at present. McAvoy has been offered use of whichever other *vardo* he wants but has resisted the generous suggestion. He wants Roisin to feel the way she did when she was a girl; travelling the backroads – saucepans and best china clinking on their hooks; hand-stitched curtains drawn across little mullioned windows; Daddy up front, chattering to the horse, sun glinting on polished leather and decorative brass. Having him sleep under the wagon is part of the aesthetic. He's done his best. He always does his best.

'Were we talking too loud?' asks McAvoy, apology in his voice. 'Sorry, we were just about to . . .'

Kush gives a shake of his head. He doesn't look his usual self. There's a seriousness about his features – something about the set of his slim, willowy frame.

'All good, Kush?' asks Roisin, looking up and switching instinctively into the role of proud matriarch and domestic goddess. 'I can make you something if you're peckish. There's ham and a couple of hard-boiled eggs . . .'

'Phone for you,' says Kush, cutting her off. 'They've been trying your mobile. Told them they wouldn't get you on it and that you'd asked not to be disturbed but he's a right persistent sod.'

'How did they get you?' asks McAvoy, sitting forward, his hand under Lilah's back. 'I never told anybody where we were going. Trish's Sophia knew, but she wouldn't . . . how did they . . .?'

Kush shrugs. He has the inherent paranoia of a person who believes in civil liberties, the coming of the revolution, and who has smoked his own bodyweight in weed. 'Coppers, innit? Always watching. You never know what they know. There's probably a tracker in your neck.'

McAvoy's mind is racing. He'd deliberately chosen not to tell anybody where they were going. If somebody has traced him to Kush's little encampment they must have had to ping his mobile phone. And to do that must have meant this is damned important.

'Detective Inspector McAvoy,' he says, and feels a shameful frisson of pleasure at being able to use his hard-earned new rank. He loses confidence immediately. Back-pedals. 'Or just Aector, whichever's easier . . .'

'It's Ben, Sarge,' comes a familiar voice. The line is crackly, the speaker doing battle with sirens and background chatter. 'You hear me, Sarge? It's Ben.'

McAvoy sticks a finger in his ear. Wonders whether his team will get used to addressing him by his new rank, or whether Neilsen will ever begin to think of himself as a bona fide sergeant. 'Ben? I can barely hear you. What's happening . . .?'

'Thank Christ,' says Neilsen, and it sounds as though he's on the verge of breaking down. 'I thought I was looking at your body. I thought it was you . . . fuck, Sarge, he's a dead ringer, I swear . . .'

McAvoy doesn't understand. He rarely does, at first. It seems as though all of the blood is draining from his body. He feels Roisin's hand on his back. Feels Lilah shrug herself from his grasp.

'Ben, sorry – you're not making sense. Where are you? What's happening?'

'It's the boss,' he says, and his voice catches again. 'We were all panicking that it was you at first. Jesus, Andy's in fucking tears . . .'

'Thought what was me? What's happened?'

There's the sound of a scuffle at the other end of the line, as if a group of excited children are trying to grab the phone to talk to a generous uncle.

'Sarge?' asks Andy Daniells. 'Sarge, you promise me you're not in an ambulance? You promise?'

'Bloody hell, Andy,' growls McAvoy, starting to stand. 'Whatever's going on, could you all try and be police officers about it? Now, chapter and verse.'

DC Andy Daniells takes a breath. 'Outside the boss's flat,' he says, pulling himself together. 'Trish's place on Vicky Ave. A man who looks just like you. He's been attacked. Critical. The resemblance . . . it's uncanny . . .'

McAvoy rubs his palm over his heard. Feels cold all of a sudden; thoughts all static and smashed glass. 'Thor Ingolfsson,' he says, quietly. 'He's a police officer in Iceland. They're friends. Maybe something more than that. You say he's been attacked? He's alive?'

'Barely,' says Daniells, and his voice becomes muffled as he jots down the details. 'DCSU Earl is on his way as we speak, Sarge . . . sorry, I mean Inspector . . .'

'Just stick with Aector,' growls McAvoy, glaring into the fire. His grip on Lilah becomes firmer. He feels her wince under his big, broken hands.

'That's no easier,' mutters Daniells, in his ear. 'You don't think you're the target, do you? I mean, if I was going to kill you and saw this bloke coming out of Pharaoh's place half dressed, I'd definitely put two and two together . . .'

McAvoy begins to colour. Wonders how much Roisin has heard. Looks towards her and sees her give him a little nod. It's acceptance. It's permission. She's heard all of it and isn't going to stand in his way. He has to be there. Has to be the man she fell for; the man she'd die for; live for – the man she'd commit murder to protect.

'Is she there?' asks McAvoy, eyes shut.

'She's in her flat,' says Neilsen. 'She needed to get clean. There was a lot of blood.'

'And she's OK?'

'She's the boss.'

McAvoy unbuttons his shirt and stops when he realizes it makes him look like Clark Kent turning into Superman. Imagines Pharaoh laughing. Hears her calling him a bloody idiot. Wonders what the hell everybody is going to say when they realize she's been sleeping with somebody who looks so much like Aector McAvoy that they could be cast as Viking brothers in a TV drama.

'Give her this number,' he says, quietly. 'I'll switch my mobile back on but there's barely any signal here other than at the top of the lane. She's going to need a friend so just stick close until I get there. Tell her I'm on my way.'

He ends the call. Looks to Roisin. To Lilah. There's a creak from the *vardo* and Fin McAvoy appears on the steps; fourteen years old but already six foot three: the double of his father. He looks at the assemblage of figures by the fireside. Makes a face. Looks at his dad. Something passes between them. Fin has been through a lot. He's wrestling with his own bad memories. There's a fear glazing the whites of his eyes.

'Is something bad happening?'

'Not to us,' says McAvoy, and hopes it's true.

'Auntie Trish,' says Lilah: a middle-aged gossip at a bus stop. 'She's been doing it with a man who looks like Daddy and somebody's attacked him. So Daddy's going to go and help, which seems a bit silly to me if somebody is trying to kill him, but I suppose he can't exactly just sit here whittling sticks while all that's going on, can he? Poor Trish.'

McAvoy throws an apologetic glance to Kush, who's busily rolling himself a cigarette and kicking unburnt sticks back into the heat of the fire. He's run this little off-grid compound for more than a decade: built himself a lodge at the top of the hill – a hodgepodge of old potato crates, reclaimed wood and sheets of corrugated iron. In daylight it looks eccentric but oddly homely, the perfect bolt-hole for the frustrated bohemian seeking to get away from the rat-race. At night, with the carousel horses leering from the lip of the porch and the rope swings transformed into so many nooses by the light of the pinkish moon, it's more akin to a horror movie.

'She all right?' asks Kush, absently. 'Didn't like to listen, but couldn't really help it.'

McAvoy chooses not to hear the question. He has been fighting the urge to ask Kush whether he knows Trish and Sophia ever since they arrived. He'd got the distinct impression that Kush would react as if he were under surveillance if McAvoy started asking him about the coppers of their mutual acquaintance. But they're not strangers, he knows that much. Can't help wondering whether Trish came here with the girls; whether Anders was with them; whether he hurt her if he was. He shakes the thought away. He can't think about what was being done to his best friend in the years before they knew one another. It makes him angry. Makes him sad.

'You don't think it was you they were looking for, do you?' asks Roisin, at his side. She cups his face. Looks into his eyes as if trying to read something on the big brown mirrors of his irises. 'So many people have tried to hurt you . . .'

McAvoy wraps himself around her. Presses her head to his chest and lets her listen to the thump of his heart. He doesn't need to say any more.

THREE

He stops running when he reaches the tunnel beneath the railway bridge. He's maybe a quarter of a mile from the big man's body and he doesn't think anybody's seen him. He's good at keeping to the shadows. Good at becoming part of the darkness. He feels more liquid than solid. In the moments that he takes notice of his own physical mass he becomes aware of a peculiar kind of molten suppleness, as if he is made of congealed ink. He doesn't remember feeling like this before, but so much of what used to be is lost to him that he knows there is little point in smashing at the locked doors in his mind. Better to think of himself as he has been these past months. Better to be this version of himself. This loyal disciple. This vengeful son. He has already been blessed with the gifts that will enable him to do what he must. He's fast. Fast and wiry and strong. He doesn't need to stop to catch his breath. He can move from a full sprint to a complete halt without having to gulp down air or rest his hands on his knees. He finds such actions to be needlessly demonstrative. He thinks that most of the things people do to express themselves physically are mere imitations of something glimpsed in childhood. He studies people very carefully and keeps seeing people act the same mannerisms. When people cry they fan their faces with a blade of hand. When they're getting worked up they run their hands through their hair. When they're tired they rub their eyes and make big, extravagant yawns. He has long since learned to imitate such actions but he cannot understand the purpose they serve.

A car trundles past nearby; the static hiss of rubber moving through dirty water. He peers out through the mouth of the tunnel. A light fall of rain is beginning to splatter in hesitant touches. He inserts himself into a pocket of absolute darkness. There's a little light set into the ceiling of the bridge but it serves no real purpose save attracting moths and illuminating a loose triangle of graffiti. He's safe here, for a moment. He can get his bearings. Make sense of the past few moments. Gather himself. Gather his selves.

He flicks out his tongue. Tastes blood and rubber and salt. Remembers.

Feels.

The ease with which the adze had penetrated the big man's back had surprised him. The blade had gone through muscle and bone as if he were chopping it into a snowman. It hadn't taken a great deal of energy. He feels oddly cheated. He's been practising for days. There's a dull ache in his right arm from the repeated swings of the blade. He's sunk the edge into tree stumps and bags of coal. He's brought it down into big piles of hardpacked earth, just to make sure that he was capable of the task he had set himself. He feels strangely cheated. It shouldn't have been so easy. His target was enormous: well-muscled, with pale skin and a huge bovine back. That he was semi-naked came as no surprise. He'd spent an hour listening to the grotesque sounds emerging from the bedroom. It had turned his stomach. Aroused him. Made him angry. Made him sad. Jealous, too, somewhere inside. It had surprised him. He hadn't thought himself capable of jealousy. The doctors have made it clear that such emotions are probably beyond him. He cannot feel the way others do. He cannot trust his impulses. He needs to breathe, and do his exercises, and take his pills, and not let himself do the things that he wants to do if there's any suggestion that they might cause harm to somebody else. He has to stop thinking of people in the way that he does. If he ever wants to be well, he has to play by the rules. He doesn't have to understand them – he just has to convince everybody that he's not the danger they all think he is. He finds it amusing that he invested so much work in proving his sanity, only to undo all of his diligence with one irreparable act. It isn't the first time he's sabotaged his own future, though this time he has no regrets. Tonight's violence was unavoidable. So is what's to come. He wishes he felt more enthusiastic about it. This is what he wants, after all. This is what he's prayed for. He'd have sacrificed a pure white lamb to whichever god vowed to give him his revenge. He just wishes he could remember the feeling. He hopes it returns soon. He fancies he will find it hard to do the things he must if he is not fuelled by an absolute and total conviction. The people he has killed so far do not weigh heavily upon him but he fancies it will be different before the end.

He realizes he's still wearing the mask. It's with reluctance that he removes it. It's made of a clammy, slightly sticky rubber and it sticks to his beard as he tugs it free. He feels himself weaken. Sag. He suffers a sudden punch of memory. He's eleven. Maybe twelve. The man is helping him out of his coat. It's too tight and the zip doesn't come all the way down. He's wearing a football top and a man's jumper underneath and he can't get himself free of the waxy, clinging material. The man's laughing. He can hear the snuffles through the thick material. There's just the two of them, but it's nice enough. Friendly. And the man is holding the cuffs of his sleeves and tugging the material up and over his head. And then he's not laughing any more, and there's a pressure at his groin, and he's being touched in a way he doesn't like. And it's just the dark, and the smell of his own tears, and the soreness and the shame and the fear it will happen again. And it does happen again. And again.

He stops looking at the memory. Draws a board rubber through the pictures in his mind and replaces the memory with something fresh. Makes space inside his brain for the new pictures; old memories shuffling up and squeezing against one another to accommodate the wet-painted newcomers. Sees the big man. Sees her. Thinks again of the look on her face and measures it against the expectation. Had she looked scared enough? Broken? He isn't sure. She'd looked horrified, of course. Had looked suitably ashen and grey. But nothing about her had suggested the utter annihilation of her happiness and peace of mind. And that, after all, is the task he has been set. She needs to understand the consequences of what she did. She needs to have her entire sense of self taken apart and remoulded into something full of hate and guilt and tears. She needs to live in the grief and flame. He experiences a moment of uncertainty. So much depends upon her reactions to the violence. So much pain is due to her before the dawn. He has to trust that she will follow where he leads. He has been instructed by a higher power; a deity with the power to grant him all that he wishes in return for his sacrifice. He has to trust that all will go as foretold, even as the older, softer voices in his head try and return him to their control. They don't like this new voice. It's too loud. Too clear. Too damn hard to resist.

He holds the mask in his hands. Looks at the rubber replica of the man who shared her bed and fathered her children. It's spattered with blood. Lifeless. It's a poor approximation of the real thing. He kisses it anyway. It feels important.

He hears the sirens now. Hears the distant wail. Lays his head back against the brick. Breathes. There's a park a little way ahead. A great matted tangle of trees and wire fencing off the scree at the side of the railway track. He's found broken bottles there. The remains of a fire. A dead cat. He watched two homeless people fuck beneath a tarpaulin tent, flea-bites on their bare legs and an absolute nothingness in their eyes. They had felt familiar, in their way. He knows how it feels to live in a medicated fog of non-existence. He has lost years within his own fuzzy numbness, adrift within the wraith-like mists of oblivion. He fancies he will return to it, in time. But for now there is a purpose within him. An energy. A sense of righteousness. An anger. A duty. He did not know how fervently he had been praying during those long years of weight-less existence. But something heard him. Something greater than himself has given him the tools to put right a great wrong. He just has to follow the instructions to the letter.

He rolls up the mask. Stuffs it inside his coat. He feels the weight of the weapon in his jacket pocket. He pulls it out. There's blood on the blade, thick as jam. He wipes it clean with his cuff. From his other pocket he takes the soft leather roll of tools. Runs his hands over the metal and wood, inserting his bloodied thumb into the grooves left by the master craftsman. Sniffs the chisels. Strokes the picks the way he used to stroke his dead pets. He touches the mortise chisel with the same reverence that a zealot would worship the bones of a martyr. Thinks of the way in which these humble pieces of decades-old equipment scarred new life into dead wood; crafting faces, fruits, flowers. It is only right that they will take the flesh from Trish Pharaoh's skeleton. Only right that they carve wheels and whorls and so much blessed agony into the bones of this fallen saint.

He wraps the soft folds around the weapon and returns it to his pocket.

He takes a breath. Hears the sirens getting closer.

He wishes he was still in the cone of yellow light outside her house. He wishes he didn't have to wear the mask. For a moment he wishes none of this was happening. He'd felt something incomprehensible inside himself when he first saw her again: those dazzling blue eyes, her soft hands, the motherly breasts and shoulders. He'd wanted her to hold him. To stroke his face. He fancies he'd have been able to make himself cry if he'd known she would wipe away his tears. He'd had to swallow down the impulse. Had to listen to the voice. It's been good to him. It's given him freedom. Given him opportunity. It will give him power, if he just keeps the faith.

From his jeans pocket he retrieves the mobile phone. The connection is still live. His God hasn't ended the video-call. They're still there, in the darkness. They're only a blur, but they're undoubtedly watching. Undoubtedly listening.

'You saw?' he asks.

'I saw.'

'Did I do well?'

'Do you believe you did well?'

He doesn't answer. He is used to such questions.

'Will she come?'

He doesn't receive a reply. The red light winks out. He's staring at his own reflection, his dead eyes glaring back at himself. He tries to smile. Can't seem to remember which muscles to use.

He pushes off from the wall. Walks towards the park; a gentleman taking a stroll in the midnight air. His car is two streets away. He'll be inside in five minutes. He'll be back with the dead man inside the hour. He'll be waiting, when she comes. And then he can make her understand. He can do what he has promised. He can carry out the fantasy that has sustained him for so long. He can help her to understand what she did. He can help her understand how it felt. He can make sure that everybody sees her for the monster that she is. And before the sun rises, those blue eyes will be black as a shark's, and those motherly arms will be carved into something so much more in keeping with the demon she holds inside.

He will be dead or in prison by the time the sun sets again.

But by then, his God will be happy.

And everybody that Trish Pharaoh cares about will be dead, or yearning for death.

FOUR

Victoria Avenue, Hull
12.52 a.m.

'And he's definitely, definitely not dead?'
        'Apparently not.'
        'He's been dead before, hasn't he? That's what I heard.'
'Not *dead* dead. Just deadish.'
'You mean he's nearly died before.'
'Same difference.'
'Not really, Matt.'
'They could be twins, though. I mean, that's a bit bloody weird, isn't it? I knew she was a bit sweet on him, but . . .'
'Sweet on him? You sound like a nana.'
'She looks at him like, well, I dunno, but like, something, definitely.'
'She's got a type, that's all. Her husband was a big lad too. I've got a mate who only goes for brunettes. Brunettes with big hips.'
'What if he fancied somebody who wasn't a brunette but had big hips?'
'Oh he'd probably still shag her, just with less – what's that word my mam uses? – aye, gusto, that's it. Less gusto.'
'But Pharaoh only goes for massive gingers?'
'Looks like. It's different for a lass, though, innit? They want, like, feelings and stuff. And they have to deal with the male gaze.'
'Are male gays a problem? I thought it would be the lezzers they worried about.'
'That's the patriarchy for you.'
'What is?'
'I don't know, I just hear people say it.'
Ben Neilsen moves away from his junior colleagues lest he find himself getting stupider by osmosis. The three uniformed

constables milling around at the rear of the closest police van,
waiting to be told what to do. He's noticed that none of them seem
able to breathe through their nose. All in their twenties and look
as though they would be more comfortable working in a phone
shop or flogging gloriously chavtastic trainers in a sports ware-
house. Matt, in particular, has the appearance of somebody who
has to poke at his face in order to find the food-hole. If he signed
up now and really pushed himself, Neilsen fancies that PC Matt
Paul could probably end his military career as a lance-private.
That, or Minister of Defence.

There's a cold wind howling down Victoria Avenue. It carries
the smell of the estuary; the sludge-and-brine reek of the waterfront. There's diesel in the air; the whiff of the bread ovens from
the bakery a mile away, just past the posh bar and the closed-down
sex shop. Blood, too. Always blood.

'Do you think she had something to do with it?' asks one of
the constables: a wiry, rodent-faced Goole lad who was clearly
bunking off when his classmates were taught to whisper.

'With what?' asks PC Paul. 'Who?

'Fuck sake,' mutters Neilsen, and opens the little gate at the
front of Pharaoh's building, crunching over pebbles and sparkling
stone and taking up a position near the big bay window. He closes
his eyes for a moment. He wants to tilt his head and pour the
second-hand stupidity from his brain. Neilsen's heard it said that
you know you're getting old when the police officers start looking
younger. He's still a couple of years off forty but today's recruits
make him feel positively geriatric. He can't help wondering what
would persuade a young, wide-eyed person with half a dozen
GCSEs and an NVQ in Health and Social Care to become a police
officer. Can't help wondering what they think the job will actually
entail, and what precisely their ability to reach the final level of
Call of Duty will bring to the service. Neilsen's been a copper for
fifteen years and still doesn't really know whether he's on the right
side. He doesn't really like the police. Can't help wondering
whether they do more harm than good, even as he takes a deep
satisfaction in the part he has played in locking up a succession
of very bad people. He knows he wouldn't have lasted had he
stayed in uniform. At least as part of the Humberside Police Serious
and Organized Unit there were fewer opportunities to equivocate.

The people he chased had done terrible, terrible things and couldn't be permitted to get away with it. He fancies he'd lose himself in a whirlpool of moral equivocations and existential *whatabout*-isms were he asked to consider bigger societal questions or the culpability of politicians and lawmakers in the creation of criminals. He wonders if he's growing up. Hopes not. He's already got himself settled into something akin to a long-term relationship; comfortably bedded down with a hairdresser named Selena and playing the role of overly earnest stepdad to her teenage son. It's a major development for a man whose previous relationships used to be over before he had the time to re-fasten his trousers.

'When do you think he'll be here?'

Neilsen spots the approaching bulk of DC Andy Daniells – a man seemingly drawn entirely in circles. He's wearing a puffer jacket, jogging trousers and a pair of garish trainers. He hasn't got much hair left but what he does have is sticking up haphazardly; little feathery tufts like the ears of a game-bird. Daniells had been asleep when the call came through about the incident outside the Boss's house. Hadn't even told his husband he was leaving. It's taken him half an hour to compose himself. He had been every bit as certain as Neilsen that the victim of the attack was Aector McAvoy. Speaking to McAvoy has done him some good but Neilsen fancies it will still take a colossal effort of will for Daniells to resist hugging him when he gets back from the frozen north. He wonders whether McAvoy's blush will be sufficient to turn the heating off in the office.

'Hard to say,' shrugs Neilsen, loosening his tie. He's still in his expensive work suit and soft leather coat. He'd been on his way back from giving evidence at a hearing in London when he was alerted to the drama by a friendly face in the Humberside Police control room. He'd only been a few streets away, already looking forward to waking Selena up in the way she has implied will always be welcome. He'd diverted to Victoria Avenue instead. Found his boss clutching the dying body of a huge, half-dressed man with red hair.

'Well, give it try,' says Daniells, joining him in the little front garden of the tall red-brick building where Pharaoh's flat takes up the second floor. There's light spilling out from every window. The neighbours are awake. There won't be any news crews for a while – not at this hour. But the street is clogged with scene-of-crime vehicles, dog units, patrol cars and riot vans. Humberside Police can never be excused of underplaying the seriousness of an incident.

'If it was you or me, we'd break every speed limit and flash every speed camera and half kill ourselves to be here before the sunrise,' says Neilsen, tiredly. 'McAvoy? He thinks so much he'll probably stick to seventy every step of the way. He can probably imagine himself being pulled over and wasting precious time explaining himself to an unfriendly traffic cop. That's the trouble with seeing every side of every story.'

Daniells doesn't say anything for a moment, mulling this over. 'So, about five, then?'

'Andy, I don't bloody know.'

Neilsen feels his phone ring in his pocket. Snatches it up and adopts his most gentle tone. 'It's OK, Helen . . . wasn't him. She's OK, I think. Hard to say. I'll let you know when I know more. Take care.'

'Tremberg,' he says, in response to the unasked question.

Daniells looks up from his own mobile. 'Bloke at 118 has got CCTV,' he says, reading his screen. 'Brought it out to a uniform and said he could have it if they promised to let him move his car outside the perimeter so he can get to the office in the morning.'

'Anything?'

'Nobody's allowed to watch it until Earl arrives.'

'Fuck sake.'

They stand in silence. They were the same rank until a few months ago but there's no awkwardness between them now that Neilsen is technically the ranking officer. Daniells could be sergeant if he wanted it. He doesn't. Neilsen isn't sure that he does either and he's damn sure that McAvoy only agreed promotion to detective inspector because it meant keeping the unit together. It's been much diminished these past few years, its function as an elite squad separate from the bulk of CID existing more in press releases and newspaper headlines than in actuality. Pharaoh was offered the job of detective chief superintendent, bossing the whole of CID. Instead she chose to stay at her existing rank, maintaining supervision of the enigmatically rebranded Major Crimes Unit. DI

McAvoy is her number two. There are two sergeants, half a dozen constables and a smattering of civilian staff. They handle big cases, high-profile cases; organized and peculiar cases. They keep themselves busy with cold cases when the people of East Yorkshire and Northern Lincolnshire take a few days off from murdering one another. Neilsen's proud to be a part of it; honoured to be learning his craft from the two police officers he admires most and who have caught more bad people than most coppers can dream of.

'People are saying stuff already,' says Neilsen, nodding towards the little cadre of uniformed officers. 'She'll hate all this.'

'She's up there?' asks Daniells, looking up.

'Cleaning the blood off.'

'Should she be?' asks Daniells. 'I mean, there'll be so much scrutiny and oversight, won't every decision have to be triple-checked?'

Neilsen nods. 'No doubt. But it won't be us doing any of that so leave it to some other bugger. And I'm not telling her she can't shower her boyfriend's blood off, are you?'

Daniells looks back up the street. A vaguely human shape in blue coveralls is standing in the glare of the lamplight, taking photographs of the thick red blood that seeps into the frost-shimmering ground.

'Dead ringer, wasn't he?' muses Daniells.

'You've said that,' sighs Neilsen.

'What if McAvoy was the target?' asks Daniells, pulling at his lip. 'It's going to have to be a line of enquiry.'

Neilsen shakes his head. 'Neighbours have already said there was a car alarm going off. He interrupted a car thief.'

'And a car thief took an axe to him?' asks Daniells, his face wrinkling in scorn. 'Come on, who goes on the rob with an axe?'

'We don't know it was an axe. We don't know what made the wounds. We don't know anything, Andy.'

'We know she's got a type, that's for certain,' mutters Daniells, lowering his voice. 'Everybody's going to be talking about this, Ben. Christ, she deserves some happiness, doesn't she? It's not like she should still be in her widow's tweeds, is it?'

'He's been dead over a year,' says Neilsen. 'And he wasn't exactly alive before that, was he? I mean, not really.'

'People will talk. You know what coppers are like.'

Neilsen turns at the sound of approaching footsteps. Feels his heart sink a little. Detective Chief Superintendent George Earl is a tall, slim, straight-backed careerist who exudes the gentle earnestness and Anglican-priest sincerity of a contrite Tony Blair. He has a habit of clasping his hands together when he talks and makes a great show of telling his staff that his door is always open and there's no such thing as a stupid question. He memorizes their names; the names of their partners and children. He clasps with both hands when offered a shake; purses his lips and presses a finger to them when thinking about some underling's interesting point. There's a picture of the King on his filing cabinet and another of Desmond Tutu on his desk. He's good at giving presentations; can deliver bad news in a way that makes it sound like a success. He can promise root-and-branch internal enquiries in a manner that makes awkward customers stop asking questions. The top brass love him.

'Ben, Ben, Ben,' he says, shaking his head and looking, for a terrible moment, as if he is about to pull him in for a consoling hug. 'Bad business. Bad, bad, bad.'

'Sir,' says Neilsen, nodding.

'And Detective Constable Daniells, I see,' says Earl, stepping back. He's wearing a suit and a cashmere overcoat, hair neatly parted, frameless glasses on his slightly too-long nose.

'I don't mind *Andy Andy Andy*,' mutters Daniells, under his breath. He doesn't get the first name treatment; Earl decided on day one that when it came to his dealings with anybody from the LGBTQ community, even a whiff of impropriety was a whiff too far. Daniells is toying with the idea of telling him that he's also mixed-race and gender-neutral, just to see what he'll do.

'You've spoken to her?' asks Earl, raising his eyes to Pharaoh's flat. 'Up in her tower, is she? Eating bread and honey?'

'Sorry, sir?'

'I take it she's not alone.'

'Uniformed officer on the door.'

Earl purses his lips. Looks for a moment as if he's pulled on a pair of slippers and felt something squelch inside the toe. 'Nobody's in there with her? That might prove problematic.'

'Nobody's taken charge, sir,' says Daniells, butting in. 'Crime scene perimeter is set up at the roundabout yonder and we've got everybody signing in and out. Ben's got PCs divvying up an immediate house to house. Dogs are active. There's the CCTV, obviously. I can take a look . . .'

Earl nods. 'And yet we have a potential suspect alone, washing the blood off her hands and potentially dispensing with the weapon, is that right?'

'Sorry, sir?' asks Neilsen, angling his head. He can feel a cold anger shimmering across his shoulders, down his arms; freezing his fingers into fists. 'You're not suggesting . . .'

'Devil's advocate, of course,' says Earl, smoothly. 'We have to think like a defence barrister – have to head off all suggestions of impropriety at the pass. No special treatment just because she's one of ours.'

Neilsen takes a moment. Swallows, hard. 'One of ours, sir? She wouldn't expect special treatment, sir – just common bloody decency. Her friend's just been hacked half to death in front of her eyes!'

'She didn't see it, did she?' asks Earl, throwing the question over his shoulder to whoever is lurking in the darkness, ready to dispense an umbrella or sun-hat, bobble-hat or windbreaker depending on the vacillations of the weather.

'She hasn't given a statement yet. We just know what she told us when the ambulance first arrived. Didn't see it. Just heard the alarm go off and then the sound of violence. Didn't see who did it. Why, what are you thinking?'

'I don't know what I think, Ben,' he says, sounding like a humanities teacher weighing up the implications of a poor piece of coursework. 'It was your good self who supplied the name, yes? An Icelandic police officer, I hear. And he's at Hull Royal, is that correct. Unlikely to survive?'

'I believe they said "critical", sir.'

'I didn't know she had a fancy piece. Did you?'

Neilsen looks down at his shoes. Counts backwards from ten, the way McAvoy has patiently instructed him.

'And Aector?' continues Earl, looking around as if he might be lurking in the shadows.

'On his way back, sir.'

'On his white charger, no doubt,' smiles Earl, his lips wet, as if he's been eating olives. 'One wonders whether he mightn't have been the intended target. I'm told her late husband was quite the hulking fellow as well. Anders Wilkie, yes?'

Neilsen isn't sure whether his senior officer is expecting a rosette for his impressive memory. He can tell the direction that the conversation is heading. Earl is going to ask him for details about Pharaoh's private life; details he doesn't want to give.

'I'm told she cared for him for a number of years,' muses Earl. 'Her husband, I mean. Aneurysm, wasn't it? Left the poor chap a fraction of his former self. It's no wonder she's so well liked – climbing the ranks, raising her children, all the while taking care of a man who sold the family silver? There'll be a blue plaque to her one day, I shouldn't wonder.'

Neilsen doesn't let himself be drawn. He went to the funeral of Pharaoh's husband but never knew him in life. He's heard the rumours, of course. Anders Wilkie was a charming bully; a businessman who liked the finer things in life and got himself in deep with the wrong people. Ended up with more debts than he could dig himself out from and suffered a catastrophic stroke when his world came crashing down. It was left to Pharaoh to negotiate the bankruptcy, the eviction, the repossessions and county court judgements. Pharaoh who found them all a little house in Grimsby and converted the garage into a specialist bedroom where she could care for the living ghost of her husband: half-paralysed, mostly mute and prone to seizures that caused him to dislocate bones and half-sever his tongue. Pharaoh never talks about her private life but police stations are a bonfire of rumour. He wishes he didn't believe everything he heard. Wishes that he didn't suspect that there's some truth to the suggestion that Anders Wilkie used to knock his wife and children about and that he only lavished them all with such luxurious gifts to compensate for the harm he did when in drink.

'I'll go on up,' says Earl, when he realizes Neilsen isn't going to fill the silence with anything that incriminates Pharaoh. He turns to the young PC who stands behind him. 'Do call Marcy and tell her that we won't be able to get in the 10k before breakfast. I fear Jeremiah will need to make his own granola this morning.'

Neilsen can feel Daniells staring at him. Can just make out his lips forming the word *'granola'*.

'It's all about family, isn't it?' asks Earl, his face a lesson in sincerity. 'Family, family, family.'

Neilsen steps aside and lets him pass. Falls into step behind him, Daniells following behind. Earl turns, looking perplexed. 'Ben? Oh goodness, sorry, did I not make my intentions plain? Do forgive me. As I said, propriety is key here. Things must be beyond reproach. Two of my old colleagues from Lincolnshire Police are already on their way to assist. We can't really have you and your little band of loyal serfs investigating her majesty, can we? This isn't the bad old days, Ben. No, I'm afraid you'd be well advised to get home and catch up on your rest. Do give my regards to Selena. And you, DC Daniells. Warm regards to Stefan, naturally.'

He's opened the door and disappeared into the light of the hall before either officer can say a word.

FIVE

Blood.

Blood on her hands; thick upon her fingers, coating her wrists and forearms as if she's had her hands inside a pig – as if her pudgy little paws were coated in fresh red wax. She can smell it. Can taste it. Can hear its accusatory whispers, each inhalation filling her with fresh waves of shame and sadness and guilt. Each iron-reek breath a fresh blow. She thinks of the slaughterhouse. Thinks of her Gran's kitchen. Thinks of Anders and the stains on his pillow and the cold, grey deadness of his skin. Thinks of McAvoy and finds herself making fists. He'll know by now. He'll be on his way back, convinced she needs him – convinced he can help.

Her grip slips as she tries to twist the tap. She tries again, biting her lip. Runs the water until it steams. Places her hands beneath the stream and feels the sting and scald. Feels her eyes blur as the water runs red. Washes her lover's blood from her skin.

She raises her head. Considers herself in the mirror. Blood on her face, too – a smear of it on her cheek, splashes in the grey that seams her dark hair. She's been sitting with her back to the bathroom door, knees drawn up, telling herself that it's not really crying if you don't give in to the sobs. She can't help it if her eyes leak like melting ice. Can't help it if there's a ball of gristle in her throat that makes it feel as though she's swallowed the stone of a peach.

She glances down at her hands. Squirts some liquid soap onto her palms. Rubs them together and works up a frothy pink lather. Begins to clean each finger in turn. She cleans herself with the artfulness of a surgeon. She's done this before.

There's a knocking at the door. She wonders if it's the young copper who's been stationed outside. Ben, maybe; the happy lump of Andy Daniells ever-present at his side. She fancies not. George Earl will take this one for himself and he won't want any of Pharaoh's team anywhere near it. She can already imagine the way he'll approach the investigation and makes a vow that if he tells her he understands how difficult this must be, she'll punch him in the throat.

She sniffs back something unpleasant. Spits into the sink. Holds up her hands for inspection and feels a stab of cold, raw emptiness as she looks upon her nails. Thinks of herself clawing at her lover's back, at his chest. Closes her eyes as she considers what they'll all fucking say.

That knock again. Louder now, more impatient. She curses herself. Curses her wasted time, sat weeping like a little kid when she should have been sorting herself out. There's stuff to be done. She's starting to think clearly again; thinking like Trish Pharaoh instead of some silly loved-up soft-shite. She needs to think like the best version of herself. Needs a drink and a fag and her boots and her sunglasses, and needs to face the world with her best fuck-you face.

On the windowsill above the sink, the little wooden statue stares at her. She shouldn't have taken it. Plucking it from the open wound on Thor's back is a sensory memory that will never leave her. But it was left for her. Made for her. It belongs to her – just like the others. She'd known as soon as she'd seen it that if any of her colleagues saw the little doll they would make a great imaginative leap and come to entirely the wrong conclusion. And she doesn't want to have to answer the questions that their mounting inaccuracies will lead them to pose. McAvoy will get it, she knows that, but the thought of talking to him is too much to take. He's the only man who's ever truly seen her cry and she will never forgive herself for allowing herself to appear so vulnerable, even in the embrace of a man she adores.

She crouches down and digs around behind the pipe behind the toilet. Finds the untraceable mobile phone and rips it free from its gaffer-taped prison. Turns it on, heart thumping. She wants to check the last messages – wants to read and re-read the same selection of words she has examined so many times that she could recite them from memory. Instead she dials a number. Waits for a moment until the voicemail service picks up. She says nothing. Hangs up. A minute later, the phone rings. She answers without a word: a stressed-out female voice hissing in her ear.

'You swore this was for emergencies! You swore . . .'

Pharaoh shushes her. Asks the question to which she already knows the answer.

'Reuben Hollow,' she states, and each syllable is a punch to the chest. 'He's there? He's in his cell.'

'Of course he's in his fucking cell,' hisses Prison Officer Dawn Peach. 'If he does anything unusual I tell you. You know I do. That's the fucking deal. He's asleep. Sleeps like a baby! You don't think I'd have told you if there'd been an escape?'

Pharaoh doesn't reply. She pictures him: sees the vigilante killer she and Aector brought to justice. Imagines him in his cell, cuddled up tight under his blanket. Looks at the marionette afresh. He's sent her one every Valentine's Day since she locked him up, each one lovingly hand-carved. He says he loves her.

'I've got to go,' comes the voice. 'Please, don't call unless . . .'

Pharaoh kills the call, holding the little phone in her palm and weighing it like a stone.

For a moment she's back in the visiting room at HMP Warcop. She's sitting opposite Hollow, with his ice-blue eyes and his neat beard, his gold tooth and his nimble hands. He's holding her gaze in that way of his – the one that brings her out in gooseflesh and varnishes her back with prickly heat. She's long since lost any sense of how much of her interaction with Hollow is a performance. She does like him, in her way. She understands how, in a different time, the balladeers might have sung about his noble, selfless acts of valour. But she also knows that he's a vain, callous bastard. He's no hero. He killed people because he wanted to know what it felt like and began to enjoy the experience. He was clever enough to find a narrative he could explain to himself. He wasn't a serial killer; wasn't giving in to a selfish, cruel indulgence. He was doing good. He was helping people. He was removing worse men than himself. He was saving people from the malevolent forces in their lives.

'. . . can't keep coming here, Reuben. Not like we're friends. Not like we're family. It's not right. You know I can't keep doing this. I have to find a reality that I can sustain.'

'I want you to be happy, Trish. You deserve to be happy. But you're all that keeps me sane. Without you? I don't know if I'll be able to keep the bad thoughts from creeping back. What is there to stay alive for without you?'

'That's emotional blackmail, Reuben. It's beneath you.'

'We're two halves of one soul, Trish. You're my muse. My inspiration. Whatever it is that's between us, it's no mortal thing. Even if I die, I'll find a way to haunt you.'

'Fuck off, Reuben.'

'You're playing games with me, I know you are. Who is it, eh? Who's wriggled inside your head? Is it the Viking? Oh it is! He's finally plucking up the courage, is he? My, my. Will you shave your legs? Throw out those baggy grey knickers? Brush your hair at the back as well as the front? God, I do hope Aector knows. What will happen if they bump into each other? It'll be like a very polite argument with a full-length reflection . . .'

She laughed at that. Laughed at the image. Blushed some more. Closed her eyes and promised she'd come back. She'd tell him everything. She'd give him every detail. All he had to do was give her something to justify it. A name. Another victim. A burial site for one of the dozen or so men she knows he put in the ground and has yet to claim responsibility for. He guards his reputation as fiercely as a true celebrity. He doesn't want to be known for the deaths that were the result of temper or jealousy or rage.

She pictures him again. Grey sweatshirt, blue jeans: ink on his knuckles. Remembers him holding the letter that, by rights, he shouldn't be permitted to read. Remembers the smell of it: and Reuben's face colouring; his pupils dilating, as the earthy scent trickled into his nostrils and lit a smouldering flame in his olfactory bulb; flooding his synapses with memory, with regret; with something terribly close to arousal.

'She's OK?' asks Trish, in her mind. 'Doing better? I know I should have read it but I'll trust you.'

'Getting there,' he says, a little smile on his face. 'Misses me. It's all apology, really. Constant regret. Is this what they're making her do? Feel like shit for every little mistake? How's that healing? How's that getting well? Maybe this is a mistake . . .'

'If she slips, they'll tell me. And she does have things to regret.'

'She was ill. You know she was ill. She's a good girl, really.'

'You think they're all good girls, Reuben. Then they let you down and you want to kill them.'

'Don't say that. I adore women. I revere women.'

'You despise women, Reuben. You just despise men more.'

'I miss her.'

'She misses you too.'

Their conversation always turns to his adopted daughter. He misses her like air and the screws know it. He doesn't get many of the letters that arrive by the sackful at HMP Warcop each week – least of all from the young woman with whom he shared the happiest years of his life. These past years she's been getting well; a succession of shrinks and mental-health nurses trying to undo the damage caused by exposure to her stepfather's twisted crimes. She's living in a halfway house, now. She has her independence, of a sort. She has a room in a nice Victorian property where young men and women with mental-health problems are able to take a major step towards true independence. She earned a degree in horticulture during her stay in the expensive mental-health facility where her anti-social personality disorder and violent outbursts were treated with a mixture of medicine, therapy and mindfulness. She has a peaceful life, now. She writes. She makes things. She keeps her world small. Waters her plants and feeds her fish and tries to make amends for her own part in Reuben's crimes. But she still writes to him. Still begs him to send her a letter or a kind word. He doesn't acquiesce to her pleading. He knows that she's better off without him in her life and resists the urge to please her. For Reuben, it's a monumental gesture. Trish tries to give him the credit he's due. But she can't find the coldness within herself to deny Delphine when she begs her to pass on a message to him on her behalf. They have been through a lot together and something exists between them. Pharaoh has almost forgiven her for trying to kill her.

'. . . *really isn't the right way to do this, Stephen, Stephen, Stephen . . .*'

She makes out the sound of muffled speech from outside the main door. She doesn't have long. She turns the tap to cold and splashes water on her face, steam rising as the cold air hits the warm. She pulls open the door to the living room and moves silently across the cluttered, high-ceilinged space. She's never really unpacked. Never properly moved in. There is a succession of tatty rag-rugs and a big plush hand-knotted Turkish rectangle covering the dusty hardwood floor. The sofa's a charity shop find, the curtains hand-stitched and expensive and hanging from too few hooks. There's a painting on the chimney breast that would be worth more than the house itself but which she's never had the courage to try and sell. Anders had taken it in lieu of payment on a deal. So too the grotesque patchwork chair: a jockey's jersey of geometric pastels stretched over a rococo-style back and Queen Anne legs. The certificate of authenticity declares it a Cappelini, which means nothing to Pharaoh, who used to think of it as the cat's bed before the fickle bastard ran off to live with the old woman at number 19. None of the items match the threadbare appearance of the rest of the property but Pharaoh spent too many years trying to keep the carpets clean and ensure that the bean tins were facing the right way in the pantry to give herself any headaches about domesticity now.

Bedroom now, moving as lightly as she can. Size 16 in Monsoon but light on her feet. She gets her bras from a specialist shop and knows that it would cost over a fiver to mail her breasts anywhere via first-class post. She's not really built for sneaking anywhere. But she doesn't make a sound as she crosses to the bed where she and Thor had made love like drowning sailors fighting over a raft. She presses her face to the tangled sheet. Breathes him in. Then she drops to her knees and reaches under the bed. It's all shoe boxes and lidless Tupperware, family albums and newspaper clippings. She finds what she's looking for at once. The brushed velvet of the jewellery box feels softly animal against her fingertips. She lifts the lid silently, closing her fist around the little spinning ballerina. She feels like a pirate opening treasure. There's a small fortune in jewellery inside: a glittering tangle of pearls, gold, platinum, sapphires. Her wedding ring is somewhere in there. Engagement ring too. The creditors took the eternity ring when Anders went bankrupt. She let it go without complaint. She'd always thought of the gaudy bauble as piss-poor compensation for what he'd been doing to her in the months leading up to their anniversary. She'd never worn it. Her fingers had still been too broken and swollen to put it on when he tossed it to her as he was walking out the door to celebrate their big day by shagging somebody else.

She pushes the jewellery aside. Opens the bottom layer of the box. Five matching wooden dolls stare up at her; each a perfect replica of the other – each a perfect imitation of her own torso. She grabs them and closes the box, shoving it back under the bed. She grabs her jeans from the floor and pulls them on. Boots, too, over sockless feet. Snatches up Thor's shirt from the floor and pulls it on, almost drowning in its folds. Spots her jacket and bag hanging on the hook on the back of the door. She stuffs the dolls inside. Moves silently back to the bathroom and picks up the new one. She takes an evidence bag from her inside pocket and deftly places them inside before transferring it to the side compartment of her bag.

'Trish, I know this is difficult but if we could just have a little chat I'm sure it would make things easier . . .'

Pharaoh mouths 'fuck off' at the front door. Reaches into the shower cubicle and turns on the tap. Cranks it up to hot. Leans back to the sink and turns the tap as cold as it will go. Steam begins to rise.

'Door's open, George. Just getting myself together. Be out in a minute.'

Her voice cracks as she talks. She tells herself that it's an affectation, that she's done it on purpose to better play a role. In truth, it's all she can do not to slide down to the floor and let somebody else take care of everything.

Silently, she slides the sash window as wide as it will go. Looks out into the cold, still dark.

'Too bloody old for this,' she mutters, and swings herself up onto the sill. She pokes around with the toe of her boot, one leg over the sill. She imagines how she looks and can't help but feel a sudden, insane urge to giggle. She fancies that giving in to madness must sometimes be quite a relief.

She finds gap in the brickwork – the same one she'd identified with a copper's eye the first time she stood in the back garden and made a mental list of all the ways she could be burgled, or murdered in her sleep. She finds the wooden trellis with her other boot, feeling her age and the cold night air in her shoulders and knees. Lowers herself down onto the tiled roof of the ground-floor flat. For a moment she feels she's about to fall, her hands slipping from the sill, but she manages to recover her balance, grabbing for the wrought-iron drainpipe that hems the kitchen wall. She slithers down, skinning her palms. Lands in the little communal garden and takes a moment to dust the brickwork and cobwebs from her front. She opens the side gate. Props it open with a stone. There's a little puddle of dirty water by the kitchen drain and she wets the soles of both boots, pressing her feet deliberately in the patina of shimmering frost that marks the little passageway between the houses. Carefully, she retraces her steps, moving backwards onto the crazy paving that leads into the dark of the garden. Moves silently, on tip-toes, barely leaving a mark as she makes her way down the path and onto the grass, ducking past the shed and under the branches of the big mulberry. She slides into the gap between the little trees and the scratchy bush and pushes through until she finds the fence. She squats down in the darkness and listens hard. Somewhere nearby, two pigeons are arguing over whatever the fuck matters to pigeons. She can hear sirens somewhere. She wonders if Earl is still talking to the bathroom door or whether he's taking the opportunity to rifle through her life. She doubts he'll find anything significant. Even if she'd left the figurines behind she doubts they would have meant anything to him. Only McAvoy knows about Hollow's little mementoes.

A wave of sadness floods her as she thinks of McAvoy. She can picture his big bovine head: his Disney princess eyes; the grim set of his jaw as if he's chewing on the stem of a pipe. He'll be trying to work things out, working his way through a mental list of people who might have attacked Thor. He'll be trying not to come to the same conclusion as everybody else and hating himself when he can come up with no other explanation. She'd love to put him out of his misery but to let him in on what she's been doing would be to put him in danger. Better to have him out of the way, hundreds of miles removed in a no-signal zone. He's precisely where she needs him to be.

There's a change to the timbre of the air. She realizes that the sound of the hissing shower has suddenly been silenced. She can just about make out Earl's voice. His upper torso appears in the frame of the open window. He looks down. She can see him doing the mental calculations; trying to decide if she's lithe enough, supple enough, brave enough to climb down the brickwork and into the garden. He looks again at the open side gate and ducks back inside. She slips through the trees to the back gate, hidden from sight. Opens the door, steps through, and closes it behind her without a sound.

She looks both ways. The little alley is deserted, all graffiti garage doors and rotting wooden fences, untended trees, fly-tipped doll's houses and the carcass of a burnt-out sofa. The main road is only a short walk away. She has money, a phone. She can get a cab to the hospital then on to sanctuary. Can get her story straight and try to make sense of things. Can talk to Tom and make things better.

She steps into the light. Walks briskly towards the footpath at the end of the street. Only when she allows herself to think that she's made it do Ben Neilsen and Andy Daniells step out from the shadow of the last garage.

'Sorry, Boss.'

SIX

HMP Warcop
January 28th

> *My darling Clementine,*
>
> You will, I trust, forgive the impudence of using your first name. Good manners dictate that we maintain the use of a formal honorific, given that we have not yet been introduced. Let us flaunt convention. Perhaps Milady would be apt. I am, after all, a mere serf within this new feudal system. You, to the manor born.
>
> It seems bizarre to think of us as strangers, given how many times I have heard you say my name, and the depth

of knowledge you claim to possess regarding my life. Perhaps I am safe to presume a friendship of sorts, or at the very least, a relationship of convenience. You have, after all, done rather well out of me of late. Am I correct in thinking that the latest episode of your podcast has been downloaded in excess of two million times? I understand that I am third in popularity, lagging behind John Wayne Gacy and Gerard Shaefer. I find myself unsure whether to be flattered or insulted. We need a word for that feeling, I think. Perhaps the Germans have already invented one. They understand human nature very well, I find. There are few complex mixtures of disparate impulses that do not have a Teutonic label.

I write entirely uncertain whether this correspondence will reach you. I cannot be sure whether the amiable gentleman of my recent acquaintance will make good upon his promise to safely convey this missive. Nor do I know whether it shall rise from the pile of similar letters that no doubt deluge your PO Box. I am no stranger to voluminous correspondence. In the weeks and months following my incarceration I was overwhelmed with letters. The poor guards responsible for enforcing the Governor's rather draconian laws were fairly stupefied by the sheer weight of correspondence intended for my eyes. There were, of course, those among my correspondents who wished me to know how revolted they were by my alleged crimes. But I am gratified to report that these were very much in the minority. I am humbled by how many people have taken the time to tell me of the esteem in which they hold me and my deeds. It astounds me how many attractive, decent-hearted women have permitted me access to the deepest recesses of their souls and shared confidences with me that their nearest and dearest would shrink from. I am immensely grateful to be chosen as a safe haven for these private revelations, though I will confess that the accompanying images do sometimes distract from the sanctity of the confession.

In the event that these words do reach your eyes, I do permit myself the fantasy that you will be slightly thrilled to find yourself in correspondence with a serial killer. It is an honour indeed to provoke a physiological response in a woman of such rarefied beauty. I sense your pupils dilating:

perfect blobs of obsidian ink spreading upon the robin's egg blue of your irises. I am there in the dryness of your mouth the spreading of heat across your capillaries; the oozing of sweat from behind your knees and in your armpits. It is imagination alone, but I fancy I know your scent: the fresh strawberries and meadowsweet cornstalks of your aroma. I taste the high, oyster-shell pungency of your excitement. It delights me to know that from this remove, trapped beneath the whisky glass with all of these enraged wasps, I have the power to alter your heartbeat; to enlarge your pupils and quicken your pulse. It pleases me that this correspondence will pour into your head like molasses into a jar; that my words will walk within you.

The purpose of my writing? I wish simply to give you my approval. You seem to comprehend the complexities of my crimes. Moreover, your voice is pleasant; your mouth strung for lullabies; your tongue honeyed with wisdom and compassion. It is strange to know that, in a different life, we could have been confidants.

In answer to your question, posed in the last episode . . . yes. Yes, I accept what I did. I took lives, Clementine. I sought out the bad men who had mistreated good women, and I delivered punishment accordingly. I have always despised bullies, Clementine. Do you not wish, from time to time, that the people who have caused you hurt could be simply expunged? Do you not wish for a benign bogeyman, an avenging angel who hears your darkest prayers and gives you the vengeance that you seek? I receive hundreds of letters from women who wish I was still able to remove their persecutors from their lives. It is a wish I share. I will confess that it is more difficult to follow my path from within the walls of HMP Warcop. The Sainted Trish Pharaoh saw to that, though I bear no ill will towards her. All things must end. My only regret is that I wasn't able to perform the task for Trish that would have made her life so much less cruel. She told me herself how frequently she yearned for a man like me to swoop in and cut out the tumour in her life. I have always taken comfort in that. I think of Trish often. When she visits, the air between us positively tingles.

'Among the flashing waves are two white birds
Which swoop, and soar, and scream for very joy.'

I shall curtail this letter now, Clementine. I hope you feel amply rewarded for your diligence. You have, indeed, reminded the ravenous public that there was, for a time, a man who wanted to liberate abused women from the chains of oppression. For that, I am grateful. Do, please, continue to resist the urge to profile my daughter. She is my one regret.

Six, you say? Oh Clementine. How I wish I could give you the satisfaction you crave.
I will be listening.
Cura, et valeas
Reuben

PS. I am told that you hold your phone in the crook of your thumb and index finger of your left hand. I would urge you alter your grip. I have suffered with carpal tunnel syndrome as a result of repetitive use of the self-same digits and would not wish such pain upon anybody. Do, please, invest in a sturdier deadbolt for the back door of your home at Copse Cross Street, Ross-on-Wye, Hereford. Honestly, one good shove and anybody could be inside. And I am, regrettably, indisposed. You might, perhaps, yearn for a man with your so-called Lancelot complex, when you find yourself on your back, and with a blade taking slices of your flesh. Food for thought.

SEVEN

I t isn't snowing, but a hard frost is beginning to set in. A sparkling rain hangs in the black air. The battered red Jeep lurches and skids, ice and grit crunching under the wheels. He's staying under the speed limit. He's got his hands exactly where they should be. He's trying to keep his gear changes smooth. He doesn't need to be pulled over by any passing cop. He doesn't need to flash any cameras. He has no doubt that the police will be examining their network of beady eyes for any vehicle seen speeding away from the scene of the horror on Victoria Avenue. So much depends upon what comes next and it would be unforgivable to spoil it by making a silly mistake at the last.

He stares out through the grimy windscreen. Presses himself against the cracked leather. The window is a little way down and he can smell the hot-oil stink of the engine over the soft yellow pungency of the frost-rimed fields, reflecting back a buttery light as he pushes the vehicle east.

He tries not to let himself think upon the outline pressed into the leather. Another man sat here. Another man pressed his flesh into the upholstery. Another man stared out through a blue haze of cigarette smoke and made his way to the places where good people asked him to remove bad men. He feels a queasiness in his gut when he thinks upon the man who drove this car; the man who wielded the tools in their soft leather roll and which he carries inside his coat. The reverence he feels for the true owner of this vehicle is incalculable. He does not see himself as an imitator. He is no acolyte. He knows himself to be a continuation: their destinies irrevocably linked by blood and destiny.

He looks at the phone on the passenger seat. Still no reply from the girl. It irks him. Hurts him. He had thought better of her. Had expected gratitude, if nothing else. He sometimes wishes he had a father figure in his life, an adult who could offer wisdom and experience. He doesn't really know how to talk to people, should they find the enthusiasm for striking up a conversation. He exudes a certain air of bone-cold menace. He doesn't look like other people. Doesn't sound like they do. He asks the wrong questions in conversation. He loves too fast and too hard. Burns himself out and retreats into numbness before the inevitable awakening of his rage and shame.

He sends her a message. Presses his bloodied fingers to the screen and chews at his lip. He probes at his teeth: both sets of molars simultaneously. His tongue is split. He can make the two halves wind together like snakes.

He pulls out the ashtray. Fumbles through the pile of paper and ash. Takes a crumpled dog-end between finger and thumb and holds it to his nose. Breathes in coal-tar and sour tobacco and feels a quickening that electrifies the marrow of every bone.

He switches on the radio. There's a CD in the slot. He's listened to it so many times he could recite it from memory but there's a certain comfort in hearing it again.

It's her. Talking. There's a slur to her voice. She's had a few and she's enjoying this quiet moment: just the two of them, sat on the steps of the little caravan in the woods.

'. . . he had this charm, y'know? Like, there was this twinkle about him. You knew he didn't really give a fuck about the rules and there's something sexy about that, even when you think you're in the business of enforcing them. And the way he looked at me – I don't think I'd ever been looked at like that. I don't think it was love at first sight but there was a lustfulness – a sort of weighing up of the options. And when I did give in, Jesus, it was like moving from a black and white movie into colour. You make allowances for a lot of things when somebody touches you like that. He lit a fire in me and it kept burning all those years. You wouldn't see it now. You wouldn't look at him and know what he was because all you'd see is what he is. But I still see it. I see him for the sexy, charming bastard who showed me what love was and I see him for the absolute cunt who used to smash me into the wall and boot my ribs when I got in his face about money or other women or where he'd been. But what do I do? I can't leave him and I sure as hell can't expect him to leave me. What's he going to do – trundle off in his mobility scooter? And he looks so bloody helpless. Do you know how many times he's begged me to kill him? To finish him off? Some days it's all I can do not to just charge up all the static I can and see if I can cause the stroke that will finish him off. And then I feel so fucking guilty because he's their dad and I love him. And how do I make time for myself? I can't meet somebody else, can I? My husband's still alive. All that he did to me . . . all he put us through . . . jealous though, did I tell you that? So fucking possessive. Always convinced I was shagging Tozer, my ex, or having a fling with Tom, or just having flings with strangers. The guy who did the landscaping at our house – he paid me a compliment and Anders went for the poor sod with half a metal railing. And me a copper, having to talk him round, asking him not to give a statement, begging him not to tell*

*anybody, and all the while I'm giving speeches about domestic
violence and locking up wife-beaters . . .'*

He turns off the CD. Noses the vehicle between two tumbledown
gateposts and crunches on up the path. He tucks it in behind the
thickest line of hedgerow and climbs out. Breathes in a lungful of
cold, damp air. Fills himself up with it. He'll be glad of it later,
he's sure. He's cranked the heating up at the little bungalow at the
end of the close. The body behind the sofa is rank now. It's coming
apart: an assemblage of greenish bones and rotten meat and a
shimmering blanket of fat, feeding flies.

He looks across the fields towards the little village. She'll come,
he knows that. This is her sanctuary. She'll need somewhere to get
away. She'll run here. She'll follow the trail and she'll walk in like
she owns the fucking place. And then he can do what he must.

He reaches back into the car. Rummages under the seat and
pulls out the taser. It's fully charged again, the wire trailing to the
cigarette lighter. It'll put her down, just like it did her lover. Then
he can come back for the car. He can take her somewhere quiet.
And he can show her that there are consequences for betrayal.

He looks again at the screen of his phone. She's active. She's
awake. She might want to talk. She might want to listen. He misses
their shared confidences. It had started as a ploy but somewhere
along the way he experienced something familiar; some softening
of his defences; some actual interest in her well-being. It had hurt
him when she changed her mind. He thought the video would
have cemented things between them: once she knew what had
been done to Anders Wilkie he felt sure she would rejoice in the
annihilation of Trish Pharaoh. It hadn't gone as he planned. He
feels empty when he thinks of her. Feels cheated. And the god
who made everything possible won't answer his questions. In such
moments, he wonders where he fits into the grand Plan. Wonders
whether he is the primary player in some great cosmic board, or
nothing more than a sacrificial pawn.

He shakes the thoughts away. Slides the CD from the slot. In
the pinkish moonlight he looks at the words written in a girlish
hand in thick black pen.

Trish and RH # 6

He takes the dog-end from the ashtray. Places it between his lips.
He takes a lighter from his pocket and manages to set fire to the

bedraggled little inch of hand-rolled cigarette. For a moment he feels the power of connection. Feels the imprint of Reuben Hollow's mouth. Closes his eyes and offers up another prayer of gratitude. He'll do what he is commanded. He will repay the debt that has freed him from the oblivion into which he had sunk like a stone.

He hefts the taser. The adze. The mask. Feels the shiver trace chill fingers on his vertebrae. Somewhere inside of him he hears the little voice that used to sing to him when things were bad. It tells him to stop. He doesn't want to do this. He's being manipulated. He's ill. He can stop. There's still time to stop.

He sets off towards Tom Spink's house. Wonders whether to give Pharaoh a chance to witness the utter devastation of his flesh before he pitches her into the earth and begins her transformation.

It is a thought which keeps him warm.

EIGHT

Amberline Haven, Gamblesby, Eden Valley
1.16 a.m.

The mobile phone service is at its best in the heart of the little wood at the top of the hill. On any other occasion, McAvoy would take a moment to muse upon the incongruity of such an occurrence; to query the placement of the phone masts, the particularities of the topography; the angle of the satellite and curvature of the Earth and marvel at the conspiracy of peculiarities that ensured a chap could only respond to an emergency in a location where he would be bugger-all use. But it's the middle of the night and it's pitch dark – the air cold and black and sparkling with gathering frost – and he's grumpy and jealous and ever so slightly afraid. He wants to be at her side. Wants to understand what's happening. Wants to know whether he's being sidelined or thrown into the heart of something destined to end in blood. So he doesn't ask himself his usual thoughts. Just thinks of Thor, and of Pharaoh, and makes a list of all the people who might want to harm her, or him. It's a depressing task. He tries his best to be a good person and yet he has no shortage of people who would rejoice at news of his brutal murder. It's a hard headspace to exist in.

He's holding up his mobile, pitching a little blue light into the air and doing his best to avoid the risen tree roots and the gnarly fingers of the outstretched branches. Woods are different entities at night. He and Fin chopped wood here yesterday afternoon. They watched a blackbird, feathers puffed up against the cold, as it hopped across hard ground and pecked ineffectually at a pebble, McAvoy providing a little voice-over that made his son laugh. *'Pebbles. Didn't care for them yesterday but this one might be different. Nope. Still yuk. I suppose that must mean I'm still a bird. What's that? Ooh, a pebble . . .'*

He waves the phone, big circles now: a lepidopterist wafting at butterflies. The shins of his jeans are getting wet as the damp snarls of grass reach up and grab at his legs. He'll have to change his outfit before he heads back. Can't remember what clothes he's brought with him. Wonders if Roisin will be able to pull something out of her bag of tricks. He needs to at least try and pass for a police officer. He hasn't shaved the boundaries of his beard in days; hasn't tried to tame the tangle of his red-grey hair. He starts to chide himself for having the gall to come away with the family in the first place. Feels the familiar gut-punch of guilt and self-reproach and screws up his face, trying to find Roisin's voice amid the din roaring in his skull. Without her, without the kids, McAvoy would be inert. She gives him just enough self-belief to stay ahead of his doubts. Everything he is, he puts down to her. Her, and Pharaoh.

'Jesus, Trish.'

He pictures her. The Boss. His best friend, his mentor and his hero. It's been almost a decade since she spotted his potential and gave him the chance to turn his career around; to come back in from the chilly wilderness where he'd found himself after exposing the old head of CID for their lifetime of wickedness and corruption. Doing the right thing cost him dear. It nearly cost him his life. But Trish Pharaoh took a chance on the big, shy Highlander. They've caught a lot of bad people together. She's saved his life. He's saved hers. They've locked up serial killers and brought down global criminal gangs. Not rushing to her side is truly unthinkable. He doesn't think he'll be able to help in any specific way – just believes in old-fashioned concepts like loyalty, duty; friendship.

Roisin has already started peppering him with questions. She'd known more about Pharaoh's love life than McAvoy, taking an interest in her occasional rival's romantic entanglements with a mixture of curiosity and concern. She may not particularly like Trish Pharaoh but she'd like to see her find a man and settle down, and possibly move to Sierra Leone, if only so she stops gazing at McAvoy like a teenager staring at a poster on their bedroom wall. McAvoy always protests when Roisin teases him about Trish's feelings for him. He sees no evidence to back up her claims – a rebuttal that Roisin sees as absolute confirmation that he's in the wrong job.

Roisin knows more than he does about Pharaoh's late husband, too. She's good friends with Trish's oldest daughter and they've spoken at length about the hulking, occasionally charming narcissist who lavished them all with gifts one moment and beat the shit out of them if they didn't say thank-you the right way. He was a bully and a coward, ambitious but inept; selfish and needy and so spectacularly wrong for Trish Pharaoh that McAvoy cannot even comprehend what it was that brought them together in the first place.

His phone beeps, locating the patch of air that the wi-fi gods have decreed a sacred space.

His inbox begins to fill; missed calls, missed messages; un-answered emails and social media notifications. He closes his eyes. Breathes in the scents of the wood; the shredded bark and the wet grass; the risen earth and the whisper of blood. Reaches out and feels the knobbled skin of the big ash tree. Fin had nicked it with the blade of the axe yesterday. It bled red.

In his hand, the phone vibrates, its song trilling loud and incongruous against the still night air. He answers automatically – any other course of action an unforgivable dereliction of responsibility.

'Aector . . . Hector . . . Aector . . .'

McAvoy screws up his face. Feels a tension creeping into his jaw. 'Speaking,' he says, unsure whether to reveal that he recognizes the voice.

'George Earl,' comes the confirmation; voice quiet, unruffled. 'Have I caught you at a bad time?'

McAvoy wonders whether the DCSU is joking. It's 1.34 a.m. and he's on his holidays. If this were indeed a good time for a conversation with the head of CID, he'd seriously need to rethink his lifestyle choices.

'I've heard, sir,' says McAvoy, aware that he has no gift for pretence.

'Heard?'

'About the incident at Detective Superintendent Pharaoh's home. How's the victim, sir?'

'Bad news travels fast, it seems.'

McAvoy lets the silence play out. Earl takes a moment. McAvoy hears him swallowing. Hears the muffled voice of an instruction being issued to an underling, Earl's hand over the mouthpiece.

'Critical,' says Earl, with an almost audible shake of the head. His manner is tailor-made for moments like these. He has a real gift for seeming quietly aghast at the things people will do to one another, as if such acts of wanton violence and rage are few and far between and that the natural order of things and catching the perpetrator will restore the world to its resting state of peace and prosperity.

'And the Boss?'

'Ah,' says Earl, and the syllable is far from reassuring.

'I thought I might make myself available, sir,' says McAvoy, scratching at his beard. 'I'm in the Lakes. Family holiday, sir. But I can be home in three hours, twenty-four minutes if there's no roadworks on the M62 . . .'

'No need for that, Aector,' says Earl, smoothly. 'We can muddle through without you, grateful as I'm sure we'd all be for your help. No, you enjoy a well-earned rest. Are the family having a nice time? Your Siobhan must be having a wonderful time.'

McAvoy breathes out, slowly. Chews at his cheek. He wonders whether Earl has misremembered the name of Roisin or Lilah. Wonders if there's an insult hidden within the DCSU's presumption that he and his Pavee wife and their half-breed diddicoy children are having a wonderful time in their gypsy wagon on the edge of the wood.

'Is that why you're calling, sir? To tell me to stay put?'

'Not entirely,' says Earl, a sigh in his voice. 'Regrettably, Trish is being distinctly uncooperative – performed a rather unfortunate disappearing act while we were still assessing the scene.'

McAvoy feels his heart sink, even as the corner of his mouth twitch into something like a smile.

'One hopes she's simply making her way to the hospital to check in on the welfare of her friend,' continues Earl. 'Obviously her first concern is for the victim, which is entirely in keeping with her reputation as a caring and dedicated officer of great esteem and experience . . .'

'Will that be in the press release, sir?' asks McAvoy, unable to help himself.

'But in her absence we do find ourselves somewhat stymied,' continues Earl, ignoring the interruption. 'We know next to nothing about the victim and there is a huge range of possible motives. Given your close relationship with her, I rather thought you might be able to fill in some of the blanks, as it were. As it were. As it were.'

McAvoy turns around. Leans his head against the bark of the tree. His mind races ahead, scanning his memory for anything that he should hold on to; any revelations that Pharaoh would thank him to keep to himself. He wants to help catch whoever has visited this brutality upon the big copper from Iceland but his loyalty is to Pharaoh. He decides to give Earl enough to seem helpful and to hold on to the more sensitive material until he's had chance to take counsel from Pharaoh.

'Do you know much about the victim?' asks Earl, and the change in the timbre of the call suggests that McAvoy is now on speakerphone. People are listening.

'They met when she was in Iceland on an investigation, sir,' says McAvoy, voice neutral. 'Four years ago? The bad winter, sir. Before your time.'

'He's a police officer, I understand.'

'Tiny rural station not far from Isafjordur. They became friends.'

'I understand there's more to their relationship than that,' says Earl, endeavouring to sound non-judgemental. 'He was half dressed when the attack happened. We understand he responded to a car alarm. They'd been in bed.'

McAvoy sniffs. Presses his lips together. 'They've maintained

their friendship, sir. As for developments, that's not really any of
my business.'

'Indeed. Sorry to put you in an awkward position, old chap. We
all feel a little, well . . . it's all a little close to home, isn't it?
None of us wants to be sifting through the life of somebody we
all admire so much. I'm enormously grateful that you can spare
her some of that.'

McAvoy closes his eyes. 'I didn't know he was visiting, sir,'
he says, and it's almost true. Pharaoh hadn't told him but there'd
been a change in her manner over the past few weeks; a giddiness;
an air of distraction. It had been Roisin who told her what her
manner indicated; Roisin who mimed being sick as she patiently
explained that Pharaoh was behaving like a woman who was
expecting to scratch a particular itch, and soon.

'There's some concern at this end that the attacker might have
made a rather rudimentary mistake,' says Earl. 'That perhaps the
intended victim might actually have been your good self.'

McAvoy snorts. 'Leaving her flat half-dressed, sir? Hardly.'

'He's a very large man. Reddish hair, pale skin. There's some
debate here whether we mightn't be advised to instigate the Threat
to Life protocol. Perhaps not full protective custody but if you
weren't already tucked away in the back of beyond I think we
would have to bring you and your lovely family into the bosom
of the station, just until we know a little more about what's
occurring.'

'I hardly think that's necessary, sir.'

'Perhaps not. One thing your personnel file makes clear is that
you can take care of yourself. Even so, guidelines are guidelines.
Guidelines. Guidelines.'

'Any witnesses, sir?' asks McAvoy, picking at the bark of the
tree. He smells sap. Feels it on his fingers.

'House to house is looking promising,' replies Earl. 'A lot of
the neighbours take their home security seriously. We have
footage of somebody leaving the scene. Dark clothing, face hard
to make out. Definitely male. We'll be trawling CCTV, naturally,
but hopefully some of the other residents will have caught the
actual attack.'

McAvoy stays silent. Wonders whether Earl is an optimist or
an idiot.

'Of course, it would make things much easier if you could contact Detective Superintendent Pharaoh and persuade her to come back to her lovely apartment and have a proper conversation. Everybody is very aware of your close friendship.'

McAvoy feels his cheeks redden. 'Of course, sir. I'll try her number straight away.'

'Her daughters,' continues Earl. 'Four, yes? Astounding to think she's raised a family while scaling the heights. Inspirational. Might she perhaps have gone to a family member?'

'Sophia, the eldest. She lives out Keyingham way with her daughter Elvie. She has a boyfriend who works away. Freddie, I think. Samantha's travelling. Thailand, last I heard. Poppy's at university. Loughborough, sports sciences. Olivia's with Trish's mum. Name's Sarah but people call her Babs. Last year of school. They live out at Laceby, outskirts of Grimsby.'

'You're an encyclopaedia,' says Earl, his manner markedly false. There's some muffled conversation. McAvoy strains to hear but Earl's hand is blocking the receiver.

'Sir?'

'Sorry, Aector. Just looking at the photographs of the victim's wounds. Looks like somebody's taken an axe to him.'

'That's awful, sir.'

'Indeed.'

McAvoy imagines the feeling of the blade working through meat and muscle. Remembers the cold pain of steel moving through his insides and wishes, for a moment, that he could have spared Thor his suffering. If the wounds were meant for him, he wonders whether he'll ever be able to live with the guilt.

'Any similar incidents of late?' he asks, trying to be useful. 'Can't be many axe attacks in the region.'

'I'm sure we'll get to that. It's the pin-pricks that worry me. I've seen them before, of course.'

'Sir?'

'Taser,' explains Earl, matter-of-factly. 'Whoever did this, they put him down with a taser. They did the rest to him when he was already down. Or at least, that's the way it looks to the people with the expertise. I'm sure they'd know more if they could actually get their hands upon the victim and poke around. Much easier with a body.'

'Thor,' he says.

'Sorry, Aector.'

'Not "the victim". Thor.'

'Yes,' says Earl, swallowing. His voice changes tone, his words becoming snake-like and insidious in McAvoy's mind. 'Thor,' he says, testing the word. 'Of course. I'll contact the Icelandic authorities as soon as the hour is reasonable.'

McAvoy can't think of anything to say. He's always felt an unfathomable jealousy at Pharaoh's friendship with the big Icelandic copper but he'd hoped they might meet some day; size each other up – share one or two anecdotes about their mutual friend; give one another a handshake designed to test the other man's grip. The thought of him laid out on the grass. bleeding from his back, bubbles in his breath . . . McAvoy feels only sorrow. Sorrow for Thor, for Trish – for Thor's wife back home. He won't proffer that little titbit unless asked. It was Roisin who discovered Thor's domestic set-up with her dedicated cyber-stalking and as far as Trish is concerned, McAvoy doesn't know. It's none of his business. So it's none of Earl's.

'Potential gangland?' asks McAvoy.

'I doubt it's a lumberjack,' says Earl, a note of chumminess creeping into his voice. 'So, you'll try and track her down, yes?'

'Of course, sir.'

'Good man,' says Earl. 'While I have you, I must ask the obvious. Known enemies – anybody who might hold a grudge against Trish? Working theory is a car theft gone wrong, but given her position in CID we can't rule out the possibility that they were expecting Pharaoh to come out in response to the alarm and that they attacked her partner in error.'

'She's been banging up criminals for thirty years, sir. She's got endless enemies. But if you're asking whether I have any immediate suspicions, no, not really. We haven't seen very much of each other the past few weeks, what with the reorganization of the department. She's been very much tied up with budgets and committees, sir. I had a quick chat with her about the podcast but she just laughed it off.'

There's a momentary pause as Earl reassembles himself; affects the very image of somebody who already knows what McAvoy is talking about.

'Ah, the podcast. Yes. Bad business.'

McAvoy curses himself. He'd figured that Earl would at least have been aware of it. Somebody as media-savvy as George Earl should have been very much up to speed with the recent episode of 'GMBD' and the return to the public consciousness of one Reuben Hollow.

'They asked her to be involved but she politely declined,' says McAvoy, a muscle in his cheek twitching as he registers the lie. 'Asked me too.'

'You'll forgive me, Aector. Lateness of the hour, mind stuffed to the gills. What specifically did the podcast deal with?'

'"GMBD", sir. "Good Murders, Bad Deaths". Reuben Hollow, sir.'

Earl swallows. He's finally up to speed. He wasn't with Humberside Police when Pharaoh and McAvoy caught the man who'd spent a great chunk of his adult life bumping off various bullies, brutes and bastards at the unspoken urging of whichever woman whose chains he wished to break. Six victims, at the last count. Catching Hollow was an investigation that cost McAvoy and Pharaoh dearly, despite the commendations and bravery awards with which they were both garlanded afterwards. Hollow's been inside more than five years – a model prisoner in the crumbling old Category A jail – a little less than an hour from where McAvoy stands. Pharaoh's visited him a few times since he was sent down. She wants him to confess to his other crimes. That's her story, at least. McAvoy's always had the unspoken suspicion that something exists between them – something unquantifiable; some mutuality of purpose; some refracted reflection. Each views the other as a glimpse of who the other could have become if they'd made different choices.

Hollow would probably have been forgotten by the public if he hadn't been profiled by 'GMBD'. Episode 13 of the true-crime show had painted him as a Romantic warrior; a righter of wrongs; a superhero lurking in the shadows and ready to dispense well-earned deaths to those who raised their hand to women and children. McAvoy can't quite believe people have bought the act. Suddenly, Hollow seems to be everywhere. Three true-crime channels have commissioned documentaries and a local writer who covered the trial has signed a book deal. The wife of one of his victims has made a tidy sum giving interviews to magazines, calling Hollow a hero and claiming that he should be given a medal instead of a life sentence.

'I don't think we can lay the blame for this at the feet of a convicted killer in a jail cell, Aector,' says Earl, with a small snort of derision. 'Anyway, sorry to have disturbed your beauty sleep. Do try and persuade Trish of the merits of thinking like a police officer, eh? It really will be a help in the long run.'

McAvoy doesn't get a chance to reply before the call is terminated. He stares at the phone and its overflowing inbox. Licks his lips. Counts backwards from ten.

Calls Ben Neilsen, who answers on the third ring.

'Have you got her?' he asks, without preamble.

There's the sound of a scuffle; of swearing and yelping and pleas to be released.

'No . . . you can't . . . stop . . . no!'

Neilsen lets out a hiss, the wince of somebody experiencing sympathy pains. 'Can I call you back in a sec, Sarge. Boss . . . let him go, he's turning blue . . . Oh bollocks, Sarge, can I call you back? I think she's killed Andy . . .'

NINE

Newland Avenue, Hull
1.19 a.m.

A ndy Daniells rubs his neck. Rubs his ribs. Counts his eyeballs and their scrotal counterparts. Finds himself all present and correct. He's still wheezing and there are pretty sparkly lights dancing in his eyes, but he won't hold a grudge. When he recounts the story of having been beaten up by Trish Pharaoh it will be with a note of pride; a campfire story retold with the same reverence as an ageing hippie holding up the hand that once brushed the rump of Stevie Nicks.

'I haven't got time for this,' says Pharaoh, rubbing his back. 'Just sips,' she adds, as gently as she can manage. 'Andy, just bloody sips.'

The three of them are tucked into a square of shadow; a patch of broken ground in the gap between two garages. Neilsen has the look of somebody who knows they are on borrowed time. He'd been trying to explain himself to the boss when Daniells had stepped out from his own place of concealment and given her a fright. She'd reacted in a windmill of kicks and punches and Neilsen fancies he can still hear the fading echo of the rusty metal door upon which Andy Daniells' head had been forcibly clanged.

'It's all right,' wheezes Daniells. 'Own fault . . . he said . . . said to approach from the side . . . like a horse . . .'

Pharaoh straightens up. 'Like a horse?'

'The Sarge said we should hang around here, just in case, like,' says Neilsen, under his breath. 'Said maybe you'd want to get away, like. Maybe get your head together, see your friend. Said you might come this way.'

'And when did he say this?' asks Pharaoh, in a voice that could turn Bridlington Beach into a sheet of gleaming glass.

'When I told him what was going on. Like, as soon as I told him, he said you might, y'know . . .'

'Need some space?' she finishes.

'Do a runner,' wheezes Daniells, ever eager to help.

'Glad to know I'm so predictable,' growls Pharaoh. She rummages inside her coat, looking for cigarettes. Curses and makes do with her vape. 'Is he OK?'

'Critical,' says Neilsen, quietly.

'No, Hector.'

Neilsen makes a face. 'On holiday but heading back . . .'

'No he's bloody not,' she insists, light flashing in her eyes. 'No, I'm not having that. Keep him out of harm's way. Call him back while you're on your way – tell him to stay put and I'll let him know what he has to do once I've decided.'

Neilsen shoots a look at his stricken colleague. 'Andy and me,' he says. 'Whatever's going on, you can count on us. Whatever you need us to do.'

'I need you to be police officers,' she snaps. 'I need you to give me a cigarette, but you're a trendy-bendy vegan bastard and don't pollute your body, so at this exact moment, you're a dead loss. As for Andy here . . .'

Daniells straightens up, tears running over his plump red

cheeks. He looks like a proud veteran on VE Day. Looks half ready to salute.

The sight of him takes the anger out of her voice. 'I'm grateful to the both of you,' she says. 'And you can help, if you're willing.'

'Of course,' says Neilsen. 'The car's that way. Andy's is by the perimeter but we're not being used so I doubt there'll be any raised voices if he goes and gets it.'

'Just shush,' says Pharaoh, rummaging in her bag. She finds her phone. Calls up her contacts list and pings half a dozen names and phone numbers to Neilsen's number. 'Check they're OK,' she explains. 'One of you might want to go and take a tour past our Sophia's, if you're feeling restless.'

'Your eldest?' asks Neilsen. 'You think somebody might be targeting your family? Christ, Boss – we need to get them into protective custody. You too . . .'

'I'm being paranoid, I'm sure of it,' mutters Pharaoh, waving a hand. 'But it would be a relief. Just a quick check, make sure there's nothing odd going on. Prowler, burglar, nutter with an axe, that kind of thing.'

'What are you going to be doing?' asks Daniells, looking up as a squad car cruises past the end of the alley.

'Don't fret about me,' she says. 'I'll talk to Earl when I want to. He doesn't like me so this will be giving him a hard-on you could play hoopla with, provided you could spare the pineapple rings.' She breathes out slowly, suddenly looking very tired. 'Fuck it, none of this was ever going to be easy. Look, lads – I just need to do a couple of things first and they're hard to do if I'm sat answering questions and explaining the complexities of a relationship I'm a bit bloody keen not to talk about. So, just kind of, y'know – leave it to me.'

'It's a relationship then?' asks Daniells, with a suggestive smile.

'Fuck off, Andy,' growls Pharaoh, for whom absence of nicotine is starting to become a potentially fatal condition.

'He looks so much like McAvoy,' says Daniells, wide-eyed. 'I mean, you must have spotted that, yeah? I don't want to shock you, or anything. There was this episode of *Friends*, where Rachel got over Ross by finding a guy called Russ, and she was the only one who didn't see it, so I just thought . . .'

'Jesus,' mutters Neilsen, under his breath.

The moment passes. Pharaoh opens her eyes. 'He's a friend,' she explains. 'We met in Iceland, stayed in touch. He came to see me. He got hurt by somebody breaking into my car. And here we are.'

'You think they were targeting the Sarge?' asks Daniells, ploughing further into the quicksand armed with bucket and spade.

'I don't know, Andy,' she says. 'I don't know what's happening, do I?'

'That podcast,' muses Daniells. 'The one about Hollow . . .'

'I haven't heard it,' lies Pharaoh, rummaging in her bag once again. She gives Neilsen her attention. 'Don't frighten anybody, OK? Don't panic them. Just let me know if there's any problem. And don't let Hector head this way, you hear me? Maybe just tootle past Olivia's place too. It's a bit of a drive but I know you'll want to be useful. She's not speaking to me, so maybe a bit of discretion, eh? God, I'm never going to hear the end of this.'

Neilsen nods. Pharaoh gives his arm a little squeeze, her eyes softening. 'I appreciate this,' she says. 'And tell Hector that I'm not doing a runner, I'm making a strategic withdrawal to permit myself the freedom to conduct my own enquiries.'

'That's what he said you'd be doing,' nods Daniells, loyally.

She looks from one to the other. Jerks a thumb over her shoulder. 'Take the long way round, would you? I've got a cab picking me up outside the Italian in about two minutes.'

'When did you order that?' asks Daniells, amazed.

Pharaoh gives him back his phone, stolen while she was banging his head off the garage door. 'You must change your pin code, Andy. You're an elite detective. *1,2,3,4* is the pin code of the simpleton.'

'Boss, I . . .'

'That'll do, Pig,' says Pharaoh, not unkindly, and she slips between them, soundless as she disappears into the darkness, only reappearing for a fraction of a second before emerging again at the end of the road. A cab is waiting, parked out of sight of the security camera on the wall of the newsagent that faces the curve of Newland Avenue. She keyed in the instruction to the taxi app as she rummaged in her bag, multi-tasking with the effortless precision of a mum of five.

She opens the door and slides inside.

'I was expecting a bloke,' says the driver. 'Andy, yeah?'

Pharaoh spots the packet of cigarettes on the front passenger seat. Leans in from the back seat and takes them. Snatches up a cheap plastic lighter. Sparks up, and inhales the smoke. Holds it deep in her rattling lungs.

She locks eyes with the driver, her expression enough to silence his protest.

'Expecting a bloke,' she mutters. Shakes her head. 'Weren't we all.'

Thirty seconds after the cab pulls away into the dimly lit silence of Newland Avenue, a black car cruises out of a side street. It follows at a respectable distance. There's a big man at the wheel. Another in the passenger seat. Two more in the back. They don't speak. They just follow. They're waiting for orders. Waiting for permission. Waiting to perform a dirty job that somebody's got to do. They're rather looking forward to it.

TEN

Needlers Way, Hull
1.44 a.m.

Detective Inspector Ashley Cross has one foot up on the ottoman, blasting his shin with a hair-dryer. His leg hair divides and reshapes, swirls and settles in complex new patterns as he moves the blast of hot air over his fur. It's like watching a whirlwind move through a cornfield. He's absurdly hairy. He swam for the county in his youth and got into the habit of shaving his legs and arms. It grew back not long after he hit thirty, intent on making up for lost time. He looks dressed even when naked: looks like he's been smeared in glue and rolled across a barber-shop floor. The only place he isn't covered in a great carpet of dark hair is on the head: perfectly bald and mottled from exposure to the sun. It looks as if it's been steeped in strong tea and onion skins.

He changes the angle of the hair-dryer. Blasts himself between the legs and enjoys the smell of singeing hair. Switches it off when he's satisfied that he's properly dry. Feels the familiar tingle as his bouffant body hair settles back into place.

'That's one for Instagram,' comes the voice from the doorway. She places her hand to her chest: a Southern belle enchanted by the sight of a handsome gentleman caller. 'I do declare . . . be still my beating fanny.'

Cross looks up, entirely unconcerned. He knows who's watching and doesn't give a toss. Detective Sergeant Emma Redmore is standing in the doorway, pulling a face, acting as if she isn't getting a tingle in the dingle at catching a sneaky peek. He doesn't make any attempt to cover up. Lets her see: the muscles, the definition; the expensive dot work on his expensive Celtic tattoos. Lets her feast her fucking eyes.

Her smile fades when Cross doesn't immediately respond to her little joke. Her expression changes: the surface of a pond reflecting a winged predator. She looks rueful. Looks a little frightened. Looks like he damn well wants her to.

'I should probably have knocked.'

Cross straightens up and puts a hand on his lower back, twisting sharply left then right. There is an explosive series of cracks. He feels a brief sense of relief. Performs a similar series of manoeuvres with his neck. Rolls his shoulders, hyper-extending the joints until he achieves the sought-for crunch. Begins working on his finger joints and wrists. He's only wearing boxer shorts but isn't remotely embarrassed about his junior officer's presence. She's seen him in far more awkward positions. Joined him in some too.

'You'll give yourself arthritis,' says Redmore, relieved. She slouches into the bedroom and plonks herself down on his bed. The sheet is bunched up and damp with sweat – the covers a mad tangle by the footboard.

'Still not made a trip to Dunelm?' she asks, chattily, staring up at the bare bulb. It illuminates a joyless cube: bed, ottoman, chest of drawers. Shirts and suits on hangers are suspended from the curtain rail, unfastened ties around the collars. There's a pile of shoes in one corner; a battered leather jacket slung in a corner. A picture of Steve McQueen, black-framed and uber-stylish, leans against one wall. There's a string on the back and a hook in the wall but the effort of marrying one to the other has so far been beyond him. He shouldn't have to think about menial tasks. Somebody should do this petty shit for him – somebody grateful for the chance to bask in his good graces.

'You're welcome to give it the *Changing Rooms* treatment any time you like,' says Cross, pulling on a pair of dark jeans. He imagines coming home one day to find that she's given him his dream boudoir: circular bed, crushed velvet furnishings: mirrored ceiling and so much leather and chrome. He'd let her be the first to break them in. He knows how to say thank you.

'That one,' she says, nodding at a blue shirt.

He ignores her. Sifts through the line of shirts that covers the window. Picks a black one embossed with little silver bicycles. Grabs a thin blue tie, striped with lines of red.

'Might take you up on that,' says Redmore, making herself comfortable. 'Could be a lovely place, this. Needs a bit of TLC, that's all.'

'Needs bloody bulldozing,' grumbles Cross, fasting his buttons. 'Needs pulverizing down to dust then dumping in the sea.'

'Still not settled in?'

'Piss off.'

Redmore is young and tough and clever. Stylish too. Her curly hair is shaved up both sides and runs down the back of her head in a mullet. She wears round wire-framed glasses and her ears are treasure chests of hoops and studs. She's wearing a woollen tank top, her arms bare; camouflage trousers and white trainers with chunky soles. She doesn't look anything like a copper. Looks like she's the lead singer in some indie band. With his leather jacket, battered boots and skinny ties, he's aware he looks like the bass player. Hates for it. Fancies her and finds her disgusting. Wants her and wants to resist her. Hates her all the more for confusing him. Hates them all, if he's honest. Hates every last fucking one.

'Turning to shit, then?' asks Cross, turning towards his colleague. He doesn't let himself look at her for more than a moment. She looks tempting, propped up in his bed, playing with her phone, all bare arms and young, gym-toned flesh. He's made a promise to himself that he won't make the same mistakes again; told himself that he'd rather maintain their friendship, their intimacy, than repeat the overtures that she's succumbed to on half a dozen occasions during their association. Trouble is, he makes those deals with himself while he's alone, and not when he's looking at her; not while she's there, looking so deliciously skanky and warm and available: not now he's single, and living in Hull, and having been roused from a pleasant sleep by the news that the operation has been compromised and that he should probably get up, shower and go blow dry his balls.

'Not exactly turned to shit,' says Redmore, waggling her hand in the air. 'Just, well . . . it's complicated.'

'Always bloody is,' says Cross, shaking his head. 'Stay there.'

He heads down the corridor. Down the stairs. Pops into the kitchen and switches on the light. His laptop's where he left it, open and lopsided amid a landmass of paperwork. There's a cork board covering one wall: an indecipherable collage of maps, phone data, financial printouts and crime-scene photographs. He locks eyes with the blue-eyed woman who sits at the centre of the artwork – dark haired, hoop earrings; a gaze that is at once motherly and intimidating.

'Bitch,' he whispers, snatching up a tissue from the table-top and stuffing it in his pocket. 'Fucking bitch.'

Cross has grown to hate Trish Pharaoh these past weeks. She's come to symbolize everything he despises about the police force in particular and the future of the planet in general. She shouldn't even be a copper. Too small. Too bloody emotional. Tits like those should belong on a tarty barmaid, dispensing pints and maternal wisdom over the varnish and spilled beer of an estate pub. She's got the Queen's Police Medal twice. She would have been Detective Chief Superintendent and in charge of all CID if she hadn't turned down the opportunity in favour of maintaining control of her unit. He doesn't understand why she doesn't just retire. She's got her thirty years. She's got her pension. Cross loathes the way everybody talks about her as if she's the perfect example of somebody who can do it all. She's raised her kids with tenderness and toughness. She nursed her husband through a decade of chronic disability. She's caught more bad people than anybody else he's worked alongside. It's no wonder they all call her St Trish. She makes a mockery of his own position; his lowly rank, his inability to hold down a relationship; the catastrophe of his family life. Christ how he's enjoying peeling back the layers. It will be so fucking sweet

to take her down. He still isn't sure whether she's actually guilty
of the things she's accused of but that's not really his problem.
He needs to give Earl enough rope to hang her with and he's
already managed that and more besides. Cross is pretty sure he'd
be able to convince a jury that she attacked her husband, caused
his brain injury and spent a decade covering it up. Since she scattered his ashes she's certainly been living the life of the merry
widow. He's seen the pictures she's sent to her lover in Iceland,
the poor bastard. Why the fuck would he want to see that? She's
past fifty. Well past a size fourteen. She's all flabby and loose and
hairy where she should be clean. It turns his stomach. He hates
himself for wanting to fuck her. Hates himself for wanting to fuck
them all.

   He makes himself a coffee. Black, two sugars. Takes a quick
glance out of the window and into the joyless symmetry of Needlers
Way. The estate looks like a computer simulation: brightly coloured
doors and timber fronts weathered down to the colour of sweaty
mushrooms. The developers had promised Scandinavian-style
living, a peaceful haven for the kind of white-collar commuters
who pad around their houses barefoot and drink red wine on white
sofas. The streets are named after the sweets that used to roll off
the production line at the nearby factory: a treasure trove of
humbugs, gobstoppers and multi-coloured lollipops. The brochures
were all Volvos and swing-parks; multi-cultural families carrying
French sticks in wicker baskets and waving hello over their trel-
lises. Cross had bought it on a sunny day, the wind whipping east
towards the water. Hadn't actually stepped inside – the negotiations
having been conducted, mid-pandemic, through laptop, phone and
email. If he'd seen it in the flesh he'd have realized that anybody
carrying a French stick on the Needlers Way estate was on their
way to a mugging or an orgy, proud of themselves for coming up
with such an effective disguise for their baseball bat or dildo. He'd
have tolerated it if not for the stench. Didn't find out about the
deep-reek fug of leather and piss until he opened the windows on
a hot day and nearly lost his biryani. No, the big-eyed estate agent
hadn't mentioned the smell from the tannery at the end of the
road. Been too busy flashing her stocking-tops and wafting her
Chloe. Sold him a lemon, more shit than sherbet. He'll get her back.
Always does, in the end.

Redmore has made herself a little more comfortable during his absence, wrapping her lower half in his quilt. She's cleaning her glasses with a loose flap of bedsheet when he returns.

'None for me?' she asks, pouting.

'You've just had one,' he says, getting into the double bed beside her and taking a sip. 'And I've no oat milk left.'

'You're weird,' she says, wrinkling her nose. 'Can you really smell it on me?'

'Be grateful I'm a gentleman or I'd mention the Snickers, the steak flavour McCoys . . .' He stops, making a show of sniffing the air. 'Tasha's home, I take it?'

Redmore laughs. She feels safe to laugh, now. Knows his moods; his mannerisms and triggers. Knows how to get the best out of him. He's worked hard on becoming the object of her infatuation and has reached the stage where he can safely with-draw, confident she'll always follow.

'Do you mind?' she asks.

'Call me next time,' he instructs. 'Let me listen.'

Gives him that cheeky smile; the one she gives him when he's pushing her face against the wall at the back of her poxy little terraced house in Gipsyville and sorting her out the way she likes. The smile that tells him he's right about this, and about everything else. He quite fancies Emma Redmore's wife. He fancies every-body, if he's honest, though the whole thing's a spectrum, if he's honest. Reckons he could get it up for just about anybody – that he could rise to the challenge of servicing just animal, vegetable or mineral if it expressed a desire or provided an opportunity. He's a red-blooded chap, after all. Red-blooded and clever, charming and sly. Deserves to be at the top of the mountain looking down. They'll want him then, that's for certain. The higher he climbs, the fewer people say no. And those who say no don't really mean it. Reckons he deserves a bloody medal for the effort he puts into curbing his appetites. He still can't quite believe that it's his few indiscretions that people have focused on – those improprieties when people have taken advantage of him at vulner-able moments. There were months at a time when he didn't do anything wrong at all – didn't try it on with anybody, didn't cheat, didn't press himself just that little bit too closely into their personal space. Didn't send a single bloody dick-pic. But did he get any credit for that? Any slap on the back from the higher-ups? No, they had to focus on the aberrations, the losses of control. Had to make a big song and dance about a couple of misunderstandings. He's made his apologies. He's compensated those who got upset over his behaviour; women whom he refuses to think of as 'victims'. *Undesired advances, inappropriate advances – behaviour not becoming a senior officer.* He hadn't understood it then, doesn't understand it now. How can he know if his advances are unwelcome until he's made them? And anyway, he's good-looking. He's clever. He's got a nice car. What sort of stuck-up bitch wouldn't welcome the chance to roll around with or bag themselves a cheap thrill in the back of a genuine vintage Alfa Romeo? Imagine the bragging rights! Be easier to say yes than to say no, wouldn't it? Why make such a fucking show of protest? He certainly doesn't feel that the punishment fits the crime. He'd been Head of CID in Leicestershire. Bumped down to detective inspector and sent to head up a poxy little intelligence unit in Humberside had seemed like overkill. Lost his wife, too. She'll take him back in the end, of course. He hasn't paid her mortgage for seven months now and he knows her well enough to be comfortably sure that she'll damn well start making nice again once the bailiffs are knocking on the door. His old bosses too. He just needs a good result. He just needs to make himself attractive again – to make an arrest that matters. Needs to reel in a fish so big that they'll think he's snared Jaws. Then he can tell them all to fuck off, take his pension and retire on a high. He's already got some consultancy work lined up. He's made friends with a publisher who's shown an interest in his memoirs. He's got a couple of bank accounts overseas and if he just does things right, he'll be rich and comfortable and living somewhere hot by the time his fortieth birthday rolls around. He fancies Thailand. He's heard a man with his particular proclivities can live very well in Thailand, provided they have money and friends in low places. He just has to keep things steady. Has to make the case watertight. Has to gift-wrap his own leaving present.

'We caught it all, then,' says Cross. 'We got it on tape.'

Redmore nods. 'She was upstairs. Didn't look out of the window until he was already on the ground.'

'And her reaction?'

'Horrified,' says Redmore, shrugging. 'Saved his life.'

'He'll live?'

'They're working on him now. Touch and go.'

'Fuck.'

'Thought you'd say that.'

Cross doesn't like complications – least of all those of his own making. He could have sent his specialist surveillance unit home for the night once Pharaoh and Thor retired upstairs. Instead he'd decided to get his money's worth. Told them to stick around. Something might turn up, he'd said. We might get some leverage.

Instead, his team had recorded an attempted murder. Not only that, they'd recorded Trish Pharaoh screaming like a banshee and doing her damnedest to save her lover's life. There are going to be questions asked – some of them quite aggressively.

'Show me,' commands Cross, his manner suddenly thuggish. 'Let's see what we're looking at.'

Redmore changes the angle of her phone screen. Presses play.

Cross doesn't speak as he watches. Redmore plays it again. Cross takes the phone from her hand.

'Easy mistake to make,' he says, at last.

'He's a dead ringer,' confirms Redmore.

Cross pauses the video. 'Is it a mask?' he asks, pulling a face. 'Looks like a gingerbread man.'

Redmore shakes her head. 'Can't say. Mike had his eye to the camera so he only saw what we're looking after. Jo saw him with fresh eyes, as it were. Said it looked like he was something from a horror movie.'

'She can bloody well change that when it comes to getting her notes down,' mutters Cross. He looks again at the screen. The surveillance camera doesn't capture the attacker's arrival. The video begins only as Thor emerges, bare-chested, from Pharaoh's building, aiming the key fob at the little convertible. It shows Thor running his finger over a dent on the bonnet, pressing his palm to the spiderweb pattern in the windscreen. Then he stiffens as if a noose has dropped around his neck and yanked him upwards. A figure in black steps from out of the frame of the recording. They hold a yellow taser in their left hand – the strings invisible to the camera but the effect on Thor's massive frame unmistakable.

The prongs stick into the back of his neck and he collapses like a tower block. The attacker doesn't pause. He raises his other hand. He's holding something like a curved axe: a glint of metal, the handle dark. He brings it down hard. Brings it down again. Again. It takes an effort to pull the blade free the final time. Then he crouches down, squatting over the injuries. Stuffs gloved hands into the wounds. His movements are staccato; crab-like, as if he's progressing in a stop-motion animation. He changes his position. Lowers himself so that he is nose to nose with the dying man. Spends a moment just breathing, close as lovers. Then he stands. Looks up at Pharaoh's window. Slips into the shadows like an actor moving from the spotlight. And then he's gone.

'And they just sat there. Didn't move?'

'Happened very fast, Ash.'

'Inconsiderate,' says Cross, still staring at the screen. 'Should have given us a fighting chance to catch him, don't you think?'

'I'm not sure they knew what to do for the best.'

Cross grunts. He can understand the indecision of the two detective constables. They've had Detective Superintendent Pharaoh under surveillance for nine days. They don't feel comfortable with it. They admire Pharaoh. Revere her, just like every other bugger in Humberside Police. But that's the nature of investigating your own – sometimes you have to slap the cuffs on your heroes. Cross doesn't make the rules, just enforces them.

'Earl is at the scene,' says Redmore, repeating the information she'd relayed when she'd woken him to reveal that an unwieldy amount of shit had just been hurled into a propeller. 'They've already received footage from some of the neighbours. House to house has produced some witness reports.'

'Showing our surveillance units, I presume.'

'No doubt.'

'And Pharaoh's made herself scarce?'

'Went into her flat after her mate turned up. Ben – the handsome one. She went in to wash the blood off. Slipped out the back not long after Earl arrived to take charge.'

Cross permits himself a smile. 'Played into his hands there, didn't she? Thought she was meant to be a shrewd operator. Doesn't look good, does it?'

'She went out the back. Unit Two picked her up getting into

an Uber on the corner of Newland Avenue. If you look out of your
window you can almost see the spot.'

Cross plays with the flap of his tie. Fiddles with the laptop.
Opens up the document that had started the ball rolling and which
still seems woefully vague.

'. . . so let's assume that the cause of his mental and physical
disability is a ruptured berry aneurysm in the brain. It was there
already, aggravated by smoking, drinking and high blood pressure,
just waiting to explode. An aneurysm may rupture through raised
blood pressure during an altercation without any physical trauma
being evident. It could also happen as a result of a blow or a fall.
The effects on brain function would depend on where the aneurysm
burst and how long it took to get him into surgery – as is the case
with any major bleed on the brain. If he had fallen/been pushed
and hit his head on something, the surgeons would probably not
be too bothered about whether the impact caused the burst or he
collapsed and hit his head after the burst, as long as he survived.
All they would have been concerned about was repairing the
damage. I would expect any visible injury to be recorded in
the notes, however. A cracked skull would be picked up on X-ray
but a crack wouldn't be needed for the aneurysm to burst. So a
third party could have covered up a row involving a blow to the
head (perhaps hidden by thick hair?) or a fall which, with elevated
blood pressure, could have caused the aneurysm to burst. Then
again, if someone had it in for a specific individual and went back
to the original surgeons' notes they could make trouble for her
– especially if there was also some circumstantial evidence
concerning rows, adultery etc. – but a successful prosecution would
be unlikely without witness corroboration or quality forensic
evidence. That said, it could be a useful lever to extricate a
colleague past their use-by date . . .'

It was written longhand by a freelance consultant – an old pal
of George Earl's – and provided little that could be used in court
or even shared with an enquiry team. Even so, Earl had deemed
it sufficient evidence to begin a covert enquiry. On its own it
would count for nothing, but coupled with the video recording,
Earl had been satisfied there was a case to answer. Cross, despite
his reservations, had been chosen as the ideal candidate to locate
the bullets which Earl could load into his gun. Personally and

professionally, Cross prefers Pharaoh to Earl. But Earl is the one
more likely to get him back to where he belongs and to that end
he's willing to do whatever it takes.

'Bit of a pickle, isn't it,' he says, thoughtfully. He wonders
whether Earl is creaming his pants or having a panic attack. He
supposes he'll find out soon enough. It's entirely possible that
the DCSU will tell him to rewrite their recent history – to make
sure they were never there and that any suggestion a highly
respected officer like DSU Trish Pharaoh was ever under surveillance could be dismissed as a scurrilous lie. Cross will play along,
of course – provided there's something in it for him. It could all
work out quite nicely for Ash Cross. And yet, it's not what he
wants. It's not the big fish. It's not the parade. It's not the glorious
fuck-you to those who did him wrong. He sucks his teeth. Sips
his coffee.

There's a buzz from Redmore's phone. She answers without
apology and he feels a bristle of indignation. He was a DCSU a
year ago. Feels the loss of rank, of respect, like the removal of
his blow-dried balls. Were he not already preoccupied with his
thoughts, he'd be tempted to show Emma Redmore the error of
her ways – to pin her down and show her that he's not some
fucking gelding; that he's still a man, still *the* man – still running
the fucking show. And what had she said about Ben being
handsome?

He blinks away the mist that fills his vision. She's saying his
name.

'Mina, from the hospital. Surgeon's removed an item from the
victim's back. It's been bagged and tagged. Picture's coming
through.' She pulls a face. Shows him the mess of gore on the
screen: a twist of bloodied root. 'Fuck's that?'

'A tuber,' he says, peering. He shrugs in the face of her
surprise. 'The wife liked garden centres, that's all. I reckon
that's a dahlia.'

Redmore consults a file on her phone. 'Doc said the same,
apparently. Plucked two fingernails from his back too. Bit of a
cougar, that one.'

Cross suck his tongue. Feels himself stiffen. Thinks of Trish
Pharaoh and her eyes upon him, staring down from this kitchen
wall. Thinks of what he did to himself before he fell asleep and

wonders whether he'll get the chance to tell her. He doesn't doubt it will turn her on.

'Attacker put this in the wound?' he asks, readjusting himself. 'Tucked it inside him like heroin up an arsehole?'

Redmore nods. Whistles as the full implications begin to dawn. 'They'll be cross-referencing . . .'

Cross takes her phone. Logs in. Navigates his way to the database and runs a search. 'Malcom Tozer,' he reads. 'Hit and run, Lodge Lane, Flixborough. January 2nd, this year. Massive cranial trauma, internal injuries . . . found by a dog walker, as if that's unusual . . . here we go – samples of vegetation removed from the cavity: notably one dahlia bulb.'

'Sounds like an unexpected item in the bagging area,' mutters Redmore. She takes her glasses off. Puts them back on.

They lie in silence for a moment. 'Go on then,' mutters Cross, after a moment.

She takes the phone back. 'Investigating officer, Detective Inspector Aector McAvoy,' she reads. She looks at her boss. 'Her knight in shining armour, isn't that what Earl called him? Location still unknown.'

'Don't make it sound so mysterious, he's just on his holidays. We'd know where he was if we were looking.'

'We all thought she was shagging McAvoy when Thor turned up, didn't we? Proper double-take moment before we found out it was her fancy piece from Iceland, popping over for a booty call.'

Cross pulls a face. 'Don't say booty call, it's very dated.'

'What I'm saying is, if Pharaoh's connected to this Malcolm Tozer somehow . . .'

Cross retrieves the phone. Scrolls through the files. 'Not much of a criminal record,' he reads, assessing the jumble of spent offences. 'Bit of dealing, some traffic incidents . . . oh.'

'Ash?'

'Arrested in June 1990 for assaulting a police officer.'

'1990? I wasn't born.'

'But Trish Pharaoh was,' says Cross. 'Police Constable Patricia Pharaoh, on the receiving end of quite the nasty beating at the hands of one Malcolm Tozer, aged twenty-four – resident of Haldane Street, Gainsborough.'

'McAvoy must have found that out when he was investigating the hit and run,' says Redmore.

Cross looks at the dates. Earl had approached him in the third week of January. *All very hush-hush*, Earl had said. *Need a chap with a bit of experience; a safe pair of hands; somebody who knows how the game is played. There's been an accusation, you see. A complaint against a very senior officer. We need to be seen to have taken it seriously. Need to have a little look into things in case it ever comes back to bite us. Serious allegation, of course, but possibly mischief. Wouldn't give it headspace if it weren't for the video . . .*

That was how Earl had first brought the matter to his attention. An opportunity, he'd said. Certain parties within the upper echelons of Humberside Police had come into possession of a video recording. It was made in June 2008. It showed a man by the name of Anders Wilkie staggering out of the big iron gates of a fancy house on the outskirts of Grimsby, bleeding from a head wound. And it showed a short, dark-haired woman running after him, then grabbing him by the arm. Showed her swinging punches, arms windmilling. Showed Wilkie turn and smash his fist into her face with the nonchalance of a man who has done it many times before. Showed two girls in nightclothes running to the side of their stricken mother, helping her up and dragging her away. A moment later, the woman ran back into the frame, tearing after Wilkie – something long and tubular clutched in her hand; disappearing out of shot as if tumbling from a stage. The clip had been sent from an anonymous email account. The accompanying message merely said that the sender believed the police needed to look into the actions of one Patricia Pharaoh. It had been kicked upstairs, and upstairs again, until George Earl took an interest. He'd ordered Cross to start digging.

Cross quickly learned that Anders Wilkie suffered his catastrophic aneurysm the day after the date on the clip. He eventually died twelve and a half years later, still wedded to Trish Pharaoh, having endured semi-paralysis, memory loss; unable to articulate save a few guttural grunts; his handsome features dragged down on one side to expose the ugly red smile beneath his eyeball. One eye was so permanently disfigured that it shone like polished obsidian. Pharaoh nursed him. Tended to him. Fed him and bathed him and changed his clothes and his bedsheets and the bags that collected his shit and piss. Cared for him tenderly, according to the endless procession of people who have told him about St Fucking Trish.

Cross has read and re-read every word in the file that George Earl slipped his way. It showed Pharaoh's financial records. Showed the full extent of Anders Wilkie's criminal connections and the volume of debts that were written off when he experienced the catastrophic event in his brain. Earl made it clear that the official debts were the tip of the iceberg. Wilkie also owed some very bad people. They were catching up with him around the time of the aneurysm. Earl and Cross had found it inconceivable that those creditors simply went away because of Wilkie's health problems. So what deal had Pharaoh made to clear the slate? There was no suggestion that Pharaoh was corrupt, Earl made that clear. But the video was compelling evidence that Anders Wilkie suffered a head injury around the time of his aneurysm. Pharaoh was there. The video appeared to show him walking away from a violent confrontation. Seemed to show Trish Pharaoh preparing to strike what would turn out to be a fatal blow, even if it took the poor bastard a dozen years to die.

'What do you think?' asks Redmore. Her cheeks are flushed. There's an energy coming off her; the excitement of a hound that has spotted a fox.

Cross cocks his head. Sees her nearness. Her warmth. Her availability. Fancies that she deserves a treat. She's worked hard. She's loyal. She does what he tells her without complaint. She's gone above and beyond in pursuit of a goal that serves him far more than it does her. He couldn't have done what he's doing without her. He understands why Pharaoh keeps McAvoy so close; the reassuring nearness of a blindly willing acolyte. He almost admires Pharaoh. Sees some of himself in her.

'The daughter,' he says, sliding his hand up her top. She slaps him away but he can tell she doesn't mean it.

'Ash, no, look . . . you said . . .'

He grabs her hair. Takes a great fistful of it. Spits on her cheek and smears it over her jawbone and pushes his thumb into her mouth. He remembers what she liked, or at least, what she told him she was into when she was still trying to get in his pants. He pushes her head down. She doesn't protest for long. None of them do.

'The daughter,' he says again, as his eyes turn glassy and he thinks of what it will be like to thrust his greatness down her throat. 'Call the daughter.'

'Now?' asks Redmore, gasping for breath.

He pushes her head back down. 'Don't be fucking stupid.'

ELEVEN

HMP Warcop, Carrshield, Hexhamshire
2.16 a.m.

R euben Hollow has always slept soundly. Wherever circumstances have insisted he lay his pretty little head, he has never struggled to sink through the black tar of his mind and into the pleasing buoyancy of quiet oblivion. His sleep is untroubled. He doesn't dream. He sleeps like a corpse, his world soft; his body sinking into the lumpy mattress and fetid air as if he were cocooned in Egyptian cotton. When he wakes it is entirely without preamble: eyes snapping open into a full and vivid consciousness – blue eyes bright and senses sharp. He always knows where he is. Always knows the hour.

This is his favourite time. He will treat himself to an hour of something close to peace. He feels free, now. Unobserved and sanguine. He can read, should he wish. Can draw. Can write a letter to one of his adoring fans. Can touch himself the way he wants to, should sufficient stimulus be present. Or he can just enjoy the quiet. The absence of silence is the privation that Hollow most despises. He is a man who prefers stillness; prefers hush. Prison offers few such moments. His days are an unceasing bombardment of harsh, raucous sounds: ugly soundscapes of squawking linoleum, slamming doors; keys in locks and expletive-laden yells, all echoing off the high stone walls to wrap around him like a whirlwind of grit and broken glass. He doesn't let it show that it bothers him. Hollow is a popular man, inside. He's respected. Most of the prisoners don't know the word 'forbearance' but they do at least think of Hollow as somebody who doesn't complain. He keeps his head down and does his time. He's a model prisoner, if such a thing exists. He eats his meals without complaint. He exercises. He works diligently on the few occasions that HMP Warcop permits any kind of vocational opportunity. He helps the less literate inmates understand their correspondence. He's been known to have a quiet word in the ear of anybody who takes the bullying of weaker men too far. He keeps himself fit. Keeps himself ready. Violence is never far away and he finds it pays to be lean and strong; his knuckles hard and numb from the hour upon hour he spends pummelling the cell wall. From time to time, he finds reason to kill somebody, quietly enjoying the nods and winks and knowing glances that are cast his way by the other lifers. He's good at killing. He doesn't necessarily enjoy it but he doesn't want the muscles to atrophy while he's inside. He looks forward to the day when circumstances and providence grant him freedom. And then he can resume his work.

Hollow lies on his bunk, hands behind his head: a rum-drunk sailor in a Tahitian hammock. His mind ticks over. The familiar sense of unease spreads out from his core. He hasn't felt entirely comfortable in recent days. He's been snappy. He's looked markedly less rehabilitated; less diffident in his dealings with staff. He's been forgetting to wear the mask: been meeting gazes with hard, angry eyes instead of the downcast subservience of a killer embracing redemption. His sense of equilibrium is off. He had vertigo a couple of years back, his eardrum bursting as the result of a hefty boot to the head during a landing brawl. He hadn't been able to stand without his whole world lurching, his vision becoming a horizon glimpsed through a porthole on rough seas. His thoughts feel the same. Something is coming. He's at the centre of a storm and he isn't sure whether he's in control or at its mercy. He cannot help but think upon the podcast. *Clementine.* He has listened to it over and over. Everybody on the wing has listened to it. He can't help but feel a little proud at the way they have framed his narrative: a working-class kid done good. He knows himself to be prone to vanity so he takes great care not to be seen to be revelling in his resurgent notoriety. But in his quiet moments he will admit to feeling almost giddy with self-regard. Finally, people are beginning to understand.

Hollow thinks of Clementine. Of Fenella. Wonders how they

smell. Wonders whether they are lying in bed thinking of him right now. Whether they're together: a sweaty assemblage of arms and legs and scent and skin. Whether he can fantasize a way to insert Trish Pharaoh into the picture. Trish, and perhaps Aector's pretty little dark-haired wife. He rubs his fingers in his armpits and smells himself. Makes-believe for a pleasant thirty seconds.

Stops himself. Smiles in the darkness, enjoying the torture of restraint. Replays the podcast in his head and wonders when the letter from the legal team will reach him. He has no doubt there will be offers, soon. Book deals. Newspaper interviews. He'll become such a fucking nuisance to the Wing Governor that he'll have no choice but to ship him out to somewhere pretty. Not a bad result, all things considered. Another big fuck-you.

Hollow has done well for himself, considering. He's not from exceptional stock. He grew up in rural Yorkshire; his childhood was spent on the family farm. The doctors have made him examine his youth from every angle and he cannot see it as anything other than a wholesome, pastoral flicker-pad of pleasant recollections. He sees himself sketching, sees Grandad telling him about the different trees and how to identify them from the edges of their leaves; sees himself helping with the birthing of the lambs; peeling apples in the warm, low-ceilinged kitchen; resting his head against her bosom and feeling her tears drip on to his head as she stared through the square windows at the smouldering pyre: two hundred and sixty-eight cows burning in a foul-smelling mound; the men from the ministry waiting with their diggers and their clipboards and their little information packs that promised to make sense of the slaughter. Dad, too. Dad, dangling from a rope in the barn, piss running down his leg, one green wellington slipping off to reveal the hand-knitted sock with the bare big toe . . .

He wonders whether he'll ever write about himself. He's a good writer, as far as he can tell. The teachers at the fancy public school praised his lyrical style of writing and he was constantly told that he was a kind and charming young man. He did fine academically. Did well at sports. He was good-looking. It was money that caused the problems. His classmates had it and he was a scholarship kid. The gifts that came from home were hand-baked or foraged. He didn't receive an allowance. When his friends from the boarding house arranged weekends away he was unable to go along. Teasing turned to taunting. Taunting turned to bullying. Bullying became a part of his life. Reuben didn't know he was a violent person until he stuck a paintbrush through the neck of a blond, piggy-eyed rich kid who wouldn't stop asking him whether his mother smelled of pastry; whether she had the red hands of a washer-woman; whether she took her bath once a week in front of the fire. He went to a Young Offenders' Institute for that moment of rage. When he came out, he was dangerous. He's been dangerous ever since. But the podcast has made it clear that Reuben Hollow is not in thrall to his demons. He can control them. He kills, but he does it with purpose. He makes people happy. He removes bad people. In another time, he'd be the sort of person that balladeers would sing about. He knows that they all see that, underneath it all. He's never doubted that Trish Pharaoh admires him. Even the big silly Scotsman who sucker-punched him and slapped the cuffs on – he knows that he doesn't really think Hollow has done anything wrong. He's just a man living in the wrong time. And he'll make amends, he's sure. He has to. Four life sentences is too much to ask of anyone.

There's a change in the quality of the air outside his cell door. He closes his eyes. Rolls on to his side. He presumes it's Mrs Peach. She's a sweet lady who really thinks he doesn't know that she reports his every movement back to Trish. He plays along, for the look of things. Sometimes he'll feed her a little titbit about this or that; somebody dealing spice on the wing or in possession of a razor blade or mobile phone. It helps to keep in with the bosses. He needs them to see that he's no trouble. Category A seems unfair. He'd like a move to somewhere a little gentler; somewhere with a better library and an art room worthy of the name. He'd like to be able to carve again. His hands miss the feel of wood; of the grooves in the handle of hammer, chisel, adze. He'd like to feel able to invite Delphine to visit. Delphine, or one of the ladies who write to him. There are plenty to choose from. Those who know his proclivities are brazen in their approaches. Mr Corcoran, his pastoral officer, has taken on the responsibility of personally overseeing his mountain of correspondence. They have a decent enough relationship and Corcoran has no compunction about telling him the assorted treats that he has to open on his behalf. Hollow understands Corcoran better than he understands himself. He has no doubt that the married, woolly-round-the-edges prison officer is beginning to enjoy his work. They send pictures. They send fantasies. They send their soiled underwear and swabs of their sweat. They offer a trade. They ask for help with their abusive partners or maintenance-shy exes. Hollow doesn't get to read the letters but Corcoran always tells him if there's something juicy. And Hollow knows just how juicy they can be.

A cigarette paper slips under the door, finding the little groove chiselled out of the floor. Silently, Hollow rolls off his bunk. Moves across the cell and gathers up the note.

He takes a moment to digest the handful of scribbled words. Breathes in and swallows, feeling the tingle of adrenaline that always precedes a kill.

He balls up the paper. Pops it into his mouth. Chews, and gulps it down.

He moves to the far wall of the cell. Gazes up through the bars. Strawberry moon, tonight. Pinkish, like a hungover eye. He likes the idea that it's looking down on all of them; a hooded leer taking in Trish and McAvoy, himself and Delphine, Mr Corcoran and Mrs Peach. It looks and sees and doesn't give a fuck who does what or why. It's a comforting thought.

For a moment he imagines her pain. Imagines Trish, bleeding and broken and begging his name. Wonders whether, in the moment, she will wish that somebody like him could ride in and save the day. Wonders whether she'll regret his incarceration before the end.

He supposes he'll be able to ask McAvoy. The big stupid bastard will be here by morning.

He returns to his bunk.

Rolls on his side.

Sleeps soundly: at peace.

TWELVE

'Do you think you can make it ring just by looking at it?' McAvoy hasn't heard Roisin's approach. He has to stifle a yell as she emerges from the darkness, ghostly in her white shawl; eyes bright as a full moon.

'Scared me,' says McAvoy, quietly, opening his arms so she can take her place inside his embrace. 'I almost unleashed the fury.'

'Almost squealed like a girl,' laughs Roisin.

'I was on the verge of whipping out a roundhouse kick.'

'I'd have kicked your arse,' says Roisin, lifting the tail of his shirt and pressing her cold hands to the small of his back. 'I know where you're vulnerable.'

McAvoy puts his phone away. Gives himself over to his wife. Leans back against the trunk of the big broad tree, Roisin slowly absorbing his warmth.

'Is she OK?'

'Won't talk to me,' says McAvoy, sounding a little like a teenage girl whose best mate won't return their calls. 'She's got Ben and Andy. She did what I said she'd do. Slipped away out the back.'

'You know her better than anybody,' shrugs Roisin. 'You've done all you can do from this far away. She's probably already got a plan.'

'But I said I'd go back.'

He feels her shake her head. 'She's gone to a lot of time and effort to make sure you're not around, Aector. Let her have her way.'

He doesn't reply at first. He tries to digest her meaning. He's always thought of Roisin as his superior when it comes to under-standing the toxicities and duplicities of the human mind. He may be the police officer but she has a better insight into the ways of the *gaujas* – the non-Gypsy folk who seem capable of such cruelty and compassion, such treachery and inelegance. Her words find their echo in his own recurring thought. Trish had more than a hand in sending the McAvoys away, after all. It was her who suggested that Roisin would benefit from a break – somewhere remote, somewhere out of contact – somewhere she could see the stars without the lights of the city obscuring the view. She needed to feel the wet grass on the soles of her feet. Needed to breathe in the good clean air that rises from the earth after a storm. She'd arranged his holiday dates, put in the paperwork. He'd seen it as the act of a caring friend. But she hadn't chosen the place, had she? That was Roisin, after all. She'd been the one to bring the campsite to his attention; to tell him that Kush's little off-grid

paradise was free on the days that he'd secured. He thinks back.
Screws up his eyes as he realizes the ease with which he has been
moved around the chessboard and wonders, temper rising, whether
she sees him as a pawn to sacrifice, or a knight to be held in
reserve.

'Sophia,' says McAvoy, jaw tight. 'Was it Sophia who told you
about this place?'

Roisin changes her position. Looks up at him, wrinkling her
nose. She pulls a face: a toddler who's been caught waist deep in
the biscuit tin. 'She was just pottering about online while the baby
had a wee sleep,' she says. 'Found this place and said we might
like it.'

McAvoy chews his cheek. 'So Trish wanted us here,' he says,
thinking aloud. 'Why here? Does she know Kush?'

'I haven't spent any time thinking of it, my love. I'm just pleased
to have you to myself.'

He holds her tight. Ponders for a spell. Breathes in the cinnamon
and tobacco of her hair. 'What does Sophia think of Thor?' he
asks, quietly.

Roisin gives a little laugh, a blast of air against his chest.
'Reckons he looks like you.'

'He doesn't really . . .'

'Feck off, you could be twins, Aector. Shame he's out of action.
You and he could have made one of my fantasies come true.'

McAvoy gives a little growl of disapproval; the noise he can't
help making when he's distinctly unimpressed. 'She knew he was
coming over?' he asks, ignoring the tease. 'All the way from
Skagastrrond?'

'Yeah, Sophia's been pretty much counting the days,' says
Roisin. 'Wants her mum to have a bit of happiness.'

'Olivia too?'

Roisin squeezes her husband a little tighter. 'Let's hope it's a
phase, eh? She'll barely speak to Sophia. Hasn't even met the baby.
There's a nastiness in that one, I swear. Every inch her father's
daughter. Making a saint of his memory now he's not around to
mess it up.'

McAvoy looks down at his feet, unsure whether to offer more.
Pharaoh hasn't confided in him regarding Olivia's recent beatifica-
tion of her dead father. He only knows about it because Sophia

has told Roisin, and Roisin tells her husband everything. He would like to raise it with Trish, but he hasn't found the right moment. He's tried to make some sense of it in his own mind. Olivia was only five or six when her dad suffered the aneurysm. For a decade he was a living ghost; angry and helpless, desperate for death – hunkered down in his hi-tech little cave in the garage and showing no inclination to maintain any kind of relationship with his children. The older kids, at least, remembered who he was before. They had memories both good and bad: recollections of the big, charming, gregarious businessman who sometimes drank too much and who beat their mum until she couldn't stand. Olivia was the only one of Anders' children who spent time with him in his later years, sitting at his bedside, reading him stories, transcribing his grunts and mumbles into something approximating conversation. It was Olivia he chose as his mouthpiece – begging, through her, that he be allowed to swallow however many pills it would take to end his suffering. It was Olivia who was there when he died.

'She'll come right,' he says, wishing he had more.

'Not everybody comes right. You should know that.'

'Nobody is all of anything,' he says. 'There's always something inside a person worth blowing a little lift into.'

'No,' says Roisin, shaking her head. 'No, some people have evil in their bones. There's nothing to save.'

'That's what Reuben thinks,' says McAvoy, staring up at the dancing branches. The moon is full and pink, like a drunken eye. He's reminded of the wood where Hollow made his home: the little tangle of trees on the outskirts of Skirlaugh. Remembers feeling the life draining out of himself as Hollow closed his hands around his throat and squeezed. McAvoy survived their bruising encounter. Got the cuffs on a dangerous man and gave the evidence that saw him banged up for the rest of his days. Most of the time he believes he did the right thing. People couldn't just go around dispensing justice as they saw fit. There had to be rules. Procedures. And yet, he cannot help but see his own hypocrisy. He's a part of the justice system. He enforces laws that he often doesn't philosophically agree with. He sometimes thinks he's doing more harm than good. He'd like to rehabilitate rather than punish, but has a duty to the dead and to the bereaved as well as to the perpetrator. Sometimes his head spins with the inconsistencies and contradictions. He'd like to talk to Reuben about them. He'd also like to never have to think about him again.

Roisin coughs suddenly: a hard, hacking bark that makes her gasp in pain and surprise; her features twisting at the sudden sharp pain in her chest. 'That bloke . . .' she wheezes. 'Dark coat . . . the funeral . . . feck, I can't get my breath.'

McAvoy looks on, helpless, his heart opening like a rose as she tries to smile at him through damp eyes; knitted brows. 'Ro, please . . .'

She waves him off as he cups her face with his hand and looks into her eyes, telling her she doesn't have to tell him, that she should rest, that he'll carry her back to the *vardo* and stroke her hair until she sleeps . . .

'Aye, she's been worrying,' continues Roisin, breathlessly, when she's finished telling him not to be such an eejit. 'Sophia, I mean. About her mum. I suppose you have too, eh? It's all right, I won't lose my shit about it. She's your mate.'

'She's yours too,' he begins.

'Feck off,' laughs Roisin.

McAvoy concedes the point. Looks up. The trees are a great black mesh against the night sky; surfaces already glinting with a hard frost. If he squints he can just about make out the light of the dying fire. He was going to leave them here: going to rush to Pharaoh's aid. Thirty years of coppering behind her and yet he can't help but imagine that she might need him. He feels sick at himself. Hates his own arrogance, his own damnable pride.

'Hasn't been herself since New Year,' continues Roisin. She's produced a roll-up from somewhere and is endeavouring to light it, shielding the flame with her hand. 'I suppose we should feel bad about that.'

McAvoy scratches at his beard. Thinks back. They'd gone away for New Year, hadn't they? He and Roisin and the kids – two nights in a posh hotel; champagne and sparklers and a verse or two of 'Auld Lang Syne' at midnight. Trish had been alone for the first time in her life.

Roisin shrugs. 'She's a grown up, Aector. Sophia had her bloke coming to stay so she couldn't go there, could she? The middle girls stayed with their university mates. And Olivia and her nan decided to have a quiet one with a couple of bottles of prosecco and a big tin of Quality Street. She said she was fine, didn't she? I suppose she might have been a bit lonely. New place, no kids for the first time in forever.'

McAvoy feels himself filling with shame and regret. Feels his reserves of guilt overflow with a fresh deluge of inadequacy. 'She couldn't exactly come with us,' he says, quietly.

'No, she bloody couldn't.'

Had she been funny with him when he came back? He can't recall anything specific, and certainly no behavioural changes that would worry Sophia. But for all her faults, he knows Pharaoh to be an expert at hiding what's going on beneath the surface. He just hadn't thought she would hide it from him.

'I haven't actually had much chance to catch up with her the past few weeks,' he muses. 'I was straight on the hit-and-run case as soon as we were back . . .'

He stops. Takes a breath. 'Malcolm Tozer,' he says, putting his head back and scratching an itch against the bark of the tree.

'Aye,' says Roisin, nipping the smouldering ember off the top of her roll-up and flicking it away with a diamante-studded false nail. 'You think they know yet?'

'It won't take long.'

McAvoy wasn't on the hit-and-run case very long. It had only come to Major Crimes because the victim had briefly been a suspect in a significant case a few years before. Pharaoh had hand-picked him for the role – his first as a bona fide detective inspector. *Total arsehole*, she'd told him, handing him the file and telling him not to lose too much sleep over it. *The world's a wanker short tonight but we'd best make sure whoever did it can't make a habit out of it. Give it a couple of days and if you get nowhere just hand it over to Traffic.*

He'd done the legwork himself. Put together a good thick wedge of intelligence on the victim, found with his skull mashed in down a country lane not far from Flixborough. Fifty-eight years old at the time of his death, living in a flat above a Chinese restaurant in Gainsborough. Separated from his second wife; six kids, all told, drinking away his disability allowance and occasionally supplementing his earnings by selling knock-off vape refills and dodgy trainers. A neighbour had given him a lift to Flixborough on the day of his death. He was on a promise, according to his pal. Meeting up with some tasty bit of stuff.

McAvoy hadn't found anything to verify the suggestion but
there was no doubt that something had drawn Tozer out into the
darkness of the quiet country road. Whoever he was expecting,
Death came instead. Somebody had driven into him as he made
his way towards whatever rendezvous he had been so looking
forward to. The forensic report showed tyre tracks across his
upper body and face. McAvoy had questioned whether Tozer
might have already been lying on the road when the vehicle in
question drove over him. Perhaps he'd been the victim of an
earlier attack. The pathologist couldn't rule anything out. The
cranial injuries were massive. If he had been struck a blow before
the car accident, the injuries were disguised by the brutal explosion of skull and skin and brains that occurred when the tyre went
over his head. *Like stepping on a grape*, the pathologist had said,
when pressed to explain himself in layman's terms.

The doctor had mentioned the presence of the dahlia bulb almost
as an afterthought: just threw it into the conversation as a peculi-
arity; an anecdote to be saved for some far-off after-dinner speech.
Mulched in among the brain matter, he'd said, marvelling at life's
little idiosyncrasies. *Dahlia coccinea*. Could have come from
anywhere. Unlikely to have been deposited there by the wheel of
the vehicle but, as McAvoy was well aware, stranger things have
happened.

McAvoy spoke to neighbours. Family. Spoke to his drinking
buddies and the customers who snaffled up his cheap refills.
Nobody particularly liked Tozer but nobody seemed to care enough
about him to kill him. His mobile-phone records showed nothing
out of the ordinary, backed up the suggestion that he was heading
into the countryside for some clandestine sexscapade. McAvoy
could find nothing in the case file to suggest that any of his former
criminal associates still cared enough about him to want to exact
some terrible revenge. He wouldn't even have found Pharaoh's
connection to the victim if he hadn't called up the victim history
on the database. He'd been going from the paper file up to then
– the one handed to him by Pharaoh when she nudged the case
his way. There was a discrepancy between the hard copy and the
digital one. The electronic criminal record showed that he had
assaulted a junior police constable in 1990. The one Pharaoh gave
him ended a page earlier – her name excluded.

'Just testing,' she'd said, when he asked her about it. 'Keeping you on your toes. Nasty bastard, like I said. Gave me a couple of good boots to the ribs when I was still green as grass. Sergeant would have taken it all the way but I reckoned a caution would be enough. He had young kids, from what I can recall. Thought I'd give him a chance to be an upstanding citizen. Christ I was naive. I shan't be shedding a tear.'

McAvoy had taken her at her word. Not long after, she'd taken the case out of his hands. *There's a department for this*, she'd said. *Let them earn their pay.*

He hadn't disputed it. He'd found the make of the tyre; canvassed for CCTV, conducted house to house and worked up an admirably detailed victim case history. The Serious Collisions Unit were delighted to have something to get their teeth into.

And then she'd booked him a holiday and had her daughter tell Roisin where to go, and when. She'd arranged for her Icelandic fancy-man to come over at the time of his absence. Even in the sanctuary of his head, he hears her snicker at his use of the phrase 'fancy-man'.

'I can hear you thinking,' says Roisin, rubbing his back.

'I thought it was the podcast,' he says, softly. 'She was jittery, wasn't she? And Sophia saw it?'

'Didn't want to hold the baby. Didn't want to come over. She still hasn't met the father and Sophia can't make head nor tail of why she's being so weird. She's not even drinking as much.'

'Sophia's heard the podcast?' asks McAvoy.

'Aector, everybody's heard the podcast. It's all bollocks but it's entertaining bollocks. I just wish they'd made a bigger deal of you. You're the mad bastard that caught him.'

'Not really,' protests McAvoy.

Roisin pinches him where he's tender. 'You did, Aector. But maybe be grateful that it's Trish who gets the focus, eh? Especially if whoever did this to Thor has got it in for her.'

McAvoy holds her closer. 'You should be a bloody detective,' he mutters.

'You're joking,' she laughs. 'Nettles, wasps, coppers and Tories – we don't need any of them, present company excepted.'

McAvoy screws up his face. He can smell fox-scat. Can smell the frost hardening the ground. Can smell Roisin. He thinks of

Reuben Hollow. Imagines him asleep in his cell. Could he really wield any influence from inside? Could one of his adoring acolytes really be willing to go after Trish Pharaoh's lover just because Hollow wanted them to?

'Why would somebody attack Thor, though?' he ponders, aloud. 'I know you're going to say that they thought he was me, but . . .'

'If they thought you were in danger you'd have been warned, wouldn't you?' asks Roisin, who seems genuinely unconcerned. 'And Hollow, for all that he did bad things, he's got a style, hasn't he? He went after bullies. Bad men. It was that mad bitch of a daughter that had the evil in her, despite what Hollow said. I dunno, I just think that he loves himself too much to sour his legend with something like this. Anyway, nobody's told you to be extra-cautious, have they? They'd tell you.'

'Theoretically,' he muses. 'But I'm out of contact, aren't I? Maybe I should call Earl back, but if he asks me where she is . . .'

'You don't think she knew, do you?' asks Roisin. 'I mean, she's always a chapter ahead of every bugger else. If she had an inkling . . .'

McAvoy's heart sinks. His worst suspicions have been trying to get his attention since he heard about the attack. He's succeeded in ignoring them. Roisin's words give them the space they need to invade his mind.

'Knew what?'

'Come on,' he says, with a sharp dig in the ribs. 'She hears some whisper you're in danger – she sends you away, out of contact, brings over a whaddyacallit, a doppelganger. You know how she can be, Aector. She always thinks she's on top of things. Perhaps she was using him as, I dunno – a decoy. Or bait. And it's gone wrong and that's why she's fucked off . . .'

McAvoy closes his eyes. She wouldn't, would she? Wouldn't manipulate him like that and play games with the life of a man she's supposed to care about. How desperate would she have to be? How irredeemably heartless.

'Can you hear something?' asks Roisin, looking up.

He forces himself to concentrate; straining his ears. She's right. He can hear a vehicle approaching. Beyond the vale, where the treeline meets the road, a vehicle has come to a dead stop. He hears the soft snap of a door closing.

Roisin doesn't say a word. Just looks up, nods, and extricates herself from his grasp. She vanishes into the darkness, moving soundlessly back towards the *vardo*, where their sleeping children wait.

McAvoy sniffs the air. Catches petrol. Churned earth. Tells himself that he's being paranoid. He's not at risk, not a target, nobody knows he's here. Whoever attacked Thor is a hundred and fifty miles away. And yet the hairs on his arms are rising as if with a static charge. He can feel that low whisper of fear, of approaching danger. He recognizes the subtle alteration in the quality of the air; the sudden silence of the birds, the stillness of the trees, as if the wood were holding its breath to see what was going to happen next.

Silently, eyes shining, he makes his way towards the road.

The forest closes around him like a grave.

THIRTEEN

Beeford Road, Skipsea
1.56 a.m.

'Bollocks,' mutters Pharaoh, pulling out her earphones and throwing the phone and cord back into her bag.

'Sorry, love?'

She glares at the driver, busy giving her the once-over in the rear-view mirror.

'Ten to two,' she says.

'Eh?'

'That's where your hands should be on the wheel. And your eyes should be at midnight.'

He looks away. She keeps glowering at the glass, daring him to ask her another stupid bloody question. She'd rather feel aggressive, rather feel persecuted and ill-used. The alternative is sadness. Fear. Grief. If she lets herself go she'll fall to sorrow and she hasn't time for any of that now. She needs to be at her best. She's sober, at least, though she's tempted to alter that deplorable state of affairs. She's not very good at sobriety. She's at her best one glass of wine from the end of the first bottle – her thoughts that little more slick and lubricated, her intuition and flights of imaginative fancy all the better for being unencumbered by the tedium of everyday concerns. She's at her best when the edges are a little softer – when the echoes of her past are muffled, the shapes drawn in pastel and their edges smudged. Here, in the full glare of unadulterated consciousness, she's struggling to get her thoughts to tie up.

She wonders if she's doing the right thing. It's such an unusual thought that she has to take a moment to fully chew upon it. She so rarely doubts herself. She may not believe herself to be much of a partner, much of a mum, but she knows to her core that she's a good copper and a good friend. She's loyal and clever and tenacious. She makes the big decisions because she's got the experience and the mental toughness to pick a path and steer herself and her team towards it. But here, on her way to a place where she can at least kid herself she feels safe, Trish Pharaoh wonders whether she's making matters worse. Perhaps she should be at the hospital, drinking black coffees, haranguing doctors, holding back tears and demanding minute by minute updates on the condition of the man she's slowly fallen for these past few years. Perhaps she should be giving her statement, repeating it over and over, answering questions posed by embarrassed, diffident junior officers, proud and embarrassed to be able to assist in a case so personal to the Boss. But Pharaoh can't stand hospitals. And she can't pretend to be somebody other than herself. She can't sit at Thor's bedside and weep. The thought sickens her. She's not his wife. She's not even his girlfriend. He flew hundreds of miles to scratch an itch and she's grateful to him. Moved by the gesture: a little proud to still provoke such an outpouring of emotion, such an exhibition of desire. She can't hold herself accountable for what happened, can she? It's not her bloody fault that some drugged-up car thief decided to make a play for a knackered old Mercedes and went to town on a visiting Viking when he got rumbled.

She picks at her nails, chewing on the thought, rehearsing the line for when she finally talks to Earl. She knows that the most important part of selling a cover story is to convince yourself of its truth. And she could, conceivably, be correct about the incident on her own front doorstep. Thor could indeed just be the victim of a petty crime transformed into a major incident by a surfeit of zeal. But car thieves don't attack giant men with tasers. They don't bring axes down into their backs. And they don't tuck little hand-carved marionettes into the puncture wounds.

Pharaoh leans back. Glares through her own reflection and into the interminable flatness of Holderness; black and featureless, cold as the grave. There's a mess of condensation on the inside of the glass and Pharaoh presses her finger to the coolness of the glass.

'Reuben,' she mutters, and turns the dot into a star. She squeaks her finger downwards. 'Podcast,' she says and bunches up one side of her face as she concentrates. She draws her own head and shoulders, woefully misshapen. 'Me,' she spits, and jabs the likeness in the face. 'Some bloody acolyte, some adoring fan, somebody out to get revenge for me locking up their poster-boy. Somebody coming for Aector, gets the wrong man. Coincidence. Just pure dumb fucking luck . . .'

She shakes her head. Thinks of Malcolm Tozer. There had to be a connection, didn't there? Some link between Tozer's death and the brutality visited upon Thor just after midnight. Whichever way she looks at it, one man is dead and another is critical and the only thing they have in common is that they've both bedded Trish Pharaoh, albeit with an interlude of thirty years. She lets herself think again of the figure in the cone of yellow light. It was a mask, she knows that. Did she transform the individual characteristics into something familiar? Was it just a random rubber mask and it was fright and imagination that turned it into Anders Wilkie? She finds herself grinding her teeth as she thinks about him. Even dead, he's at the centre of every problem she has to face. He's the only person who would want to kill Tozer and Thor and his motives wouldn't be anything complex. He was simply a jealous bastard. He didn't mind fooling around with other women but in the moments when he thought somebody else had touched what was his, he responded with fury and violence. He would have killed Tozer years ago, had Pharaoh not been a copper. He'd have gone for Tom Spink, too – forever convinced that there was something between Pharaoh and her mentor. He found ways to make his feelings known about Aector, even with the paralysis; his face twisting with revulsion and hatred whenever Pharaoh mentioned her protégé within earshot. And now Thor. But Anders is dead. She scattered his ashes himself: doling him out in litter gritty parcels to his four daughters and telling them that they could give him to the wind or line the litter tray for all she cared. Only Olivia had treated them as something worth revering.

She feels hot tears prickle at her eyes. Bites her tongue until they stop. Tastes blood. Thinks back to the bad man she'd dallied with around the time she became a cop. He'd loved the idea of fucking a WPC and she'd let him enjoy the novelty until something better came along. He hadn't reacted well. Spink knows what he did to her, and what she did in return. Reuben Hollow, too. She spilled most of her secrets to the charming bastard when she was trying to get him to confess to what he did in between carving gorgeous gothic sculptures. She hadn't held back. He knew exactly who to put on the list if she ever wanted to take revenge against those who wronged her. So is somebody setting her up? Is she being framed, or primed for murder herself? She hates this. She wants a fucking drink.

'Fucking hell, Hector . . .'

She should have told McAvoy about her connection to Tozer as soon as she gave him the case. Instead she'd made a cack-handed attempt to obscure their connection, even while she knew that an officer as thorough as McAvoy would leave no stone unturned in his quest for answers. She should have given it to somebody incompetent, but to do that would be out-and-out corruption and she couldn't bring herself to do that. So she gave it to her best detective and left it to providence. If he found out about their connection, she could deal with the fall-out. And if he missed it, well – she couldn't be held accountable if even her best officer fell some way short of her own investigative brilliance, could she?

She wipes her hand through the jumble of lines and dots. 'Bollocks,' she mutters. Crosses to the other window and tries again on the clean surface of the far window.

'Delphine,' she mutters. Closes her eyes. 'How the fuck could you . . .?'

'This one, is it love?'

Pharaoh glances up. They've arrived on the little cul-de-sac where she knows she'll always be guaranteed a warm welcome – even in the middle of the night. Tom Spink was her mentor and boss for the first twenty years of her career. She's long since surpassed the rank at which he retired but she still thinks of him as the senior officer. He's her mentor and one of her closest allies and friends. He's godfather to her eldest daughter and she calls him at least once a week to see if old age is taking the lash to him. He hasn't had much luck these past few years. The retirement cottage that he and his wife purchased is slowly slipping into the sea, half garden long since washed away. He's not entitled to any compensation – the powers-that-be declaring the erosion of the Yorkshire coastline an unavoidable act of God. But the Almighty moves in mysterious ways, compensating Tom for the loss of his home by ensuring that he got beaten half to death by corrupt police officers while assisting Humberside Police with a cold case. An out-of-court compensation payment was inveigled from a publicity-averse Home Secretary. Tom ploughed the money into their crumbling home: the equivalent of tossing the cash into the sea. He has a stubbornness about him that Pharaoh has always adored. Pharaoh doesn't visit as often as she should but somehow whenever she arrives it feels like visiting Mum and Dad.

'Card payment, is it?' asks the cabbie, leaning back. 'Fuck, it's like the end of the world up here, innit? Did you hear about the young lad that drove down the road he'd always used? Weren't there any more. Drove off the cliff like a cannonball. I'd best be wary on the three-point turn, eh?'

Pharaoh flicks a glance out the back window. 'You see that black car?' she asks, conversationally. 'The one that's trying to find a way of looking like it hasn't been following us from Hull, yeah? Doing laps back where the sign says not to come any further?'

He nods. 'Spotted that, did you?'

'There's an extra twenty in it for you if you lead them back the way they came. Go via the seaside, if you like.'

He smiles: yellow teeth, yellow eyes, sallow, jaundiced skin. She can tell why he works nights – the bloke has the look of a malnourished vampire.

'Won't they see you getting out?'

'End of the road there,' she says, nodding into the darkness. 'Spot for a three-point turn. When you're backing into the little hedge bit I'll tuck and roll.'

He looks at her as if she's mad. Sees she's serious. 'Aye, all right.'

Pharaoh wonders whether he'll ask her who she's trying to avoid. Feels oddly gratified when the question isn't forthcoming.

Thirty seconds later, Pharaoh is slipping out the back door and performing an inelegant tumble across the soft grass at the end of the lane. She hurts her shoulder, jars her knee. Lies still and looks up. She watches the cab indicate right and turn on to the straight road out of the estate. Sees it continue on, vanishing amid a line of trees then reappearing at the junction of the main road. She's gratified to see the dark car following after a moment later. She hopes she'll have the opportunity to tell whichever unit has been tailing her that their surveillance skills are a bag of shite.

She walks. Shudders. Feels the wet grass pull at her legs. She's always liked it up here. She and Tom have done walk to the little church half a dozen times over the years. She's never been inside. There's nothing in there she wants to see.

There's no front gate at Tom's property. No wall to mark the perimeter. She steps from the footpath onto the paving slabs that demark the parking area and moves silently over the gravel towards the front door. She'd like to imagine that he's already up – that he's been reading, or writing, and that he's wrapped in his old dressing gown, glasses halfway down his nose, silly little fez on his grey hair to stop the pipe smoke staining his still-luscious locks. But the house looks empty. Looks dead.

Pharaoh knocks on the uPVC front door, the sound loud against the absolute stillness of the night. Knocks again, louder now, and for a moment she thinks of raised fists on a coffin lid. She opens the letter box. Puts her mouth to the gap and opens her mouth to say his name.

She breathes in a scent she knows too well. Inhales a mouthful of sweet, cloying foulness; mulched rose petals and bad meat.

She tries the door handle. It opens without complaint. She opens the door without a sound. Steps in to the warm, foul-smelling fug of the hallway.

Down the hall, boots silent on the carpet. She can hear her heart hammering in her chest. Tears prick her eyes; hot acid rising up her gullet.

'Please, Tom,' she whispers, to herself. 'Come on, you're trying to scare me, aren't you . . . playing silly beggars . . .'

She reaches out, fingers finding the edge of the doorway. Sidles right into the living room. Raises her hands to her face as the stench hits her in a hot gust of putrid reek.

He's been dead for days. Dead and rotting and puddling down into rancid green meat and liquid entrails. The remains of his flesh and blood cling to the sodden remains of his clothing like raw meat in a canvas bag. He's staring at her with eyes that used to twinkle when he laughed. Eyes that are sunken in a putrefying face: the irises dyed black as coal.

The flies rise in a swarm. It's as if the world is dissolving into pixels, as if the picture in front of her were fragmenting into ash.

Her head becomes a buzz of wings; flies landing upon her face, her hair, in her mouth, her eyes, her nose.

Through the swirl she sees a figure move towards her. Sees a tall, broad-shouldered man dressed all in black.

She looks at his face through the maelstrom of swarming flies. Looks at the gaping holes around the eyes and mouth; the brown blood and rotten-parchment skin. Sees the ragged mouth open, the red tongue and white teeth a slash of livid colour against the marbled whiteness of his face.

Something stirs. A memory; a whisper of familiarity.

She looks into the face of her dead husband; a face cut from his corpse and worn like an ill-fitting glove.

She opens her mouth. Takes a lungful of dancing flies. Gags and coughs and raises her hands.

And then the electric prongs take her in the face and everything is pain and fire and lightning.

Then there is just the dark.

PART TWO

FOURTEEN

Victoria Avenue, Hull
3.33 a.m.

Detective Chief Superintendent George Earl presses his palms together, the tips of both index fingers softly brushing his lower lip. He looks as though he is standing in front of a particularly arresting work of Renaissance art, absorbing the individual striations in the brushwork; lost in liminal blush and angel-breath *sfumato*. He looks earnest. Intense. Looks as though he is thinking of matters that it is his burden, his duty, to address.

'. . . hard to say if there is any permanent mobility damage. The fragments of vertebra are completely irreparable.'

Earl realizes that the young officer with the short blonde hair has come to a halt and is expecting him to say something. He wishes he'd been paying attention instead of thinking of the best way to look enthralled.

'He'll live, sir,' says DC Sasha Trent, with an encouraging nod. She looks a little flushed: pink around the cheeks, a little sweaty at the temples. Earl wonders whether she's up to this. Makes a mental note to check her personnel file. Forgets immediately.

'Once more, please,' he says, diffidently. He taps his cranium with a long, slender finger. 'I need it to go in. Forgive me if this is tiresome, Sasha. Sasha. Sasha.'

'Three distinct wounds, delivered while he was prone. The burns around the puncture marks all but confirm the use of a taser, sir.'

'And the weapon, Sasha?'

She looks confused for a moment. Her eyes flicker to the little pencil sketch laid out on the table in front of Earl. He picks it up with a little smile, trying to indicate that he, as a very senior officer, has his own eccentric way of doing things and that she would do better to ask God why the rain falls than to question him about his process. He needs her to repeat herself and she will simply have to make space for his eccentricities.

'An adze, sir,' says Trent. 'The surgeon remembered seeing a similar injury during his time in Uganda, sir. Can't say for certain but he said he would dig out some old case notes for comparison. Pardon the pun, of course.'

'He did this, did he?' asks Earl, considering the little pencil sketch. 'It's rather good.'

'Googled it on the way over,' says Trent, with the look of somebody who isn't sure whether they are showing initiative or being bloody presumptuous. 'It's a cutting tool – halfway between an axe and a trowel, I suppose. Curved blade. It's used a lot in woodworking, sir. Been used since ancient times . . .' She stops, seemingly unsure whether to carry on.

'Something else, Sasha?'

'One of the murders attributed to Reuben Hollow, sir . . . from the documentary, sir. The podcast. An adze was used.'

Earl rubs his finger down the length of his nose. 'Reuben Hollow is in prison, Sasha.'

'He seems quite popular,' says Earl, apologetically. 'Somebody could be getting revenge, sir. Setting Detective Superintendent Pharaoh up – or going after somebody she cares about . . .'

'Or it could be a car theft gone wrong, Sasha,' says Earl, wagging his finger. 'Exciting as it would be to have a copycat out there intent upon some blood feud, I have my doubts.'

'If you look on the message boards, there are lots of people claiming he shouldn't be in prison – that he should be given a medal for getting rid of bullies . . . that he was the victim of a honey trap . . .'

'I don't think DSU Pharaoh could be accused of wafting her nectar, Sasha. Perhaps of acting like a queen bee.'

Sasha stops talking. Looks momentarily taken aback. Earl replays his words and fights the rising panic. God, could she misinterpret that? Could she make a fuss about his use of the 'wafting her nectar' phrase. God, he'll be looking at a complaint over this. Looking at a bloody tribunal. A chap can't say a bloody word without it upsetting somebody these days.

'Just a thought, sir,' says Sasha, respectfully, and the moment passes.

Earl sits back. He feels rather comfortable here, on the sofa in Trish Pharaoh's rather shabby living room. Two white-suited science officers are at her work in her bedroom, taking pictures of her rumpled sheets, her stained mattress, conducting tests for spilled fluids on every conceivable surface. They've already found blood. Urine. Semen. He imagines how it would feel to have an investigations team working their way through his own innermost sanctum. He imagines he would take the Roman emperor approach – draw a hot bath and open a vein, bleeding out in an attempt to retain some honour and avoid being a witness to his own humiliation. He doesn't think Pharaoh will do the same. She'll brazen it out. She doesn't seem to care very much what people think of her. Earl can't understand it. He doesn't give a fig for the opinions of his underlings but he has always sought the approval of his betters and has done everything in his power to reach a tier of authority that permits a quiet sense of invulnerability. But Pharaoh? She seems entirely genuine in her ambivalence towards the top brass. She doesn't seek their approval. She does things the way she thinks they should be done. Her first duty seems to be towards the victims of crime and everything else is of entirely secondary concern. He almost envies her naivety. And yet she was first choice! Humberside Police picked her for the role of Detective Chief Superintendent. The regional Murder Squad wanted her as top dog. She was head-hunted by the Met and the National Crime Agency. And she chose to stay where she was! Picked her little unit and declined a whopping great pay rise and a vastly improved pension. He can't stand the thought that he was second choice. Every time she calls him 'sir' he can hear the sneer in her voice. And that fucking award! The British Association for Women in Policing is an organization that he has publicly applauded. In his private moments he yearns for its awards evening to be selected as a target by some well-stocked suicide bomber. And Pharaoh – the only serving officer to ever win the Leadership Awards and Bravery Awards twice. Why not just make her a fucking baroness and have done with it? And now the documentary, making out she's halfway between Jane Tennison and Jason Bourne. Earl doesn't believe in hatred. He works hard at his yoga and his breathing exercises and he doesn't let himself eat red meat. He doesn't let toxins into his body. And yet the feelings that bubble

up and eat away at the lining of his gut, at the opening of his
oesophagus; the acid that spills into his lungs and wakes him with
hard bouts of coughing at 3 a.m. – they're all the result of Trish
Pharaoh and her ilk.

But things are changing, thinks Earl, trying to catch his smile.
Somebody out there feels just as strongly about Trish Pharaoh as
he does. Has given him a smoking gun. All he has to do is let
things play out. Watching her lover get hacked to bits in the street
might just be one small part of the suffering Trish Pharaoh is
destined to endure at the hands of whoever it is that wants to rob
her of her happiness; her legacy; her piece of mind. And Earl
doesn't think he can justify the resources needed to stop them.

Earl tells himself that he didn't allow his personal feelings to
bleed into his operational decisions when instructing DI Ashley
Cross to begin a covert operation into the circumstances of her
husband's long, lingering death. He doesn't know where the
video came from but it had fallen into his lap like a bag of gold.
Whatever happens now, she's finished, isn't she? He has to hope
so. She wasn't under arrest but she fled the scene of a crime.
That can't look good. And Cross is making good progress digging
into her past. Even if she manages to wriggle her way out of
any criminal charges they've got proof that she was married to
a serious criminal and that she overlooked continued violence
towards her children and herself. She knew about her husband's
dodgy dealings. She may have fled the family home half a dozen
times after his bouts of violence but she always went back –
always brought the kids back into a dangerous environment. St
Fucking Trish! He's never understood women who stay with
abusers. Why not just leave? He's politic enough to keep such
thoughts to himself but there have been occasions at the golf
club or after one too many brandies with his old university chums
when he's confided that women must, on some deep, atavistic
level, prefer to be dominated than free. He doesn't need to raise
his hands to his own wife and children. They do as they are told.
If they don't, he withholds the little envelopes. And without the
little envelopes, the bills don't get paid. They don't eat. They
behave much better when they're hungry.

'I'm not sure there's much more going to happen before the 8
a.m. briefing, sir,' says Trent, respectfully.

Earl nods, taking her opinions on board, listening effectively, the way they showed him on the leadership course. For something to do with his hands, he picks up one of the photograph albums from the box in front of him. He has no compunction about going through Pharaoh's possessions. He's a detective, looking for clues. He tries not to wrinkle his nose as he leafs through the plastic pages, looking at picture after picture of Pharaoh and her girls; building dens in the woods, celebrating victory at a ten-pin bowling centre; dressing up for the wedding of some unnamed family member. Some of the pictures have dates and places but most are stuffed in haphazardly. Anders Wilkie seems to be the man charged with taking the pictures. He appears nowhere. Earl feels a wave of pure loathing for Pharaoh as he looks at her lying on a sun-lounger by the side of a pool in Kefalonia. She's chubby, busty, all squishy and Jelly-Baby-like, but she looks extraordinarily beguiling in her little two-piece, floppy hat and big sunglasses. One of the children is painting her toenails, slathered in sun-cream and her hair braided into tight corn-rows beneath a bandana made of a T-shirt. An older girl is in the back of the shot, reading a book. There's a boy beside her; pale and dark-haired; white shins and forearms poking out of black T-shirt, black shorts. There are stark white whorls on his skin: fossils and ammonites pressed into the rock of his skin. He's staring at nothing. Earl looks at the date. July 2010. He slides the picture from the protective sleeve. Notices Trent shuffling her feet and realizes why she's looking flushed. She feels awkward, here, in the hallowed ground of the saintly Trish Fucking Pharaoh. Doesn't like that he's looking so closely at a pic of her hero in a bathing suit.

'Best get back to the hospital,' says Earl, apologetically. He would like to give her a squeeze on the forearm to show that they are all in this together. Knows from the career curtailment of several of his peers that physical contact is entirely unacceptable. Unacceptable, unless you're Trish Fucking Pharaoh and you can dish out motherly hugs and Chinese burns as and when the mood takes you. 'One never knows.'

Trent doesn't protest. He imagines she's tired and would like to go and get a few hours of shut-eye before the morning briefing. And now she can't, because he said so. It's a good feeling.

Alone again, Earl takes his phone from his pocket. It's the

private one – the unregistered spare. He snaps a picture of Pharaoh in her swimsuit. Zooms in on the thickness of her thighs; the little overspill of belly fat at the lip of her trunks. Fancies he can make out a stray dark hair curling up near her belly-button and finds himself feeling all fizzy and light-headed. He takes a couple more as he leafs through the album: a candid snap taken by a cheeky daughter as she's rising from the toilet, pyjama bottoms around her ankles; another where she's leaning on the table of a country pub, leaning forward with her arms crushing her breasts together. She's smiling, knowing precisely what she's doing. He can't wait to get a look at Thor's mobile-phone records. He wonders just how many pictures of herself she's sent him over their interminable courtship. She won't be the first fucking choice then, will she. Won't be able to lord it over him when everybody knows that he's seen her touching herself, flaunting herself, flashing her flesh for her Icelandic bit of rough. He's no doubt that her neutered Rottweiler will come to her aid and that anybody caught making fun of her will find themselves in serious pain, but Earl doesn't think it will be a problem. He has plans for McAvoy. And so does the person who sent him the video.

The tinging of his phone interrupts his thoughts. It's the work phone – the number not recognized by the software but known to Earl. He sighs, irritated that his train of thoughts has been derailed. He's getting rather tired of having to speak to Ashley Cross. He thinks there's an ugliness about the man's character; something unashamedly sly and venal. But he can't help but recognize him as somebody who knows how to play the game. Cross may have footage showing the attack on Thor Ingolfsson, but he's had the good sense to call Earl on his private phone and enquire whether he would like to be told officially, or whether it mightn't serve his DCSU's purpose to have suffered some technical difficulties. Earl had told him to delay. At present, there are larger matters at play. Cross had the good sense not to question him.

'Ashley,' he says, endeavouring to make it sound as though he had been busy with something important. 'I thought we said . . .'

'The daughter,' says Cross, without preamble. 'She's in contact with him.'

Earl pauses, trying to move the pieces around in his head without sounding stupid. 'The daughter?'

'The youngest,' explains Cross. 'Olivia. She's on-line. She's talking to him now.'

'Talking to whom?' asks Earl, impatiently.

There is a pause as Cross mentally recalibrates – reminding himself that Earl went to a school for the gifted. Says it slowly, to be sure.

'The attacker, sir. She's talking to him now . . .'

FIFTEEN

Milton Road, Grimsby
3.01 a.m.

Olivia Wilkie. Seventeen. Five feet nothing and big blue eyes. Stocky legs, like a well-fed pit pony. Boobs. Round shoulders. Olive skin, beneath the make-up. Eyeliner and glasses; piercings and an undercut; fingerless gloves and a pentagram necklace. A Halloween Jelly Baby. Village weirdo. Sad case. The one with the dead dad. Odd-bod. Wilhelmina No-Mates. She's the creepy one – the emo girl with the eerie eyes. She's a loner. Kooky. Bookish and catty. She's so fucking enigmatic that it's all the basic bitches can do not to cut her open and look for answers in her entrails.

Olivia isn't entirely sure whether anybody says any of these things about her, but she's spent the last year working damn hard on her Princess of Darkness aesthetic and she'd be devastated if nobody noticed. She had to throw away an awful lot of pink and pop when she made the transition. Had to strip the posters of Korean boy bands from her wall and embrace the absolute starkness instead. She's all big hoodies and baseball boots now. She's big round glasses and thick volumes of metaphysical poetry. She may still watch romantic dramas on her laptop but she does so with a post-ironic sneer, content in the knowledge that she's entirely a-romantic and that love is a social construction – a patriarchal concept designed to control a gullible, grateful populace. She has her final A-level Drama exam in June and is working on a performance piece based around a school shooting. She intends to blast her more popular classmates with a confetti cannon, provided she can find one, or that she doesn't forget, or that she doesn't wake up tomorrow and decide that the idea is derivative, passé and *soooo* yesterday.

Olivia's sitting on the windowsill, knees tucked up to her chest, staring out over the quiet little road and watching the frost gather on the grey-black hardness of the pavement beneath the street-light. She feels comfortable here, arms around her knees, head haloed in the folds of her dressing gown, the light of her mobile reflecting in the greasy lenses of her glasses. Hopes that somebody will be out walking the dog and look up and see her, squatting behind the curtain like a troll. She'd like to give them a little wave; a Joker smile. Would like to seriously unnerve the neighbours. Would like to be reading a book on serial killers with a pet rat on her shoulder. She has the feeling that she's going to have to start killing the neighbourhood cats to get people to take her seriously as a threat, which is a shame, given that she loves cats and frequently spends her own limited resources on buying them little treats and giving them all better, more suitable names.

Olivia looks at her phone. Snarls at the time. Fishes some crisp fragments from a back molar and swallows them. Thinks about her mum. About St Trish. Thinks about Reuben Hollow and the podcast and the handsome young man at the funeral. Thinks about Snapchat and college and the thing she did that she wishes she could undo. Blinks back tears. Swallows again; her throat tight. Thinks about calling Sophia. About listening to her voicemails. About making a hot chocolate and reading a book, or maybe even going the fuck back to sleep. Can't bring herself to move.

She went to bed around 8 p.m. Slept for a bit. Woke up and read for a while. Dropped off again and sat bolt upright an hour later, one hand stuck in a tube of Pringles. She bashed out a little character arc for a story she's writing. Filled a Pinterest board with pictures of shoes. Drew a pixie on the back of a shrew and then scribbled it out. Slithered back off to a sleep peopled with thick, ropy tree-roots. Woke up again twenty minutes ago and started searching for an illegal streaming site that sometimes shows American horror shows. She's got some missed calls from her sister. One from Mum. She thinks Nana might have knocked on the door a wee while ago but it might have just been part of the dream. She doesn't interact with her nan as much as she used to. Nan doesn't really know what to make of the shaved head and the endless piercings and the great thick silver hoops in her earlobes. She tells her she looks nice no matter what aesthetic she's rocking. So does Mum. They're all so fucking supportive of her choices it makes her want to scream. She can't understand how they don't see how mercilessly they're disenfranchising her. She's an artist; a creative; a subversive and a rebel. They're denying her the chance to kick out against their illiberal, outdated forms of coercion and control. And that's impossible if they keep telling her she's pretty and doing well and can be anything she wants to be. She doesn't mind the tea and the biscuits and having her clothes washed, ironed and put away in her drawers, but she'd give her right arm for one of them to look at her with outrage.

Thoughts rise. Her gut pops like hot mud: bubbles of guilt and shame explode into her throat. There had been a moment there when she'd thought it was all a nightmare, some fevered imagining – a movie in which she did something that she could never take back. For a moment she experienced the wave of cooling peace, the flood of relief, the sense that she'd been given the chance to pick a different path. Then the truth hit her like a fist.

Olivia looks at the little icon in the corner of her phone screen. Him again. So many messages unanswered – the number climbing every few moments as he makes another plea for her to acknowledge him, to respond, to answer his plaintive cries. She can't bring herself to open the app. A few weeks ago she wouldn't have been able to conceive of leaving his messages unanswered – her stomach flip-flopping with excitement every time her phone vibrated and she opened another poetry-laced missive. It had felt as if they were two sides of the same person – the head and tail of a heavy old gold coin. Everything he said made so much sense. She had never felt so seen. So special. Never felt so damn interesting. Sometimes the messages numbered in their hundreds. She'd lose hours, whole mornings, afternoons, evenings, nights, lose huge chunks of her reality engaged in passionate, fascinating discourse with the only person in the universe who really knew what it felt like to be her. He questioned her with such gentleness that she gave up all of her secrets without a moment's thought. Everything she felt, everything she wanted, everything she feared – it all tumbled out in great spumes of tears and laughter, of acid and snot. She hadn't realized just how lonely she was until he stepped into her life. It wasn't romantic love; wasn't desire – that would be just too fucking weird. But their bones vibrated at the same tension; their thoughts found an echo in one another's words. She'd missed him even during the long years when she'd barely remembered that he existed. Together they've rewritten the narrative. With his help, she's seen through the lies. With his careful tutelage she's seen her mother for what she is. And she's taken a course of action from which there is no return.

So why not answer his messages, Olivia, she asks herself, all sneer and pout. *If you know you've done the right thing, why leave the poor sod hanging?*

She tucks herself deeper into her hoodie. Looks again at the icon in the corner of the screen. He's still trying to get her attention. Sophia too. A call from a number she doesn't recognize. Christ, it's the middle of the night and everybody's trying to get her attention. She just wants to be left alone. Wants to go back to how things were, when Dad was just the poorly man in the garage and her sisters were still at home and Mum wasn't sending pictures of her tits to some big bastard in Iceland who looks the spit of Uncle Hector. She tries to find the heat and loathing within herself. Tries to feel the rage that had churned in her belly like hot rocks just a few weeks ago. It had made sense when he spoke to her. She had learned to see her father differently. Learned to hate herself for having so little to do with him while he lived; for the guileless way she had accepted her mum's version of events. He'd blown upon the embers of her doubts and ignited a fire within her. Over the course of a few weeks she began to remember things differently. Images long since buried began to rise to the surface. She had questions that nobody wanted to answer. She put the pieces together with the help of her new friend and realized that Trish Pharaoh had sold her a lie. Olivia hadn't even fought it. Hadn't stuck up her mum, or her sisters, or her nan. She fell in love with her dad's ghost, even as the podcast producers were turning her mum into a fucking hero. Olivia rewrote her entire sense of him, of family life; of who she truly is. She began to see Anders Wilkie as Trish Pharaoh's victim. Slowly, under his careful tutelage, she began to question the events that led up to his aneurysm. She researched the potential causes of the catastrophic brain injury. She started looking through her mum's old love letters, old bank statements; correspondence with doctors; with social services. She didn't know what the tape was when she found it. It looked like something out of a museum: a chunky square of plastic and shimmering tape. She'd had to send it off to her new friend. He knew about these things. And then he sent her the footage. She watched herself, just five years old, trying to yank her mum upright; to staunch the blood from her nose and wipe the tears from her eyes. She'd watched Sophia putting herself between her mother and father with the air of somebody who'd lost count of the amount of times she'd seen violence. She'd seen him – pale limbs and dark clothes and the blackness in his eyes. And she'd felt a shiver of uncertainty. She'd asked herself whether or not she mightn't have been misled. Perhaps her friend had a different agenda. Perhaps she'd betrayed her mother, her sisters, her nan. Perhaps Anders Wilkie was a horrible, horrible man and that whoever had bludgeoned him across the head and left him to a lingering death might just have had a good reason.

She looks again at the screen. She can sense his anger. His rage. The last time she spoke to him was a few days ago, reaching out to him for some words of comfort. The Icelandic bloke's coming over, she'd typed, alongside a string of 'yuk' emojis. She's all loved up. She's like a terrier in heat.

Something had changed, then. Something in his manner. The way he spoke about her – the fire and fury and sheer raw loathing had frightened her. She'd signed off quickly. Quietly. For a moment she'd seen an ugliness about his soul – the suggestion that he was capable of hate as he was of love.

She looks again at the screen. Screws up her eyes. She wants to call her mum. She hates herself for it but she wants to make her laugh, and share memories, and just be silly and naughty and daft together. She wants to tell her that she's in danger – that somebody from their past has video footage of what she did to Anders on the night when she couldn't take any more. She wants to tell her that there is somebody out there who has never forgiven her betrayal – somebody who approached her after Dad's funeral and told her she mattered; she was the one who might just understand.

She looks up, startled. There's a car pulling up outside. She's been lost in her own head. Lost in ugly thinking and regret.

She shakes her head. Wipes her eyes. Tells herself that she's the local weirdo; the Goth girl, the Enigmatic Emo. She opens the file. Sees page after page of threats; of rage; froth and flame and bile. She's just like her bitch mum. She's a betrayer. She's a cunt. A whore. A liar. A spoiled fucking slut. And she'll pay. She'll pay like the rest of them.

She opens the new video file.

Watches the footage.

Watches again.

Feels herself come apart; blood thudding in her head, numb with the whump-whump-whump of her own slowing heart.

He's wearing her father's face.

And he's taking a blade to her mum.

SIXTEEN

Amberline Haven, Gamblesby, Eden Valley
3.47 a.m.

McAvoy moves like smoke through the darkness of the wood. He plants his feet carefully, forcing himself to keep his eyes on the coal-black air in front of him rather than to glance up at the fat church candle of moon. He can't lose the little night vision he has and even a flash of light would be enough to tear jagged lines through the blurred, slowly developing photograph of his line of sight.

He reaches out. Touches the bark of the crooked oak. Feels something sharp clutch at the hems of his trousers. Feels something squelch beneath his feet. He steps over a snarl of roots, the slope beginning to even out now. He gets a sense of where he is. Remembers the journey from the little country lane, Lilah on his back and bags clutched in both hands, knuckles white. It had been a quarter of a mile, mostly uphill: Kush's off-grid compound tucked into a fold of the patchwork landscape. The trees had served as a summit marker; thinning out and drifting to scrub around the parking area by the road.

A sharp, sudden stab of scent. The meat and ammonia reek. He looks to his left. Sees the furred outline of a fox, eyes reflecting back. McAvoy jerks his head. The fox pads on without a backwards glance.

The woods are thinning out here. He ducks under a branch; wet spindles tip dirty water down his collar. He wipes a hand over his face. Feels the ground change underfoot and has to stifle a yell as he slips on the damp gravel. He recovers his balance and moves forward, quicker now, more urgent. He feels the two sides of his nature doing battle within him. He tries to be rational. Tells himself that something bad has happened back home but that Trish is dealing with it; that a robbery has gone wrong and a decent man has paid the blood price. But there is a primal, atavistic knowledge within him; a vibration in his very marrow – some instinct born in the cauldron of violence seen and heard and felt. He knows that Roisin has gifts that defy logical explanation. Knows that there is no scientific evidence for the existence of such abstract concepts of love and justice and forgiveness and that people live their lives taking the concepts for granted. Some people can look into a stranger's eyes and know that they mean them harm. And he knows that there are those who can detect the slightest change in the quality of the air in the moments that precede violence. He counts himself among them, for better and worse.

Slowly, the strip of road comes into view. He can make out the lumps of three vehicles. His own minivan is parked where they left it. Kush's little Suzuki Jimny is tucked in underneath the canopy of the silver birch. The third car is new. The doors are open; the lights on. On the passenger side, a figure is upright, standing between the door and the chassis. There's enough light to make out the presence of a second figure at the wheel. From this distance it's impossible to make out any details but there is the suggestion of solidity about him; an air of a big man crammed into a too-small space that McAvoy knows only too well.

He stops. Tries to gather his thoughts. There's no reason to believe that the arrival signals danger. They're far from home, whereabouts largely unknown, and there has been no real threat to his safety or that of his family. There's no reason to believe that whoever attacked Thor outside Pharaoh's flat is now intent on doing him harm. He doubts that the attacker could even make it from Pharaoh's place to this remote pocket of the Lake District in the time provided. But his heart is beating fast and there's a fizziness beneath his skin; sweat pooling between his shoulder blades and at his temples. He tastes the acid and pennies of rising fear.

He stops, perhaps sixty metres away from the parking area. The nearest house is a further quarter of a mile away, hidden away behind dry-stone walls and screened by the rising hummock of a sheep field. The only people who use this road are on their way to Kush's compound. And Kush hadn't said to expect guests.

There's movement by the car. The vehicle rocks slightly and a large, solidly built man pulls himself out of the passenger seat. McAvoy squints. The light inside the vehicle is soft and yellow but McAvoy can just about discern enough about his appearance to feel satisfied that it's nobody he knows. He's bald; head shaved smooth as an egg. There's a bulkiness to him, ripples at the neck and shoulders: hooded top under a dark coat.

McAvoy tucks himself in behind a stand of recently planted cherry trees. Strains his senses. Watches as the figure in the passenger seat closes the door and walks around the front of the vehicle to take their place beside the bigger figure. If they're talking, McAvoy can't make out the words.

He considers his options. He could walk down the slope, bold as you like: make a big show of greeting and ask them if they're lost; weary travellers eager for the help of a passing stranger. But if they're here for him? If they're armed? If they put a bullet in his head and carry on straight up towards the compound? He needs to know who they are and what they want before he can decide how to respond.

'. . . keep it steady, yeah. Leave it to me. Being here is enough.'

'No. No fucking way. The debt's mine.'

'It's not. He doesn't know you. It's me that owes.'

'He said you should bring me. He asked for me, John. I'm pulling the trigger.'

'There's no trigger to pull, boy. It's different when you have to get up close – when you see the light go out.'

'It just needs doing. That's the end of it. So I'm gonna blasted well do it, yeah?'

McAvoy raises his head. The two figures have detached themselves from the darkness of their vehicle and are making their way up the slope towards the treeline. The smaller of the two is holding their phone out ahead, using the thin white beam as a torch. It swings wildly, cutting lines in the darkness. McAvoy frowns into the strobing darkness, squinting as he tries to get a sense of who they are. He racks his brains for a more innocent explanation. Could they be poachers? Perhaps they're out lamping – light-blinding rabbits. Perhaps they're in the employ of some local landowner who wants Kush and his eco-friendly ideas as far away from the Eden Valley as possible. Kush has his secrets, he knows that. He has a shotgun, too. McAvoy wishes he'd thought to run up to the main lodge and ask to borrow it the second he heard the vehicle. Wonders what good it would have done him. He'd never pull the trigger.

The two figures come into focus. The big man is younger than he'd first thought. Flabbier too. It's not so much muscle as fat pressed into ill-fitting clothes. He's well over six feet. Pug nose. A scrappy beard. A tattoo curling around one pink cauliflower ear. The other figure is older. Forties, maybe. T-shirt tucked into straight-leg jeans. Glasses. Sensible hair cut, thinning on top.

McAvoy opens his phone. Starts recording. Slithers lower to the ground and raises the phone, angling it so that he's recording them as they make their way up the slope. He can hear their laboured breathing. Can make out the mutterings of conversation. Slows his breathing down and forces every ounce of concentration into picking up the details of their words.

'You think we'll keep the signal? If they want to watch – to see the whole show?'

'Just record it. Send it when we're back in the land of the living.'

'It's asking for trouble, though. What are they going to do with it?'

'None of our business, lad – now shush, it's over that rise, yeah? Breathe. Don't be sick if you can help it.'

In his hand, McAvoy's phone trills into life. The cold dark air is suddenly bright with sound, the screen garish against the absolute dark.

'Right there,' barks the smaller man, turning towards the spot where McAvoy shelters. 'Get the sneaky bastard . . .'

McAvoy hauls himself upright, stuffing the phone into his pocket. There isn't time to run back into the woods. He stumbles forward, foot slipping in fox shit.

'I'm Aector . . . I'm a police officer . . .'

One foot goes out from under him. He slithers down to one knee.

'Put him down.'

The big man doesn't wait for further instructions. Runs towards McAvoy as if trying to knock down a wall with his shoulder.

McAvoy is only halfway back to his feet when the big man crashes into him. McAvoy feels like he's back on the rugby pitch: experiences the sudden, bone-jarring collision as the big man ploughs into his middle and takes him around the waist. McAvoy's head snaps back, feet leaving the floor, all the breath rushing from his gut in a great whoosh of breath and spit. For a moment there is a sensation of something close to flight; the rush and high of elevation. He twists, the big man's shoulder in his belly, and then he is slammed to the ground so hard that his teeth mash together around his tongue. He feels something break. Sees stars. Feels lightning in his fingertips, blood in his throat.

The big man grabs McAvoy's beard; big fat hands gripping his chin. There's a sudden stinging hiss of agony and then he's being hauled upright: all nineteen stone of him being lugged to his feet as if he is made of paper and cloth.

A fist in his stomach. Again. Again. A great chopping blow smashes into his jaw. For a moment he can't hear. Can't tell if he's upright or lying down.

McAvoy throws a punch. Lurches forward, swinging at air. Something strikes him behind the knee. He feels a hand in his hair, yanking him backwards. Feels the sudden hammer blow as the big man slams his forehead into the back of McAvoy's neck. His legs go out from under him. For a moment he's sitting on his backside at the entrance to the wood, wet and bleeding; head ringing; his vision all static and snow.

Roisin, he thinks, clinging to the certainty of her name. Roisin . . .

He tries to stand. Somebody hits him in the face. Hits him again. In the corner of his vision he makes out the smaller figure moving towards him. Sees the little object in his hand. It's police issue. It dispenses 50,000 volts.

'Out the way, boy . . .'

McAvoy raises a hand, desperately, just as the smaller man presses the trigger. The barbed strings shoot forward like a striking snake. It is pure luck that McAvoy catches them, whipping his head back and snatching the trailing wires from the air: fizzing barbs snapping uselessly in the air around his massive fist. Desperately, he yanks at the strings. The smaller man is too stunned to drop the device. He tumbles forward and McAvoy, rising from the ground, hits him beneath the chin with the flat of his hand. His head snaps backwards like the lid of a pedal bin.

'No! No . . . Da!'

McAvoy turns. The big man is right behind him. He's staring at the fallen figure, eyes streaming, face pale. He turns his face to McAvoy; a look of utter, abject loathing. Swings a fist. McAvoy catches him by the wrist. He slams his other hand into his attacker's armpit, numbing the limb all the way to the fingertips. Hits him once. Twice. Feels his nose break in a meaty explosion of snot and blood.

A sharp pain in his gut now; the clear sting of a blade slicing through skin, striking bone.

McAvoy staggers back. Feels warm wetness on his hand. Feels the strength leeching from his legs. Looks up with glassy eyes. Sees the man who's going to kill him. There's something sharp in his hand and he's bringing his arm down directly towards McAvoy's exposed neck.

There's a flicker of movement to his left; a sudden explosion of colour and power; of pelt and muscle: a blurring insanity of fury and speed.

'Aector . . . fecking move!'

He throws himself sideways. Looks up to see Roisin, impossibly tiny upon the great ridged back of the carthorse as it stampedes from the treeline; fingers in the horse's mane, her hair streaming out like spilled ink; face set in the wordless scream of an ancient warrior summoned in a ritual of blood.

'What the f . . .?'

The big man never gets to finish the question.

Bob ploughs through him like a train.

SEVENTEEN

The feeling returns to her feet first of all – a sensation of something not yet pain, but a tingling, skin-prickling prelude. She realizes she is thirsty – that her tongue is lolling in her mouth like a piece of dried fruit. She becomes aware of a sharp point of pressure at the base of her skull. She hears voices somewhere.

Fear, now. *Memory.*

She'd been in Tom Spink's living room, out at the little cottage on the edge of the world. She'd been looking for sanctuary, a place to feel cosseted and safe and where she could start making sense of things. Somebody had attacked Thor, hadn't they? Put an axe in him while she watched from her bedroom window. Somebody had killed Malcolm Tozer, too.

And then she remembers Anders. Remembers the figure stepping out from behind the grotesque mound of flesh and flies, their face obscured by the ragged, parchment-yellowed flesh of her dead husband's excised face. There had been pain, then. Lightning in her fingertips; a paralysis in every cell. And then there had been the darkness.

She opens her eyes into blackness. Feels pain flood her senses. Numbness. Heat. She feels a pressure at her sides, as if she is being held too long in a too-tight hug.

She swallows. Tastes blood and metal. Tries to make sense of herself. She's on her back, she thinks. On her back and staring up. Her hands aren't responding to her commands. She tries to roll herself sideways but her legs won't cooperate. Panic trills in her chest. She forces herself to concentrate. Tries to push her arms out from her sides. Something holds her fast. She rolls her head from side to side and a sudden sharp pain shoots from the top of her skull to the base of her spine. She gasps and her chest constricts. Her eyes start to water. She can smell mud and damp. Can smell bad meat. Can smell her blood and piss.

She stops. Closes her eyes. Slows her breathing and wills herself to stay calm. She's frightened, but she doesn't have to give in to it. She's alive, and that's a start. Somebody has electrocuted her with a taser. They've tied her up and dumped her somewhere in the dark. Somebody will find her. She may have lost the vehicle that was following her but it wouldn't take a great detective to figure out that she'd been making her way to Spink's place. Any of her team would be able to fill in the blanks. But what if the bastard's moved her? She doesn't know how long she was unconscious. She might be miles away from Tom's house by now. Whoever has done this to her might be several steps ahead of her pursuers. They might have as much time as they want.

She wriggles where she lies. Tries to focus on the material that touches her skin. She's not dressed as she was. She's wrapped in something rough and unyielding, as if wound in a sheet. She's naked beneath. She's been stripped. Bound in sailcloth. There's something sharp beneath her head. Everything tingles but doesn't respond to her commands.

The fear rises. She wants to scream. She wants to snivel and beg and shout into the darkness; to plead with her captor for mercy. She won't let herself. If that's what they want from her then the only power she has is denying them the satisfaction.

She swallows again. Tries to work some saliva into her mouth.

'Water,' she says, and suddenly her mouth is afire. It feels as though she has drunk acid. She gags, eyes streaming; her throat closing up so swiftly that for a moment she can barely catch her breath.

She tries to slow her heartbeat. Her whole body is a phantom limb. She can't communicate. Can't reach out and touch. A memory stirs. She thinks of the specialist who had first explained the extent of her husband's paralysis to her in the weeks after his brain split down the middle. He'd made her lay her hand flat on the table and wiggle her ring finger. Then he'd made her make a fist with the same finger extended. He'd told her to move it. She hadn't been able to. She'd sat there entranced, focusing all of her energies on to the solitary digit, instructing it to move, to lift, to wiggle side to side. It had stayed obstinately still. Anders felt like that down all of one side of his body, said the doctor. And it's unlikely to change.

Slowly, Pharaoh begins to understand. The mask. The attacks

on men she cared about. The not-so-covert investigation into the events surrounding Anders' initial injury. And now the paralysis. The darkness. The absolute helplessness . . .

There's a movement nearby – a change in the quality of the air. She jerks to the right and the pain cuts into her skull. She tries to cry out and her throat closes up. She smells chemicals. Flesh. And then there is a weight at her side, a pressure against her shoulder, and somebody is lying down beside her, close as a lover. She feels their breath upon her cheek. Hears them swallow. Hears the rasp of their tongue across their teeth.

Pharaoh lies still as death. She knows, now. Perhaps she has known all along. She has faced down so many bad people and yet she is sure she glimpsed real evil only once. She had thought she had taken steps to eliminate the threat. She had believed them all to be safe. All he had been doing was biding his time.

She feels something moving on her stomach. Hears the slip and slither of leather against metal. Feels a sudden coldness, a sense of exposure. Feels shame and powerlessness. She wants to fight him. Wants to writhe and roar and bite. All she can do is lie still, weeping her silent tears, as he exposes her breast.

She wants to say his name. Wants to tell him that whatever he does to her, it must end with her. Wants to tell him that she'll acquiesce to whatever he wants but that he has to leave the people that she loves alone.

And then she hears the laughter; that little snuffling, simian whoop; a nose like a hacksaw cutting into hard wood. Thinks of the big house. Thinks of Anders. Thinks of the children playing in the big garden, feet dangling in the fish pond; koi carp moving fatly against their bare toes and wrinkled soles. Thinks of white legs and dark eyes and scars upon alabaster flesh. Thinks of Olivia, eyes wide, face blue, hair streaming out like pondweed. Remembers that laugh. That laugh, and the dark, dead eyes.

She feels wetness at her breast. Feels the warmth of his mouth.

She fights the pain. Pushes her head back into the sharpness beneath her skull. Turns the agony into something approaching a cry.

And then the laughter is in her face; the breath; the wet lips; the reek of the mask, all meat and piss and formaldehyde.

Hands on her face now; palms upon her cheeks.

She feels the rubber of the mask against her neck, hands in her hair; leathery softness caressing her jawline; spit-smeared lips at her ear.

And then he speaks.

Says the word that opens her insides like a blade.

'Mother.'

EIGHTEEN

McAvoy peels his shirt away from the wound at his hip. Tries not to grimace. Fails.

'Feck,' says Roisin, kneeling in front of him and holding her phone up to the knife wound. 'Jesus, Aector, could you not go a week or three without getting stabbed?'

McAvoy pulls a face. 'It's been ages,' he mutters, leaning back against the tree. 'Will it need stitches?'

'Of course it will,' grumbles Roisin. She pulls his shirt a little further up and takes a look at his big, broad stomach. She shakes her head. 'It's like seeing somebody draw a cock and balls on a Van Gogh, it really is. The state of you!'

He helps her back to her feet. She shines the light of the phone into his face. 'That's going to swell.'

He pulls her close to him, enjoying her warmth. 'What is?' he asks.

'Your cheek, eejit,' smiles Roisin. She puts her palm on his face. Rubs his beard softly. 'He pulled you up by the beard, Aector. I didn't like that.'

McAvoy looks away, embarrassed. 'You saw that?'

'Bob was being an arsehole,' she says, matter-of-factly. 'Who was it rang?'

McAvoy has spent the past few moments waiting for his heart rate to return to normal. He takes stock. His hand hurts. Ribs. There's a bit of beard missing. Some unhelpful sod had called him as he hid in the bushes like a flasher. He looks at the phone. George Earl. He wonders if he should return the call straight away or use a bit of sense and work out what the hell to say.

Decides that Pharaoh would favour the latter course of action so he will too.

'He's groaning,' says Roisin, nodding in the direction of the thinner man. He's been lying on his side, one leg drawn up, a hand to his face. It was Roisin who put him in the recovery position, though she did so under duress. The bigger man is a crumpled mess at the bottom of the slope: shin bones sticking through his jeans and his head facing the wrong way. One arm is folded under his mangled middle like a broken wing.

'Did he call him Dad?' asks McAvoy, rubbing his jaw. 'I hope I misheard.'

Roisin rubs the small of his back. 'You are so soft, my love.'

McAvoy looks back down the slope. He doubts there's an official form for this kind of incident. A different kind of man would make up a lie – fabricate a cover story to explain away any hint of wrongdoing. McAvoy isn't that kind of man. He always tells the truth. If it weren't for Pharaoh spending the past decade finessing his confessions into something more laudable, he'd have been out on the street or banged up in prison long since.

'You broke my jaw.'

McAvoy glances down at the smaller man, cupping his cheek as if suffering with the worst toothache of his life. His teeth are clamped together, his words coming out of just one side of his pressed-together lips.

'Fecking right he did,' says Roisin, pushing her hair back from her face. She glares at the man, nostrils flaring. 'Big lad's dead, if you're wondering. Mangled and tangled at the bottom of the slope, there. Should have stayed in your car, I'm guessing.'

He looks to McAvoy for confirmation. McAvoy nods. Wonders if he should apologize. Wonders if he should just back away into the woods and leave it to his wife.

'You'll die for that,' says the man, eyes fixed on McAvoy. 'I swear to you, you'll die for it.'

McAvoy pushes his hair back from his face. Feels frost and sweat and blood upon his palm. He takes the phone from Roisin. Squats down in front of the man and looks at him properly. He has him pegged as around fifty. Gold earring. Gold chain made up of big chain-mail hoops. Short greying hair gelled over a bald spot. A line of smudged blue ink tattooed across his neck. Stubble.

Deep-set eyes and bad skin. McAvoy doesn't know him, but he recognizes a man who's no stranger to criminality and its consequences.

'What's your name?' asks McAvoy, quietly.

'Fuck off,' he says, almost conversationally. He grimaces as pain grips his jaw.

'I'll find out,' says McAvoy. 'I can go through your pockets . . .'

'Try it.'

McAvoy sighs, disappointed. 'That's a downy birch,' he says, using the voice he employs when telling the children something they're not interested in but might need to know. He nods towards the straight trunk of a glistening tree. '*Betula pubescens*, as it goes. Soft on the outside. Tough on the inside. Fuzzy leaf stalks, shoots and twigs. It actually grows further north than any other broadleaf species.'

'What the fuck do I care . . .?' he asks, looking like a hedge-fund manager trying to fit the concept of altruism into an Excel spreadsheet.

'Thanks,' says McAvoy, giving Roisin's hand a squeeze. She's taken his wallet from inside his jacket and a phone from his waistband. Neither man saw her move.

'You fucking bitch!'

McAvoy shakes his head. 'None of that,' he says, inflexibly. 'Call me what you like, but don't insult her.'

'Yeah, what you going to do?'

'Me? Nothing. But she would take a dim view and there's a chance that . . .'

McAvoy winces in sympathy as Roisin takes the opportunity to physically express herself. Gives Roisin a warning look. Takes her bruised hand and kisses the knuckles. 'Could you not?'

'Sorry.'

McAvoy changes the angle of the light and starts looking through the wallet. It's dark leather, stuffed full of old Lottery tickets, bus tickets, betting slips; scraps of paper with long-faded numbers; a couple of credit cards. Phone cards, too. Phone cards, and a blue rectangle of plastic emblazoned with Blockbuster in yellow lettering.

'You've been inside a long time,' says McAvoy.

'I'm not going back,' he growls. 'Not after this.' He squirms upright. Tries to stand and slips back down to the floor with a bump. The last of the fight goes out of him. 'Copper, are you?'

McAvoy doesn't change his expression. 'What makes you ask that?'

The man shrugs. 'Big lad. Dirty fighter. One brain cell more than your average traffic warden. Stands to reason.'

McAvoy reads the name on the card. John Lee Prince. Says it aloud.

'Like you didn't fucking know,' growls Prince. 'Where are they, eh? Rest of 'em?'

McAvoy finds a folded-up piece of paper tucked into a flap in the wallet. It's headed HMP Warcop. There's an address written across the top in blue ink. A set of coordinates. A phone number. The number of a B-road.

'You reading me my rights, then?' he asks. 'You may as well just fucking chuck me down the hill with Stalker there. You send me back and I'm dead anyway.'

McAvoy doesn't reply. He doesn't want Prince to realize that he has no back-up and absolutely no idea why he's here. He tosses the phone to Roisin. She squints at the make and model. Rolls her eyes and keys in a universal pin. Tosses it back to her husband. There are no contacts saved. There's a Snapchat app flashing on the home screen. McAvoy uses his own phone, accesses the video recorder and points it at Prince's phone. Opens the message.

Flowers and Flames. Show me every moment. Live it for me. This is what you were born to do.

McAvoy reads it again. Watches it disappear from the screen. Recites it aloud to Prince. The scrawny man's features crumple, eyes pricking.

'He'll take me apart piece by piece,' he says. 'This was my chance.'

He swallows. Spits.

'Just break my neck now. Save me the pain of it.'

McAvoy trudges a little way back up the hill, waiting for his mobile phone to find a signal. He calls Ben Neilsen. It takes what seems like an age for him to answer and when he does, his manner is rushed, his voice hushed.

'Sarge, it's really not the best . . .'

'John Lee Prince,' says McAvoy, a finger in his ear. 'First priority. Chapter and verse.'

'I'm just pulling up to the Boss's mum's house,' says Neilsen, exasperated. 'I got sat-navved about ninety miles the wrong way. I haven't spoken to Andy yet and as for Olivia I doubt . . .'

'Quick as you can,' says McAvoy, and ends the call. He blushes instantly, ashamed of his manner and the ease with which he had imitated Pharaoh's approach to rank. He walks back down to where Prince is lying on the cold, hard ground. Roisin has given him her vape and he's puffing, awkwardly; the mouthpiece wedged in his broken jaw.

'Never seen him take a beating,' says Prince, wincing – drool leaking from his lower lip. He nods his head towards where the big bruiser named Stalker lies in a tangle of twisted bones. 'Not once. You must be a right hard bastard. What's your name?'

McAvoy licks his lips. 'You don't know?'

Prince shrugs. 'You're none of my fucking business, are you? Just another copper.'

'Detective Inspector Aector McAvoy,' he says, feeling daft. 'Humberside Police.'

Slowly, Prince rises back into a sitting position, his face inscrutable. He looks upon McAvoy as if seeing him for the first time. 'The one who caught him?' he asks. He inhales, nostrils flaring, anger and outrage etched on his face. 'Pharaoh's fucking poodle? I've been put down by Pharaoh's fucking poodle?'

'What did you call him?' asks Roisin, starting towards him.

Prince is ranting now, spit frothing at his lips, his words hard to decipher, eyes sunken deep in his skull. 'Does she know? Know what's coming for her? That bitch, that fucking bitch . . . she's set this up, hasn't she? Set this up from the fucking start! She thinks she's in charge but she's so fucking wrong. She'll pay, I swear to you. You too. Proud of yourself, are you? Locking up the one man who was doing any fucking good! One chance, I had – one chance to do something right and now the lad's dead and I'm . . . I'm . . .'

McAvoy wishes he had some cuffs. Or a gag. Adrenaline is flooding the stricken man. He'll be able to stand soon. Will be able to turn his rage into action.

'Why are you here?' asks McAvoy, raising his voice over the

sound of the shouts and curses and threats. 'What are you here to
do? If you're not here for me, then . . .'

Kush steps out of the treeline. Bare-chested under a donkey
jacket, patchwork trousers and big biker boots, hair sticking out
madly from the great stained dome of his bald head. He's holding
a shotgun. There's a half-smoked joint in his mouth, ember glowing
red.

'Kush?'

He shrugs an apology. Turns the gun on John Lee Prince.

'How did he find me?' asks Kush.

'Doesn't matter,' says Prince. He takes a breath. Closes his eyes.
'Whatever you do, he'll come for you.'

'Who?' demands McAvoy. 'Who's coming for you? What are
you here to do? And Trish, what do you . . .'

Prince springs to his feet. Darts towards Kush.

Kush pulls the trigger.

And the forest is just noise and smoke and blood.

NINETEEN

She's alone again. Alone and motionless: a corpse wound in
sailcloth and dumped in an unquiet grave.

He left as soon as she said his name. Left her to think
about things for a while.

Stuff to do, he'd said, his lips rubbing at the rubber of the mask:
the sound of moth-wings against flame. *People to see.*

Pharaoh can't feel her legs any more. Her fingers are numb.
The headache behind her eyes feels like it's drilling through to
her brain. Her throat is still fire, irises gritty with soil and tears.
She tries to get a sense of herself, to picture her surroundings.
The smell is all old stones and damp; the soft reek of a boulder
hefted from its berth. She can catch the faintest trace of something
familiar. Some sense of home, insinuating itself into her nostrils.
Furniture polish, maybe? Beeswax?

Doesn't matter, she tells herself. Doesn't matter whether you
work out where you are or whether you don't. Nobody's coming

for you, Trish. Anybody who fears for your safety will follow the wrong trail. They'll be waking up Reuben Hollow and demanding that he spill his guts; tell them how he's done it and why. And the clever bastard will enjoy every moment of it. All the while she'll be here, in this cold, dark space, while the man who calls her Mother revenges himself upon her for her betrayal.

She can't fight the memories any longer. They rise as if she were sinking into the earth. Helpless, desperate to pull herself out of her own mind, she peers out through the eyes of memory. She's in the big four-poster bed that Anders ordered for them with his first big payday. French and luxurious. The best cotton; the softest blankets; pillows fit for a queen. She's holding Olivia to her breast, stroking her cheek with the back of her knuckle. She's conscious of the memory of pain – the dull ache of bruises at her ribs; a burn at the small of her back; a red patch on the back of her head where her hair came out in a clump. Anders has been gone for three days. He hasn't called. Hasn't sent flowers. Sophia's in her bedroom. She won't come out. Daddy went too far this time. She doesn't think he should be allowed near the new baby. She's too precious; too sweet. It doesn't matter how expensive a gift he gets her to say sorry – she isn't going to forgive him. Nor should Mum.

She can hear his car, now. Can hear the big throaty rumble of the powerful VW Phaeton as it crunches over the polished stones of the driveway. She feels her heart lurch: feathers thrumming against the bars of her ribcage. He's home. Home, where he should be. Home to make it up to them. He'll be so bloody sorry. He'll sob with sheer, raw regret. He'll make excuses and she'll acquiesce to let him hold her. He'll tell her that she's the one; that this is passion; this is true love; that he hits her because she makes him crazy and that he'll never do it again, no matter how hard she's pummelling him, screaming at him, telling him that there are other men out there who would treat her better; treat his girls better; telling him that she's leaving; that she wants a divorce; that she'll take all she's owed and more besides. He'll be nice as pie for weeks. He'll be the best version of himself. They'll make good memories together. He'll love her the way he used to. She crosses to the window and looks down into the immaculate garden: red-green leaves floating on the pond; hedges shaped like chess pieces

holding back rhododendrons; wisteria tumbling gloriously from
the trellis by the big arched front door. She watches him get out
of the car. Still handsome, despite the gut. Dark beard, wavy hair,
broad across the shoulders. There's the same thuggishness to him,
even in his neat blue jumper and pressed jeans; the suggestion
that he'd be happier in jogging trousers and a wife-beater vest.
She imagines him coming upstairs and pressing her against him.
Imagines his lips upon the places where he hurt her. She knows
that she should leave him. He's dangerous. He's unpredictable.
He's hurt her badly and will again. But they have kids. There's
the house. And she loves him, despite everything. She'll be going
back to a detective inspector position when her maternity leave is
over and part of her job will be persuading battered wives to give
evidence against their abusers. She'll fight down her own shame.
She'll persuade herself that her situation is different.

She lifts Olivia. Takes her pudgy little hand and prepares to
wave it at Daddy.

A little boy gets out of the car. He's been sitting in the back
seat. He's five, maybe. Dark hair. Dark eyes. Skin white as fleece.

Anders crunches over the gravel. Puts his hand out. The boy
takes it. They head towards the front door without looking up.

Pharaoh feels her heart thudding against her chest. Her vision
blurs; pain in her back teeth, a tightness across her sinuses like a
steel band.

The door opening. Closing. Footsteps on the black-and-white
tiles. A soft muttering. The waft of lilies from the huge vase in the
picture window.

Pharaoh turns from the window. Puts Olivia into her cot at
the foot of the bed. She doesn't want to be holding the baby for
what comes next.

'Sweetheart,' says Anders, opening the door and jerking his
chin towards her; the greeting of a bloke in a pub seeing an old
drinking buddy. 'Surprise for you. Don't go mad.'

He'd crept into the room like mist. His eyes are downcast, his
limbs the colour of wood beneath the bark. He looks underfed.
Malnourished, even. He's wearing a bright T-shirt and some combat
trousers, the tag still clinging to the waist. He's wearing plimsolls.
He looks like a chimney sweep who's been scrubbed clean with
a wet brick.

'This is Trish,' says Anders, putting his hand on the boy's shoulders. 'She'll be taking care of you.'

Pharaoh looks to her husband for an explanation. She knows, of course. She's a detective. She'd made her accommodations with her husband's extra-curricular activities. But now he is in their home. Her bedroom. And he is being proffered like a bunch of flowers.

'This is Madoc,' says Anders, taking his cigarette case from his back pocket. He likes a long, thin panatela. Waves the match and gives his wife a smile. He looks like a schoolboy who knows he's done wrong but fancies that he'll be able to bat his eyelids in a way that gets him out of trouble. 'Madoc is Dulcie's boy. You remember Dulcie, yeah? Worked for me, yonks ago.'

Pharaoh does the maths. He's been making support payments for five years and two months – a standing order from the account she's not supposed to know about.

'We're babysitting, are we?' asks Pharaoh, trying to keep herself steady. She can see herself charging forward and pushing the smug bastard over the railing and down the stairs. Can see herself smashing a fist into his face and daring him to hit her back. And she can see herself broken and bloodied, laid out on the floor of the bedroom; Sophia running out to see what all the noise is about and taking a kicking for her trouble.

'Madoc's got nowhere to go,' says Anders, blowing out a cloud of smoke. 'His mum's not well. They want to put him into care.'

'They?'

'Busybodies. Social workers. Council. They reckon she's a danger to him. Can't take care of him properly. Got herself a bit messed up. Can't do the mum stuff. And you're so good at all that. I reckoned you'd rather offer him a roof than see him shunted off to some bloody orphanage or a paedo foster-dad. We've got the room.'

Pharaoh looks at the boy. He doesn't raise his head. Madoc puts a hand on his crown and forces him to look up. 'She's nice,' he says to the boy. 'She's a copper. Saint Fucking Trish, that's what they call her.'

Pharaoh sees her husband's eyes staring back at her from the face of the small, ghostly features. She holds his gaze. Looks up at Anders and sees the little half smile on his face, daring her to ask him; challenging her to make a fuss and see what fucking happens. No apologies this time. No regrets. She's pushed him further than he can stand and now he is going to make her play mum to the child he'd put in the belly of a drug-addicted prostitute on the East Marsh estate.

'Yours?' she asks, and she has to stop herself from baring her teeth. Has to turn it into a little chuckle; a big white-toothed smile. That's what he married, after all. That's what he liked best about her. Liked her big smile and her blue eyes and her fight. Liked her slim hips and big tits. Liked her gratitude. He hadn't married what she's become. Doesn't like her figure since the girls came along. Doesn't like being married to a detective who keeps winning commendations. Doesn't like that she has male friends and that her boss is her confidant. He's a jealous man, is Anders. He believes in the sanctity of their union. She's his wife and the mother of his girls. She'll belong to him until her last breath.

'Do you like ice cream?' asks Pharaoh, holding out her hand and plastering on a smile. 'Shall we see what's in the freezer?'

Anders slaps her on the arse as she passes him. She breathes him in as she eases herself past him. Smells somebody else's perfume. Smells the wrong brand of cigarettes. Smells somebody else's sweat.

'Introduce him to the girls, yeah?' instructs Anders. 'It'll be nice for them to have a brother.'

Here, now, on the cold floor, Pharaoh remembers the clammy, wax-like feel of the boy's palm against her own. She remembers that dreadful instant when she looked at his fragile limbs and his dark hair and his black, shark-like eyes, and she remembers wanting to push him down the stairs. Wanted to see the poor little bugger come apart like a china doll.

He didn't speak to them for the first few days. Ate. Slept. Filled out. He read books in his new room. Drew. Sometimes, she'd find him looking at Olivia in her cot. When he finally started to speak, it was at her bedside, muttering gentle nothings through the bars of her crib; a strange smile on his face as she sucked, gummily, at the tip of his index finger.

Pharaoh tried to be his mother. For nigh on seven years she raised her husband's love-child. He wasn't a difficult boy. He was quiet. Didn't play much. Spent most of his time trotting around after his dad. He did well at school. He was good at art. Good at sport. When he was twelve, he started to really fill out. Became his father's double. He even began to exhibit some charm; reciting poetry, mimicking comedians, talking about politics and police work and thinking of the man he wanted to become. Anders never raised a hand to him. Rarely raised a hand to his wife any more. He had bigger problems than family life. He was in debt to some terrible people and his world was about to come crashing down around him.

Six months after Anders suffered the stroke that left him voiceless and immobile, Madoc tried to suffocate his little sister. Sophia said he scared her. Samantha spoke about the time she had seen Madoc trying to force Olivia's head under the water of the lily pond. Pharaoh's world was already a catastrophe of bankruptcy petitions, County Court judgements, bailiffs and court enforcement officers. Her girls were starting to go hungry. They needed round-the-clock medical treatment for Anders. She had nothing left inside of her for Madoc. So she drove him back to Dulcie's shit-box little flat on the outskirts of Scunthorpe. Left him on the doorstep and drove away. Weeks later, appalled at herself, she drove to Dulcie's to bring him home. He wasn't there. Dulcie had allowed her case worker to take him. He was in the system now. And Pharaoh, despite herself, couldn't find the fight to look for him. He was dangerous. She'd always known he was dangerous. He was somebody else's problem, now. She'd pick up the pieces if he ever broke the law.

Pharaoh gives in to the sobs. Guilt and shame and regret puddle out of her. Tears trickle into her ears. She sobs, soundlessly. Sobs until there's nothing left.

She'll take her punishment when it comes.

She hears Anders' voice; a vibration inside her chest.

Look what you're making me do.

TWENTY

Ben Neilsen is beginning to wish he'd switched his phone to silent when the well-meaning dispatcher first told him about the attack on Park Avenue. Wishes he'd opened the window and thrown the bloody thing into the Humber. He could have been in bed now. Could have been spooned up behind the woman he's trying to love; a lullaby in his head and a breast or two in his hand. Instead, he's parked up here, loitering in the black-on-black shadow of a big, silent pub on the outskirts of Grimsby, shivering as the cold seeps into his bones and trying to decide whether he should urinate into his stainless-steel water bottle. He should have been outside Olivia's house a couple of hours ago but there were roadworks coming over the Humber Bridge and he got diverted halfway to Scunthorpe before he could find his way back towards his actual destination. Then Earl had started pestering him, asking for endless information about Pharaoh's friends and family; information he'd been reluctant to give. He reveres his boss and knows to his bones that she's not involved in whatever has happened to her boyfriend. She was never going to sit there snivelling like a victim when she could be doing something practical, like tracking down the person responsible. Now she's off the radar. The Americans would say she's 'in the wind'. And the last instruction she gave him was to go and keep a watchful eye over her youngest daughter – a command he has so far failed to follow. And now McAvoy's being all gruff and enigmatic and asking him for information that he could damn well find for himself if he wasn't tucked away in the cleavage of the Pennines and the Lakes, imagining himself a Celtic warrior and cosied up with his perfect bloody family.

Neilsen stops his train of thought. He's being horribly unfair. He's cold and hungry and he needs a piss and if McAvoy wants him to do something there must be a damn good reason for it. But still, the grumbling is keeping him warm . . .

Neilsen's phone rings. He answers swiftly. It's one of the civilian staff in the intelligence unit, a retired detective by the name of Diane: blonde and broad-shouldered, Scottish and motherly. She didn't mind being woken by her favourite sergeant. Told him that in her perfect world, he'd wake her up most nights and help send her off into a happy sleep. Neilsen had played along. He always plays along.

'Diane,' he says, trying to put some sparkle in his voice, 'I was just thinking about you.'

'Quelle surprise,' she says, mangling the French enunciation. 'I would say the same but I haven't had a chance to think happy thoughts. Been too busy with this wee job you shoved my way.' She lowers her voice, as if afraid of being overheard. 'Is it true what they're saying about Trish?'

'Depends who you're listening to,' says Neilsen, his head in his palm. The condensation on the glass is already starting to freeze. He switches on the wipers and winces as they screech across the sparkling darkness.

'The WhatsApp group's pinging like a xylophone. Some big lad from Iceland that she's been shagging – left for dead outside her flat. Dead ringer for Aector McAvoy.'

'Aye, that's about the size of it,' sighs Neilsen.

'And she's done a bunk, is that right?'

'Not really,' he says, trying to downplay events. 'She just needed to be with the people she loves, that's all. She'll give a proper witness statement when she's got her head together.'

'Poor lass,' says Diane, with feeling. 'She deserved a bloody knighthood or whatever for the way she cared for that husband of hers. Can you imagine? Ten years taking care of him like he was a baby, and after all he put her through. Worst-kept secret at Grimsby nick, that was. Stuck with him even when he was knocking lumps out of her. If that was me, once he was an invalid I'd have showed him who was boss. Not right, is it – cuckoo in the nest like that and her expected to just go along with it . . .'

'Did you get anything on Prince?' asks Neilsen, glancing at his watch. 'So sorry to rush you but it's a bit on the urgent side.'

'Och, don't apologize,' says Diane, brightly. 'I can be a gas bag if you don't stop me. Give me a moment . . .' There's a pause and Neilsen hears her fingers moving over the keyboard of her laptop. Pictures her sitting up in bed, perhaps in a big purple dressing gown, dipping shortbread in a mug of tea. Wonders whether his imagination might be racist. 'Righto, John Lee Prince. Seven of them in the system but I have a feeling I've got the one you're after. Born 11 August 1970, Carlisle Maternity Hospital. Dad Malcom, mum Simone, third of five children . . . first conviction 1989, assault with a deadly weapon, theft, burglary, graduated to a wounding, affray, Lancaster nick from 1993 to 1995, released, nose clean until 2001, did a stretch for possession, another for a minor role in the illegal import of cigarettes . . . sent down in June 09, attempted murder of one Maurice Bruce . . .'

'Attempted murder?' asks Neilsen. 'You have the particulars?'

'Quick cross-check with the case file and a Google search on the trial report,' she says. 'I know enough. Prince beat him bloody with a steering-wheel lock at his home in Maryport, West Cumbria. Gave "no comment" replies throughout the interviews and didn't protest when he was charged. Got fourteen years. At trial, defence barrister said that Bruce was financially responsible for a common-law wife and three children and was working as a joiner for a small firm of furniture manufacturers. He was endeavouring to get his life in order. Wouldn't say what led to the attack. Bruce suffered multiple skull fractures and a bleed on the brain. Pulled through, though I doubt anybody celebrated that. He was charged with rape of a minor two years later. Tip of the iceberg, from what I read between the lines. Bruce had been abusing kids since his teens.'

Neilsen sucks his cheek. 'Still inside?'

'Which one? Bruce, you mean? No, killed himself in his cell at HMP Warcop in 2019. Some suggestion of third-party involvement but no charges brought.'

'And Prince?'

'Been in Category C at Grantham for the past nine months. Working at a charity shop in Mablethorpe and coming back at evenings and weekends. Released on licence mid-January, this year, to an address in Kendal. That's the Lake District, isn't it? Bottom end.'

Neilsen lowers his head to the steering wheel. He hasn't made any notes but the information will stay fresh in his brain for a good few hours. He's lucky that way. It means that he can write up his official notes at his leisure and ensure they say what they need to rather than the unvarnished truth. He's a straight operator as a detective and would never willingly break the rules. But sometimes they need to be twisted.

'Anything else I can do for you?' asks Diane, optimistically. 'Shoulder rub? Feet? I'm awake now and I'll only spend the next couple of hours gossiping with my pals if you don't distract me.'

'You go and gossip,' says Neilsen, tucking the phone under his chin and turning the key in the ignition. A blast of hot air takes him in a warm embrace. He turns it up to full, angling the blowers towards the windscreen. He sticks a finger in his ear while he talks. The windscreen isn't clear yet. He has a couple of moments to make conversation. 'You must have known Trish since she was a rookie, I suppose.'

'Tough as boots from day one,' says Diane, admiringly. 'Had to be, in those days. Never let anybody get one over on her. She had the piss taken something rotten those first few months. I mean, she's five foot and a peanut if she's an inch – didn't exactly look the part. Mind like a whip, though. Always saw the best and the worst in people. Tom knew it at once. Obviously he was trying to shag her, just like everybody else, but she was all loved up with some nasty bastard from Crowle and Tom didn't push it. Took her under his wing instead. You know how good you have to be to rise as high as she did when you've been off on maternity leave four times and your husband's a vegetable?'

'You don't sound like you mourned him,' says Neilsen, only half-listening.

'Can't believe he hung on as long as he did,' says Diane, admiringly. 'Loved the bones of him, for better and worse.'

'He was the nasty bastard, was he? From Crowle?'

'No, she traded up when Anders fluttered his eyelashes at her. Anders was a posh boy, y'know. Very well-to-do. Bit of money in his pocket and a swagger in his stride. Bit of a chancer, if you follow me. Didn't always do things as they should have been done.'

'I can't see the boss swooning for that kind of flash bastard,' says Neilsen, with a frown. 'She wouldn't have let him get away with dodgy dealing.'

'She wasn't always the person you know,' says Diane. 'She was young and daft, like we all were. Threw her lot in with Anders and her boyfriend got the heave-ho. Didn't take it well, from what we heard at the time. He'd have gone down for what he did if she'd made a fuss but as far as she was concerned, he was within his rights after she broke his heart. I doubt she'd think the same now. We're all a work in progress, aren't we? You ask me, she'd have been better off with Tozer, God rest him. She may have got the big house with Anders but it all turned to shit in the end, didn't it? Poor lass. And now this? God, she'd be forgiven for thinking she was cursed.'

Neilsen doesn't speak for a moment. The name 'Tozer' rings a bell. He digests it all. Wonders whether the dates match. Sighs, and turns off the engine. He's going to have to phone McAvoy at once. Olivia is going to have to wait.

'You are a life-saver,' he says. 'I owe you one.'

'I'll look forward to it.'

TWENTY-ONE

Olivia is stamping back and forth across the living room, hands in her hair, tugging at her scalp. She's breathing heavy, breathing hard. She can feel her own heartbeat smashing against her ribcage; a pain behind her eyes.

'Come on, love, come on now . . .'

Nana Babs keeps trying to put her arm around her. Keeps trying to get her to look her in the face, to meet her eyes; to tell her what's happening, why she's so scared, why she screamed as if somebody were twisting her arms from the sockets.

'Please, Liv, please . . . you're scaring me, whatever it is, whatever it is . . .'

Olivia's temper breaks like a glass flung at a wall. 'I told you! I told you what I saw! Why won't you listen, why won't you believe me – he's killing her, right now, he's killing her . . .'

'It's a bad dream, love. That's all. We get 'em and they feel real, but if there were owt on your phone you'd show me, and there's nowt there . . .'

'It's Snapchat!' she screams, tugging a lock of her hair from behind her ear. Why won't the silly old bat listen? Why does she have to be so bloody pointless, so clueless; so fucking old!

'I don't know what that is!' protests Nana Babs, throwing up her hands. She was dead to the world when Olivia's screams woke her. She's got a dozen or more missed calls on her own phone and the world feels fuzzy and off-kilter. There's a strange feeling behind her heart; some sense that something is wrong in the vibrations of her own particular universe. She wants to make everything better but other than offering teas and cuddles she's entirely out of her depth. She has a horrible feeling she's going to have to phone Trish, and Trish has made it plain that tonight, of all nights, she has plans that aren't to be disturbed. Her big lump of Scandinavian beefsteak has flown a thousand miles just to dance the cervix rhumba and God alone knows that she's entitled to a bit of happiness, or at the very least, a night pretending she's snuggled up tight with the silly Scottish lummox she's been in love with for the best part of a decade.

'I can't,' sobs Olivia. 'Just . . . just . . .' She stops herself, looking at her nan; all wrinkles and tears and skin like dried-out paper. She presses her head against her chest and lets herself be hugged.

'Come on, love. Come on.'

She's wearing her winceyette nightie and a soft blue dressing gown. She's got her teeth in but no make-up and she looks every one of her seventy-nine years. 'Bloody phones. You just get the hang of one thing and they bring out something new . . .'

Olivia raises her head. She's still holding her phone, pressed against her palm even as she scraped her nails through her scalp. She holds it up in her grandmother's face. 'Once you watch it, it's gone. You can only see it once.'

'Well what bloody use is that?' asks Nana Babs, making a face. She's pretty tech-savvy, for her age, but she does still sometimes try and change the TV channel with her glasses case.

'He had Mum,' says Olivia, her voice cracking. 'I saw it. It was dark and he was wearing a weird mask but he had her on the floor and he was cutting off her clothes.'

Nana Babs wrinkles her nose. 'Sounds like something from a film, love. Have you been watching something scary?'

'It was him!' she shouts.

'Your mum's just fine, love,' says Nana Babs, softening her tone and perching on the arm of the chair. She puts an arm around her granddaughter. 'Nobody could hurt your mum. She's tough as nails. Never had none of this with her. She wouldn't have taken a hug from me when she was your age, I tell you that. Already thought she knew it all.'

Olivia stares at the horrible pattern in the carpet: a maze of reds, greens and golds. The leather three-piece suite doesn't really fit in the boxy living room and she truly hates the glass coffee table that rests on the paws of an upturned panther. There's a big glitter painting hung above the electric fire: a handsome couple

locked in a steamy clinch, their outline studded with crystals and
points of light. She would be too embarrassed to bring a friend
back, if she had any – would hate to explain why her nana, in her
baby-hued nightie, has the same taste in furniture as a serial seducer
in a silk kimono. Nana Babs claimed all of it when Trish discovered the Cleethorpes shag-pad that her dad had been paying for;
laser-disc players, globe-shaped drinks cabinets; a circular bed and
a mirrored ceiling. Nana Babs had refused to see it go to the
bailiffs along with everything else. The big circular bed takes up
the entirety of her bedroom but she says she's never slept so well.

'Come on, love,' says Nana, giving her a squeeze. She smells
of rose-scented hand cream and breath-mints. 'This boy you've
been chatting with – is he the sort to try and scare you? Boys can
be silly when they like a girl.'

Olivia screws up her eyes. She knows she'll have to tell somebody who she's been talking to and what she's done. She just isn't
sure she can find the right words.

'Maybe a tea, eh? And then we can send him a message and
tell him he's been a silly beggar and that if he wants you to carry
on talking to him he'll start treating you with a bit of respect, eh?
The lasses in this family have taken enough of men's nonsense
over the years and I'll be buggered if . . .'

'He's not interested in me like that,' says Olivia, a sob making
her hoarse. She swallows. Wipes her eyes. 'He couldn't be. It's
illegal.'

Nana Babs gives her a funny look. 'Sorry, love, you've lost me.
You spend half your life sending messages back and forth. Don't
go giving me that "just good friends" stuff.'

Olivia hugs her arms to her sides. 'I've done something stupid,
I think, Nana. I really think I've fucked up.'

Nana Babs softens her face. 'We all make mistakes over boys,
my girl. Your mum! Honestly, when she were your age I couldn't
keep up with who she was seeing and who was last week's Romeo.
Of course, you could get a reputation in those days and there were
those who said nasty things about her. Never off her back! I swear,
when my dad heard what people were saying he'd have leathered
half the town if it wasn't going to cost him his job. Not easy being
a copper's daughter and not much easier to be a granddaughter
– not least when you're putting yourself about. Sorted herself out

though, didn't she? Look at her now! Proud as punch, we are. So whatever you've done, there's nothing can't be undone . . .'

'Did she cause Dad's injury?' asks Olivia, suddenly – the words out of her mouth before she can stop herself. 'Sophia says they used to hit each other. Did she make him have the stroke?'

Nana Babs' expression hardens. 'Who said that? Where did you hear such nonsense?'

'Something must have happened to cause it,' says Olivia, squeezing at the hems of her trousers with her fingertips. 'Nobody would ever talk about it. I hardly remember what he was like before the aneurysm. All those years, it was like having a ghost in the house. It wasn't like he even tried! I'd come home and tell myself I was going to be a good daughter. I'd sit with him and read to him and listen to the music he liked or put a film on and I swear he never wanted me near him. He never wanted anybody but Mum. I'd find stuff online, things to help him communicate, and Mum would just nod and smile and say that he loved me but he was ashamed of how he was and that I should just go and play and enjoy myself. But she spent her life at his bedside. I'd go in and see her stroking his hair or bathing him or watching old movies and it was like she was happier with him that way than who he'd been before. But if he hit her, why did she stay? She was a copper! And when he said that maybe it was guilt – that maybe she'd hurt him, that she was keeping him close so he couldn't find a way to tell anybody, it made sense, and I . . .'

'When who said?' asks Nana Babs. Her pupils are pin-pricks now, tiny perforations in the same blue irises as her mum. 'Who's been saying this horrible shit?'

'After the funeral,' says Olivia, and lowers her eyes. Her mind fills with images of him. Dark hair. Dark eyes. Pale skin. Black suit. He'd looked like a singer from an emo band: black nail polish and eyeliner, key-chain and a bandana around his wrist. Sunglasses, even in the rain. He hadn't joined the mourners. Only saw him because she'd taken herself off for a little stroll, trying to find a place where she could smoke a joint away from prying eyes. He'd appeared from behind a stand of trees like a genie conjured from a bottle. She'd fancied him at once. And then the sense of recognition had taken hold. So many memories; so many scraps of unfinished, disjointed recollection. She remembered him.

Remembered the boy who used to read her stories and push her on the swings; the boy who Sophia found creepy and Samantha refused to sit next to in the car. His name was on the tip of her tongue. When she spoke it aloud, his pale face had creased into a smile of such pure delight that she'd wrapped him in a spontaneous hug; eyes filling with tears. It had felt as if some obstruction had been excised from a nerve; as if she'd been massaged in the right spot and suddenly she was awash with a strange, teary emotion. He'd talked to her as if they were already close as hand and glove. Had spoken of the ache that lived inside him; the bruising around his soul; the constant nagging agony of being far from the only people who'd ever tried to love him. He'd only heard about his father's death because his mother had told him there might be some money coming his way. He didn't want it. But he did want to say goodbye. He'd come back to England just to loiter, silently, at the edges of the funeral – to see the smoke and the dust and the ash fill the cold blue air. Olivia had told him that they were going to scatter his ashes in the car park. She would keep some for him, if he wanted. It had been one of the strangest things she could ever remember saying, but it had been oddly right, in the moment. He'd smiled, properly. Thanked her. Taken her details. Told her not to tell anybody that he had been at the service. He wouldn't be welcome, he said. Trish would kill him if she saw him. That was how it started. And it ends with her mum alone in the dark, her cuckoo child cutting off her clothes with a knife.

Nana Babs takes Olivia's chin between finger and thumb. Forces her to look at her. 'Tell me,' she says. 'Tell me who's been filling your head.'

Olivia can't meet her gaze. Her eyeballs feel like they are trying to climb out of their sockets. But the word escapes her anyway.

'Madoc,' she says. 'My brother.'

There is a moment of absolute silence, the words spreading into the air like smoke.

Nana Babs doesn't speak. Just gulps, face set in stone.

She blinks once.

Twice.

Then she hits her across the cheek so hard that Olivia feels her teeth rattle in their gums. Flatters out of the chair and sprawls on the nasty carpet; eyes filling with tears; great red hand-print on her pale, pale skin.

'I'm sorry,' she whispers, into the flutt and the grime and the swirls of wool. 'I'm so, so sorry. He said she tried to kill him. Said there was a video. It made so much sense. And when I saw it . . . she's meant to be police – meant to be better than that – they had to see, didn't they? Had to investigate it properly. She sent him away – dumped him like he was nothing so she could have Dad all to herself. I didn't know he was so angry. I didn't know!'

Nana Babs isn't listening. She's already reaching for the phone.

'Sophia,' she says, all urgency and breathless relief, 'Sophia, are you safe, my love? Are you safe? Oh thanks Christ. He's back, baby-girl. That fucking monster. He's out. I think he's got your mum . . .'

TWENTY-TWO

McAvoy feels the kick of the shotgun all the way up his arm; feels the heat in his palm as he jerks the barrel up and away. There's a roar of pain as the explosion of shot grazes Prince's shoulder, takes a chunk of ear and a strip of skin from his neck.

'Bastard,' growls Kush, trying to wrestle the gun back out of McAvoy's hand. He kicks at the bigger man, boot connecting beneath the knee. McAvoy holds on tight. Jerks his arm upwards and for a moment Kush's feet are off the floor. Shakes him loose as if trying to dislodge a stick from the jaws of a terrier.

'He's shot my fucking ear off! My fucking ear!'

Kush lunges for the gun again and McAvoy kicks his legs out from under him. Catches him by his shirt-front and lowers him down so he doesn't hurt himself.

'Please, stop it, Kush . . . stop, you'll get hurt . . .'

Roisin stands by the tree, the light from the phone angled into the clearing, reflecting off the silvered branches; the frost-dusted earth. The darkness has taken on the appearance of an X-ray;

smudges of black muscle and fat bisected with delicate lines of white. She can see Prince trying to get up, his palm to his bloody ear. Can see him thinking about making a run for it.

McAvoy drops Kush and ambles over to Prince. He grabs him by the shirt and pulls him upright as inoffensively as he can. Looks at the damage to the side of his face. 'That's nasty.'

'I fucking told you!' bellows Prince. 'I said just kill me!'

'I thought you were being dramatic,' mutters McAvoy, rummaging in his pocket for a handkerchief. He finds a tissue. Presses it to Prince's ear. Puts himself in Prince's line of sight and jerks his head at Kush. 'You were here for him?'

'I'm not telling you anything,' spits Prince. 'Arrest me. Fit me up, like you did Reuben. Doesn't matter to me.'

'Shut your mouth,' says Kush, from the floor. 'Don't confuse the poor sod any more. He looks like a Labrador doing a fucking Sudoku.'

McAvoy looks from one man to the other then gives his attention to Roisin. She shrugs. Spreads his hands, wondering whether she can make any sense of the situation. She shakes her head. 'No, my love – I've no bloody idea what's happening. Would you like me to kick anybody until they stop being so . . . what's that word? Oblong?'

'Obtuse,' mutters McAvoy, feeling hopeless. He looks at Kush. Escorts Prince towards the old hippy. Helps him up and dusts him off. Kush is skinny beneath his clothes: fragile; his ribs like an undernourished cat. His heart's beating hard. Roisin joins them and for a moment they stand in a loose circle, four people connected by something that none seem able to identify. There's a soft squelching sound as a loose piece of Prince's ear detaches itself from the rest of the lope and drops, gorily, onto his shoulder. McAvoy pretends not to notice.

'Trish Pharaoh,' says McAvoy, at last. He directs the name at Kush. 'You know her.'

'That cunt,' growls Prince, under his breath.

McAvoy doesn't respond. Just glares at Kush. 'Now,' he says, coldly. 'Tell me something useful or things are going to take a turn.'

Kush rubs at his head, his hair sticking up in clumps. He looks like all the fight has gone out of him. He glares at Prince. Shakes his head. 'I didn't think I'd be able to pull the trigger. Did though, didn't I? I'd have blown a hole right through you.'

'Do you want a bloody medal?' asks Prince, petulant. 'Take me on without a shooter, you raggedy prick – see how you get on without your pet bear here.'

'I thought I was a pacifist,' says Kush, marvelling at himself. He holds up his hands, chapped and weathered, inked and bloodless. They tremble slightly as he inspects them. 'Guess you never really know.'

McAvoy can't decide whether he should bang their heads together or start to cry. 'Trish Pharaoh,' he says again. 'If somebody doesn't give me a straight answer I'm going to really lose my temper.'

'She deserves all that's coming to her,' growls Prince, licking blood from his teeth. 'Bitch won't ever sleep easy again, I swear – not with all this blood on her hands. Say goodbye to St Fucking Trish, big lad. She'll be with the devils by morning. Flowers and fire, mate, grief and flame.'

'And you think she'd weep for me?' asks Kush, staring past McAvoy at the man who came here to kill him. 'Christ, it would be a weight off her mind if I was in the ground. You don't think she's wanted me six feet under for the past ten bloody years?'

'Yeah, that's kind of the point, dickhead.' Prince twists in McAvoy's grasp. Swears as he catches his bloody neck on his collar. 'Won't take long, will it, eh? She's prime suspect material, if you ask me. Proper motive. Bang to rights.'

'He's setting up Trish?' asks Kush, incredulous. 'She's miles away! And why now? Why risk everything just when she's flavour of the month? If I was ever going to tell, I'd have done it before now.'

Prince sneers at him, disgust carving lines in his features. 'Got greedy, didn't you, lad? Old lag like you, got old debts, felt entitled to a cosy retirement. Asked for a bit extra. And she sent somebody to make sure you could tell no tales. Sent a couple of dangerous men after you as punishment for breaking your agreement.'

McAvoy looks from one to the other, umpiring a game of tennis played with obscure rules. He's trying to keep up but fancies that if he asks any questions he'll just make things worse. He's trying to make a mental note of the things he doesn't understand but on the jotter of his mind, it's all scribbles, question marks and Tipp-Ex.

'Old lag?' he asks, quietly.

'Kush is a nickname,' he says, as if explaining something to a particularly hard-of-thinking six-year-old. 'It's Laurence Kidd. Laurence with a "U". Kidd-double-D. I don't expect it to mean anything to you but no doubt you'll be riffling through the system. I'm in there somewhere, unless Trish has made me disappear.'

'Oh this is so fucking boring,' says Roisin, pinching the bridge of her nose. 'I'm not a well woman and my patience isn't great at the best of times. My husband's bleeding, my ears are ringing and I just watched a horse commit murder. Now, you . . .' She glares at Kush. 'Why did you try and shoot this silly bollocks here?'

Kush looks to the floor. 'I always told myself that I would fight if it came to it – that whoever he sent, I'd make sure I took them out before they got to me.'

Roisin makes a thin line of her lips. 'You're being obtuse again. You said "he", as if I know who you're fecking talking about. Do you mean Reuben Hollow?'

Kush scrumples up his face. Looks at McAvoy. 'You really don't know what's happening, dude? About the recording? The boy?' He shakes his head. 'All the stress to keep everything wrapped up tight and you don't even know what she's accused of, do you?'

McAvoy takes a breath. He considers the pain in his hip and the sting of the new bald patch in his beard. He thinks about the campfire and the wagon and his children asleep under hand-made quilts. He thinks of home, and the caravan in the back garden where he likes to go and read poetry and listen to Radio Three. He thinks about Trish and the way she teases him and makes him laugh and shows him how to walk the line between being a good copper and a good person.

McAvoy increases the pressure of his grip on Prince's shirt. Pulls him closer. 'Do you know who attacked Thor Ingolfsson tonight?'

'Weren't me, was it?' shouts Prince, face twisted. 'I've been sitting in a service station most of the night, ask anybody.'

'But somebody's trying to set her up,' says McAvoy, trying to cling to something tangible. 'Setting her up for the attack on Thor – coming after Kush, here? But why Kush?' He looks at the old, scrawny man. 'You weren't an item, were you? I'm not judging, but . . .'

'She's getting what's coming,' says Prince. 'Count yourself lucky, big lad – be grateful he doesn't have his sights set on you.'

'And this is all revenge for her putting him inside?' asks McAvoy. 'Last time I checked, Reuben Hollow was still professing his undying love for Trish.'

'She's not what he thought she was,' shrugs Prince. 'Reuben's different too. Seeing things clearly again. Feels duped. Feels a bit of a mug, truth be told. You don't want to upset a man like that. Makes a lad like me feel honoured just to be able to play a part.'

Roisin snorts. Chuckles and lets out a long, low sigh. She peers at him. Looks him up and down. 'You're one of his fan-boys, are you? One of the Hollow Men? Doing his bidding? Find you on Incels Anonymous, did he? Or is it more old-fashioned? Just paying you to do his dirty work?'

Prince is about to protest, drawing in a breath to launch a stream of frothing invective. The air catches in his throat and he starts to cough, pain gripping him. McAvoy finds himself rubbing his back. He tries to get his breath, hands on his knees. When he raises his head his face is white; the hollows so deep they seem to be drawn in charcoal. He sags, the fight seeming to drain out of him. He looks past McAvoy, down the slope. 'He was a good lad, under it all. Easily led. Shouldn't have brought him. His mum'll be fucking heartbroken.'

'You brought him to kill me,' says Kush, pointedly. 'Came to do me in. You'll forgive me if I don't shed a tear.'

'Rough life, that one,' says Prince, softly. 'Thought this would give him a chance to move on. Didn't deserve any of this. Should never have come to this.'

'You said his name was Stalker?' asks McAvoy.

'Nickname, daft lad. He's Kian. Kian Stempel. Not even twenty-two till next May. Only just got me back in his life and look where he's at. Begged me to come, I swear to you. Begged. Wanted to do right by the bloke who did right by him. Silly sod.'

McAvoy breathes out heavily. The adrenaline has worn off. He needs sugar and a rest. He feels an anxiety fluttering inside him.

He needs to know if Trish is safe; to warn her that Reuben Hollow is trying to destroy her. But he can't help himself asking how much she already knows. It can't just be coincidence that he's found himself at the little compound run by somebody whose death she would take as a blessing. Has she manoeuvred her pieces so that he's here as a witness or as a protector? Has he aided her scheme or made things worse? He needs answers but doesn't even know which questions to ask.

'You look all funny around the edges,' says Kush, looking at McAvoy. 'All sort of grey.'

'I'm fine,' he says, automatically. 'And if I do happen to pass out, I swear, Roisin will be a lot less bloody amenable than I am, so don't be thinking that your world will all be peaches and cream if I happen to be unconscious for a while.'

Kush gives a little laugh. 'Christ, she's not wrong about you, is she? Said you weren't like anybody else. Anders would have bloody hated you. Shame she didn't know you years ago. The boy might have stood a chance.'

McAvoy takes a moment. Digests. Closes his eyes until the desire to fall down dissipates for long enough to talk.

'Anders? Her husband?'

'Killed him, didn't she?' snarls Prince. 'Bangs up a good man and all the while she's got blood on her hands. Tortured the poor sod for a decade and him in his sick bed, unable to move or defend himself. Twelve years it took. Twelve years of torture and then she acts like the victim! Broke his heart, I told you, just when he was starting to get himself right in the head. Said I'd do anything he asked, didn't I? That's the deal you make. And if he wanted this prick dead then that's a small price, innit?' He looks down the slope again. 'All for nowt, now. What a mess.'

McAvoy looks to Kush, who shrugs. Looks up at the big white moon. 'I tried,' he says, staring straight up. 'I didn't get greedy. I didn't ask for more. I swear.'

McAvoy curses as his phone starts to ring in Roisin's hand. She looks at the number. 'Ben,' she says. 'You want me to?'

McAvoy wonders whether he wouldn't be better served just letting his wife take care of everything. He'd like to sit down at the base of the tree and have a nice little nap. He's getting a little tired of being a police officer, truth be told. He's tired of feeling beaten up and bewildered. He'd quite like a job showing people around stately homes, or writing articles for a history magazine. Wonders whether he's too old to re-train. Wonders whether he should go and be a lighthouse-keeper or a custodian of a tiny island in some distant loch back home. He would like people to stop trying to kill him. Would like to stop having to make life or death calls.

'I'll take it,' he says, and lets go of Prince, taking the phone from his wife. 'Ben, where are we at?'

For a little while, nobody speaks. McAvoy holds the phone to his ear and absorbs everything Neilsen has learned. He doesn't reply. Kush and Prince watch each other like cats. Roisin gives her attention to one, then the other, smiling as if this is all tremendous fun and occasionally putting her finger to her lips if either of them looks like they're going to interrupt.

'Tom's place,' says McAvoy, at last. 'If she's gone somewhere to get her head down, she will be at Tom Spink's.'

Prince sniggers. It's a nasty little snuffling sound, like a pug with a cold. He bites it back a moment later but McAvoy has already seen something in his expression that chills him right through.

'I'll call you back,' says McAvoy, and ends the call.

'No,' says Prince, raising his hands. 'No, whatever you're thinking, I swear, I don't know a thing . . .'

McAvoy looks down the slope. Does the dates in his head. Takes a wild stab in the dark.

'Reuben Hollow killed the man who abused your stepson,' he says. 'You're here to repay that favour. What I don't know is why anybody would think that Trish would want Kush here dead. And I sure as hell don't know why the name Tom Spink should mean anything to you. So, please, John. Do yourself a favour. Tell me what I need to know. If Trish is heading to Tom's place, is she walking into a trap?'

Prince holds his gaze. Slowly, his eyes start to fill with tears. He glances again at the body at the foot of the hill. 'By the time he's done with her there'll be nowt left but grief and tears. That's what she left with him with and that's what he'll take in return. She'll be in a jail cell with nothing but the guilt and the grief. By the time he's done, even you won't recognize her.'

McAvoy breathes deep. Smells sap and ice and blood. Smells fox piss and gunpowder. Smells the sour reek of fear.

'How do I stop him?' he asks, under his breath. 'What does he want?'

Prince laughs, blood frothing on his chin. 'He's a clever bastard, I tell you that. He must have known you'd be here and waiting. Must have known you'd show your face. I didn't understand what he meant until just this fucking moment. He said that if her warrior poet got in the way, I was to extend you an invitation. To tell you he's waiting. And Christ, she's made it easy for you, hasn't she? Put you just where he wants you to be. You set off now you can be face to face with him in an hour. Won't that be nice, eh? You and him, across the table from one another. Just like old times.'

McAvoy feels Roisin slip her hand into his. She's cold and clammy. When she squeezes his broken knuckles he feels the warning implicit in the caress. Please, Aector. Please don't go and see that evil bastard. Please.

He looks up at the moon and knows, to his bones, that he's going to have to disappoint her.

He needs to look Reuben Hollow in those cold blue eyes.

TWENTY-THREE

Pharaoh jerks awake, her body one great shuddering spasm of agony. It pushes the air from her lungs. Crushes her. Sweat oozes from her every pore. She feels the blood rush into her limbs. Feels the gritty air settle back in her lungs. Breathes through the fire of the constriction in her throat. Hears the whispered croak of her scream.

There's light, now. A soft yellow cone of light somewhere off to her left. She tries to turn her head but something is holding her fast. She can only stare straight up into nothingness, the light dwindling a few feet above her face. She can just make out the fuzzy outline of a curving roof and an old timber joist. She senses she's underground. It smells damp and cold and forgotten. She lets herself hope for a moment: hope that this is what he wants.

He's going to leave her here. He's going to walk away and leave her to expire in the quiet beneath the earth. She starts to wonder who'll find her. She hopes it's a stranger. She hopes somebody places a coat over her body before anybody she knows sees her like this: bloodied and naked and broken. She imagines Aector kicking in the door. Imagines the look on his face when he bends down and wraps his fingers around her wrist: her pulse motionless beneath his calloused thumb. She imagines his tears splashing onto her rictus face. Sees herself in a fairy tale. Imagines him stroking her cheek and the colour returning to her dead flesh.

She forces herself to stop. She knows that she's taken a blow to her head. She's injured. She has open lesions where she's been dragged across a rough surface. She's at risk of infection. She can't let herself sink into hallucination; has to keep the confusion from leaking in.

Madoc, she tells herself. Madoc's doing this. The boy you took in. The boy you gave away.

She coughs and hot pincers of pain squeeze her throat. She uses the agony to clear the grogginess from her head. Forces herself to think about what she truly knows, and what she has only suspected. But her thoughts are all swirled up with her feelings. She can't separate the man who attacked Thor from the little boy she betrayed.

No, she tells herself. No, that's not how it was . . .

Pharaoh has never allowed herself to indulge in regret. She has no time to look back: no inclination. But she has always known that she did wrong by the boy who called her Mother for a time. She took him in and gave him a family. And then she sent him away. It was the hardest decision she'd ever had to make. She knew he was damaged; that he was dangerous. But after all he'd endured at the hands of his biological mother, she knew that the darkness within him was the product of an absence of nurture, and not an intrinsic evil. She could help him, she knew that. She could bring him home. It was his father who forbade it, using whatever means of communication he could employ. He wouldn't have the boy back under his roof. And if Trish tried to do it without his blessing, he'd tell. He'd tell everybody what she did.

She makes herself think like a copper. Like Trish Fucking Pharaoh. Tries to work out why here and why now? She thinks of Olivia and the way she has been towards her these past months. Thinks of her youngest daughter and her endless questions about her dad, and how he was, and who he used to be. Thinks of the funeral. Of how she let herself down. Tries to untangle that chunk of time when she'd been not far off unconscious, pissed out of her mind and sobbing into her cigarettes in the driving rain on Cleethorpes beach. She'd left her daughters at the crematorium. She couldn't stand to be there: couldn't stand to imagine Anders' body being reduced to clumps of smouldering ash behind the velvet curtain. It made a mockery of the past decade of her life. All those years she fought to keep him alive, just for his heart to give out after contracting a simple infection. It made every sacrifice seem pointless. McAvoy had found her. Held her. Took her home. Had Madoc come to the funeral? Could he have contacted Olivia? If he got inside her head, he might be the reason why she has been so damn cold towards her; why the distance between them has been getting wider and wider. And if she somehow saw the video, if she watched the footage of the night that Anders suffered his injury, the poor girl's head must be reeling.

She thinks of Tom. Feels her whole body rise as the flood of emotions and memories and chemicals fills her and spills out of her eyes.

'Comfy? Perhaps we could have a bedtime story.'

Pharaoh stiffens where she lies. She becomes aware in a change in the quality of the air. Smells him; the cat-piss reek of sweat; the old coins and offal of old blood. She recognizes her own voice in his words: his imitation of her Mexborough accent, flat vowels and hard consonants.

She tries to speak. Tries to say his name. The noise that emerges is the creak of a church door.

'Spurge,' he says. '*Euphorbia helioscopia*. It won't kill you, but it'll steal your voice, just like you stole Father's. Suggestion from a friend. A good one, like always. You'll be amazed at how effective their suggestions have been, as it goes. You won't like all of them, but you'll definitely admire their efficacy. I wasn't sure they'd be able to deliver the Succinylcholine. But it was here and waiting. Did it sting going in? Another 10mg and you'd be already starting to die. Instead, you're just nice and still. Nice and helpless. Just like you wanted Dad.'

She senses him move. Hears the whisper of footsteps upon uneven ground. She hears a rustling: clothes being removed, replaced. Her nostrils fill with him. With the sweat and musk of a sweat-soaked young man. Terror grips her: a panic unlike any she has ever known. She uses every ounce of strength, tries to push up or down; to wriggle into the earth. Her body doesn't respond. She's totally immobile.

And then he's standing over her, bare feet planted either side of her shoulders. He's wearing a soft leather apron with a pocket in the front – a selection of blades poking out of the top like paintbrushes from a pot of dirty water. She can't make out his face. There's ink on his bare legs: flower petals and intricate feathers lending a shimmer to his hairless legs.

He squats down in a swift, fluid motion. For an instant his face is directly above hers. Without the mask, he somehow looks more like Anders. He's every inch his father's son. But Anders didn't have the scars. He didn't have the haunted hollows and sunken cheeks. He had brown eyes. But Madoc's are black. Utterly black, like the shell casings of a scarab beetle, the whites a shimmering obsidian. His hair is short and dark and sticks up in sweaty clumps from where he's pulled off the mask of his father's face. He smiles, now. Smiles to show her the other modifications he's made to himself on her behalf. Opens his mouth and reveals the two wriggling points of his neatly bisected tongue, worming out from between teeth that he has filed into points. He's a thing of nightmares. He's a fear made flesh.

He drops something at her side. Reaches out to touch it. Stands up again and moves away.

There's silence, for a moment. And then she hears herself. Hears her own voice.

'. . . *he was always trying it on at first. They all do, don't they? Even if they don't think you're going to go for it they kind of like the chase. Even the best ones – they have to make it about whether you fancy them, whether you're stuck up, whether you're a slut. All these sweet old men with the crinkly eyes and the polyester slacks, placing their carnations on the wife's commemorative bench – I swear to you, thirty years earlier those same blokes were trying to get in the knickers of the lass at work or the woman from the corner shop or that tasty barmaid from The Sailmaker's. It's how*

*it was. So Anders wasn't wrong, really. And he wasn't unique. And
he did love me, I know that. Loves me now. I only ever saw passion
in him when he thought somebody was trying to get inside me.
Tom was the one he couldn't ever get over. Tom, and maybe
Mally Tozer. I'd taunt him with them, sometimes. I'd shrug and
tell him that maybe I really had done all the things he accused
me of, just to see his face. Who was it that said a kiss with a fist
is better than none? He'd kill the pair of them given the chance.
He'd hate you, I think. He'd admire you, but hate you. He hates
Hector, that's for sure. Won't let us say his name if he can hear,
though there isn't a lot he can do about it laid out in his bed like
a hot dog in a fucking bun . . .'*

Pharaoh closes her eyes. She can see herself sitting on the steps
of Reuben Hollow's caravan, ringed by trees, breathing in his
tobacco and cider, the air pungent with wild garlic. She's reeling
him in. She's spinning a yarn. She's trying to get Reuben Hollow
to admit what he is, what he's done. She recorded their every
word. How the hell had Madoc got hold of it? She needs to explain.
She needs to tell him that it isn't how it sounds.

He's at her side, now. He's lying down beside her: two figures
on the lid of a tomb.

'You betrayed him,' says Madoc. 'I told you. I gave you a
chance.'

Pharaoh grits her teeth. Swallows fire. 'No . . .' she manages.

'Dahlias,' he says, quietly. 'Black, for betrayal. You know the
language of flowers, don't you? Every bloom has a symbol. And
these were extra-special, Mother. They were grown in his ashes.
It took work. So much work; neutralizing the acid, the salt, freeing
the correct chemicals from the roots. But the blooms are radiant,
truly. To have grown from the remains of my father – to be made
a gift for you, the woman who betrayed me, betrayed him – betrayed
the one who has made things right . . . there is a pleasing synergy,
don't you think? It's a word I like a lot. Mr Bruce used to use
large words like that. He liked to show off. He wanted to impress
us as much as he wanted to do the other things. Sometimes he'd
leave me alone if I used a word or phrase that impressed him.
He'd pick on one of the others instead. It didn't always work. I
had to make myself repulsive to him. To stop washing; to piss in
my clothes until they rotted. Have you ever felt worms crawling

out of yourself? Do you know how it feels to prefer that sensation to the alternative? You did that, Mother. You turned my dad into a vegetable and you sent me away to the devil . . .'

Pharaoh tries again. Forces herself to swallow the agony. 'Madoc . . . I didn't . . . I tried . . . you were ill . . .'

He isn't listening. He rolls away from her. Stands up and looks down at her with his black, shark-like eyes.

'You're going to feel just what you did to him, Mother. You're going to know how it feels to be crippled and helpless and afraid. You're going to lie there and watch everything that ever mattered to you burn to the ground. I've done right by my father. I've killed the men you sullied yourself with. Before morning, the police will know what you did to him. The cases you made, the men and women you put away – their convictions will be overturned. And he'll be out. He'll be free. And he'll see what I've done in his name.'

Pharaoh feels as though her every thought is suddenly being drawn together by an irresistible force. Suddenly, she understands. Reuben Hollow killed the man who abused Madoc. Reuben has found his apostle. Reuben has sent him forth to destroy everything that matters to her. It's all been a lie. His every protestation of love has been a way to mask the white heat of his loathing for her.

'They'll need to see,' says Madoc, suddenly astride her again. 'They'll all need to see what's really under the surface. Those blue eyes keep people from seeing what you are. I can't let you keep them. I just can't . . .'

He pulls a hypodermic needle from the pocket in his apron. Pharaoh catches sight of the elaborate stitchwork on the pocket: a monogram: **RH**.

'It doesn't hurt as you'd think it would,' says Madoc, with a note of apology in his voice. 'It's not nice, but you've had worse pains. But don't wriggle about. If I go too deep you'll go blind. I don't care, but you might.'

He presses the plunger on the end of the syringe. Black ink trickles down the glinting needle. He angles his head and stares into her, as if reading something off the back of her skull.

'Please, Madoc . . . please . . .'

The needle comes closer. She pushes herself back into the ground. Tries to will her eyeball to sink into her skull.

The point pricks the lens of her left eye. It slides under the lens. He smiles, and slowly depresses the plunger. Black floods her vision like sadness.

He stands up. Drops the syringe back into his pocket. Rubs his hands together as if satisfied with a job well done. He snatches up the phone from beside her and looks at the screen.

'You saw?'

The voice is tinny. Far away. But Pharaoh recognizes it. Knows how wrong she's been from the start.

'Put her in the mask.'

Madoc does as he's told. It's sticky and sweaty and stinks of blood and rancid meat. It's silicon: a perfect replica of Anders Wilkie. It tugs at her hair and smears her black tears onto her cheeks. She feels his fingers in her mouth. She tries to breathe. Feels herself growing hotter, fainter.

Madoc stands. Considers her. Considers the half-naked woman who lies motionless on the floor, wearing his father's face and looking out into nothingness with his own black, black eyes.

He picks up the phone. Shows his handiwork to the God who commands his every action.

'Oh, Trish,' comes the voice. 'Are you a sight for sore eyes . . .'

TWENTY-FOUR

McAvoy waits until he's out of sight before he gives in to the pain. Only when he's sure that Roisin has led Kush and Prince up the hill towards the compound does he let himself sag, bending over as if he's run a marathon and letting great strings of blood and saliva fall from his mouth. His head's reeling and one of his ribs feels as if it's been snapped across somebody's knee. His arms ache all the way up to the shoulders. He feels as if he's made of gristle and brick dust; that the skeleton beneath his skin is no more robust than a scarecrow stuffed in a wetsuit.

He waits for the thudding pain to subside. Wipes his mouth. Stands and stares at the big pink moon. She'd promised him something was coming. Full moons are bad enough. He remembers reading that staff at mental-health facilities go out of their way to avoid working on the nights when the moon is fattest. He heard a radio show, months ago, with various experts offering their opinions as to why instances of mania and suicide are so much more prevalent beneath the bright lunar eye. They had spoken of the waves in the brain; how they might be affected by gravitational pull, like the tides. Roisin has never had any time for such scientific nonsense. She believes that the same ancient impulses that forced humankind to sacrifice white lambs and fair maidens to celestial bodies are still present in people today. The sight of the clear moon or the blazing sun simply unleashes that primal force. McAvoy isn't sure who to believe. McAvoy's never really sure of anything. He sometimes fears he's a Liberal Democrat.

Stalker's body hasn't moved. It lies in a mangled heap at the foot of the slope: spears of white rib sticking through his shirt-front in a mess of red and pink. Steam rises from the open wounds, mingling with the sparkling white frost. McAvoy isn't really sure what action would be appropriate to take. He should probably take off his shirt and cover him up: close his eyes so he stops staring sightlessly upwards into the blackness above. But he's also a police officer, and this is a crime scene, and Stalker has just tried to kill him. More importantly, McAvoy's wife has just trampled the big sod to death and there are probably going to be awkward questions to answer once the world wakes up. He probably shouldn't interfere with the body, all things told.

McAvoy squats down. Slips finger and thumb into the dead man's trouser pocket. Feels a pouch of tobacco and a cheap plastic lighter. He moves to the far side of the body and checks the other pocket. Unearths two empty crisp packets and a blister pack of pills. He holds them up and feels a gut punch of remorse. The young man was on citalopram, commonly prescribed for anxiety and depression. McAvoy wishes he could take back the past half hour of his life. The kid called Stalker shouldn't be dead. Kush shouldn't have emerged from the woods with a shotgun. Roisin shouldn't have had to come to his aid. He'd rewind all of it, if he could. He'd go all the way back to the day when Trish asked him to look into the suspicious death of Malcolm Tozer, and he told her he didn't feel ready and that she should ask somebody else.

McAvoy can't help himself. He leans forward and closes the dead man's eyes. There'll be hell to pay for that, at some point. But McAvoy can't help but feel there's always hell to pay – it's just a question of which creditor is most to fear.

He leaves Stalker on the ground and picks his way carefully down towards the vehicle. The engine's still warm, the underside of the chassis dripping sloppy mud onto the hard, sparkling earth. He opens the door with the hem of his shirt and takes a swift look inside. It smells of spicy food and unwashed men; cheap tobacco and wet wool. There are blankets in the back seat, one of them a multi-coloured jumble of crochet squares. There's a packed-lunch box in the rear footwell. McAvoy changes the angle of his neck to try and read the words on the square of paper tucked in between the apple core and the discarded crusts. He fishes a pen from his shirt pocket and manages to use it to spear the edge of the paper, moving it into the light from his phone. The message is simple and heartfelt.

I'm proud of you, love always, Mum.

McAvoy lets the note slip back into the box. His eyes feel hot and his bones ache. He can feel something in his gut that might be temper; might be shame. He feels as though he has done something unforgivable but he can't quite make sense of what it is he needs to lash himself over. Pharaoh tells him he's always feeling guilty about something: tells him that it's his inner Catholic. He sometimes wonders if she might be right. Everybody else in the western Highland community where he grew up was a member of the Free Church of Scotland: drifting in to cold, dour little kirks to worship a miserly God with joyless words of praise and offerings of quiet suffering. McAvoy's mother had brought the gift of Catholicism instead: no less full of self-loathing, but with considerably more glamorous pageantry. McAvoy is dispiritingly agnostic, now: hopeful of something more, but also fearful that there could be greater consequences to people's actions. He likes the idea of an afterlife if it means he gets to keep Roisin and Fin and Lilah by his side for the rest of eternity. But he fancies that after the fifth or sixth millennium, they might get a bit snappy with one another.

'Anything?'

McAvoy bangs his head on the doorframe. Turns around and sees his son making his way down the path. He's wearing his coat over rugby shirt and jogging pants and looks so much like his father that McAvoy feels like he might be staring down the wrong end of a telescope, gazing thirty years into the past.

'What are you doing, son?' asks McAvoy, rubbing his head. 'You shouldn't . . . did you see?'

Fin stops a few paces away. His face is pale, eyes shining. He saw Stalker's body. McAvoy feels his heart sink. Fin's known too much violence. He's seen too much horror.

'It's OK,' says Fin, quietly. 'I tried not to look.'

'It was an accident,' says McAvoy. 'Mammy didn't see him . . . it could have happened to anybody . . .'

Fin manages a weak smile. 'Lilah's with her. She's making hot chocolate. Kush is holding the gun, if you're wondering. I don't think he quite knows who to point it at.'

McAvoy takes a breath. For a moment, Fin's five again, and they're sitting in Hull's Holy Trinity Square. It's a bitterly cold day, snow in the air, and they're making each other laugh while they wait for Mammy to finish the Christmas shopping: Lilah in her belly and three credit cards in her purse. And they hear a scream. They hear the sound of pure and perfect suffering emerging from the open mouth of Holy Trinity church. McAvoy is up and out of his chair and running towards the sounds of danger before he even stops to consider his son. The look on the boy's face is forever imprinted in McAvoy's mind: his features twisted in shock and fright; an accusation in his tear-filled eyes – the question, forever unasked: who matters to you more, Daddy, the living or the dead?

Fin readjusts his coat. He takes McAvoy's poetry book from inside its voluminous folds. 'I can't get into it,' he says, apologetically. 'I think I'll stick with Heaney.'

'You'll write your own verses some day,' says McAvoy, a fond smile crinkling the edges of his eyes. 'You'll have the courage to say what you think.'

Fin gives a little shrug. McAvoy wants to hug him. He doesn't know whether it's for himself or the boy.

'You're going to see Reuben Hollow, aren't you?' asks Fin, without emotion. 'Mammy said.'

McAvoy feels his pulse quicken. 'He knows what's happening. He's involved. I can't make sense of it, but he's involved.'

Fin nods. 'Did you know that Lilah's first memory is of what
we found in the fog? At home? Outside?'

McAvoy's lips become a line. He thinks back to that mist-
wreathed spring night: the rotting body of the missing girl laid
out in a floral haycart on the strip of grass outside the McAvoys'
front door. Lilah had been little more than a toddler. But she'd
seen. She'd glimpsed the flesh and bones and ragged strips of
cloth. She'd breathed in the dead woman; taken particles of her
putrefying body inside herself.

'I'm not seeing him because I want to,' mutters McAvoy. 'I
need answers. Nobody knows where Auntie Trish has gone and if
these two are trying to set her up for murder, for what's happened
to the man who was visiting her; to her ex . . . it has to be him,
somehow. I don't know how it fits but I'll make him tell me.'

Fin's eyes widen in surprise. 'You'll make him? What are you
going to do? You're going to beat it out of him, are you? In a prison?'

McAvoy closes his eyes. Pinches the bridge of his nose. 'I'm
not like that, Fin – you know that.'

'I've seen you hurt people, Dad.'

'I've done what I've had to. I've never hurt anybody out of
choice.'

'I heard the podcast,' says Fin, scratching at the little shadow
of soft red beard that's sprouting on his Adam's apple. 'They don't
say it like it was. They make him out to be a hero or something.
People at school have heard it. They know you caught him and
some of them think you've put a good person in jail. All he was
doing was getting rid of bad people.'

McAvoy feels as if the blood in his veins is slowing: coagu-
lating: freezing. He can't stand to hear this. Hasn't got time. And
yet he wants to be a good man more than he wants to be a good
police officer. And if he can't find a way to be either, he can at
least be the best dad he can imagine.

'And you?' he asks, quietly. 'What did you make of it?'

'I think he's just as bad as the people he killed,' says Fin,
quietly. 'The man who took me – he had his own reasons for
wanting blood, didn't he? In his mind, what he wanted to do to
me was entirely justified. But you didn't let him do it. You came
for me and you stopped him. And I don't really know if you did
that as a police officer or just as my dad but I do know there's a

difference between what you did, and what Reuben Hollow does. And I know that the way you love me and Lilah and the way he loves his stepdaughter – they're different, aren't they? He's just about himself, really. And you don't think about yourself at all.'

McAvoy's mouth is dry as ash. He can't seem to remember how to swallow. Doesn't know what to say.

'You look all lost,' says Fin, with a little smile. 'That's the look you get that Auntie Trish makes fun of; when you go all sort of goldfishy.'

McAvoy feels himself beginning to thaw. 'Auntie Trish makes fun of me whatever I do. It's just her way.'

'Is she really in trouble?'

McAvoy gives a little nod of his head. He suddenly can't stand the idea of sitting across from Reuben Hollow. He can't abide the idea of grubbing around in the poisoned garden of his mind. He can't stand the thought of his handsome, self-satisfied face: can't watch him play the role that he enjoys so very much. He tries to think of a way that he can do something of use without having to spend time with the multiple killer who almost cost him his life. He's never understood how Pharaoh manages to tolerate his company: to flirt with him, indulge him; go along with his fantasies in the fading hope that he will give her the name and location of another body, and bring peace to another family. McAvoy doesn't believe himself capable of such performance. His blush always gives him away. And yet, he knows to his very bones that if Hollow tells him what is in store for Trish and is willing to make a deal to call off the dogs, McAvoy will give him whatever he wants. He wonders whether there really is such a difference between them and has to grip on tight to Fin's words so that he doesn't descend into the swirl of guilty introspection that so often leaves him inert.

'Mammy will be tired,' says McAvoy. 'I'll make sure the police come as soon as I know what's for the best. For now, just help her. Just make sure that the man with the missing earlobe doesn't try anything.'

Fin nods. He gives his dad an encouraging smile. 'You know how I once thought about becoming a police officer . . .?'

McAvoy nods, starting to untangle the braid from his beard and to brush the worst of the mess off his front. 'Aye?'

'I think I've gone off the idea,' says Fin, with a little grin.

McAvoy ducks back inside the vehicle, running his torch over the contents of the car one more time. He spots the button for the boot release and pushes down, hearing the satisfying clunk from the rear of the vehicle. Fin joins him by the open boot. McAvoy uses the tail of his shirt to lift the lid. It's empty save a clear plastic bag, its opening hanging loose, a trail of string leading to a label. It's marked as the property of HMP Bull Sands Fort and shows the name John Lee Prince. McAvoy has seen such bags before, clutched in the hands of prisoners on release day: their meagre possessions bundled up and dumped inside, along with anything that they had in their possession on their first day of incarceration. McAvoy looks inside. Gets the familiar whiff of soap and sweat and detergent. It's mostly clothes and a few items of crockery: a plastic mug and two hand-painted plates: sticky blobs of gaudy paint colouring in a honey bee and a flower and signed by Rosie, aged three. McAvoy reaches to the bottom of the bag. There are some paperback books and a stack of envelopes bound with string. McAvoy tugs them free. Takes the books and holds them up to the light. There are two adventure stories and a book on dealing with anxiety. McAvoy opens it up. It's a lightweight tome: a simplistic guide to helping people overcome trauma. McAvoy flicks through the pages. Some of the passages are underlined. There are asterisks against key sections and the tops of certain pages are turned down.

'I've read that one,' says Fin, peering at the book. 'It was one the doctor gave me. It was OK. A bit basic, but OK.'

McAvoy looks at the inside cover. It's not marked as being prison property. Somebody must have sent him it, along with the stack of correspondence. There would be no reason for the censors to block access to it.

McAvoy turns the pages. Midway down page six, the word 'time' is circled. On page 12, the second digit of the page number is similarly ringed. On page 32, the word 'repay' is underlined, twice. It takes McAvoy less than five minutes to turn it into a coherent message.

Time 2 repay your debts. You know what I did for you and I want just this in return. L C. Address will follow. You end him and you don't ask why. Take the boy – let him understand what it's

like to take a life. What I did was for him as much as you. You
know I remember my friends. But I remember those who let me
down. You do this, we're square. You let me down, I'll turn you
inside out. You'll be contacted. Don't let me down.

McAvoy reads it aloud to his son. Reads it again.

'And that's from Reuben?' asks Fin, making a face.

McAvoy straightens up. Fastens his top button and tries to brush
the sweat and leaves and blood from his hair. 'Somebody wanted
him to think so,' he mutters. He can't quite hold on to the tail of
his thoughts. He feels as though somebody is playing with him,
toying with him: feels like he's a dead leaf thrown to the breeze.

'He'll tell me,' says McAvoy. 'I know he will. He loves to talk.
Trish and him, they spent hours talking when she was trying to
reel him in. Told him things she's only shared with her closest
friends . . . things she wouldn't even tell me . . .'

He stops himself. Sucks his teeth and tastes blood. 'That book,'
he says, nodding to Fin. 'The poet . . .'

Fin rummages in his coat and retrieves the book of poetry.
McAvoy joins him. He's only a little taller than the boy. He shines
the light on the fly leaf. At the inscription.

For the only good man I know . . .

He angles the torch on the first page. The second. Flicks forward
at random and spots a faint circle around the word '*My*'. On the
following page, somebody has underlined the word '*solitary*' in
wavering pencil.

My solitary delight. I yearn for you. The world is weak and
asinine without your nearness. Please find a way to tell me that
I am still your one and only love. Nobody else understands. I shall
make them see. And you will know that in all things, I remain
yours to command. Command me, I beg you. Make me your instru-
ment. Give me a reason to hope. Yours eternally, RH.

'And he sent you that for your birthday?' asks Fin, giving his
father a funny look. 'That's a weird gift, Dad.'

'He sent it to Trish,' mutters McAvoy. 'And she gave it to me.'

'Why did she do that?'

'Because she thought I'd like it.'

'So he really is in love with her? Because, y'know, some people,
when they're in love, it's like . . . well, it's more like hate. If she
didn't respond to him, maybe he really would send somebody to

get her back, to hurt the people she cares about – to set her up or hurt her, or even . . .'

McAvoy takes his son in a bear-hug. Holds him so hard that his ribs sing with pain. Breathes him in and gets the same rush of scents and memories and feelings. Breathes in the cut grass and soap and feathers of his son's crown. 'Take care of your mammy,' he says. 'I promise, I'll be . . .'

He hears Fin give a hug of laughter against his shirtfront. 'You nearly said it,' he smiles. 'Nearly went all Terminator.'

McAvoy picks up the books from the boot of the car. Grabs the hardback of poetry. Reaches into the back seat and removes the crocheted blanket. He passes it to his son. 'Cover him up,' he says. 'He doesn't deserve to lie there cold.'

'Even though he tried to kill you?' asks Fin.

'He didn't,' says McAvoy, shaking his head. 'He was set up. Manipulated.' He turns and walks towards his own car, his parting words almost lost on the cold air.

'We all were.'

TWENTY-FIVE

They stand and smoke in silence, listening to the soft rumble of the waves caressing the sands; the pizzicato of rain on aluminium; the admonishing shush of waves rearranging pebbles on the shore.

Cross waits for Earl to say something. It feels strange, seeing him unbuttoned like this. He's let go of his accoutrements; shed the skin of his perfect political policeman. Here, now, in the shadow of the docks and the silent iceberg of the bobbing ferry, he looks like the copper he used to be, when he'd smoke and drink and talk shit with the lads. Cross is rather enjoying seeing him let himself go. Likes knowing that the man who can change his future is starting to panic, and that Cross has the power to make his life better, or worse.

A few steps away, Emma Redmore is sipping from a cardboard cup. From time to time she changes her position so she can see down to the waterfront; a shifting black mass beneath a riot of gulls, rising off the water like flakes of ash from a fire.

'It might be something else completely,' says Earl, flicking the cigarette butt into the water. He gives Cross a hopeful look – begs him with his eyes. Please, he's saying. Please tell me that you can make all this go away.

'Of course, sir,' says Cross, smoothly. 'It could be a clip from a film. It might not even have been live when it was sent. You and I might not even be chatting right now. It's all a matter of getting the narrative right.'

Earl presses his lips together into a line. Shoots a look at Redmore. 'And she's sound?'

'She saw it, sir. Better to have her inside pissing out than outside pissing in. And she's very loyal.' He gives a leer and a wink; two men of the world. 'I've taken steps, sir. She only opens her mouth when I tell her to.'

Earl runs his hand over his throat as if looking for a noose. 'A decorated officer, Ashley. Bit of a legend to many. If she's in danger . . .'

'If she's in danger, it could be viewed as her own silly fault, sir. She buggered off from the scene of a serious crime. She took steps to lose the officers tailing her. She ran straight into the mouth of the dragon, if you ask me. And given that we were running a covert operation that she had clearly sussed out, I reckon St Fucking Trish had plenty to hide and might just be getting what's coming to her.'

Earl shivers, drawing in his elbows. He clearly doesn't want to be here. He'd thought that having Cross dig into Pharaoh's past would give him the tools to lever her out of CID for good. Cross has done a good job in building a case. It's unlikely that they would be able to prove her complicity in her husband's death but he could at least trash her reputation and expose her for who he has long suspected her to be. He could threaten her pension, if nothing else. Threaten a full audit on her life and expose her for her extra-marital affairs and the blind eye she turned to her husband's dodgy business dealings. He could even make the case that she knocked him about and spread the rumour that she attacked him in the days before his stroke. Things were going absolutely fine. Now she's missing, and Cross has just watched a Snapchat video of a dark-haired, blue-eyed woman having her clothes cut off by a hulking great man in a mask. He knows he should be using all available resources to find her. But to do so would lead to so many questions and he isn't entirely sure his answers would stand up to scrutiny. He's grateful to Cross for being so discreet; for asking for this clandestine meeting and the opportunity to deal with things more privately.

'I can see how much you're struggling with this, sir,' says Cross, sympathetically. 'It's a huge call. And to have to make it because you ordered covert surveillance of a minor – the daughter of a senior officer . . . you'd need balls of stone, sir. And I know you have them. That's what we all admire about you. But you've got to think about a bigger picture than a mere underling like me could even hold in my head. Reputational damage to the Force, sir. Repercussions. All the cases that could be undone if it was found that Pharaoh was a bent copper . . . I don't know how you stay so calm.'

Earl knows he's being flattered. Cross makes no attempt to hide it.

'You have a suggestion?' asks Earl, carefully.

'Where she lost the tail, sir – out at Wawne. I've checked for a connection and her old boss, Tom Spink, shows up on the electoral register at a property not fifty yards from where she slipped away. I could do things discreetly, sir. He was on the list of people to speak to if we ever made the investigation public. I could be there inside half an hour.'

'And if somebody's snatched her? Hurt her? Killed her?'

'We were just a moment too late, sir. Good police work led us to track her down but the damage had already been done. In the aftermath, we tell whatever story works best. She was a hero who paid the price, or she was corrupt and it cost her life. I don't mind either way.'

Earl looks uncertain. He'd wanted Pharaoh humiliated. Wanted her embarrassed. Wanted her gone. He didn't want her brutally murdered by the same man who's already taken an adze to her Icelandic lover.

'McAvoy,' says Earl, carefully. 'He'll never accept that she was corrupt. None of her team will. It will have to be the hero narrative.'

'Hero it is, sir,' smiles Cross. He offers another cigarette to Earl, who declines. Looks to where Redmore is waiting, ready to be told how they're going to play things. He enjoys a moment's sense of satisfaction. She looks tough as leather but she comes apart like spun sugar now he knows where she likes to be squeezed. She'll convince herself of whatever lie best serves Cross's purpose. He finds it unfathomable just how badly people will allow themselves to be treated when they are in love. Hopes he never finds himself similarly compromised. 'As you say, it might be nothing.'

'Cuckoo in the nest,' says Earl, sadness in his voice. 'Never ends well, does it? Do you think she'll work it out? If he has her, he'll tell her who he is. The sheer brass neck of that husband of hers – no wonder the boy idolizes his memory and wants a bit of vengeance on his behalf.' He shakes his head, marvelling at the late Anders Wilkie's ability to show his wife who's boss, even from beyond the grave. A frown creases his forehead. 'The daughter. Olivia. She's going to call a friendly face, I presume? She watched the same video. She'll go straight to McAvoy.'

'He's far away, sir.'

Earl nods. 'It's entirely possible that she's about to walk into the hospital and sit at Thor's bedside. Then we carry on as before. We even get to arrest her cuckoo child for the attack on Thor, as planned. It could all go perfectly.'

'And if Madoc has her?'

Earl makes a face. 'I should imagine she's having a rather terrible time.'

Cross scratches his face. In a perfect world, things would be different. But it's not a perfect world, and if he has to choose between himself and Trish Pharaoh, he'll choose himself every time.

'St Fucking Trish,' marvels Earl. A little smile plays across his lips. 'That's the thing with the beatified. They do seem to die such horrible deaths.'

Cross nods. 'I'm Catholic, sir. Drowned in the blood of the martyrs.'

Earl claps him on the arm. Walks away.

A moment later, Redmore puts her hand around his waist. 'He really is going to let her die?'

Cross ignores the question. Slides his hand inside her coat and twists her nipple. Bites her neck.

'Dirty job,' he says, licking the salt from her throat. 'But somebody's got to do it.'

A686, Gilbern Bridge, Alston
6.14 a.m.

McAvoy scans the horizon for the first whisperings of sunrise. Finds none. It's still black as tar beyond the glass: the road shimmers with frost and the stars glisten pink beneath the big, blushing moon.

He glances in the rear-view mirror of the people-carrier. There are no vehicles behind. None in front. He presses the accelerator and allows himself to drift a little above the speed limit. Manages it for a mile until the extra tension in his arms brings on the beginnings of a migraine. He slows down again, double-checking that he hasn't been flashed by a concealed speed camera, or inadvertently run over a nun with a pushchair.

He catches a glimpse of himself in the darkened glass. Hates what he sees.

'. . . *I mean, this guy knows how to write a letter, yeah? That's some serious Dickens meets C. S. Lewis shit right there. Have you ever been threatened so gently? It's like being kerb-stomped with your mouth around a thesaurus . . .*'

He's listening to the latest update to 'Good Murders, Bad Deaths'. The host, Clementine, has received a letter from Reuben Hollow. It's wordy and theatrical and McAvoy isn't sure it's genuine. He'll get a chance to ask him, soon enough. He'll look into those blue eyes and beg him to stop whatever it is he's started. He'll offer him whatever he wants. He needs Trish to be safe. He needs her to be the police officer who has always shown him how to walk the line; how to be a good copper and a good person at once. In the decade that she's been steering him he has put real distance between himself and the catastrophically shy introvert who used to tie himself in knots trying to follow the letter of the law. He no longer hides behind the rules and regulations. He tries to uphold the law but there are times when he knows that he is committing a greater sin by following the prescriptions of an intractable justice system. He carries the scars of a man who isn't afraid to follow the evidence into dangerous situations. He doesn't know whether he will be able to be a police officer without Pharaoh to guide him. There was a time last year when he thought she was about to retire. She seemed to have lost all enthusiasm for the job and was drinking herself to death in her lonely little flat – ignoring her girls and paying only lip-service to her job as head of the unit. She turned down a promotion that would have given her authority over the entirety of CID. But he would accept her retirement, however grudgingly, rather than this grotesque alternative. Could she really be in danger? Could somebody really be hurting her? Could they be setting her up? He's heard endless whispers that she's being looked into by some of the higher-ups; that her late husband's business dealings are still the subject of some concern. He's tried to be the best friend he can be but she never wants to talk about her problems. He wishes she'd confide in him. Why the hell has she been seeing Reuben? What does she make of the podcast? She's his best friend and she's gone back to treating him like a barely tolerated colleague. Roisin claims that she's trying to toughen him up: to demonstrate that he doesn't need her, so he's ready to fill her shoes when she does step down. McAvoy takes no comfort in that. She either rates him by now, or she doesn't. And given how he's handled the Tozer case, he can't help but feel like he's failed some kind of a test.

The podcast cuts out as his phone rings. He jerks, startled. Glances up and sees that he's about to plough into the back of a delivery van. He jerks the wheel to the right and skids across the white line in a blare of honking and hissing brakes.

'Aector McAvoy,' he says, breathlessly, as he jabs at the controls on the panel and switches his phone to the speaker. He spots a sign telling him he's three miles from Alston. He's forty minutes away from Reuben.

'Is it really? Gosh.'

McAvoy turns up the volume. He doesn't recognize the number. Doesn't recognize the voice: female and cheerful and slightly Bristolian in its pronunciation.

'Yes, hello. Detective Inspector McAvoy, Major Crimes.'

'I didn't expect to get you at this hour. I was expecting a voicemail service – thought I could check if it was the right number then hang up. And here you are.'

McAvoy peers at the speaker. He hasn't got time for riddles.

'To whom am I speaking, please?'

There's a little laugh at the end of the line. 'To "whom". I like that. And it's Aector like Hector, is it? I wasn't sure.'

McAvoy turns the air conditioning down. Slows a little so that the tyres don't make such a racket on the road surface. He concentrates on the voice. There's something familiar there: a faint trace of blurred memory. 'I'm sorry, I'm on my way to somewhere important, so if you could please state your business I can see whether I'm able to help.'

There's a pause, as if the speaker is thinking about it. 'Finn,' she says, at last. 'Short for Fenella. I run the podcast with Clemmy. I sort of produce it too, if that isn't too fancy a word. Um, we wrote to you. Wrote a couple of times, actually. Do you know our show?'

McAvoy takes a moment. Marvels at the neatness of the moment. He'd been listening to her reading Reuben's letter a moment ago. And now she's calling. But her voice is markedly less polished now she's on the phone. Could it be a prank? A hoax? He certainly hasn't had any letters.

'I'm sorry . . . did you say it was Finn? Might I ask how you got this number?'

'I have your business card, as it goes,' she says, brightly. 'You gave it to a mutual acquaintance on a case a few weeks ago. I hope you don't mind.'

'No, no, it's no secret, but . . .'

'Good, good. Like I say, we've written to you.'

McAvoy has no reason not to believe her. He wonders whether Trish has been up to her old tricks – keeping things from him so he doesn't get overloaded with moral conundrums. He wouldn't put it past her to have insisted his post be redirected to her pigeon-hole. Emails too. She's more tech-savvy than she lets on.

'And how can I help, you please?'

There's a pause, stretched out and laden with things unsaid.

'It's tricky,' she says, at last. 'It's just, well, some of our regular listeners have been hitting our social-media account in the past couple of hours. We've had a few anonymous tips. Am I right in thinking that there's a warrant out for the arrest of Trish Pharaoh?'

McAvoy focuses on the road. Chews his cheek. Tries to keep his thoughts from sloshing out of his ears.

'I'm sorry, but there's a press office to deal with any questions like that. I'm actually on leave, at present, so I wouldn't be in the loop . . .'

'That's not a denial,' says Finn, a smile in her voice. 'We've been trying to get her on the show for an age but she's been very blunt in response to our enquiries – even when we've offered to pay a sum to the charity of her choice. We did speak to an old colleague of hers who was able to give us a little information and he suggested we try you instead, but I'm guessing from the lack of response to our emails and letters that you weren't keen either. May I ask why? Is there something to hide?'

McAvoy looks up to see the faint pink smudge of the sunrise creeping over the lip of the earth, casting a soft glow on the rises and dips; the rugged nothingness of the landscape. Forces himself to focus. He needs to hang up. Needs to do so right now.

'I'm right, aren't I?' asks Finn, her voice altering so she sounds more like her podcast persona. 'Is Reuben still where he's meant to be? Clementine reckons it's only a matter of time until he's out. Trish's reputation will be dirt if what we're hearing is true. Maybe now would be a good time to get ahead of the bad publicity and nail your colours to the mast. Tell me the truth. Is she really this crusading cop or is she the demon in disguise? We can make it sound however we want so maybe you help us out and we do you a good turn, and . . .'

'She's the best person I know,' says McAvoy, through gritted teeth. 'She deserves better than this.'

There's a little laugh from the speaker. 'Deserve? How can a police officer talk about the word "deserve" as anything other than an abstract concept? You're all scars and heartache and there are people living in mansions on the proceeds of crime without a single whiff of self-doubt. What's deserve got to do with anything?'

McAvoy buzzes down the window. Lets the cold air cool the sweat on his cheeks and brow. He aches all over. He fixes his gaze on the road ahead. Signals right and forces the people-carrier up the steep road through the little market town: picture-postcard shops twinkling in the frost; dead flowers in hanging baskets and colourless bunting flapping from boarded-up pubs.

'I'm hanging up. I hope Clementine has a bit more about her

than you. You're a psychiatrist, aren't you? Isn't there some ethical aspect to a job like that?'

She laughs again, a sound that chimes weirdly off-key, as if it's from a different time; a different place. 'I'm not really a shrink, Aector. It just gives us an air of legitimacy. And Clemmy, well – she reads a lot of books and has a fantasy about Ted Bundy and Karla Homolka. We met in a chat-room. We've never actually met in the flesh. The way the podcast took off – it caught us by surprise. We're just riding the dragon as long as we can, y'know? And it doesn't do us any harm to have Reuben Hollow's name on people's tongues.'

'You know nothing about Reuben Hollow,' says McAvoy. 'Christ, you must have read between the lines by now, haven't you? He took the fall for two murders that weren't anything to do with him and the rest were just to make him feel good. He's a monster.'

'Oh, you're one of these saps who blames the daughter, are you? What was she? Seventeen? And she was carving the armpits off the women who wronged her dad, was she? She was helping him pick his victims? She had that power, did she?'

McAvoy is about to respond when he glimpses the sign for HMP Warcop. His mind fills with a flicker-pad of images. Thinks of the big red-brick building with the slitty-eyed tower and the big black gates: the rust-coloured double-doors; the lime-green corridors and the endless clang and squeak of keys and doors and training shoes on rubber. He thinks of the darkness beneath the courtyard: the old cells, where the condemned were left to consider their mortality before a noose was placed around their necks and their problems ended for ever. He wonders how many times Hollow has wished for that sweet release; whether he ever cries in his cell – whether he has the wit and the guile to plot the righteous execution of everybody whom Trish Pharaoh cares about.

'Aector? Tell me about Delphine. Tell me what you really think.'

McAvoy kills the call. He grips the steering wheel until his knuckles gleam: rodent skulls pushing against his pale flesh. He locks his teeth.

A message pings through. It's from Ben Neilsen. He's made the appropriate arrangements. Hollow will be waiting in an interview room as soon as McAvoy arrives. Ben's had to pull some strings, but he's good at that.

McAvoy thinks about sending back some words of thanks but he knows he'll have to pull over if he wants to send a text message and he can't help but hate himself for that. He keeps driving. Tries to reach out in his mind; to grab at the different pieces of the puzzle and guide them together.

His phone rings again. It's Sophia, Trish's eldest daughter. He doesn't want to answer it. He doesn't want to know what she has to tell him.

'Sophia?'

Her voice is reedy, her throat tight. She's trying to control her breathing. A baby is crying in the background. He fancies he can hear the gentle cooing of Andy Daniells, doing his damnedest to be useful while the world tumbles down around him.

'Olivia just called me,' she says, trying to control herself. 'I didn't know. I swear I didn't. But she met this boy, you see. At Dad's funeral. We didn't know, I swear, I didn't know . . .'

'Didn't know what, Sophia.'

'My dad's son. Madoc. She's been talking to him. And then she stopped. He's really angry, Aector. And she's just opened a message from him. I think he's got Mum.'

McAvoy feels the hot coals in his guts turn to ice. His head fills with memories. For a moment, he and Trish are in the wine bar on Newland Avenue and she's laughing at him because he's twirling his hair around his finger. *My son does that*, she's saying. *He's ten.* He doesn't probe. Not then. Not even when he meets her four daughters and the shell of her husband. She'll tell him when she's ready, he thinks. And she never does.

'Where are you?' asks Sophia, urgently. 'Are you still with Kush? She was desperate for you to be there – to protect him in case anything happened. Is something happening, Aector? Is he really doing this? After all this time? It wasn't Mum who sent him away. He was dangerous. He tried to kill Olivia when she was a baby. He's out of his fucking mind!'

McAvoy pulls over. Rests his head on the steering wheel.

'Tell me,' he says, quietly. 'Tell me everything.'

PART THREE

TWENTY-SIX

M cAvoy hates prisons. Hates prisons like this most of all, squatting in the middle of the bare, bleak nothingness like a black tooth in a gummy smile. It's old and forbidding. Haunted, if you believe the stories. Men and women have been hanged here. There were three suspicious deaths last year. It has that smell: that boarded-up-school stench; something beyond the range of the normal senses. It feels like stepping into a black-and-white photograph of a lunatic asylum.

It hasn't affected Reuben Hollow. He looks well. Looks fighting fit. Leaner, prettier: his eyes two sparkling sapphires in a wolfish face.

Mrs Peach, a mumsy, incongruously cuddly prison officer in her mid-forties, leads him into the art room. He's holding a coffee in a plastic beaker: grey sweatshirt and blue jeans. He has a red handkerchief knotted at his throat. There's a cross on a gold chain winking out of his top. He still wears an earring. McAvoy looks down at himself. Hates everything he sees.

'Well,' says Hollow, with a grin. 'This is a surprise.'

He takes a seat on a hard plastic chair. Stretches, extravagantly, his top riding up to show off his lean stomach. Mrs Peach gives his shoulder a squeeze and throws McAvoy a warning look. Closes the door behind her and leaves them to it: a harassed mum hoping that her son and the neighbour's kid can be trusted to play nicely while she does the dishes.

McAvoy swallows, his throat dry. Scans the room for the umpteenth time. The art on the walls was painted by killers. There's a big cross-stitch praising the Lord; a series of gaudy flowers picked out in big daubs of poster-paint. There are books on the shelves: guides to form and figure, watercolours and animal-sketching. McAvoy tries to picture Hollow spending his days in such a place. He was a master craftsman, whatever else he did with his spare time. He wonders if they let him carve. Wonders whether he thinks they should, or to revel in the fact that they don't. He can never make up his mind about what to do with the people he arrests. He loves the idea of rehabilitation; has written reports on the benefits of treating drug addicts as medical patients rather than law-breakers. But what to do with the genuinely despicable? Where to house the dangerous? How to redeem the irredeemable? He's grateful that the solution isn't his to find.

'You're looking well,' says McAvoy. His voice sounds wrong. Sounds dry and weak. Sounds like a man who's had the stuffing knocked out of him.

'That's kind of you,' smiles Hollow, unblinking. 'I wish I could say the same.'

'It's nothing,' shrugs McAvoy, before he can stop himself.

Hollow lets out a little groan, rolling his eyes like a teenager who's just seen their parents singing along to a song they shouldn't know. 'It's nothing,' he repeats, grinning. 'Trish thinks you may have a masochistic streak, y'know?' He narrows his eyes, inspecting him properly. 'The scar above the eye – that's new. I bet those hands feel agony on cold mornings.'

McAvoy combs his hair with his fingers. Tries to keep the colour from his cheeks. 'I took a new scratch in the early hours, as it happens. Knife.'

Hollow lifts his top and inspects his stomach. Looks up, all innocence. 'Roisin patch you up, did she? Knocked up a poultice of cobwebs, dandelion heads and spit, did she? Honestly, Aector – you'll believe anything.'

McAvoy feels the moisture evaporate from his mouth. Feels his tongue sticking behind his teeth. He holds Hollow's gaze. 'I can't say I like it when you mention Roisin's name,' he says, quietly. 'Or Trish's, for that matter.'

Hollow offers him the cup of coffee. McAvoy shakes his head. Hollow grins again, utterly unconcerned. 'Really?' he asks. 'You'll forgive me if I don't quite give a tinker's fuck for what bothers you and what doesn't.'

McAvoy hopes he's touched a nerve. 'You sound bitter.'

Hollow raises his hands, palms up. 'Four life sentences will do that to a person.'

McAvoy picks up a paintbrush from a pot. Strokes the hard, paint-stiffened bristles against his palm. He's surprised that Category A prisoners are allowed access. In Hollow's hands, such an object could kill. In McAvoy's too.

'I'd have thought you were living your best life,' says McAvoy, swallowing hard. He works some spit back into his mouth. Tries to be a police officer. 'Infamy. Notoriety. Adoration, here and there.'

Hollow breathes out, long and slow. 'I'd swap it for a little patch of woodland and my bare feet planted in the wet grass.'

McAvoy stops thinking. Lets the words flow. 'I don't think you would, Reuben,' he says, shaking his head. 'I think you'd be bored inside half an hour and need to go and find some vulnerable young beauty who would give you a noble reason to take a life.'

Hollow stretches again. He seems to be enjoying himself. 'I've waited years to see you again, Aector. Now I'm looking at you I can't work out the fascination. You're a big toddler really, aren't you? Wouldn't move a step in any direction unless Trish or Roisin were holding your hand.'

McAvoy feels his temper rise. He puts his hands beneath the Formica-topped table. Grabs at the material of his trousers until his knuckles are white. 'I know what you've been doing, Reuben,' he says, quietly. 'Your thugs didn't get the job done. Stalker's dead. And Prince has told us everything.'

Hollow wrinkles his nose. 'Everything? I don't think that's likely. He has to close his eyes when he's got his mouth full, poor sod. Not a great thinker, that one.'

McAvoy looks up at the clock above the door. Wonders how it feels to mark time when you know you're sitting in the place where you will see out your days.

'You manipulated him,' says McAvoy. 'John Lee Prince. He's under arrest as we speak. I know what you did for him. Ensured he was in debt to you; that he became another of your adoring fans. You killed the one person he'd have given anything to get his hands on. Maurice Bruce, yes? And then you sent him out to kill on your behalf the moment he got his release papers.'

Hollow inspects the back of his hands. 'I've killed somebody, have I? Thought I'd remember.' He narrows his eyes, as if trying to place a face. 'Stalker, you say? Big lad? John's stepson? He's dead? That's tragic.'

'You sent him to his death,' snaps McAvoy, grinding his teeth.

Hollow rolls his eyes again, bored of the conversation. 'I wouldn't even send that big lump for chips, Aector. Who was he supposed to be bumping off on my behalf?'

'Kush,' says McAvoy. 'Laurence Kidd, on his birth certificate.'

Hollow makes a show of thinking. Scratches at his chin. 'I think I've smoked kush, in my time. It's a strong weed, that one. Helps you see things.'

McAvoy sits forward. 'Why are you doing this, Reuben? Trish has always played fair with you. She got all the help she could for Delphine. How many detectives come and visit the serial killers they've put away? But she comes to see you, doesn't she?'

Hollow lets the echo of McAvoy's rising voice fade away. Sits forward. They face each other like two chess players hunched over a board.

'You sound jealous,' he says, smoothly. 'Can't understand what she sees in you. Still, we all have a type.'

McAvoy's temper frays. 'You're still into women with hairy armpits, I take it?'

Hollow grins, licking his lips. 'That's an over-simplification. I like the natural look. The scent. The carnality of sweat. What's your thing? Teenage Gypsies?'

McAvoy feels it like a punch to the gut. 'Don't,' he says, feeling pitiful.

'Sorry, that wasn't necessary,' says Hollow, looking momentarily sincere. He breathes out, slowly, as if considering his options. 'I really don't wish you any ill, Aector. Trish neither. We will always disagree about whether I deserve punishment for what I've done. I enjoy the cut and thrust of debate. Some days I feel something close to shame. But honestly, the amount of people who send me pictures of themselves, or their wives; the begging letters, wishing I was still outside, able to lend a hand.'

McAvoy isn't sure whether to let the conversation play out or steer it back in the direction he needs. He plays along. 'To kill, you mean?'

'To serve as a warning to bad people,' says Hollow, simply.

'You're bad people, Reuben,' says McAvoy, and manages a smile.

'Oh shush, you silly man,' says Hollow, shaking his head. 'It's like arguing with a sponge . . .' He stops, midway through the insult. A different look passes across his face, as if he's just woken from a dream and is trying to remember the details before it fades. 'Is Trish OK?'

'Trish?'

He looks frustrated, suddenly. Impatient. 'I can't think why she'd send you to talk to me unless she was indisposed. What's happened? Did the Viking give her more than she could take?'

McAvoy almost admires the performance. He looks genuinely concerned. He's seen this look on plenty of people's faces over the years; has stood on no shortage of doorsteps and asked the residents whether they are related to the dead and the dying. Hollow has the same look on his face. He looks afraid.

'The Viking's in intensive care,' says McAvoy, coldly. 'Somebody took an adze to him as he was leaving her flat in the early hours of this morning.'

'An adze?' asks Hollow, pushing himself back in the chair and rocking on two legs. 'You saw it?'

'We've analysed the shape of the wound,' says McAvoy. 'Woodcarver's implement, yes?'

Hollow nods, as if he's an expert witness rather than a suspect. 'Yeah, yeah it is. I had a vintage one. Absolute beauty. Great heft to it and the tang of the blade was beautiful. Fuck, poor bloke. Is she coping?'

McAvoy lets the sourness in his gut bleed into his expression. 'Don't act like you care.'

Hollow shakes his head. Licks his lips. Some of the colour's gone from his face. 'One thing you can take to the grave with you, Aector – I care about Trish. I care about her the same as you do. Is she at his bedside?'

McAvoy wants to grab him by the throat. Wants to smash his fist into his handsome face.

'We don't know where she is,' he says, teeth bared. 'That's why I'm here.'

Hollow looks at him like he's simple. 'Well, she's not bloody here, is she? Have you asked the kids? I know she was putting down the drink but maybe she'd gone off on one like she did when they buried Anders . . .'

McAvoy pushes away from the table. Stands up. Paces back and forth to keep his anger from spilling out.

'I didn't come here for suggestions, Reuben. I want answers. You're doing this, we know that. Where is she?'

Hollow stands up. He's smaller than McAvoy but he seems to take up just as much room. He glares back at him, eyes so like Trish Pharaoh's that it makes him want to look away.

'Done what?' he demands. 'I'm locked up, you silly bastard. And what's this Kush got to do with it? And Stalker? Have you got some mad theory in your head? Bloody hell, I haven't even had my second coffee yet. I can try and ring her, if you want. She might pick up for me . . .'

McAvoy feels like his brain is going to spill out of his ears: feels it rising like pudding batter inside the oven of his skull. 'Malcolm Tozer,' he says, hoping to wrong-foot him.

'No, I'm Reuben Hollow,' he says, enunciating each syllable. 'Used to be Oliver Millichamp but I changed it. Much prefer this, thanks.'

McAvoy slams his fist down on the table. The coffee cup jumps up. Hollow snatches it from the air before it spills.

'You know the name,' growls McAvoy. 'Malcolm Tozer. You know her so well, you know that name.'

Hollow shrugs. Sips his coffee. 'Her first boyfriend?' he asks, as if dredging up the memory. 'Bit of a lump? Ratty fellow from Crowle, wasn't he? Her husband had a bee in his bonnet about him. So what?'

'He's dead,' says McAvoy, simply.

'That's tragic,' says Hollow, without emotion. 'And?'

McAvoy feels himself losing control. He needs Trish. Needs her to be safe and at his side. 'Why did you send your acolytes after Kush?'

Hollow shakes his head. He talks without temper. 'I don't know who Kush is, Aector.'

'Real name Laurence Kidd,' he insists, and realizes he's got his hands in his hair, tugging at the roots.

'Nope, still . . .' He stops himself. Something passes over the blue of his eyes, the shadow of a bird of prey.

'I saw that,' spits McAvoy. 'Saw the flicker.'

Hollow sits down again. Chews his lip.

McAvoy forces himself to calm down. Sits. Tries again.

'Reuben, somebody killed Malcolm Tozer a couple of weeks

back. Possible hit and run. It was a bad death. And last night, John Lee Prince and the lad he cares about, they came to kill Kush at his little encampment in the Lakes. They were acting on your orders. You didn't tell them the whys or the wherefores but he joined up the dots when he heard her name. You were setting her up for his murder. And they knew what would happen if they didn't do as they were told. I've seen the letter, Reuben, the clever little coded messages. You set him up.'

Hollow looks pained, as if his thoughts are twisting around themselves. 'Coded messages? Are you having a stroke, Aector? You're talking gibberish. Scottish gibberish, which is worse.'

'Malcom Tozer,' growls McAvoy, his head all smashed glass and static. 'Thor Ingolfsson. This is you. This is all you!'

Hollow looks blank. Looks like a little boy who doesn't know why people are shouting at him and doesn't think it's fair. He wrinkles his nose. 'You'll have checked to see if she's at Tom's, yeah?'

McAvoy scowls, hating the fact that this killer knows where Trish would run to. 'Don't change the subject.'

'Tom Spink,' he says again. 'Is he still in that place that's falling into the sea? It's there or her Sophia's for certain. Or she could even be at your place, if you've been away, which you clearly have. You look like a woodsman . . .'

McAvoy presses his hands into the table, splaying his fingers. He looks as though he's about to start chopping his own digits off in sheer frustration. 'Reuben,' he pleads, weakly, 'please, stop playing games.'

'Who's with her daughter right now?' he asks, quietly. 'With her youngest. Olivia.'

'She's safe.'

'You're sure?' he asks, like a doting dad. 'And what about Sophia?'

'I know how much you know about her,' says McAvoy. He wants to leave. He hates the smell of this place. The cold, regurgitated air. 'You don't have to show off. You're so smart, tell me about the dahlia tubers. About your little sculptures.'

Hollow seems to freeze. For a full five seconds he just stares at nothing. Something seems to sag inside him, as if a fire has gone out. Slowly, he puts his hands on the table in imitation of

McAvoy. Looks into his eyes. His eyes seem less blue, somehow. For a moment, he looks genuinely sorry for him.

'He'll come for you last,' he says, quietly. 'He'll take everything, then take away the last drops of hope.'

McAvoy grinds the heel of his hand into his eye. He can't get his breath. 'Who will?'

'He's going to make her pay for every betrayal.'

'Betrayal of whom?' asks McAvoy, trying to work out what he's said that has changed the course of the interview.

'He's taking revenge against all the men she's ever cared about,' says Hollow, and he closes his eyes, face turning the grey of a church roof. 'Every man she's shared a connection with. Everybody she's slept with . . .'

McAvoy stops. Closes his eyes. Pulls the different strands together in his mind.

'Madoc,' he says, at last. 'Her husband's child.'

Hollow nods, running his tongue over his teeth. 'She's never forgiven herself, you know that, yeah?'

McAvoy recalls the fire and flame in Sophia's voice; the fear as she spoke of the boy with the dark eyes. 'She sent him away,' he says, quietly. 'That's right, isn't it?'

'She had too much to deal with,' says Hollow, and the way his face looks when he speaks about Pharaoh is almost too much to bear. 'She would have taken him back, in the end. But he was already in the system. He was dangerous. And once they get in there . . . they don't come out the same.'

McAvoy scratches his beard. Watches a flake of dried blood pinwheel down and land on the table between them. 'She spoke to you about him?'

'She spoke to me about everything. But I wasn't the only one listening.'

'And you're telling me you don't know him? That you haven't tracked him down and wound him up and sent him out to do your bidding?'

'I'm not Hannibal Fucking Lecter,' says Hollow, looking confused. 'Yeah, I know about him because she told me most of her life story within an hour of us meeting. She was trying to trap me, remember? But she used the truth to do it. We shared something. But I had to take steps just like she did.'

'I don't understand,' says McAvoy, kneading his knuckles with his palm.

'He's insane, Aector,' says Hollow. 'If he was in and out of facilities when he was a teenager I wouldn't be surprised to learn that he's only recently been released. And if he's been inside the mental-health system, well . . . he might have met somebody who knows a lot about dahlias.'

McAvoy feels his pulse slow. Thinks of a red-haired girl. Broad shoulders; that earthy smell; the dirt beneath her fingernails; her tinctures and potions and the cherry wine they found in the stomach of two dead women.

'She's better, isn't she?' asks McAvoy, wishing it was true. 'Your daughter. She's well.'

Hollow laughs. 'What's well, Aector? She killed two people to try and protect me from prison. She cut their armpits off because she was jealous that I liked their scent. She tried to kill Trish the same night you caught me. And she's very good at getting people to believe her stories. You think some mood-stabilizing drug and talking therapy is going to change that?'

McAvoy can't bring himself to believe him. 'And you're telling me this because?'

'Because I care about Trish,' he says.

'One of your sculptures was left in the wound,' growls McAvoy. 'Pushed deep into Thor's back. Dahlia tuber, too. Same with Tozer.'

'Black dahlias are what you would give somebody in Victorian times if you believed they had betrayed you.'

McAvoy swallows. Tastes blood. 'Would she know where you kept your tools?'

'We buried them together – when we thought you might be getting close. There's a little church about ten miles from where we used to keep the caravan. I had a commission to tart up the gargoyles and carve a new lectern. Good money. There was a grave, still fresh.' He glares at McAvoy. 'The bastard no doubt used my bloody adze.'

McAvoy wipes his nose on the back of his hand: a smear of blood on his knuckle. 'Trish knows the place?'

'It's out Speeton way. Mile or so from her mate's house. Tom.'

McAvoy stands. His limbs feel numb. His mind is all ripped pictures and loose threads.

Hollow looks up at him. 'This is all for me, isn't it? This is Delphine's way of getting my attention. She sent flowers to Trish and you to me. This is what she's wanted since you arrested me. You and me, together. No sucker-punches.'

'I never sucker-punched you. I just got lucky.'

'Bollocks,' snarls Hollow. He shakes his head, trying to focus on what matters. 'She never did understand what I was trying to do. I only ever killed people who were doing harm.'

'Hannah Kelly didn't do any harm. Ava Delaney.'

'That's not true,' says Hollow, shaking his head. 'They black-mailed me. Delphine was doing what she thought was right.'

'That fucking podcast . . .' grunts McAvoy.

'Don't swear, Aector – it doesn't suit you. Pharaoh says you're the only good person she knows.'

McAvoy thinks of the poetry book. Closes his eyes.

'I think, if you look, you'll find Madoc was briefly fostered by Maurice Bruce,' says Hollow. 'Making sense, now?'

'So Madoc would hero-worship the man who killed him, yes?'

'Probably. You're the poet. You understand human beings better than I do.'

McAvoy pinches the bridge of his nose. 'Why do you call me a poet?'

'Come on, with the sad eyes and the true love and the deep, dark chasm in your heart? You're a poet in your bones. A Romantic, certainly. I think I'm probably Byron to your Shelley.'

'You can make her stop,' says McAvoy.

'I can't make Delphine do anything.'

'You said you did. At the trial, you said it was all you.'

'I'm not a total bastard, Aector.'

'You need to contact her,' says McAvoy, rounding the table and taking Hollow by the arm. 'I'll speak to the governor. You can call her off. However she's done it, she needs to know this isn't what you want.'

Hollow slips inside McAvoy's grasp. Finds the spot where the blade went in. Jabs it, delicately, with his thumb. He slips away as McAvoy doubles over. Wipes the blood on his jeans.

'You don't touch me, Aector. Nobody touches me. There are people here who want me dead. Others who think I'm a fucking hero. I take steps, you understand that. I didn't know what he was up to; what he had planned. Fuck, the dirty bastard must have been having a ball.'

'Who?' wheezes McAvoy. 'What are you talking about?'

Hollow bends down. Angles his head so he can smile into McAvoy's face. 'Bad things are going to happen, Aector. But it can work out if you trust me.'

'Trust you . . .'

Hollow walks to the far side of the room. From the back of the tapestry, he removes a tiny mobile phone. He tosses it to McAvoy, who catches it from the floor.

'Don't look at me like that,' says Hollow. 'Now, you tell whoever's looking where to find her, OK? And then you do exactly as I say.'

McAvoy looks at the phone. Looks at Hollow. Thinks of the dead and the dying, the living and the damned. He nods. Calls George Earl's number from memory.

'Sir. It's McAvoy. I know where she is . . .'

Hollow nods. Grins. Blows a kiss into the air and hopes it flaps its way, butterfly-like, to the cheek of his brilliant daughter.

It's all going exactly to plan.

TWENTY-SEVEN

St Oswald's Church, Buckton, East Yorkshire
6.46 a.m.

Trish Pharaoh and Delphine Hollow are sitting in high hard-backed chairs, watching the glowing coals in the fireplace. The only other light in this square, sturdy room comes from the fat church candles at the centre of the long table. Shadows dance upon a ceiling the colour of home-made butter. The room smells of bread and fresh flowers, of Pharaoh's cigarettes and the perfume she has sprayed in her hair. Smells of a teenage girl who spends her days outside and didn't shower this morning. Smells of dried grass, burning on hot stone. It's a hot, dark and comfortable space, and makes Pharaoh imagine horse brasses and cider.

She feels somehow transplanted, as though she has been shoved, bodily, into another time, where women darn socks by the fire and the men swig ale from pewter tankards. Both she and Delphine are drinking pear brandy. Pharaoh is holding her customary black cigarette in her right hand and her mobile phone in her left. Occasionally, she reaches up to push her hair back from her face, or to bat at the moth which keeps fluttering against her cheek.

And now Trish is sixteen. She's got bare brick against her cheek and her knickers around her knees and Mally Tozer is pulling at her bra straps like they're reins and he's grunting and telling her she's the best at this; the fucking best and . . .

. . . first day in her blues. Silly and proud and self-conscious and scared all at once; walking the same streets she grew up on, listening to the jeers; the shouts from old school-mates telling her she looks like an Oompa-Loompa in uniform. Mally, trying to feel her up through her blouse; pissed outside the chip shop, telling her he doesn't care what she calls herself now, she's still his, still the same slag she always was, and he's pushing his greasy hand into her face and pushing her down and she's on her back and he's holding her down, laughing, laughing, spitting right in her fucking eye, and then she can breathe again and a big lad with a dark beard and a gold earring is smacking the shit out of Mally and there are coppers everywhere and she can't work out if she's angry or scared . . .

. . . a proper copper, now. Detective. Tom Spink's blue-eyed girl. Drinker. Smoker. Couple of collars under her belt and hand-some, suave Anders Wilkie at home in her bed. Ring on her finger now. Fancy meals out and swish holidays and a cleaner twice a week. Pregnant, now. Playing mum. Playing housewife. Bigger house, bigger car, bigger belly as the babies come along again and again. And Anders is getting nasty. He's lashing out. He's glaring at her when she's not looking; snapping at the kids, keeping secrets, telling lies. He's spending like crazy and the numbers in the account are falling, falling. He's taking calls late at night and asking her to find out dirt on rivals, enemies, investors, partners. And she's doing what he says because he's started hurting her. Slaps first. Then punches in the places that won't bruise. He's started pulling her ear so hard that the cartilage keeps breaking. No visible injury but the pain makes her head ring. He's fucking around. Drinking too much. People are coming to the house asking for money and all the while she's locking up villains and climbing the ladder to the pinnacle of CID . . .

Madoc, now. The boy with the dark eyes. The silent, brooding, dangerous boy who used to touch Sophia while she slept; who stabbed the goldfish in the ornamental pond; who tried to drown his own sister and left her wide-eyed and blue, staring at the sky . . .

And now it's that night. Anders coming home and telling her it was all over. He'd lost everything. There was no money left and bad people were coming for him. He was leaving. Going to one of the girls who still thought he'd deliver on his promises. And she's hitting him in the back, slapping him, sobbing, begging him to stay; telling him that she loves him; they need him; that they can get through it all together; that they're all here for him; his wife, his girls, his son. And he punches her full in the face. Smashes his hand into her nose like she's a mugger with a knife. He turns and walks away. Instinct takes over. She runs after him – the kids holding her back. He hits her again. Sophia drags her back towards the house. She sees the pipe; the length of steel railing that the workman has just cut from the fencing around the garage . . .

And now she's looking down at Anders in his hospital bed. Catastrophic brain aneurysm, they say. Could have happened at any moment, they say. He can't move. Can't communicate. He's going to need round-the-clock care. The creditors are coming calling. They business is sunk; the girls' school fees haven't been paid in months. Credit cards, loans; emergency loans; deals with loan-sharks and money-lenders. And then the handyman's on the doorstep, telling her he's got this video; something she needs to see.

Now it's just McAvoy. McAvoy and his big silly face and his stupid brown eyes and his desperate desire to please, and the people they've caught and the lives they've saved and the things they've done. And it's Anders, shrivelling away in the bed in the garage. Sophia, screaming in her face that she's a terrible mum. Olivia, asking her about the night it happened; about what happened to Dad.

And then she's in the living room of Tom Spink's bungalow, and it's all flies and the smell of dead meat. It's a man with the

face of Anders Wilkie. It's pain and fire and paralysis and a fear
that she's going to end her days like her husband; trapped and
alone and with nothing but regrets for company.

Here. Now.

This chill, dank space beneath the earth. A straitjacket around
her upper body; leather straps holding her legs. She can't talk for
the fire in her throat. Can't see in this absolute blackness. Can't
hear him any more. Can't even find the strength to shake the bad
memories away. She pictures Thor. Wonders if he's made it through.
Thinks of Tom, and weeps. Of Malcolm Tozer. Of Reuben and
Delphine. Thinks of Kush, and the video he shot by accident.
Thinks of Anders, and the way he first held her.

Sobs, silently, and her tears run into her ears, and down, to fall
upon the cold earth.

And Madoc Wilkie watches, wearing his father's face. Watches,
and smiles, and rubs his black eyes with fingers that taste and
smell of the dead man upstairs. Sometimes he plays with the adze.
Sometimes he fondles the chisels and the blades and the awl from
the soft leather roll of craftsman's tools. The man who used to
own them has shown him the way. He has set him on the path
to peace of mind. He did him a great service, and now expects
one in return. And Madoc is performing his task with gusto. He
didn't even know he wanted to kill Trish Pharaoh. Now he finds
it extraordinary that it took him so long to see the truth. He's eager
to start, now. Eager to perform the transformation that has been
demanded.

He looks at the phone on his knee. Waits for the call. They
want to see. Where would be the fun if he were to perform these
ministrations without an audience?

He wonders if Kush is dead yet. Hopes so. Hopes the Icelandic
man is dead also, though it doesn't really matter any more. It was
always going to come down to what happens next. It was always
going to be about Trish, and the man whose name she whispers,
silently, in the grip of her suffering.

Madoc strikes the mask with his fingertips. Wishes he could
conjure a good memory of his father. Wishes he could think of
some ill carried out upon himself by Trish or the girls. It would
be easier, he thinks, if he could remember what they'd done to
him. But he knows that his mind cannot be trusted. He's ill. He's

damaged. He's endured more trauma than anybody should have to. It's only right that he should trust somebody with the sense of conviction and purpose that Madoc lacks. It's right that he put his faith in the master craftsman, and in so doing, honour the father that she murdered over so many years.

From time to time, he crosses, silently, to where she lies. Takes her nipple in his mouth. Strokes her face. She doesn't fight him. All the stories he's heard about her and she doesn't even try to fight. Just cries, and dies, in pitiful little increments.

Madoc's getting bored.

He can't wait to hear what she'll say when she finds out just what a transformation is in store.

TWENTY-EIGHT

6 .57 a.m. Three minutes and then it all starts again. Same shit, different . . .

No, he thinks, adrenaline flooding him: a kid at Christmas; a Muslim at Eid. No, today's the fucking day. Today's the day it changes for ever. Today's the day the world stops, and rotates, and turns back the way it fucking came.

He keeps his eyes closed. Listens to the shouts from the landing. The threats. The promises that today's the day. Feels the dreams recede: a tide of black petals and rotten tubers; thorns pricking skin and eyeballs turning blue.

He yawns. Takes a chunk out of the air. Swills and swallows. Takes the fetid grey air inside of himself and feels it seep into his flesh. Smells disinfectant. Piss. A whisper of burning toast. Smells his own self; brine and onion skins, gingivitis and clay.

He says his prayers. They're not to any particular god. He doesn't trouble himself with questions of monotheism; polytheism; agnosticism. He believes in the indecipherable something. He has to believe there's something more than this. He doesn't want a Heaven or a Hell but he'd be happy with a second chance. Reincarnation might be nice. Prayers seem important, no matter the recipient. He finds that he can't lie in his prayers. He knows precisely how he feels about himself when communing with the great unknown. There is no dissembling when he talks directly from the heart. And it seems somehow important that prayers be the first action of his day. Promises are easy to keep when they're made at night. It's no hardship to fall asleep knowing that you'll be able to keep your word for at least the next few hours. They mean more at dawn. It's harder to keep your vows when you've got to spend your day on the nonce wing surrounded by people who want to kill you. Try being a good man then. Try praising God with acts of decency when you've got to sift through your dinner for ground glass and half a dozen lads want to take a toothbrush shank to your throat.

Thank you, he says, under his breath. *Thank you for the gift of life. Thank you for the beauty of the world. Thank you for listening to me and for granting me these moments outside the same bare walls. Forgive me my transgressions. I cannot pretend to know what you find sinful but for any and all actions committed against your wishes, I am truly sorry. I hope I am atoning, in some small way. I hope to be the best version of myself. I hope to lead a life that pleases you. I hope to do more good than harm. I do not imagine that you will be offended by the harm I must do. The blood I must spill will fall upon a righteous path. This much I know above all else. Thank you for the love I have known and the hate that keeps me alive. Thou art with me, and I am with thee. Amen.*

Bang. Bang. Bang.

'Rise and shine. Up and at 'em.'

A muttered reply from the top bunk. 'Fuck off, Cartmel.'

A snort, from the doorway. 'Put it away, Foster. You'll go blind.'

Guttering breath. The sound of bananas being peeled. Wet snufflings and the squeak of bedsprings. Foster, starting the day he always does.

The man in the bottom bunk pulls his covers back. Yawns extravagantly. Aims a kick at the place where Foster's arse should be. The noise stops.

'Amen.'

'And you, Handsome. Alarm not go off?'

'Two sugars, if you have a spare moment.'

'You're a cheeky bastard, you know that?'

He swings his legs around and puts his feet on the cold floor. Stands.

Cartmel looks him up and down. Cartmel's old-school. 'Meeting with your personal officer this morning, laddo. Legal rep this afternoon. I feel like your fucking secretary. Solicitor's letter here, too.'

He feels his pulse quicken. Feels the excitement crawling up his throat like a blush.

Looks at the name on the envelope. *Reuben Hollow*. HMP Warcop. Cumbria. It's stamped with the official ink-blot of Dolan and Finlay. It hasn't been opened. It's for his eyes and his alone.

Cartmel scowls. Shoots a look at the nonce on the top bunk and shakes his head. Walks back onto the wing as if fleeing an infected space.

He sits back on his bed. Slides his finger under the sealed flap. Does it slowly, as if the envelope is knicker elastic and he is prolonging the excitement for some lucky lady. Raises it to his nose and breathes in. Inhales. Sucks her scent right down into himself. Breathes out like a smoker – a long, slow exhalation; a miasma of sweat and sex, tobacco and lip gloss.

He removes the letter from its sheath. Finds himself smiling. It's all been so fucking easy.

Everything is in place. I'll be watching. So will she. Enjoy yourself, my love. Take out every last frustration. He's timber, waiting to be carved into a more pleasing shape. I love you. X

There's a sanitary towel folded into the single sheet of paper. It contains her scent. He holds it to his nose. Hardens at once.

He stands. Touches himself. Looks in the little mirror over the sink and likes what he sees. Prison has agreed with him. He enjoys the gym. Has the library to himself most of the time. He attends poetry classes; creative-writing classes. He's got a cushy job in the Education Department, opening letters and filing. Sometimes he writes to the families of other inmates: birthday cards, anniversaries; plaintive missives about life and jail and hope and loss. He gets to teach people with their writing. He's doing a six-week pottery course after the Easter break. He's got correspondents aplenty. He'd be happy enough inside if it wasn't for the absence of purpose. He's always been a man with particular needs. And prison doesn't satisfy them. Speaking to the prisoners makes him feel jealous. He knows this means he's probably made wrong. Knows that the things he wants to do mark him out as somebody for whom normality would only ever be a facade. But these past weeks he's been permitted to be himself. *She* understands. She likes him just the way he is. She rewards him in the ways he needs. A few letters; a little turning a blind eye; the occasional misdirected envelope. It's been so easy to make her happy. He feels nothing for the people who'll have to suffer in order to give her what she wants.

Sometimes, Mr Corcoran thinks he's got more in common with the inmates than with the rest of the staff. It's not a thought he enjoys. He would not survive prison were he unable to open the cell doors. And yet, he's willing to risk everything to make her happy. He's willing to risk his liberty just to please the only person who has ever understood what goes on inside his head.

Mr Corcoran shadow-boxes for a full five minutes; his hands a flurry. Works up a fine sheen of sweat. Rubs his hands into his wet armpits and rubs them over his nose, enjoying his own rankness. Thinks of her. Takes a piss. Brushes his teeth. Spits blood and froth into the sink. Tucks the sanitary towel into his boxer shorts and feels it settle. Feels their scents mingle.

The prison's waking up, now. Murderers. Rapists. Armed robbers. Terrorists. The worst of the worst. Household names, some of them. Notorious. Famous, even. He's listened to the podcast over and over. Read every damn word about the crimes attributed to Reuben Hollow. They don't know the half of it. Less than that. He could make himself a lot of money with the information sloshing around inside his head. His mind is awash with visions of dead men and frightened women; of sexy coppers spilling their secrets against his neck and big, scarred warriors holding him down and wrapping the cuffs around his tattooed wrists. He'll probably tell the truth, eventually. He'll get himself privileges. A single cell. A TV and fewer restrictions on his laptop. He'll be glad to be able to use a mobile phone that hasn't been previously hidden inside his, or somebody else's, rectum. But they are all pleasures for another day. For now, there is work to do. He sits at the centre of a vast web: a malignant spider, waving an ornate tapestry that will capture a whole host of fat flies. He has followed her instructions to the letter. She rewards him in ways that satisfy his thirsts while leaving him desperate for more. He wonders if they'll ever meet. Whether she'll find a way to visit him; to make good on her promise to let him smell the real thing.

'Are you coming?'

He opens the cupboard. Pulls out a shirt. Soft cords. Loafers. Puts on a cardigan that reaches almost to his knees. Puts on his lanyard.

Heads onto the wing.

'Morning, sir.'

It's the pretty boy. The celebrity. The one with the twinkly eyes and the wolfish grin who's serving life for six murders. The one who doesn't even know what's being done on his behalf. Who doesn't know the care and attention that has gone in to serving him up a gift he'll never forget.

'Morning, Hollow. Sleep well?'

'Rudely awakened, sir. Feeling a bit rattled, to tell the truth. Copper who locked me up – he gave me some news that doesn't sit right. I'd be glad of a chat, sir.'

He makes sure his features don't betray him.

'I'm on my way to the Wing Governor as we speak. You did right to come to me. Pop along with me – we'll see if we can get to the bottom of it.'

He looks grateful. Looks so pitiably relieved. He doesn't deserve the esteem in which he's held. Doesn't deserve to have all those pretty fucking whores sending him their pictures and their filthy words and bag after bag of their underwear. Doesn't deserve to be the star of a podcast. Doesn't deserve to get visits from detectives and psychologists who think he's Sir Fucking Lancelot.

He'll get what's coming to him. He'll make her happy.

Everything's going exactly the way they've planned.

'Was it that McAvoy chap you spoke about in our sessions?'

'He claims that our mutual friend is in danger. I don't know what to believe. It's properly taking my peace of mind, if I'm honest.'

'Can't have that, can we?' says Mr Corcoran, with his soft voice and kind eyes. 'You can tell me about the church at Great Middleton as we walk.'

'A beautiful place,' he confirms. 'I replaced the vaulted ceiling in the crypt. I don't think anybody else even knows it's there.'

Yes they do, smiles Corcoran, falling into step by his side. They really do.

TWENTY-NINE

HMP Warcop
7.43 a.m.

The Wing Governor's secretary isn't in yet so it falls to one of the early risers from the Education Department to deal with the large, red-faced Scotsman who is insisting on seeing all correspondence to and from Reuben Hollow for the past six months, and making outlandish claims about immediate threats to life. He's bleeding, underneath his shirt. He looks like he's been dragged behind a car. There's horse-hair and dead leaves on his brow. He's got big sad eyes and he's trying to keep his temper, and she likes him for it. She's trying to help, she really is. But it's early and nobody's up and she can't help him without authorization. She can get him a coffee, if it helps. She might even be able to manage some chamomile tea. There are some magazines to read, if he's bored. Some copies of *Inside Time*. And no, she can't get him his phone, because there are protocols, and she knows it's a pain but she's way down the pecking order when it comes to decision-making so all she can do is follow the pesky rules.

McAvoy sits down in one of the spongy green chairs. Stands up again. Reads one of the posters on the faded yellow wall. Sneers, then feels bad about it. Sits back down again. Fastens his shirt all the way to the top. Unfastens it again.

'Dreadful weather, isn't it? Days like these, you're almost glad to be inside. Always the same with a strawberry moon, isn't it? Rustles up a storm.'

Her name's Cat. Forties. Redhead, though it's a shade only found in a bottle. She's wearing a cardigan over an expensive silk blouse. She's got a husky voice. She smokes, by the sound of her, though there's no way of detecting the scent of cigarettes through the fog of perfume that surrounds her. McAvoy realizes he is staring at her. Trying to get a read on her. Glares, the way Roisin taught him; picks a spot just behind her head and lets his consciousness blur. For an instant he fancies that he can see a smudge of something ochre. It is a second outline, a heat-haze of yellows and silvers; a silhouette of her seated form. He sees her as a Russian doll at its centre. He blinks and it's gone. He's left feeling sick. Dizzy. Lost.

'I can have somebody walk you down to the front. Or you're welcome to wait in one of the new classrooms, though it means somebody will have to stay with you. Category A, I'm afraid. Sounds frightening, doesn't it? Most of them are more broken than dangerous. Lost sheep. Scary, when their blood's up, but they were all babies once and I don't think anybody's born bad. Some in here – they'd better suit a medal than handcuffs. That's not one of my pet phrases, by the way. Mr Corcoran, the pastoral officer, he has a lovely way with words.'

'If I could use your phone, perhaps,' says McAvoy, looking hopeful. 'There's a live operation; an officer in danger.'

She halts whatever it is she's doing behind the computer screen, and looks at him with green eyes that are framed by a mascara too harsh for her plump, doughy face. 'That's awful. Honestly. Let me try another number – see if I can't hurry somebody up. It's Aector, you said?'

'Aye.'

She gives a little nod, and a flicker of sympathy crosses her face, as if she understands. As if she thinks it's rotten his parents didn't have the decency to call him Paul. 'Please, just take a seat. At least Mr Corcoran will be able to give a yea or nay. It's all very touchy-feely, if you catch my drift. We've got the shrinks and the counsellors but Corky is really doing a good job on, well, whaddyacallit . . . the holistic front. Or do I mean homeopathic? He's done a lot on behalf of your man.'

'My man?'

'Your Hollow. You should see the man's mail-bag. Full-time job for half a dozen staff but Corky's taken the responsibility on himself. Wing Governor won't hear a word against him. Gives him the budget for any extra-curricular course he reckons the Lifers will get something out of. You wouldn't catch me taking on a job like that. Some of the things he used to get sent. Honestly, these women . . . brazen!'

'. . . if you stick it in the multi-storey you might be able to claim back . . .'

The conversation is interrupted by the sudden whispered clatter of manila folders and loose pages hitting the polished, tiled floor. Castro looks up to see a mousy-looking woman in her early thirties emerging from the glass doors, bent almost double as she claws up fistfuls of paper and stuffs them back under arms already bulging, like the flanks of a camel, with documents and clutter. McAvoy crosses the floor to help. Bends down and takes a handful of papers in his palm. Ducks his head into her eye-line. She mutters a thanks, blows wispy hair from the corner of her mouth, and stands up, nodding to McAvoy that he should place the remaining paper in her hand, which is opening and closing like the beak of a baby bird.

McAvoy steps back. Manages a smile. She has an air of manic energy about her that suggests she's not a tea-drinker. She's short and dumpy, with a stubby nose that only just manages to bear the weight of her designer spectacles. A mess of curly brown hair starts only three inches above her unplucked eyebrows, and taken with her floral blouse, knee-length skirt and sensible, clumpy shoes, McAvoy is put in mind of a wartime secretary.

'Morning, Izzy,' says Cat, waving a hand. 'Don't mind the detective, here. Just waiting for a nod from on high before I can release some of Hollow's correspondence.'

'Not just Hollow. Anybody else who's shared a cell or been on the wing with him.'

Cat looks at Izzy and something passes between them: some unspoken intuition that the Inspector is living in Cloud Cuckoo Land if he thinks he's going to get what he wants.

'Corky's on his way up, as it happens,' says Izzy, breathlessly. She dumps her papers on a desk. Untucks an Extra Strong Mint from her cheek. Huffs a curl of hair from her eyes. 'You're Sergeant McAvoy,' she says, accusingly, as she looks him up and down.

'Inspector, now,' says McAvoy, colouring.

'It's normally Trish,' says Izzy. 'Force of nature, isn't she? I can see why Reuben's so taken.'

McAvoy scratches at his beard. Her voice sounds familiar.

'You know the names of the investigating officers of all your inmates?' he asks.

'Just the celebrities,' she smiles. 'And Reuben does talk about you a lot. Your name comes up in his letters almost as often as Trish's.'

McAvoy glances up at the clock. It's getting on for 8 a.m. Trish has been missing for hours.

'Ah, the very chap.'

A tall man in baggy, bohemian clothes is standing in the doorway, palms against the frame. He looks like he's doing press-ups in the air. He's got an air of athleticism about him; good skin and bright eyes, scruffily fashionable hair and three days of beard. McAvoy stands. Notices Reuben standing behind him, looking at the floor: a child who's had no choice but to tell a teacher about his naughty friend.

'Mr Corcoran,' he says. 'I'm Detective Inspector McAvoy. Aector, or Hector, if it's easier. I've reason to believe . . .'

'No need for any of that,' says Corcoran, smiling. 'I've no doubt you're going to give me all manner of good reasons why I should let you go snuffling about in Reuben's private correspondence. Unfortunately, it won't make any difference. The Wing Governor will have to make that call, and in the meantime, I've got the rather more pressing matter of Reuben's well-being to consider. I honestly can't believe you had this poor man woken and brought to an interrogation in the early hours of the morning and I certainly can't get my head around the fact that the night staff went along with it. I'm not an angry man, Inspector McAvoy, but I'm growing rather tired of police officers stomping in here and undoing all the hard work of the education and psychological staff who are endeavouring to repair these broken people. Reuben has been working very hard on taking ownership of the past and outlining a future with real meaning.'

'He's serving life, Mr Corcoran.'

He shakes his head, disgusted. 'I'd rather believed you were on the progressive side of the fence, Inspector. We're just here to punish, is that right? We're just a deterrent, and a place to stick society's problem people.'

McAvoy pushes his hair out of his face. Gets a sudden whiff of Mr Corcoran. Turns his head away. The man reeks. The clothes are fine and his hair doesn't seem to need washing but there's waft of stale sweat coming off him that is making McAvoy's eyes water. He understands the strong perfume now. Understands the Strong Mint.

'I've reason to believe that Detective Superintendent Trish . . .'

'No,' says the pastoral officer, shaking his head. 'No, this simply isn't acceptable. I'm going to escort you back to the Family area where you can take the opportunity to do things properly. There will be a complaint, believe me.'

McAvoy looks past him. Reuben raises his head. Wrinkles his nose. Tightens his jaw.

McAvoy looks to the two female members of staff. Nods an embarrassed apology and thanks them for their time. Follows Mr Corcoran down the wide, empty corridor and past the library. Reuben's at his side. McAvoy follows like an unloved child.

'. . . thought you might like to give a reading at the next session, Reuben. Young Graves got so much out of hearing his work spoken aloud . . .'

McAvoy listens as the officer and the serial killer talk about poetry. Glances to his left and into the dead air of the prison library. The doors are locked. Some of the posters on the windows are peeling. Others tell of the joys of reading, of writing; of how easy it is to request a book or some help with literacy. One hangs loose, advertising the visit of a memoir writer; a former inmate returning to talk about the healing properties of confessional journaling.

'This way, please . . .'

'You sure, Mr Corcoran? Across the yard, yeah?'

'I think I know the way, Reuben.'

Mr Corcoran is holding an iron door open. It's set into a brick archway. The flooring here is an old blue linoleum. It's dark: unlit bulbs hang on long cords from a high ceiling.

'Got a Vulnerable Prisoner on exercise,' explains Corcoran. 'Best to go round. Treat, this, for you, Reuben. Bit of inspiration next time you get your turn with the crayons.'

McAvoy steps through the gate. Reuben too. Corcoran closes it behind them. Locks it. Drops the keys back into the depths of his pocket.

'Old part of the prison,' he says, walking into the dark. 'Haunted,

so they'll tell you. Old poisoner by the name of Mo Wharton took
the long drop in 1906 and swore that she wouldn't be taking it
lying down. She still gets spotted from time to time: just this grey
shape and eyes like plums in a rice pudding. Don't know if I
believe it myself but they've investigated twice and there were no
complaints when they closed this whole area down. Apparently
there was a cell found behind one of the walls with scratches in
the brick and a pile of bones in the dirt at the bottom – some
escape gone wrong. Good story for a campfire but it might
be balls.'

Reuben drops back. Looks to McAvoy. 'Stinks, doesn't he,' he
whispers.

'Like a midden in July.'

'Mr Corcoran opens my post, Aector. Chooses to do it himself.
Very diligent about it.'

'What are you trying to do, Reuben?'

'I'm trying to help you, you stubborn bastard. You do understand, don't you? You do know what she's done?'

'What who's done?' mutters McAvoy, feeling the wound in his
stomach start to weep. He feels ill. Weak. His head's spinning. He
knows that Hollow is to blame for all of it, he just can't make
sense of why, or how, or what he hopes to get other than a chance
to enjoy some extra exposure. He needs Trish beside him, and her
absence is gnawing away at him. He can't stand the thought of
her in pain. He wonders whether Fin would forgive him if he just
picked Hollow up by the throat and smashed him against the wall
until he told him everything he wanted to know.

'Watch your step here,' says Corcoran, leading them further
down the sloping path. 'Ah, yes, just right here and . . .'

McAvoy follows. Turns the corner. The walls are painted white,
here. Bare brickwork, wet and cold. He hurries forward, eyes
adjusting to the sudden change in the quality of the gloom.

'Mr Corcoran, I'd be grateful if you could slow down. I wanted
to talk to you about a particular correspondent of Reuben's? One
Madoc Fulmar, possibly going by the surname Wilkie, possibly
Pharaoh – perhaps even Hollow, now I think of it, and I think you
might know more than you think you do . . .'

Corcoran stops dead. Pulls up like a lame horse and McAvoy
clatters into the back of him.

'Sorry, is something . . .?'

Corcoran is looking up. McAvoy follows his gaze. There's a trapdoor in the ceiling. A door to their right. Bare brick ahead. He's led them to a dead end in the cold and the murk beneath the old hanging yard.

'Fuck sake, Corky, you got lost?' asks Reuben, at McAvoy's side.

The door to their right opens. The men who emerge are wearing prison greys. Big men. Ripples in their necks; rounded shoulders, fists the size of house-bricks.

'Mr Corcoran?' asks McAvoy, putting an arm across the officer. 'Radio it in. Quick. Radio it in . . .'

Corcoran looks at him. Gives him a pitying look. Then he pulls the keys from his pocket and wraps the chain around his fist; a great knuckle duster of jagged metal.

'Reuben, go for help . . . run . . .'

Reuben looks at the odds. At the big men who fill the little chamber. At the big copper who doesn't know how to retreat. At Mr Corcoran.

Weighs the odds.

'Sorry, Aector. Give her my best, yeah?'

He turns on his heel and walks away.

'You don't have to do this,' says McAvoy, desperately, to the nearest thug. He's got a bald head with a heraldic lion tattooed around his ear. He has the look of a bodybuilder gone to seed; has the yellow eyes and sweaty lip of a steroid addict. They all do.

'Don't take it personally, big lad,' says Lionhead, diplomatically. 'Are you going to cooperate or are you going to be a silly sod and fight back?'

McAvoy turns to Corcoran. 'Radio it in, for God's sake, man . . .'

And Corcoran punches him in the side of the face with his fist of serrated metal.

McAvoy feels his skin tear. Feels metal hit bone. Hears his face rip like paper.

And then it's all fists and boots and the thud and stamp of skin on skin; muscle on bone; steel against unprotected flesh.

Only one of the men doesn't involve himself. He's holding up a camera, replaying the whole show.

Were he able to hear above the grunts and thumps of violence, McAvoy might just hear the sound of Delphine Hollow telling Mr Corcoran that he's done so very well.

He might just hear Madoc telling his prisoner that she has to watch; that she can't look away; that this is all for her; all because of her; all down to her betrayals and lies.

And he might just hear Trish Pharaoh gasping for breath. Fighting for air. Swallowing and choking and trying to find her voice. Might hear her make a promise. Make a deal with the devil. Might hear her tell Madoc, tell Delphine, that she'll do whatever they want if they'll just make this stop.

They won't stop.

They were never going to stop.

THIRTY

'Look,' he says, holding the camera in front of her face. 'Look at your hero.'

Pharaoh can't focus. Her vision swims, head full of blood and fear and hurt.

'You stopped caring. Soon as this big bastard came into your life you let my father start to die.'

Pharaoh feels her lashes scrape the mask. His words seem to be coming from far away. She feels like she's underwater, staring up at a rippling, indistinct world. She can just about make out his words but she can't make any sense of them. There's an accusation, she thinks. She's done something wrong. But she can't seem to get the two ends of the thread to tie together.

'How many times did you betray him? That's what you do, isn't it? You make yourself irreplaceable when you turn your back.'

There's a sob in his voice. He's staring at the phone he holds in his gloved hand, watching as the one called Corcoran drags the unconscious detective up the spiral staircase, grunting with the effort. Two big men are holding his feet.

'Do you think the rope will break?' asks Madoc. 'I've read

about times when even Pierrepoint misjudged the drop. Head can come clean off, if you get it wrong.'

Pharaoh's tongue sits fat and swollen in her aching mouth. She tries to work some saliva from her palate. Swallows and feels a momentary easing of the fiery pain in her throat.

'Look,' hisses Madoc, spit frothing from his bared teeth to patter down on the reeking mask. 'Look at him. Another one, dying for you. How many people will you put in the ground, Mother?'

Pharaoh flinches at the name, surfaces from beneath the mess of pain and confusion and manages to focus on the image on the screen. For a moment she isn't sure what she's looking at. Then she recognizes McAvoy, blood-spattered, head hanging to the side. A fit-looking man is fastening a rope around his neck. A group of big, broad-shouldered prison thugs are standing by, waiting for whatever comes next. One of them is holding a bloodied cuff to his bleeding nose. McAvoy got some digs in before he fell.

She feels herself flooding with a desperate rage. She would give her life to save his. Would fire her heart like a cannonball if it stopped them hurting him any more.

She tries to find her voice. 'Madoc . . . stop, you don't have to . . .'

'Oh, Mother,' grins Madoc, looming over her and staring down. 'You sound demonic! Where's the silver tongue, eh? Where's the little quips?'

'Kill me, Madoc. Kill me, not him.'

He creases his features in a snarl of disgust. 'Ever the martyr, Mother. St Fucking Trish, eh? Sorry – you don't get to save him. He's not my prize. You are.'

Pharaoh tries to force some feeling into her limbs. Her lower half is completely dead and her arms are numb inside the strait-jacket. She wriggles. Pushes with the little strength she has left. Licks her lips and tastes the rubber of the mask. Feels the grit and tears in her eyes.

'She's lied to you,' says Pharaoh. 'That's what she does. She lies!'

'Foot on your throat, is there, Mum? Can't quite make out the words.'

'She's set you up, Madoc. She's playing with you. She's filled your head with her poison. You're not this person. You can stop. Cut me free and I can stop what's going to happen. You don't need to be who she's making you.'

Madoc shakes his head. Looks back at the screen. 'She's watching,' he says, quietly. 'She's watching this, and she's watching you, now. She's seeing you suffer. She made it all make sense for me – why I hear the voice; why you sent me away – why you never came looking.'

'I did! Madoc, I swear, I wanted to take care of you.'

'You're a liar!' screams Madoc. 'Dad took me away from all that ugliness, all that suffering. He gave me a home and a future and a family. He worked so hard to provide for us all and you couldn't stand it. You attacked him. Caused the stroke. Covered it all up. Kept him like your prisoner all those years, making his every day more miserable. I'd have taken care of him. But you didn't want me – you sent me back to her, and she sent me to him!'

Pharaoh starts to choke. She can't breathe. Her words are forming a lump of gristle in her throat. She glances at the phone in Madoc's hand. McAvoy is on his knees, rope around his neck. In the corner of the screen there's a little red dot showing that the live stream is being broadcast to a third party.

'Let me talk to her,' pleads Pharaoh, coughing up blood and mucus. 'Let her see. Take this fucking thing off – let her see properly . . .'

Madoc hesitates. This is how he's fantasized about seeing her. But he only has his chance at retribution because of the girl who talks to him in his dreams. Perhaps she would like to see Pharaoh's true face.

'Shall I?' he asks. 'Delphine? Shall I take the mask off her?'

The image on the screen changes. Suddenly Madoc is looking at a young woman with long red hair and freckles. She has an air of sweetness about her; the look of a country girl or farmer's wife; red cheeks and pale shoulders, neat white teeth and an unlined forehead. She's smiling out from the screen like a favourite auntie saying a hello from the far side of the world.

Madoc reaches down and puts his fingers under the edge of the rubber mask. Pulls it free. Pharaoh flops down to the earth, banging her head on the hard floor. She's all sweat and blood and dirt: red-black ink leaking from her eyes.

Madoc holds the phone in front of Pharaoh's face. She looks up. Sees Delphine Hollow smiling back at her.

'You did this,' says Pharaoh. 'You told him it was me.'

'Oh, Patricia,' says Delphine, sadly. 'You look such a mess.'

'You've played with his head. Convinced him I killed his father.'

'You did kill his father, Patricia. Took a decade to do it, too. And you're killing mine, now. It may take forty years, but you're killing him every day he's in that place – every day you pretend you don't care.'

Pharaoh spits. Tries to use the pain as a mooring; a way to guide herself through the fog.

'You think you're doing this for Reuben?'

Delphine pouts a little. Sticks out her lower lip. 'He won't talk to me. He's very cross. I think he's feeling a little hard done by. The podcast – it could have made him a bona fide hero. Ava and Hannah are two black marks against his name. He did the right thing but it's come at a price.'

'And you're serving up Aector and me like we're a bunch of flowers?'

Delphine grins. 'I do like you, Patricia. I know what Dad sees in you. The thing is, Madoc here deserves his revenge, don't you think? You sent him away. You took a metal pole to his father's head. We've both seen the footage.'

'All of it?' snarls Pharaoh. 'You've seen what he did?'

Delphine's expression changes. Her face hardens. She scowls. 'That'll do, Madoc. Flip the stream. Let's watch Aector's dance, shall we?'

'You know what he did!' roars Pharaoh, tasting blood. 'Madoc, watch this whole video. I've tried so hard to protect you, I swear. I know you did it for me. You did it because you saw what he was becoming. But I didn't attack him, I swear. Madoc, it wasn't me.' Her voice cracks. Black tears spill from her eyes and she remembers with absolute clarity the moment that Kush handed her the video and told her that he didn't know what to do. Told her it was up to her how she proceeded. She remembers the feeling of her insides turning to ice and steam as she watched Madoc run after his father and pick up the metal railing that Sophia had wrestled out of her mother's hands. She can see it now; can see Anders bending down to re-lace his brogues, wiping the blood from his hand, turning back towards the family home with a look of absolute revulsion on his face. And then Madoc hits him from behind. Brings the railing down right across his crown. Turns and runs, even as his father slumps forward and collapses onto the road.

'I tried to protect you,' she says again. 'You know what you did, Madoc. I'd go to my grave not telling. You were a child. You'd been through so much. You didn't mean to, I know that. I'd have brought you home, I swear, but I didn't know how to protect you from yourself or how to keep the other children safe while we got you well. And Anders knew. He wouldn't let you stay. Even when he couldn't speak; when it was just grunts and twitches, all he kept asking about was whether I was going to send you away. I'm so sorry, Madoc. I'm so fucking sorry . . .'

Madoc stares at the screen. He's holding Delphine's gaze. They are listening to the voices.

'Don't spoil it,' says Delphine, sulkily. 'Don't deny yourself what you truly want.'

From somewhere nearby, Pharaoh hears the sound of voices. There's a thudding sound: a muffled fist on a wooden door.

'Madoc, you can stop this. I can help you. I can take care of you. Delphine – tell them to stop. Tell them to let him go!'

The voices are growing louder now. She hears footsteps on flagstones. Hears floorboards creaking: catches the faint trace of the open air on the sudden waft of cool breeze.

'Madoc, stop them,' begs Pharaoh. 'Delphine. It's not what he wants! This isn't what he wants!'

Delphine's face twists. For an instant she is a being transformed: a hydra of absolute malevolence and rage. 'It's what I want,' she says. And smiles. 'Mr Corcoran. Do it.'

Somewhere to Pharaoh's left, a door bursts open.

Madoc doesn't turn. He's still watching the lady on the screen. She'd been so kind to him. She'd told him how things were. She'd told him it wasn't his fault. She'd told him about Trish Pharaoh, and what she'd done to his dad. She'd told him that she needed to know what his father had been through and everybody needed to see her for the monster she truly was. He had a duty to honour his dad. He had a duty to hurt those men she'd betrayed him with so that his father could sleep soundly in his grave. He had a duty to tell her children the truth about who she was and what she did. She made everything feel better, for a while. She gave him a sense of something he'd never known. She told him he was special. She loved him. He could make her love him more by doing the things she asked. He needed to be brave. Needed to be the kind of man his father would be proud of . . .

'Police! Don't fucking move!'

Pharaoh stretches her neck, desperately looking towards the door. There are two of them: a bald man in a black suit and a younger woman in a bomber jacket with spiky, punky hair.

Madoc doesn't turn. Just watches, as Delphine looks at him with the eyes of a god betrayed.

'What a pity,' says Delphine. 'What a silly, silly boy.'

Redmore pushes past DI Cross. Closes the space between herself and Madoc in four strides. Kicks him in the side of the face with the sole of her boot then pins him to the ground, face pressed into the earth.

'The phone,' shouts Pharaoh. 'McAvoy's got a rope around his neck! Stop them. Fucking stop them!'

DI Cross snatches up the phone. For an instant he looks into the eyes of a tall, red-haired girl. Then she vanishes from the screen and all he's looking at is an empty room: a rope swaying lazily above a darkened platform. The image jolts, as if the phone has been knocked from somebody's hand. Cross's face creases in puzzlement. He feels like he's watching a horror film. A big man with blood running from a wound on his neck is staggering down a half-dark corridor. He stumbles over a fallen body; the leg sticking out at a grotesque angle. He watches as the angle of the phone changes. Stares for a moment into a handsome, wolfish face: long hair, paint-flecked beard: blue eyes and a gold tooth. Reuben winks at him. And ends the call.

'Is he alive?' begs Pharaoh, from the ground. 'Is he alive?'

Redmore slips tie-wrap cuffs over the wrists of the unresponsive Madoc. Leaves him where he lies and scurries over to Pharaoh. Her features crease in horror as she sees what has been done.

'Can you see?' she asks, trying to unfasten the straps. 'Has he blinded you?'

'I can see,' whispers Pharaoh. She swallows. Spits. 'Did you hear?'

Redmore nods. Unbuckles the straitjacket and Pharaoh feels the blessed agony as the blood rushes back into her limbs. She tries to haul herself upright but she can't find any strength. Can't get her legs to work.

She can hear DI Ross talking into a mobile phone. He's whispering. He's being discreet. He's not calling for urgent assistance – he's telling George Earl that she's alive, they've found her, and he doesn't know what to do.

Redmore drags the bulky restraints off Pharaoh's torso. Shrugs out of her jacket and passes it to her, helping to cover her nakedness.

'He injected me,' she says. 'Made me swallow something. My throat's on fire.'

Redmore looks around her. There's a half-full bottle of water over by the curved wall. She hurries over and snatches it up, running back to Pharaoh. She takes it and drinks deep. Coughs. Feels the agony recede.

'Did they kill him?' asks Pharaoh, from the floor. 'Those men. Did they kill him?'

Cross turns. Looks at her and his face turns pale. Shakes his head and finds his voice.

'Not yet.'

THIRTY-ONE

McAvoy wipes the blood from his eyes. Squints through the blur of pain and darkness. The air has a gloopy, opaque quality to it, as if he's looking out through a Tupperware box. He can smell blood. His throat is agony. His hands feel like two useless lumps of gristle at the end of his wrists. There's a dull pain in his ribs; a sharp, bright agony in his cheek.

'Wakey-wakey, there's a good lad. Come on. Follow my voice,

yeah? It's not Roisin so don't wake up all fruity, yeah? I like you but not in that way . . .'

Reuben Hollow's face swims in his vision. McAvoy freezes, his heart turning to a fist in his chest. Memories flood back. Corcoran had set him up. There were half a dozen of them. They'd beaten him bloody and wrapped a noose around his neck. They'd made him look straight into a camera. Made him open his eyes. Then they'd pushed him into the darkness. There had been a moment of rapid descent; the lurching terror of the sudden fall. Then his feet had hit the hard floor and he'd clattered sideways and smashed his head on the broken brick of the hanging cell. He'd been unable to hold on to his thoughts. Had been unable to make sense of what he had just witnessed; what he had been put through. There had been a face, hadn't there? On the screen? Watching? And Trish, too. A young man with black eyes. And there had been the sounds of violence and blood and the screech of people being hurt in ways that would never heal . . .

'You're welcome,' says Reuben, smiling. His tooth glints in his smile. There's blood on his face but no wounds.

'You came back,' rasps McAvoy, his throat aflame.

'Course I bloody did,' says Hollow, and he produces a flask. He dribbles water into McAvoy's mouth. 'Not much point in going to all this trouble if I was going to bugger off and leave you. I'm pleased you're so heavy. If the rope hadn't broken you'd be a lot taller and a little more dead.'

McAvoy swirls the water around his mouth. Tastes the butcher's-shop reek of blood. Swallows, his eyes watering.

'Corcoran,' he says, at last. 'He's dead?'

'I should certainly think so,' nods Hollow. 'A person shouldn't be able to look at their own arse, should they? I thought it would be harder. Wasn't really difficult at all.'

McAvoy blinks, his thoughts lining up like bullets. 'You set all this up?'

Hollow wrinkles his nose. Makes a face. 'I wish I was some sort of criminal mastermind, I really do. Wish I was one step ahead and always had an ace up my sleeve. Truth is, I'm really rather ordinary in that regard. Some days I can't even do the crossword in the *Guardian*. But I do hear things, and for some reason, people like to be in my good graces. I knew Corcoran here was having a great time pretending he was me. Do you know how many ladies he's had sending him their underwear? I mean, it's a lot to ask of anybody, isn't it? Giving them access to that kind of temptation. Got a bit above himself though, if you ask me. You can't recruit a load of thugs for a hatchet job in a prison and not expect somebody like me to hear about it.'

McAvoy rubs his neck. 'You cut the rope?'

'Not me personally, no. But not all of Corcoran's recruits were on his side. Pal of mine frayed it, just in case it was going to be me that was facing the long drop.'

McAvoy holds his gaze. Glares into him. 'You ran,' he says.

'I don't think I did,' says Hollow, with a twitch of a smile. 'I think I withdrew momentarily to get a gander at the situation and to retrieve a piece of masonry from that crumbling wall. Sorry if it took a little longer than I expected. Perhaps some part of me didn't entirely object to seeing you take a right fucking kicking.'

McAvoy feels a hot lance of pain in his ribs. Shuffles himself upright and leans back against the wall. Hollow is squatting down in front of him. Between his legs is a blood-soaked, prison-issue sock. There's half a brick inside it; rough edges matted with brain matter and skull fragments.

McAvoy swallows again. Takes the offer of the water bottle and takes a drink.

'Trish?' he asks.

'Delphine's going to be furious.'

McAvoy moves the pieces around in his head. 'Who attacked Thor?' he asks, at last.

'Delphine is very good at getting people to do what she wants,' says Hollow. 'No doubt she'll have persuaded some poor sap to throw his life away just for her amusement. He won't be the first.'

'You took the blame for her,' says McAvoy. 'You admitted to the murders of Hannah and Ava.'

Hollow looks pained. 'I made an agreement. I wanted her to get the help she needed and if everybody knew she'd killed them, well – she was going to prison for life. A bit of time in a nice facility, getting well, learning to control her impulses – Trish thought it was best for everybody and I've kept my word.'

'She didn't get well,' says McAvoy.

Hollow gives a dry laugh. 'No, I think it would be fair to say she's still very much a work in progress.'

McAvoy rubs the blood from his beard. Looks at the murder weapon dangling between Hollow's legs. 'What now?'

Hollow shrugs. 'Ideal world? I get a pardon for saving your life. But that won't happen because this isn't America and most of the people who work here are bent or stupid or hooked on self-preservation.'

'This isn't an escape?'

'Escape to where?' asks Hollow. 'I'm a tad notorious. No, like I said, none of this is really very much to do with me. Delphine's the big thinker. She's played poor Prince like a fucking fiddle.'

'You did kill the man who abused his son . . .'

'Did I?' asks Hollow, flashing his teeth. 'You know that, do you? It would be very easy to take credit for a thing like that – to get somebody in your debt. Delphine's letters don't reach me any more. She has to find other ways of showing she still cares. So she did all this to Trish. She sent me you.'

'Sent you me?' asks McAvoy, holding his ribs. 'Nobody sent me anywhere.'

'She did a bit,' says Hollow, with a look that suggests he's trying to spare McAvoy's feelings. 'I mean, if I really wanted to get you alone, all I'd really have to do is threaten somebody you care about. Trish, Roisin, even one of your pals. You were always going to come tearing across here to get in my face about it, weren't you? Not a strategic thinker really, are you? For a shy man you're very gung-ho.'

McAvoy folds his arms in at his side. From somewhere nearby he hears the sound of somebody in pain.

'Survivor!' grins Hollow. 'That's one less life sentence. Might almost be back in single digits now. If I eat a balanced diet and practise mindfulness, do you think I'll make nine hundred? Might be a bit past it by then but it's good to hope.'

McAvoy casts around in his mind. Finds the right name. 'Malcolm Tozer,' he says. He flashes angry eyes at Hollow. 'Tom Spink. Is he . . .?'

'I've no idea,' says Hollow, apologetically. 'I know the name

Tozer though. You do know that Trish and I talk a lot, don't you? We told each other a lot of stories when she was trying to trap me. Told me all about Anders and what he did to her. About who she was with when she was young. About Anders being jealous of Tom. She gave me a perfect little list of who a chap would have to kill if he was trying to get in her good books.'

'Delphine overheard?'

'Delphine recorded it all,' says Hollow. 'I didn't know, of course. Not until after. Not until she told me what she'd done to Hannah and Ava. She did it for me, of course. Very much a daddy's girl. What was I to do? Turn her in? I was happily going about my own business, doing what I could to make the world a little safer, and all the while Delphine knew exactly what I was up to and was taking steps to make sure nobody made life difficult for me. A love like that is a beautiful thing.'

'Why now?' asks McAvoy. 'Why suddenly kill the people Trish cares about?'

'Delphine's a little bit of a peculiar creature,' says Hollow, apologetically. 'Always a bit of a mystery to me. She'll have her reasons. Opportunity, perhaps. She may have found the right person to carry out her dirty work. Wherever she is, she'll be absolutely furious that Trish is alive, if not exactly kicking. She loathes her. She'd have had her killed long since if she didn't think I would be furious about it. I have a horrible feeling that somebody has been telling her things that aren't true. If Corcoran wasn't dead I could ask him what he's told her while he's been pretending to be me. I could also give him a serious ticking off for the tone of that letter he wrote to the podcast. So over the top, wasn't it? Sounded like he'd swallowed a thesaurus.'

There are shouts from the other end of the corridor: the thunder of footsteps and the clanging of keys against metal railings.

'Cavalry are here,' says Hollow, ruefully. 'I can rely on your support, I presume. I'd hate to have come and saved your life just for you to suddenly be a twat about it all.'

McAvoy rubs his throat. Swallows and grimaces. Swallows again.

'Where is she?' he asks, at last. 'Where would she go?'

'I'm not telling you that, Aector,' says Hollow. 'She's not cut out for prison. She likes the open spaces. Likes nature. Likes the

great outdoors. You go after her and she ends up in prison and I
can't have that on my conscience.'

'What fucking conscience,' grumbles McAvoy.

'Steady now,' warns Hollow. 'Hearing you swear is like hearing
a nana say cunt. Rubs me up the wrong way.'

'Will she stop now?' asks McAvoy. 'She's had some of her
revenge, hasn't she? Will she just leave things alone?'

A trace of pity flickers upon the lenses of Hollow's piercing
eyes. A thought rises up like an eel. 'Who's with Roisin?' he asks,
quietly, over the sound of bellows and bangs and the clatter of
feet upon stone. 'Are they safe?'

McAvoy clutches at his chest. Grits his teeth. 'Why are you
asking about Roisin? What's Roisin got to do with anything?'

'She sent you to me in the hope I'd be grateful and take a
chance at revenge. I've declined her offer. So now she has to hurt
you herself. And you're here. Which means that your family aren't
being held in your big strong arms. The way she thinks? Maybe
it was your Roisin she wanted all along. Honestly, I know it's
wrong, but it's hard not to feel a little proud at the way she plays
the game . . .'

McAvoy hauls himself upright just as the squad of prison
officers in full riot gear clatters into Hollow and takes him to the
ground in a welter of helmets and shields, boots and sticks. In a
moment there are torches in his face, gloved hands probing the
puncture wound on his face; a medic examining his neck and
the ugly bruise gathering at his throat.

McAvoy pushes past them. Barges through the sea of people,
tottering like a drunk. Careers into the wall and rights himself;
prison officers pulling at his arms, trying to block his path. He
hears sirens. Becomes aware of flashing lights. A ringing phone.
Somebody saying his name over and over.

He falls to the ground, blood fogging his vision.

One word, over and over, expanding like spilled ink, until the
blackness spreads to consume his whole vision, his whole world.

Roisin.

THIRTY-TWO

Pharaoh sits in the front pew, shivering. She's wearing Emma Redmore's coat, a blanket around her legs. Her body isn't really responding to her commands yet. She's a puppet with its strings cut; a discarded scarecrow bleeding straw.

'On their way,' says Cross, for the fifth time. Madoc is kneeling in front of him, hands behind his back, tied at the wrist. He looks like a supplicant taking communion.

'Here,' says Redmore, bursting in through the front door and darting down the centre of the church. She holds out a paper bag. 'Knew they'd come in handy.'

Pharaoh makes a face. Gestures at her own rubbery limbs. Redmore grimaces in response, all apologies. She rummages in the bag and pulls out a handful of little cartons of long-life milk. She rips the top off one and holds it to Pharaoh's mouth. She drinks. She'll probably feel embarrassed to be seen this way, given time. But right now, if Redmore pulled her close and laid her head on her shoulder, she'd accept the kindness.

'More,' says Pharaoh, as the milk coats her throat. 'Please.'

Redmore does as she's asked. Pharaoh manages to swallow down six cartons of the sweet milk. Her eyes water. Her nose runs.

'Better?'

Pharaoh nods. Licks her lips. She looks around the little church as if seeing it for the first time. It's cold and small and the walls look haphazard and lumpy. There are birds' nests in the ancient timber eaves. There's a wooden font in front of the slitty windows. There's a lectern, illuminated by the pale morning light that lances in through the coloured glass. She recognizes the curved fretwork on the plinth.

'Reuben's,' she says, and the word is bitter on her tongue. She looks at Redmore; at her punky hair and sparkly eyes. Wishes she could do a better impression of herself.

'How did you find me?'

'Your friend,' says Redmore, looking down at the dusty

flagstones. 'Phoned Earl. Earl phoned us just as we were turning up at Mr Spink's address. And when we saw the vehicle . . .'

Pharaoh manages a smile. 'It was Tom, then? No tricks? No little game to play with my mind?'

'He hasn't been identified,' says Redmore, as gently as she can. 'Maybe . . .'

Pharaoh shakes her neck. Feels the tingle of pins-and-needles rush across her scalp. A black tear leaks from her eye. Redmore moves to wipe it away and stops herself. Pharaoh's a senior officer. She's St Trish.

'I wish we'd got here sooner,' mutters Redmore, kicking at a stone. 'Before he did the things you went through.'

'I'll live,' says Pharaoh. 'I didn't think I was going to.'

She hears Cross muttering to himself. Looks past Redmore and glares at the man in the black coat as he plays with his phone and casts furtive glances at the door.

'I owe you a thanks too, Ashley,' says Pharaoh, sweetly.

Cross shrugs. 'We'll talk about who owes what to whom some other time.'

Pharaoh manages a smile. Keeps her eyes fixed on his. 'Did you catch it on film, then? What he did to Thor?'

Cross's brows furrow. He stops playing with his phone. 'What are you talking about?'

'Boss,' she says, her voice still not much more than a croak. 'You call me Boss, or Guv. Trish, if you're somebody I like.'

'Sorry,' says Cross, his voice oozing disdain. 'What are you talking about, Boss?'

'You've had me under surveillance for ten days, isn't that right? Maybe eleven, I'm not sure where I'm at. Unless your team are absolutely hopeless, they must have videoed the attack. I'd imagine we'll be grateful for that, come the trial.'

Cross shoots Redmore a puzzled look. Gives his attention back to Pharaoh. 'I have no idea what you're talking about.'

'You do, Ashley,' says Pharaoh. 'You've been doing George Earl's bidding, I know that much. He's incompetent but he's enough of a strategic thinker to see the potential of a bastard like you, eh? All he had to do was dangle the chance of a bit of payback in front of you and you were his to toy with. Is that how it went?'

Cross looks down at Madoc. The killer is staring at the floor, utterly motionless. 'I honestly don't know what . . .'

'It was my daughter who sent you the video clip, as it happens,' says Pharaoh. She nods at the unopened carton of long-life milk and Redmore dutifully rips the top off and pours it into Pharaoh's mouth. She spots a packet of cigarettes sticking out of Redmore's inside pocket and gives her a meaningful glare. Redmore lights one with a plastic lighter and places it between Pharaoh's cracked lips.

'What video?' asks Cross, trying to twist his features into a mocking smile and ending up looking like a toddler with wind.

'The video that got Earl's underpants elastic all distended,' says Pharaoh, through a cloud of smoke. 'It was taken by a man called Laurence. Kush, to his mates. Years ago, of course. We owed him money, you see. Well, Anders did. Kush was our handyman and Anders reckoned that a drippy hippy wasn't the sort to get all capitalist and make a fuss so he kept him hanging and kept refusing to pay up. Kush knew Anders was a bit happy with his fists. He knew that he had a temper. Kush, God bless him – he figured he could get a bit of leverage if he had some footage of him giving me a hiding. So he set up the camera in the big fancy hedges near the house. Motion-activated, which wasn't as advanced a technology as you'd think. And he got more than he bargained for. He saw Anders hitting me, just like he wanted. He turned up at the house bold as brass, ready to tell Anders that if he didn't give him what was owed, he'd plaster it on Facebook and send it to his wife's bosses – his wife being head of the Domestic Violence unit at Humberside Police. Of course, Anders was in a coma at this point. His brain had half ripped itself in two. He showed me the video instead. Showed me what Anders did to me and what it looked like to an outsider. Turned my stomach. And it showed Madoc, there. Showed Madoc smashing him over the head with a metal railing . . .'

'No,' says Cross, shaking his head. 'No, that's not . . .'

'I know it's fucking not,' snaps Pharaoh. 'I know that because I made a deal with Kush. He wiped the end of the video and I'd pay him what was owed. It would take years but he'd get it all back. And I'd keep the clip that remained.'

'Why?' asks Redmore, face creased.

'I needed to remind myself,' says Pharaoh, and a black tear runs from her ruined eye like a line of text. 'I didn't know what would be coming home to me. I didn't know how to raise the girls the right way. Sophia knew what he was but the younger kids? And I needed to have something I could reach for if I felt myself loving him the wrong way. I needed to keep a record of what he was.'

'It was this man who sent it to us?' asks Redmore, looking at Madoc, mute and immobile.

Pharaoh shakes her head. She can hear sirens: the diphthong blare of police and ambulance calls rushing across the flat clifftop and tumbling into the sea. 'I told you, Olivia sent it. Madoc told her to do it, but Madoc hasn't had an independent thought since he met Delphine.'

Redmore snaps her head up. 'Delphine Hollow?'

'She must have thought all her Christmases had come at once,' says Pharaoh, bitterly. 'My husband's love-child in the same halfway house where she'd washed up when she convinced them she was well. She'll have done all this to make her daddy happy – she's like a rich kid going off with a bad boy so her doting father will buy her a new pony. She's done well, of course. She only had a couple of recordings of me chatting with Daddy and she managed to mess with Madoc's head so badly he forgot what he did. All this theatricality – it's Delphine playing with her dolls. Look what she's done to him. Look what she told him to do to me. All the shit with the dahlias and the adze and Reuben's fucking woodworking apron. We're just points on one of her zentangles.'

'You're saying you didn't smash your husband over the head with a railing,' snaps Cross. He looks down at Madoc. 'You're saying he did it.'

'You may be one of the thickest people I've ever met,' says Pharaoh. She can feel some life coming back into her hand. Wonders if she could make a fist. Whether she could swing it. 'Extraordinary, really, given that I work for Humberside Police.'

'You'll get your say,' spits Cross. 'There's a case to answer. For all we know, you lured that poor McAvoy-lookalike over for more than some rumpy-pumpy.'

'Rumpy-pumpy?' Pharaoh manages a smile. It tears her lip. 'I like that phrase. I might use it. He's OK, is he? Not too Thor?'

Redmore grimaces at the casual cruelty of the question. 'He's stable,' she says, after a moment. 'There might be nerve damage, but . . .'

'That's all right then,' says Pharaoh, her eyes still on Cross. 'He's not the love of my life, you do understand that? He's a friend, and we had a nice time together. He's separated from his wife and I'm a merry bloody widow. If we want to have some rumpy-pumpy we bloody can. You'll have some of it on tape, I think. I kept the windows open so you'd hear me having a lovely time. Tom told me about your cack-handed attempt to get some info out of him. If you hadn't, I might have noticed Madoc here. As it was, every time I saw a shadow I thought it was you doing Earl's bidding and trying to get something on me.'

Cars are pulling up outside. Pharaoh can hear shouts and instructions and the blare of sirens.

'But the video,' says Cross, confused. 'How did you know that's what we had?'

'Because somebody had moved it,' says Pharaoh, with a shrug. 'Somebody had been in my box of precious things. Olivia, as it happens. And Olivia might be a very clever girl with a temper like a honey badger but she lacks a bit of common sense. Maybe it's a generational thing. Teenagers all seem thick as mince to me. Either way, she didn't seem to remember that the laptop she uses used to belong to her sister and that it was set up through my account. So I get to have a look through her emails whenever I want. And when she Googles things like "set up an untraceable email account" I do take notice. I'd have put a stop to it already, if it hadn't been such a good opportunity.'

Cross moves away from Madoc. He towers over Pharaoh. Over Redmore. The door to the church opens and George Earl strides in, suited and clean and looking fresh enough to face the cameras at a moment's notice.

'Patricia,' he says, arms wide, like the chap on the cross. 'Patricia.' He stops and takes in the damage to her eyes and the rubberiness of her bloodied limbs. 'Patricia.'

'Cunt,' she says, conversationally. 'Cunt. Cunt.'

Earl bristles. Cross glares daggers at him. Emma Redmore stands. She looks from Cross, to Earl, and back again. Slowly, she lifts her jumper. There's a microphone taped below the underwire of her bra.

'Every word?' asks Pharaoh.

Redmore turns to her boss and mentor; the copper she most wants to be like in the world. 'Every word,' she says.

'I don't understand,' says Earl. 'Ashley, what's happening?'

'You'll work it out, in time,' says Redmore. 'My name is Karin Hogarth. I'm Anti-Corruption. And Ashley Cross, you are very much under arrest . . .'

'Arrest for what?' spits Cross, face twisting. 'Arrest for what, you fucking slut?'

'We'll start with rape,' she says, her eyes flashing fire. 'Multiple counts. Primarily, one PC Gaynor Hilyard. The same Gaynor Hilyard who took her own life eight months ago because she went to her boss and told him what happened and he did fucking nothing about it. Moved her on. Covered things up, like you always fucking do. Ringing any bells, George?'

Earl is shaking his head. 'No,' he says. 'No, we were running this operation on her – not the other way around . . .'

'Ever wondered why I didn't take the top job, George?' asks Pharaoh, face twisting. 'It's because if I was one rung above you, you'd bow and scrape and kiss my fucking arse. But one rung below? I get to see you for what you are. You're a fucking moron, mate. And I think that before very long, you and I and some very powerful people are going to have a chat about your future options. None of them involve staying in the police force, I tell you that.'

'No,' says Cross. 'No, this isn't happening, this isn't right . . .'

Pharaoh senses movement behind him. Sees Madoc stand.

There's a moment when their eyes meet: his black eyes upon hers. There is a connection. There is the heat and light of something indecipherable; a language of love and regret and sorrow and prayer.

Nobody is close enough to grab him. He nods, once, at the woman who tried to be his mother. His gaze lingers for an instant on the intricate fretwork of the lectern. For a time, he had thought that the man who killed Maurice Bruce saw him as his successor: had fantasized of a father figure who would nurture him, reward him; love him. But Reuben Hollow barely knows that Madoc exists. It's all been a game. It's all been Delphine. He doesn't want to live in a world so full of cruelty and deception. He's tried to make himself a demon and found that the angels are far more terrifying than his reflection.

Six steps, that's all. Six desperate steps, and . . .

Madoc hurls himself through the glass.

There is pain and impact; smashed glass and coloured beads. There's stone upon his cheek, rocks smashing his knees together. There is the thud and soar and dizzying impact of flesh upon grass, upon stone, upon jagged rock.

He pulls himself to his feet: blood and dust and glass patterning his skin. Stands for a moment, looking down at the rocks; at the sea.

Steps out into nothingness.

Drops like a stone towards the grey, grey oblivion so far below.

Pharaoh will never know whether she believes it or not but she is sure, in the moment of his death, that she feels her heart lurch: a mother sensing the loss of a true-born son. Her grief will spill out in so many black tears. She will grieve for what he could have been as much as she will regret what he was.

But that will come later. In solitude. In drink.

For now, there is just the sound of the sirens, and the crashing of the waves.

THIRTY-THREE

Delphine Hollow sits in a swivel chair, staring at her own reflection in the blackness of the computer screen. She's comfortable. Relaxed. In another life, she could have lived somewhere like this: could have made a home here, in the living room of the small terraced house at the far end of a nondescript street. The property belongs to Clementine Lippman. There's good money in podcasts, if you find the right formula. The advertisers have been fairly falling over one another to line her pockets since she received the letter from Reuben Hollow and the number of subscribers passed the half-million mark. Delphine wonders if

she'll ever hear a thank-you. Somehow, she doubts it. She contents
herself with the knowledge that her daddy will be proud of her.
It was an immaculate forgery. He couldn't have done any better
himself.

Delphine wonders when Clementine planned to spend the
profits. She certainly hasn't splashed the cash on interior decor-
ating. The walls are a strange kind of purple colour and decorated
with poorly hung movie posters in clip-frames. There's a bookcase
full of true crime and battered paperbacks: a stack of dusty DVDs
in a cardboard box by the little table with its patina of stains. The
boxy brown sofa carries the imprint of Clementine's ample arse.
Her magazines are all piled up on the other seat: a sure sign of
solitary living. One of the cats is prowling around the dead yucca
plant in front of the closed curtains. It's a friendly little thing and
has made itself perfectly at home in Delphine's lap. The other
was less welcoming, scratching her across the back of the hand
with its sharp little claws. It's dead now, its skeleton grotesquely
twisted: an accordion stretched beyond its parameters. She fancies
she'll regret killing the nasty little bastard. She always regrets the
killing of animals. But they're so damn fragile. Things tend to
come apart in her hands.

Delphine's wearing a dressing gown. It's borrowed. Blood-
spattered. Comfortable, if a little careworn. It smells of Clementine.
Her dad would like it.

Delphine has been calling herself Finn for a couple of years. It
doesn't suit her but the new moniker provides a degree of separ-
ation between who she used to be, and who she's had to become.
It's also the name of Aector McAvoy's only son, and she rather
likes the synergies of that almost accidental occurrence. She likes
patterns. She enjoys solitaire. Patience. She used to spend her
spare time drawing zentangles – letting the pen make haphazard
doodles on a blank page and then trying to transform them into
something approximating a picture. It's a game she's good at. She
can make pictures out of anything. She has never looked at a cloud
without seeing her mother's face or a hill of burning sheep; her
brother's corpse or a fat man half-swallowed by a whale. She finds
coincidences fascinating. Sometimes she engineers her own, just
to marvel at the ease with which events can be rearranged into a
more intriguing shape. She's spoken with the doctors about her

infatuation with symbols. They tell her that she should try not to make a pattern out of disparate events. The connections she sees are wild stretches and flights of fancy. She gathers independent events onto a single string and marvels at the beauty of the necklace. Events are random, they tell her. One thing happens, then another.

Were Delphine not utterly committed to the role that she has played these past years, such asinine quackery would lead to outburst. She knows herself capable of great and artful harm. Instead she has taught herself to smile her soft smile and angle her head as if fascinated; to squeeze out a tear and grip the tissue in her palm; to let silvery beads of regret trickle down her nose and land in her lap. She is regret made manifest. She looks upon the deeds she was party to with horror. She is inconsolable. She longs for redemption. She longs for mental wellness. She longs to leave Delphine Hollow behind and to go forward as if born anew. It's taken time to convince the sceptics. Not all of the doctors she has encountered have been sympathetic and earnest in their dealings with her. Some of the more experienced nurses look at her with outright disdain, utterly convinced that she is a charlatan. They've seen it all, they say. She doesn't regret a bit of it. She's got an evil that goes down to the bone and if they permit her to leave they won't see her until she's caught for whatever brutality she inflicts away from prying eyes. Delphine has had to take significant steps to convince the senior staff that she is genuine. She's almost killed herself three times – the most recent coming uncomfortably close to success. She still carries the scars in her wrists: two great diagonal slashes across the pale blue rivers of vein. She'd frightened herself, last time. She'd come dangerously close to letting go; to sinking into the warm black ink of nothingness – of returning to the place she was before. If it wasn't for the young man, she'd be dead. He found her on the floor of the potting shed, bleeding into the cracked tiles and the soft brown loamy earth. He'd wrapped his hand around her wounds and held her blood inside her body, eyes upon hers as the life pumped out of her. It had been their connection that brought her back. She saw herself in the dark mirror of his irises. Saw herself in them, reflecting back: a pale, red-haired shield-maiden; broad shoulders and strong arms, bone-white flesh and a pleasant, scampish face; all freckles and rosy cheeks, snub-nose and laughing eyes. He saved her, in his way. It seemed only right that when she returned from the hospital wing she'd do him a good turn in gratitude.

His name was Madoc, he said. He'd been in and out of hospitals since he was twelve. He heard voices, he said. Saw things that probably weren't really there. He hurt people, from time to time. He was angry. They gave him pills to help him calm down and to quieten the voices. If he stopped taking the pills, the voices grew louder and the impulses became harder to resist. Sometimes, he wasn't sure whether to believe his own memories. He'd been happy, once. He'd had a home and a family and a mother who made him feel loved. But she sent him away for being bad. Sent him to be with the useless bitch who'd birthed him. Then care homes. Orphanages, as if his parents were dead instead of fucking useless. He was fostered, for a while. But a bad man did things to him that made him wish he wasn't alive any more and he ran away. He started tattooing himself because he liked the sting of the needle. He got ill. Tried drugs that the doctors wouldn't have wanted him to take. Lost himself, somewhere. Served time. Got sectioned. Lost whole months of life to absolute nothingness and returned to himself with new scars and new ink and memories that were more akin to dreams.

Delphine had listened. She'd nodded. She'd held him and told him that he was her friend; her saviour – she wanted to make things better for him. He was entitled to his hatred. He was entitled to his thirst for revenge. He owed it to the poor abused child he used to be to demand redress from those who wronged him and transformed him into the creature he was to become. She spoke of transformation. She told him of her father, and the way he lived, and of the lives they took together. She moved the pieces around as if playing solitaire. She used her new-found liberties. Made sure she was just behind him in the line for medication each morning and evening, breathing in his ear. He didn't need it, she said. They were trying to control him. They were trying to stifle his rage.

He put a baby inside her the very first time she climbed on top of him.

Don't take the pills, she said. *Don't let them close you down.*

Listen to me. You can trust me. Do as I say and you won't ever be scared again. Take your revenge and you'll sleep soundly. Let me lead you, Madoc. Let me show you all you can become.

She spoke of transformation. What he had to do, and why. She told him that Trish Pharaoh needed to know what she had done. She needed to understand his father's paralysis; his impotence and rage. She needed to be shown up as the true demon that she was. She wove a new narrative. His father was a good man. He loved him. Cared for him. The injury that he suffered was all part of Trish Pharaoh's cruel scheme. She battered him bloody so she could torture him until his heart gave out. She was the wicked stepmother. She sent him away. She made sure he went to the worst person in the world. Engineered his suffering and pain. And she was out there now, still a malign influence in so many lives. She injected black ink into his eyeballs and split his tongue with a pair of garden shears. She wrote to the silly man who wouldn't let her letters reach her father, and she brought him under her spell. It wasn't difficult. Little for Delphine has ever been difficult. She orchestrated the death of Maurice Bruce without ever speaking to her father. She knew his type. The man who abused Madoc was in the vulnerable prisoners' wing at the self-same nick where her father was serving his time. It was as if the universe was lending a hand. She knew that he would always respond to a plea for help from a suitably pathetic maiden. She wrote her letter in a way that would be guaranteed to get past the censorious eye of Mr Corcoran. Reuben reacted as she knew he would. In so doing, she gave Madoc proof that she could deliver him a different destiny. She also gained the fealty of John Lee Prince, even if he didn't realize it. He was Reuben's disciple, but it wasn't hard to imitate her father. She sat at the centre of her web and wove her concentric circles. She made a pattern. She found a way to hurt those she despised and to serve up a gift to her father along the way. At no point did it ever feel taxing. Nothing changed in her manner. She continued to improve; to get well – to take her tablets and write her journal and submit for the reports that the mental-health service insisted on. And then they let her walk out of the gates and into sheltered accommodation.

Delphine's six-months pregnant now. Her back aches and her joints are swollen and she feels sick a lot of the time. She needs

to urinate almost constantly and sometimes the sensation of the
baby moving inside her is positively grotesque, as if her stomach
were a burlap sack and the unborn child a coil of writhing snakes.
And yet there are moments when she holds her bump and feels
the child press their face against her palm, and tears come unbidden.
She loses sight of herself in such moments. She thinks of the
people she has killed and she wishes she had taken a different
path. Such moments are fleeting. It doesn't take her long to rewrite
herself. She is simply a person born in the wrong time. In another
age, she would have been revered as an angel of vengeance.
Her father told her this the day she admitted that she had killed her
brother and hastened her mother's death. Reuben hadn't shouted.
He hadn't told. He just changed the lessons that he taught her.
And she was a singularly apt pupil.

Delphine looks at the blank screen. She has seen enough.
McAvoy isn't dead but she has witnessed his near-annihilation.
Her father came to his aid, just as she had hoped. Corcoran is
dead. The prisoners he recruited to attack the visiting detective
inspector will have no compunction about spilling their guts.
They'll tell the authorities that Corcoran was a corrupt officer who
became obsessed with taking revenge upon the copper who put
away Reuben Hollow. He formulated an elaborate plan to bring
McAvoy to the prison for overdue retribution. Hollow refused to
go along with it. Saved him from the noose. If he doesn't get a
reduction in his sentence he'll at least get more privileges and
he'll have Delphine to thank for that. She's sure he's grateful. And
Trish is still alive. Madoc won't tell, she knows that. The poor
bastard's head is so messed up that the only voice he listens to
any more is hers, and she certainly won't be talking to him again.
She's done with him. She doesn't care for the way he seemed to
lose his nerve at the end. She'd wanted to see what Trish Pharaoh's
bones looked like. Wanted to see her eyes turn black. Wanted her
to know that her daughter had such a low opinion of her that it
barely took any effort to convince her to steal the recording from
her mother's stash of personal belongings, and to pass it to her
half-brother. She would like to have seen the original – the one
that showed the young boy smashing his father's head in with a
metal railing. She fancies there is time for such pleasures somewhere down the road. She has other priorities for now. Trish will

know who did these things to her. McAvoy too. But nobody else will. There's no case to build against Delphine Hollow, or her new avatar. She doesn't really exist. They'll look for her, she's sure of that. But they won't find her until she's ready. She'll definitely send them a photo of the child when it's born. She rather hopes that it's a boy, complete with Anders Wilkie's dark, dark eyes.

Delphine spins around, slowly, in the swivel chair. She has her hands in her lap, thumbs rubbing the swelling of her belly. She looks around, blinking in the half light, as if coming back to herself from far away. She sucks at her cheek. She's hungry, she thinks. She's always hungry. She can't quite recall whether there was anything left in the kitchen. She might have to order in a takeaway, though doing so brings its own problems, and besides, she can't imagine she'll be able to persuade anybody to deliver here, at this hour. She realizes she's tired. She's been up nearly twenty-four hours. She imagines that the woman is hungry too. Thirsty. She's definitely pissed herself. There's a reek of fear and sweat and ammonia bleeding through from the bedroom. At least she's stopped struggling now. She seems almost resigned to what's going to happen. The thought of such meek acceptance angers Delphine. She thinks it's important to fight for your life. That's what she likes about McAvoy. He won't die quietly. Trish neither. There's something there to admire. It had been strange hearing the big Scotsman's voice again after all this time. He'd been very brusque with her on the phone. She imagines he'll feel guilty about tonight's events until his dying day. And that is a win, of a sort.

Clementine has been a less impressive victim. She hadn't even understood what was going on. How could her podcasting partner Finn also be the stepdaughter of Reuben Hollow? Was it coincidence? No, it couldn't be. And if it wasn't coincidence, that must mean it was intentional, and that the rumours were true, and it really was the young woman who had guided Hollow's blade . . .

She didn't even fight. Gave up as soon as she saw the knife, submitting to the ropes and the gag and the delicate ministrations of the blade without any of the thrashing she had expected. Delphine's tempted to let her live, just so she can feel the shame of her own worthlessness. But to let her live would be to deny herself the sport that she has promised herself these past months. And she doesn't really think she has any right to complain.

Clementine has brought this on herself. She shouldn't have said those things about her father. They were rude. And all Delphine needs to commit murder is a half-decent reason.

She stands. Stretches. Rolls her shoulders. She huffs her red hair out of her eyes. Then she lets the dressing gown fall to the floor. She walks into the bedroom naked, her belly pointing out ahead of her like the nose of a shark. She looks upon Clementine, starfished in her own bed. She gives her a look that is almost apology.

She takes the recording device from the dressing table. Activates the microphone. She wants to record every single whisper and shriek. Then she can send it to her dad. It'll make a nice addition to the podcast, she thinks. A Bad Person, with a Good Death.

Eventually, Delphine will sleep. By sunset, she'll have showered and stolen a new set of clothes. She'll have taken Clementine's car and driven in whichever direction feels most in keeping with her mood. She'll cut off her hair and dye what's left. She'll change her walk. She'll adopt an accent until it becomes tiresome. She'll eat and she'll drink and she'll watch the news. She'll hear about the horror at the prison, and her father's heroics. She'll hear that an escaped mental patient has been arrested for killing a man called Malcolm Tozer and a retired cop called Tom Spink and for the attempted murder of Thor Ingolfsson, among others. She'll ring the helpline, just to show willing. She might even leave a message for Trish. She'll tell her not to get too comfy. There's still unfinished business between them. She'll post her some pieces of Clementine. She'll send the armpits to her father, inside. She fancies he'll get a kick out of that.

'Oh my darling, oh my darling . . .' whispers Delphine, as she begins to carve.

The blade goes into her flesh as if she were slicing ripe fruit.

EPILOGUE

The strawberry moon has been devoured. Above the flat, lonely countryside it shines a dull, silvery-grey: a rusting sickle blade arcing down into clouds that rest atop the city like a pie crust. There's a touch of spring in the air; a scent of bluebells and wild garlic drifting out of the big black mass of the Country Park. It slips elegantly over the row of white-painted fishermen's cottages, picking up fresh scents as it goes. At the house with the red door and the too-big hanging basket, it captures the aroma of a young, dark-haired woman. She lies on top of a caravan, squashed into the back garden as if dropped by a crane. She's wearing a purple bikini and Ugg boots, big hoop earrings and sunglasses. It's not remotely warm enough for such a get-up, but Roisin McAvoy needs little encouragement to allow the sun to touch her flesh. She's happy, here. The kids are in the caravan, arguing merrily. Fin seems happy enough. Lilah is painting his fingernails and telling him to stop wriggling. Sophia will be here soon, with the baby. Olivia's coming too. Nana will play the role of peacemaker. There'll be drink and good food and as many arguments as tearful hugs. She'll go and get changed soon; slip into something that will make Trish Pharaoh feel frumpy. She thinks it's important to demonstrate that nothing has changed between them. She's sure that what she went through was horrible, but she feels sure Trish wouldn't want her to sugar-coat their exchanges. They like each other too much to pretend there's any affection between them. She's looking forward to the afternoon. Thor will be arriving by taxi in an hour or so. He's heading back to Iceland to see if he can patch things up with his wife, but Roisin had refused to let him go without getting the chance to meet him. The idea of an afternoon spent with McAvoy and his mirror image is just too delightful. She won't need the heating on – she'll be able to warm the house just from the blush.

When she's sure that nobody is watching, Roisin rolls onto her stomach. She picks up the binoculars from beneath her magazine and trains them on the spot where McAvoy and Trish are walking, slowly, towards the ice-cream van. They're sheltered beneath the colossal splendour of the Humber Bridge, where the green grass disappears and the muddy beach begins. Pharaoh is shuffling like a little old lady. McAvoy is doing his best to support her but she knows that he's in as much pain as she is. They look like promenaders: a Victorian gentleman and his aged mother.

Roisin doesn't need to hear what they're saying to one another. She knows how they interact. She knows what they mean to each other. She'll be teasing him and he'll be looking hurt and they'll both be trying to pretend that they don't want to get it out of their system and just fuck until they catch fire. Roisin doesn't mind. He'll never cheat. Trish would, in a flash. But it takes two to tango.

She settles back down. Thinks of Delphine Hollow. Kush. John Lee Prince, back inside. Of poor Tom Spink. There's talk of Reuben having his case re-opened. Talk of a medal for bravery. The papers are doing their nut trying to work out where to fire their moral outrage. Trish is going to be detective chief superintendent when she comes back to work. McAvoy her number two. 'Good Murders, Bad Deaths' is the number one rated podcast in the world, despite the global petition to have it taken down. Record numbers have downloaded the final episode: an hour-long audio file of Clementine Lippman's gruesome death. The message boards are alive with conspiracy theories. McAvoy's been offered six-figure sums to talk about what happened in the tunnel beneath the prison. Roisin has handled such requests. Kept them from him, to save his worn-out brain.

She lies down. Stares up at the sky.

They'll scatter Tom's ashes, later. They weren't allowed to bury him at the clifftop church. The plots are all sliding into the sea. Somebody's going to have to dig up the bones and have them reinterred somewhere else. They'd settled on cremation instead.

She thinks of Madoc. Lights a cigarette. Inhales, and suddenly decides that she hates smoking. She extinguishes it on the roof of the caravan. Decides that, as of now, she's a non-smoker. She'll stick to it. She knows who she is. Doesn't know how to be anybody else. Mother. Wife. Traveller. Killer, when she has to be. Non-smoker, now. She likes it.

She hears a thump from the caravan. Hears Lilah, threatening her brother with bloody retribution; the dire consequences if he doesn't sit still. Feels the warmth spread across herself as she thinks upon her children, her man. Wonders whether Lilah would kill for her father the way Delphine has for Reuben. Wonders whether vengeance is right, or wrong, or nature or fucking nurture. Wonders, for a moment, if this is how he always feels. How it is to be her Aector.

She settles down. Clears her mind.

Hears his voice inside her head; the soft whisper of poetry against her hip. Loves him. Loves him to *death*.

Roisin would kill anybody who tries to take this from her.

And if that's a sin, she'll gladly take her place among the legions of the damned.

'You're sure we did the right thing?' asks McAvoy. He feels cold. Aches to his bones. He'd like to lie down for a hundred years. Hopes he'll get forty winks in his favourite armchair once everybody's gone home.

'No,' growls Pharaoh, grimacing as she swallows. 'Of course I'm not sure. I'm not even sure what size shoe I am any more. I'm not sure if I want to be a police officer any more. I'm not sure if I'm a good person or the fucking devil. But I think it's all tied up neatly enough to please the powers that be and these days, that's really all that bloody matters. It's all about the look of the thing, after all.'

McAvoy glances over at her to see whether she's being serious. He's never really sure any more. He wonders whether things used to make more sense, or whether they were always a complicated mess of contradictions and conflicts. Wonders when he started to see the world in so many shades of grey.

'Bollocks to this,' mutters Pharaoh. She stops and stretches, both hands in the small of her back: a house-proud Hessle Road fishwife rising from scrubbing the front step with a wet stone. 'Light this, would you?'

McAvoy takes the cigarette and lighter. Places the filter tip against his lower lip and flips the wheel on the lighter. Sucks the smoke into his lungs. His mouth fills with the taste of Roisin's kisses. He breaths out a great plume of smoke and hands the cigarette back to Pharaoh. Her hands shake as she takes it with a nod of thanks.

'You think he'll die in there?' asks McAvoy, limping to the sea wall and leaning against it. He's downwind of Pharaoh and can smell the sweat and perfume and the cold, greasy pain that emanates from her skin.

'Reuben? Nah. He'll be out some day. Men like him don't go quietly.'

'Think he'll send you another sculpture on your birthday?'

Pharaoh shrugs. Glares at the tip of her cigarette. 'I think I'd be sorry if he didn't.'

McAvoy fights the urge to ask more questions. He wants to know what she planned and what she thought and what she did to keep him safe. He wants to ask so badly that it pains him. But he knows the answers will hurt them both. So he stays quiet. Says nothing. Just stares at the water.

'They still haven't found him,' says Pharaoh, following his gaze. 'Madoc. Went out with the tide and by the time the boat got out there was no trace. Blood on the rocks though.'

'He couldn't have survived,' says McAvoy. 'In cuffs? That impact . . .?'

Pharaoh breathes out smoke through her nostrils. Gives the faintest shake of her head. 'Whoever he was at the end, he wasn't the boy I tried to be a mother to. When I think of the man who tried to kill me – who killed poor Tom . . . I can't make the two shapes fit together in my head. It's like something dark, something evil – it just climbed inside him like he was a Russian doll. Just squatted there, waiting . . .' She tails off. Flicks her cigarette butt at a damp, grey stone. 'I'm just talking bollocks now. I sound like you.'

'I hate the thoughts that keep rising up,' says McAvoy, hoarse. 'I keep thinking about that hanging cell. About the simplicity of it – the long drop and the broken neck and then suddenly the problem's gone away. The monster's dead. I hate that I'm seeing the appeal of it. I'm supposed to believe in humanity; in decency – I'm supposed to be a good man. And yet, I can't help thinking that if Reuben had died all those years ago, all the people he infects . . .'

'Welcome to the world of the ethical conundrum, Detective

Inspector McAvoy,' smiles Pharaoh. She rests her head on his shoulder. He presses his cheek to her crown.

'For a moment, I really thought Delphine was going to go after Roisin.'

'Aye,' says Pharaoh, softly. 'One can only hope, eh?'

McAvoy frowns. Says nothing. Wonders if she's watching. Wonders what he would do if Delphine came for her now. Hopes that she'll give him time to heal before she comes back to tear out his soul.

'Will you visit him?' asks McAvoy. 'He'll be good company while he's still high on his new fame. They'll be making a film next, I shouldn't wonder.'

'Wonder who'll play you,' says Pharaoh, moving away and peering at him. 'Meryl Streep, I reckon. She's proper versatile.'

McAvoy bites down on his smile. Shakes his head at the enormity of it all. He doesn't want any of this any more. Doesn't want to be fighting for his life and battling to protect those he loves. Doesn't want to feel the accusing eyes of the dead staring at the back of his neck; their voices whispering at his ear; tugging at the tails of his coat – demanding justice, restitution, vengeance.

'You can't quit,' says Pharaoh, matter-of-factly. 'Neither can I. What fucking use are we if we're not doing this?'

They sit in silence. Listen to the sea.

'Did you bring him over here as a decoy?' asks McAvoy, unable to help himself. 'Did you put him in harm's way to save me?'

Pharaoh laughs. Rolls her eyes. 'Jesus, the world doesn't revolve around you, Hector. I brought him over because I was absolutely gagging.'

McAvoy's cheeks begin to colour. 'Oh,' he says. 'Sorry. I mean . . . that's not really any of my . . .'

Pharaoh looks at him over the top of her sunglasses. Narrows her eyes. 'That's the exact shade I want for the bathroom carpet.'

He stops talking. Stops thinking. Turns his head away from her the moment he sees the lie in her eyes.

There's a sudden trilling from Pharaoh's pocket. A moment later, it finds its echo within the folds of McAvoy's coat. Both sigh as they recognize the ring-tones.

'Major Crimes, Detective Inspector McAvoy . . .'

'This is Trish. Somebody dead?'

A minute later they're hobbling back up the beach. By the time they reach the road, they're barely limping. Pharaoh's still on the phone, barking orders. McAvoy's fingers are moving over the screen. Suspicious death. Stab wounds. DS Neilsen already on the way. It's a bad one. A young woman. Ex-boyfriend recently released from HMP Lincoln. Her four-year-old found her. Held her hand until the dead fingers turned cold and immobile. Then he called for help. Still hasn't cried. Still hasn't spoken . . .

And inside McAvoy's head, another voice joins the chorus of the dead.